I0710396

THE Painted DAISIES
Royal
HAZE
WRITER'S DIGEST AWARD WINNING AUTHOR
LJ EVANS

The Painted Daisies, Book V

Royal Haze

L J Evans

This book is a work of fiction. While reference might be made to actual historical events or existing people and locations, the events, names, characters, places, and incidents are either the product of the author's imagination or are used fictitiously, and any resemblance to actual persons, living or dead, business establishments, events, or locales is entirely coincidental.

ROYAL HAZE © 2023 by LJ Evans

Published by LJ EVANS BOOKS
www.ljevansbooks.com

Cover Design: © Emily Wittig
Cover Images: © Unsplash | weston m, Deposit Photos | Vadim Vasenin, Dekues, and Flower Studio, and iStock| Punnarong
Chapter Image: © iStock Vidok
Content & Line Editor: Evans Editing
Copy Editor: Jenn Lockwood Editing Services
Proofing: Karen Hrdlicka

ISBN: 978-1-962499-15-6

Library of Congress Cataloging in process.

https://spoti.fi/3IWaDPK

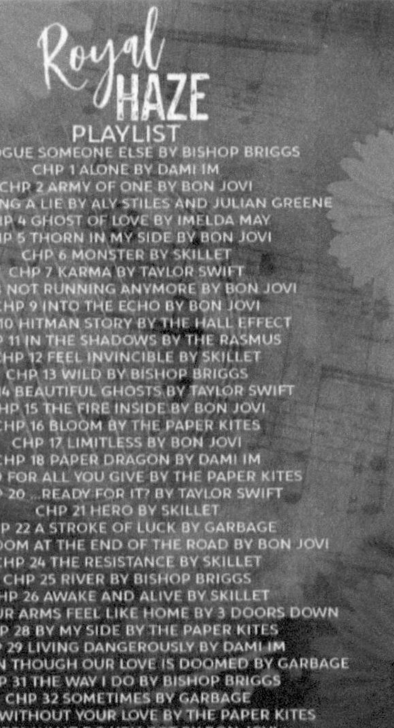

Dedication

To my family, who cared and encouraged me while I disappeared for months on end to bring this adventure to life, thank you from the bottom of my heart for being my calm in the storm. For being the light guiding me home.

To the Daisy Detectives who made the release of this series one of the most joyous experiences of my publishing career. You've all earned life-long badges.

To my readers, may the only real superpower that exists in this world be at your side every moment of every day—may you be loved.

 Prologue

SOMEONE ELSE
Performed by Bishop Briggs

TWENTY YEARS BEFORE

SAN FIORE 65: I just learned some disturbing news about the heirs of Prince Dario. They may be a problem.

SEGRETI: Meet me in our old spot at the library of Sapienza. We'll figure out how to take care of it.

SEVENTEEN YEARS BEFORE

SEGRETI: I've searched the entire house, gone through every message, photo album, diary. I'm fairly certain he doesn't know.

SAN FIORE 65: I need one-hundred-percent sure.

SEGRETI: You mean, WE need one-hundred-percent sure.

SAN FIORE 65: Don't be ridiculous. You know that's what I meant.

NINE YEARS BEFORE

SEGRETI: He fucking knows! He plans to go to San Fiore.

SAN FIORE 65: We should have taken care of him and the girl as soon as we found out about them.

SEGRETI: I'll take care of it.

SEGRETI: It's done.

SAN FIORE 65: We should have taken them both out.

SEGRETI: She won't be a problem. She knows nothing, and we'll ensure it stays that way. We started the countdown. That's what truly matters. It gave us what we needed with the least amount of risk.

SAN FIORE 65: You said he didn't know either, and look what happened.

SEGRETI: This is different. She's a child. She wouldn't be able to keep this kind of a secret. She doesn't know.

THREE YEARS BEFORE

Dear Sir,

It is my understanding that the San Fiore government has established a two-million-dollar reward for information leading to the discovery of any progeny of Prince Dario Alberto Gregorio Fiorani after his abdication and disappearance in 1940.

I believe I may have information pertinent to your search. Please advise on how you'd like to proceed.

Sincerely,

Dr. Parker Maynard

Professor of Social Anthropology

Wilson-Jacobs University

Grand Orchard, NY

SAN FIORE 65: We left a loose thread, and now there's a professor threatening to unravel it. Finish this.

SEGRETI: If I do, and this professor knows the truth, eliminating her could expose us. I'll deal with the professor instead. Send me his details.

SAN FIORE 65: You can't do it, can you? You're too close. Damn it, I knew it. I knew it nine years ago when you deviated from the plan and only took him out instead of both of them.

SEGRETI: I'll handle it.

♫ ♫ ♫

TWO AND A HALF YEARS BEFORE

Nikki rubbed her temples, the ache in them a slow, flashing burn. Her phone buzzed, and she looked down to see Professor Maynard's name and number appear over the white and yellow daisies on her lock screen. She forgot she'd agreed to meet with him this afternoon. He'd been so determined and persistent ever since she'd arrived in Grand Orchard, and if she was truthful with herself, he'd weaved a fairy tale that was hard to resist.

She should put him off. In all likelihood, whatever he had to say would only increase the chances of her headache developing into a full-on, throbbing monster refusing to be tamed. But she'd already postponed meeting with him twice, each time doubting herself. Wondering if the inner romantic she'd tried to bury ages ago was letting her believe a whole lot of hogwash. Wondering if she was being scammed. Plus, if she believed him, then she'd have to come to terms with the fact her dad had lied to her for years before he'd died. Or at least, he'd kept enormous secrets from both her and her stepmom—life-altering ones.

But what if the professor is right? The little girl in her who'd loved all the princess movies couldn't help asking while her older, more cynical self, denied it being possible.

She sighed. She had to go. She couldn't leave this huge unknown hovering over her for the rest of her life. She had to hear him out. The only good thing about the start of her headache was she could use it as an excuse to leave the studio and her bandmates without giving away that she was meeting up with him.

"I'm going to the café to get a coffee. Anyone want anything?" Nikki asked the others.

"No. Go take care of your headache before it turns into a beast," Fiadh said, shaking her head and causing her mahogany curls layered with purple to dance around.

Nikki waved, shouldered her bag, and left her friends at the studio along with the drama that had been building between them ever since arriving in New York. A weird uneasiness was growing inside her that she couldn't shake as she made her way past the charming old storefronts of downtown Grand Orchard to the ivy-covered buildings of Wilson-Jacobs University. Neither having her bodyguard with her nor her faith in her own ability to defend herself seemed to lessen the disquiet, and for half a second, she debated turning back.

The university wasn't nearly as busy as it would be when the fall semester kicked in, but there were still students and faculty wandering the campus during the heat of the summer. In another lifetime, Nikki might have blended in with them, but instead her life felt light-years away from the normalcy of these twentysomethings.

She'd looked up the professor's office on a site map earlier and headed for the hundred-year-old, stone Humanities building as if she'd been there before. Her pace fast, maybe because of the nervousness clinging to her or just because she wanted this done. To find out and move on. When she reached the second floor, she hesitated. She had no desire for her bodyguard to be anywhere near the conversation she was going to have.

"I'd like you to wait here," she told Andy.

He frowned, unhappy with this development.

"You know I can handle myself better than even some of the members of the detail," she said. This wasn't her bragging, and Andy knew it from working out with her several times since he'd joined Garner Security. She'd needed a sparring partner, and he'd volunteered. A lifetime of training with her dad, Jerome, and a host of martial arts instructors had made sure Andy had ended up on the bottom of the mat with her foot on his neck on more than one occasion.

He raised a brow, gave her a curt nod, and leaned up against the wall near the stairs while she continued down to Maynard's office near the opposite end of the corridor.

She knocked before twisting the knob and entering, only to freeze.

The office was a disaster. Books had been tossed from the shelves, and the file cabinets were open with their contents spread about the room. The two chairs in front of Maynard's large walnut desk had their cushions sliced open, and everything on the desktop had been pushed onto the polished wood floor.

Professor Maynard was standing amidst the mess, laptop clutched to his chest and his trendy, black-framed glasses slipping down his nose. Anger and fear were roaring through his eyes as they met hers.

"Close the door!" he demanded.

She hesitated but then did as he'd asked, trying to find a spot to stand where she wouldn't be on his strewn belongings.

"What happened?" Nikki asked, the surprise melting into concern.

"You. You happened." His words sent a chill running up her spine as fear curled through her.

"What are you talking about?" she demanded.

The last time she'd met him, she'd thought he'd had a nice smile, which only added to his Indiana-Jones-like appeal she was sure made him popular with his students. Now, his wild gaze made him look unhinged.

"How did they find out? They must know how close I am to the truth about you. They must know what I found in LA. They must be searching for it." It was a rushed ramble of words that she wasn't sure she followed.

"Who's they? What are you talking about?" Nikki asked, stomach clenching as the obvious truth finally sank in. His office had been ransacked by someone searching for something tied to her.

The office door crashed open, and Nikki's natural instinct was to whirl to face the sound with her arms coming up in a protective stance. Another man burst in, and her heartbeat kicked up ever so slightly. He was taller and lankier than the professor, but there was a marked resemblance between them. Except, this man had an aura of roughness about him that a scar along the side of his jaw emphasized. As if he was used to fights in bars and back alleys. Dark, beady eyes took in the entire room before coming back to land on her. He simply ignored her raised fists, stepping around her to right a chair that had been knocked over.

"What happened?" the new man demanded.

"I must have tipped them off when I asked for the report on the shooting at the gas station," he told the other man, almost forgetting Nikki was there.

Her heart stopped and started. Was he talking about the gas station where her dad had been killed? A wave of pain hit her in the chest. It had been years since she'd lost him, but it sliced through her almost as if she was hearing it again for the first time.

"I told you we needed to drop this entire notion," the man with the scar growled. "Nothing good will come of it now. You're going to ruin your life. You could end up dead too."

"I'm sorry. This was a mistake," Nikki said quietly, easing her way back toward the door and opening it.

The professor moved with a skilled ease that surprised her, slamming the door shut and grabbing her arm. Without a thought, she batted his hand away, while assessing just how to leverage his weight against him.

He stepped back, pushing his glasses up. "I'm sorry. It's just… It's important. Please. I have proof. I can show it to you."

She looked around the destroyed office.

"What proof?" the scarred man asked, face scrunching into a scowl.

"It's not here. I wouldn't be stupid enough to just leave it laying around," the professor insisted, and the other man's eyes squinted at the desperation in Maynard's voice.

Every alarm bell in Nikki's body was telling her to get the hell out of there.

"I…I think it's best if we just drop this," she said

quietly, hand slowly moving toward the doorknob again.

"Please," the professor begged once more. "Give me another chance. We're so close to the truth. Closer than anyone has been in decades. My brother and I…we need this."

The two men exchanged a strange look that only increased the turmoil inside her. Nikki wanted to tell him to go to hell. She wanted to leave and never think about any of it again. But the little things Professor Maynard had told her about her family had all rung true in a way that seemed both impossible and probable at the same time.

If she had him come to the farmhouse tonight, there would be a host of bodyguards and her friends around. She'd be safe. She'd have to tell the band something about him or just let them assume she had a thing for the attractive college professor.

"Tonight. At the farmhouse. Any time after seven," she said before stepping through the door. "But only you, Professor. If you both show up, I won't be able to explain it."

"Thank you! You won't regret it," Professor Maynard called after her, relief coasting over his face, but his brother looked wary and thoughtful.

Nikki already regretted it. Regretted ever letting him close. Acid burned in her throat, the situation and her migraine twining together, causing the nausea to spike. Her head was throbbing mercilessly. White lights flickered through her vision. She needed to climb into bed, shut all the blinds, and sleep until it disappeared.

She slipped out the door before either of the men could stop her again and found her way to Andy, who—she was relieved to see—was none the wiser. He led her back through the campus and the streets of downtown to one of the security detail's SUVs waiting for her at the recording studio.

As she went to get in, her skin prickled. A sensation

of being watched washed over her, and she glanced behind her to find a man leaning up against the white pillar of the bakery across the street. She'd seen him when she'd arrived at the studio this morning too, and she'd had the same thought as she did now—he was beautiful. He had black hair, hooded eyes, and an imperious nose that screamed of some ancient-Egyptian lineage. Except, instead of being lean like a pharaoh, he was enormous. Not only in height but in the breadth of his frame. His arms were crossed over his massive chest, bulging forearms showcasing a swirl of tattoos.

He should have frightened her. She should have mentioned it to the others, especially with the creepy notes arriving daily, but she hadn't. It was like she knew, inexplicably, he wasn't there to hurt her, which was ludicrous. But there was something almost mythical about the man, as if she'd blink and he'd disappear.

After she'd climbed into the SUV, and Andy had backed out of the spot, she looked again only to find he had disappeared, just like she'd expected. A mirage. A figment of her imagination.

She reached into her bag for the nose spray that only seemed to help with her migraine symptoms fifty percent of the time. She used it, and then closed her eyes and rested her head on the seat back. The pain gripping her pushed everything else out of her mind. The fear. The doubts. Nothing remained but the knowledge that if she didn't lose herself to sleep soon, she'd never shake the agony swallowing her.

When she got to the early-twentieth-century mansion the locals called "The Farmhouse," the sun had started to fall below the mountains, lengthening the shadows of the apple trees as if they were crawling out of the orchard. The white-planked house with its wraparound porch waited silently, and the same unease she'd had all day settled again over Nikki's shoulders.

When she walked in the door and called out, no one answered. Not even Landry who'd headed back to the house long before Nikki had left to meet the professor. Landry's running shoes weren't by the door, which meant she was likely out jogging around the pond as she had almost daily since they'd arrived in town. The quiet was a relief to Nikki's pounding head. It was exactly what she needed.

She made her way up the stairs, desperate to close her eyes.

Even with the sun going down, the bedroom she'd claimed at the front of the house was still too bright. She needed the pitch-black of oblivion, so she shut the blinds and drew the curtains before fumbling her way to the bed. She stripped to her underwear as she went and slid into the cool sheets, resting her fevered brow on the pillowcase. Everything that had happened today and everything hovering around the edges of her life drifted away as she let sleep claim her.

♫ ♫ ♫

She'd been jolted from her sleep to a waking nightmare she was still struggling to comprehend.

Landry was dead…

God…it seemed impossible. So desperately wrong.

And now she sat with tears streaming down her face, trying to hold Paisley up while Nikki was falling apart herself. Her heart hurt. Her stomach was a pit of snarling vipers. Paisley's tortured screams from the backyard still echoed through her along with Jonas's heartbroken face as he'd picked Paisley up and carried her toward the house. He'd grabbed Nikki's hand and dragged her along with them as if to prevent either of them from seeing Landry's body on the ground.

But it was too late. It would be embedded in her memories for the rest of her life.

How could this be happening?

One of the police officers approached them, leaning

toward Nikki to say softly, "There's a Professor Maynard here to see you. He insists it's important. Do you want me to send him away?"

Nikki turned a wide-eyed gaze toward the open front door and the sea of officials who'd been pouring in and around the property. She'd forgotten about the professor. Forgotten about the torn-up office and the rough man who'd been with him and who he'd said was his brother. A chill raced over her.

She didn't know if she wanted to see him. Not now. Not after what had happened.

Her eyes landed on Maynard at the foot of the steps. He was even more wild-eyed than earlier, and he was pacing back and forth. If she refused to see him, would he create a scene? Would he spill the words she certainly didn't want anyone else to hear? She pulled herself from the couch and joined him on the porch.

He grasped her arm tightly, tugging her farther from the steps.

"They thought she was you!"

His words caused her blood to run cold, ice filling her veins. "What?"

"You look the same from the back. I almost approached her instead of you that first day until she turned around. This is *THEM*, Ms. Rani. I've led them straight to you! You're lucky to be alive."

Bile hit her throat.

No. Her mind revolted. She shook her head. Was Landry dead because of her? Because of her family and the secrets the professor hinted her father had kept? Had this all been a gigantic mistake? Should it be her on the ground by the pond and not her friend?

God, no. Please no. A new sort of agony whirled through her chest.

"I didn't know until you left my office today, but my brother…he received a death threat. They promised to kill everyone we know, even our mom who's in a nursing home, if we continued down this path. We can take care of ourselves—our dad made sure of that—but it isn't worth the risk to you," the professor whispered. "You need to let this go. Don't tell anyone. If you do, you'll put your loved ones in danger. You don't know who you can trust. They have people everywhere. In law enforcement. In the government. Maybe even in your own security team. They came for your father. They'll come for you and kill whoever is in their path."

At his office, he'd seemed afraid but still eager, almost desperate. Now, there was a strangely horrified resignation to his voice. As if he'd stumbled into a conspiracy bigger than he'd expected and was now back pedaling to get out before everything crashed down.

A tremor of fear went through her.

With a sickening clarity, she realized he was telling the truth. About her. About her family. And Landry was dead because of it! She was dead even though they'd had a host of bodyguards and law enforcement agencies watching over them.

"I'm walking away from the entire debacle. This"— he shoved a small package at her—"it belongs to you. It proves who you are. Take it, but don't show it to anyone. Not ever."

Nikki tried to push it away, but he pried her fingers open and placed it in her palm.

"Good luck, Ms. Rani. I hope you stay safe," he said, stepping back.

She would have protested. She would have thrown the package at him if two people hadn't emerged behind him in the darkness. One was a tall and somber woman with her brown hair pulled back into a bun, and the other was a wide-shouldered man with a frame that screamed military. Sadness and relief flew through her as she rushed toward them, suddenly overwhelmingly glad her mom and Jerome had decided to come see her. They'd been worried about the stalker notes the band had been receiving, but maybe they really should have been worried about Nikki. About a forgotten history that had come back to terrorize them.

"Mom!" Nikki cried, throwing herself into her mom's arms.

"What's happened?" her father's best friend asked, placing a hand to her back.

Anxiety bloomed, burning through her entire being. Just like the professor had said at the college—she'd happened. Her curiosity. The damn romantic child inside her. Her desire to learn more about a family she would never know because her father was no longer alive to answer the questions.

The loss of Lan was her fault!

It sent pain crashing through her. Worse than any migraine. It was as bad as the day the police had shown up at their house in Orange and told them about her father. This was going to leave an impenetrable black mark on her soul. She promised herself right then that she'd forget it all. That she would never again risk her friends…her mom…herself… to chase a fairy tale.

Her mind flashed back to the muscled, tattooed man she'd seen outside the studio and Maynard's brother with his beady eyes.

She hadn't said anything about either of them to her security team.

She should have said something.

Now, it was too late. Now, she could only bite her tongue and hope the swells of guilt and sorrow didn't drown her.

♫ ♫ ♫

SEGRETI: You sent someone after her? We just needed to get rid of the professor! I told you I had it handled, and now look at the mess your stooge left in his wake!

SAN FIORE 65: If you'd done your job years ago, I wouldn't have had to contract out.

SEGRETI: Well, that worked out brilliantly. And now there's another person who can tie this to us. No one was supposed to know.

SAN FIORE 65: He has no clue who I am, and he's easily eliminated.

SEGRETI: Is that your answer to everything? Will you say that about me once you finally get what you want?

SAN FIORE 65: Don't be ridiculous. We've been in this together for almost thirty years. You're the one who first opened my eyes to the possibilities.

SEGRETI: I opened your eyes and helped create the plan you keep deviating from! Don't go behind my back again!

SAN FIORE 65: I'm not the only one who's deviated. You didn't take care of this nine years ago. Besides, we both know that new information often requires adjustments.

SEGRETI: The only good thing to come out of this is that she's terrified. Whatever she knew, she's too afraid to pursue it. What about the professor?

SAN FIORE 65: I've got someone on him.

SEGRETI: Who? The same screwup? Let's hope he does a better job this time.

SAN FIORE 65: He knows he messed up. He's motivated to make it right, otherwise he doesn't get his money.

EIGHTEEN MONTHS BEFORE

SEGRETI: If I had any doubts before about what she knew, I've confirmed it's nothing. I tested her, and there wasn't even a flicker of recognition.

SAN FIORE 65: What test?

SEGRETI: Let's just say San Fiore means nothing to her.

SAN FIORE 65: I don't trust your objectivity when it comes to her.

SEGRETI: I want this as much as you do.

SAN FIORE 65: Prove it.

SEVEN MONTHS BEFORE:

SEGRETI: She has the brooch. But she doesn't know what it means.

SAN FIORE 65: Merda! Get it.

SEGRETI: I have a plan, and if it doesn't work out, I have a backup. It'll put us close to the deadline, but it'll get done.

THREE MONTHS BEFORE:

SEGRETI: The Cavalieri have eyes on her.

SAN FIORE 65: Don't worry about them.

SEGRETI: They sent a massive beast to tail her, and you say don't worry?

SAN FIORE 65: Castelli isn't a threat.

SEGRETI: You have someone on the inside?

SAN FIORE 65: Just concentrate on your part of the plan, and don't worry about mine.

SEGRETI: Don't keep things from me. I promise you it won't end well for either of us if you do.

SAN FIORE 65: We're too close to have anything go wrong now. Let's just finish it.

Chapter One

Nikki

ALONE
Performed by Dami Im

EIGHT DAYS BEFORE

The seventy-five thousand people in the stadium's seats took a collective breath, and silence settled over the arena as the video of Landry faded with the last notes of "The Legacy." Nikki's eyes filled with tears, but she held them back, closing her lids to capture them. Then, thundering feet, hands, and voices filled the air, chanting Landry's name, chanting for all of them…

Remorse filled her.

Self-hatred.

Disgust.

She could never fix it. She could never make it right, but she could be here to honor Landry every day. She could help Paisley accomplish the dreams the two sisters had built together.

Nikki left her guitar by the drum kit and joined her bandmates at the front of the stage. She locked hands with Adria, and then they all took a bow before walking offstage. The crowd went wild. As soon as they were out of sight, the five of them formed a circle, hugging each other and holding on tight.

They used to do something similar before each performance to help Paisley with her stage fright, but these days, she battled it differently—with Jonas, who was part of their tour-management duo and her boyfriend. Now, he was the first of the small group of men waiting in the wings to step forward, swallowing them with his muscled arms and joining their circle.

When they broke apart, they all wiped their eyes, and Paisley fell into Jonas. He dwarfed her, making her look even smaller than her barely five feet. He had almost thirteen inches on her and doubled her in width. As tiny as she was, Paisley's personality was huge these days. Strong and vibrant. She'd stepped into Landry's missing shoes, filling them in a way Nikki didn't think her sister could ever have imagined.

As Jonas's hair slipped over his brows, he pushed it back to reveal bright-green eyes that settled on Paisley. He brushed aside her straight, black strands and kissed her forehead before linking their fingers together.

Adria threw an arm over Nikki's shoulders. While each of them was hot and sweaty from the performance, banging on the drums worked Adria out more than any of them, so her black hair was practically adhered to her face and neck.

"They're cute together," Adria said with her bright, blue-eyed gaze on Paisley and Jonas. "I used to worry they'd hurt each other all over again."

"But?"

"I guess I understand second-chance love better these days," her friend replied with a shrug as her eyes landed on another man who'd been waiting for them. Ronan was wearing faded designer jeans and an old-school *Goonies* T-shirt that made him look more like the film director he once was rather than the president of a production studio he'd become. His cinnamon-colored hair with its thick waves was brushed back carefully, his beard was trimmed neat, and his gray eyes were glued to Adria.

Nikki chuckled but didn't respond. She was laughing on the outside while, deep inside her, the little girl she'd once been was throwing a tantrum, aching for the love all her friends had found but had eluded her. The way the men in her friends' lives looked at them, like they were the only thing worth living for…she wanted that. She'd wanted it from the time she'd watched her very first fairy tale.

But her fairy-tale dreams had cost them everything. It had cost them Landry.

She certainly didn't deserve a happily-ever-after story. Not when Landry would never have one. Forever after wouldn't be hers. She could barely allow herself moments of pleasure and peace these days without the guilt tearing her apart.

"Want to go out tonight?" Adria asked. "I've heard the Pygmalion has a great house band and even better bar food."

Instead of an after-party full of media and important guests, they'd held the VIP gathering before the concert today. The two-night stand in Dublin was the last of their concerts in the calendar year. Tomorrow, everyone was heading off in different directions for the holidays. The fact they were going to be apart for a few weeks wasn't the reason Adria was asking her to go out though. This was her friend keeping the promise she'd made in November to not leave Nikki without a wingwoman just because the entire band now had a man to go home with at the end of the day.

"Nah," Nikki replied. "I want to be sure I'm packed and ready to go for our early flight. Besides, I think your man might literally explode if he doesn't have you in his arms in the next ten seconds."

Adria snorted. "Ronan will survive."

Nikki turned laughing eyes to her friend. "But will you?"

Adria's smile grew, giving Nikki the signature wink

the world associated with her. "Maybe. Maybe not."

Nikki hugged Adria tightly before letting her go, and they started over to where Ronan was standing with Nikki's stepmom. Her height was the only thing that made her mom stand out in a crowd. It certainly wasn't the medium-length brown hair she almost always had tied back in a tight bun or her hazel eyes hidden behind simple black-framed glasses that drew attention to her. She was quiet, and many would say she was plain-looking—forgettable—but Nikki had seen her mom standing in the face of a storm, holding the tiller of a sailboat, and keeping them on course. She was a quiet power. One Nikki admired deeply.

Her stepmom had been there when the worst hit—when they'd lost Nikki's father. She'd gotten them through it one day, one plan at a time. Then, she'd continued to be there for Nikki as the darkness came after her friends. Sometimes, she ached to tell her mom everything. To unburden all her secrets.

Nikki slid her hand into the pocket of her ripped-up jeans, finger landing on the sharp point of the clasp on the tiny bird-of-paradise-shaped pin she kept there. The pain was a reminder that she needed to stay silent. For a long time after Landry's death, she'd hidden the sapphire-encrusted brooch away in her luggage, unable to stomach looking at it without being torn apart by her deadly mistake. But ever since she'd seen the picture Holden had shown the band of the professor's brother meeting up with Angel Carter, she'd been tempted to tell everyone the truth. But she couldn't afford to do so. She wouldn't be the reason any of them got hurt again.

Ronan's arm went around Adria's waist, tucking her close. "Showering here or going back to the hotel?" he asked, hope gleaming in his eyes, and Nikki barely held back a laugh.

"Hotel. But I need to say goodbye to everyone. I'm not sure we'll see each other in the morning," Adria answered, turning toward the rest of the band gathered near the stage.

Fiadh's dark-mahogany hair lined with purple was a vibrant splash of color against Asher's black suit jacket as he held her to him. The couple was listening to something Holden was saying as Paisley, Jonas, and Leya looked on.

The former Secret Service agent who was now in charge of the multiple security companies and agencies trailing the band looked fierce tonight, like the superhero they sometimes teased him about being. He'd been especially on edge since Colombia, increasing their security until it was a tight knot around them and running the entire organization with an iron fist. If any of the detail made one mistake, they were let go. There'd been too many things that had gone wrong already this year. The only softness you saw in Holden was when he reached for Leya, as he did now, grabbing her hand and stopping her from playing with the leather and beaded bracelets layered on her arms.

Nikki and Adria made their way over to the others to say goodbye. The men were already offering each other backslaps and handshakes. They'd become almost as close as Nikki and her bandmates, forming a group Jonas laughingly called the Painted Daisies Ultimate Fan Club. Four men who'd do anything to ensure her friends' lives ran smoothly from now on. No more drama. No more kidnappings or death.

Nikki swore it too, but she was a club of one. A very lonely club.

She was the only person who knew the truth about Landry's death, except the killer himself.

You don't know for sure, a tiny voice inside her tried to scream. But she squashed it with a sharp prick to her finger. This time, the pierce drew blood. She felt it along the tip. She had dozens of matching pinhole marks now.

But at least she was alive to have them.

"See you in two weeks," Nikki said, hugging Leya before moving on to do the same with the others.

Then, each of the band members made their way to their separate vehicles that would take them and their partners to different entrances at the hotel. More security precautions. More things pulling them apart instead of keeping them together.

Tears pricked at her eyes. The goodbye left her unexpectedly emotional when, really, she should feel less so. Her loneliness would be temporarily broken tonight as Mom was staying with her. Since Ronan had hired her as his executive assistant last month, her mom had been traveling with them, helping him do his job remotely so he could be at Adria's side. Normally, her mom had her own room, close to Ronan's. But tonight, she was staying with Nikki so they could leave bright and early for the French Riviera, Nikki's sailboat, and the meandering trip around the Mediterranean they had scheduled for the holidays.

They'd spend Christmas on deep blue seas. Just the idea of it, of having the smell of the salty air surrounding her and the wind on her face while basking in the tradition her father had once started, brought a sense of calm to her. It was a respite Nikki needed even when she felt guilty for taking it.

The more Holden and the team had dug into Landry's death recently, the more she'd felt the need to tell them everything. But she knew, deep in her heart, doing so would only lead more darkness to their doors, and she refused to be the reason another one of them died.

Nikki had been able to hide her tension from her bandmates because they were lost in their new relationships. But her mom had been eyeing her funny lately, as if she knew there was a dam inside Nikki that was leaking. She was desperately trying to patch it, hoping she had what it took to hold back the swells.

You're stronger than you know, Nik. Training can help you, her father's voice came back to her. He'd pressed his palm to her chest at the time. *But your heart will give you more strength than any skill Jerome or I will teach you. Men have lifted cars off children because of it. It won't fail you when you need it most. It will be the one thing that saves you.*

More tears poked at her eyes. Damn did she miss him. It had been over nine years, and it still hurt enough to rip through her with a simple memory.

"You look worried. What's wrong?" her mom asked.

Nikki's finger settled on the pin again inside her pocket, and she shook her head. "I'm just tired. The sun and rest will be good for me."

"The weather shows a storm hitting us for a couple of days, but the rest should be clear."

Nikki turned to really take in her mom in the shadows of the back seat. "You look tired also. Is working for Ronan wearing you down?"

Her mom fidgeted with the arm of her glasses, adjusting them, a move Nikki had watched so many times that it brought an unexpected comfort. Like walking into the house and smelling cookies baking. "I have a lot I'm juggling, but I wouldn't change it. The job was perfectly timed."

Nikki rested her head on her mom's shoulder. After her dad had died, the structure Clarissa had brought to their lives was the only way they had made it through. One task, one goal, one moment. It was what made her extremely good at her work as an executive assistant, juggling high-powered people's worlds. But in the last two years, her mom had changed companies three times. Sometimes, Nikki wondered if what had happened with Landry, the way she'd had to step in once again to keep Nikki on an even keel, had brought back her mom's grief at losing her husband.

More guilt settled over her.

Nikki closed her eyes. When her life was over, she wondered how many negatives would be added up. Was she doomed to an afterlife of torment for the sins she'd been responsible for? Whether she'd known about them or not, she'd still been the catalyst…

Her temples throbbed.

No flickering white lights though.

Maybe it wouldn't become a migraine.

Maybe she'd get through a week without one.

She'd never tell anyone they were getting worse. Like the pinpricks to her fingertips, they felt justified. Earned.

She should find a therapist before everything she was holding in destroyed her inch by inch. Maybe when the tour was over, she'd make an appointment. She'd pick a different person than the one she'd gone to after her dad's death. That one had been useless, advising her to journal and tell everyone how she was truly feeling. If she'd done that, if she'd told anyone how she felt, she would have been screaming at the top of her lungs for days on end.

No.

She'd buried her emotions just like she'd buried the truth. She'd do the same now, and somehow, she'd survive it. She had to. She needed to be there for the people who were counting on her. Her mom. The band. Their team. It was the only penance she could pay that wouldn't cause more pain and grief.

Chapter Two

D'Angelo

ARMY OF ONE
Performed by Bon Jovi

D'Angelo watched from the shadows as a man eased out of the alley. Dressed similarly to D'Angelo, all in black, the man settled at the side of a dumpster with a clear view of the hotel's entrance. The man opened a rifle case he'd had slung over his back, quickly adding a scope and suppressor to the weapon. He checked the clip, and D'Angelo noted it was full. There were enough bullets there to kill a dozen people and make it look like yet another mass shooting. But D'Angelo knew the real truth because he'd seen the ruby pin on the man's jacket.

As the SUV containing Nicolette and her mother pulled underneath the hotel's portico, the man shifted the rifle in the direction of the vehicle. An unexpected wave of anger overtook D'Angelo. Sharp. Bitter. Strong. This asshole thought he could snuff out the bright light that was Nicolette without thought or consequence. The fury that hit him was stronger than he'd felt in over a decade. The emotion was unwelcome. It was even more dangerous than the man standing in front of him.

As if to taunt him, D'Angelo's father's voice came back to him. *You're angry, Son, and that's okay. Your emotions are powerful tools. Harness them, wield them like a sword. Just don't let your enemy see them, as they'll use them against you.* His father had been right, because his dad's enemies had used his love for his family in just that way. He'd been blind to the attack. He hadn't seen them coming.

And that was the job. To see it all. To be prepared for anything and everything. It was easier to have no emotions and rely solely on your skills to get the job done. It was safer. If he allowed feelings to sneak in, not only might he miss something, but the guilt and regret might raise their heads as well, and he'd never be able to function if he started doubting himself now.

As Nicolette emerged from the armored vehicle, D'Angelo moved forward on feet that made no sound, hand sliding under his jacket to the bandolier that held rows of knives instead of bullets. The assassin never heard him coming. Never knew until the knife had already silenced him.

Another kill. Another death. His soul was black with it.

He tossed the man and his gun into the dumpster. Instead of the nothing he'd trained himself to feel on the job, the rage still simmered. They'd come for her and may have succeeded if D'Angelo hadn't been there.

When he turned to find Nicolette with his eyes, her mother had also stepped out of the vehicle, and the two women had been surrounded by their bodyguards. The anti-royalists were getting desperate. The sniper would have had to take out several men before he'd gotten to the women. It had been a risky play at best because her detail would have reacted instantly after the first shot. The security surrounding the Daisies had gotten tighter and significantly better since Holden Kent had taken over. D'Angelo didn't want to like the man, but there was a piece of him that did, or at least respected what he'd done. The band was safer than it had ever been.

And yet, it was in even more danger.

The man in the dumpster was just the start of it as the clock counted down the last few minutes of the year.

D'Angelo caught a glimpse of Nicolette's black corkscrews blowing in the breeze as she stepped toward the lobby doors in torn jeans, heeled boots, and a leather jacket with her white-and-yellow daisy embroidered on the back. A Royal Haze daisy. If he was a person to find humor in anything, he would have found it amusing she'd unwittingly chosen that particular flower to represent her in the band.

His gaze followed her as she headed inside with a grace that couldn't be taught. Her shoulders were pulled back, stance straight, showing off her small curves that swayed delightfully as she walked. She was stunningly beautiful. Regal. She'd make a picturesque queen. His queen. He had to remind himself of that whenever watching her poked at some wolfish part of him that wanted to devour her. It was simply desire, and yet, it felt like something more. Something that could turn into a different emotion if he let it. An emotion he had no intention of feeling.

He tugged the hood of his jacket down farther over his brows and stepped out of the alley just as Nicolette's mother turned toward the street, searching it, and he cursed silently, stepping back into the welcoming shadows. Clarissa Rani had spotted him the other day as well. Either he was slipping, or she had a sixth sense when it came to her stepdaughter.

When she finally turned to follow Nicolette into the hotel, he eased back out of the alley, crossed the road, and moved around to the employee entrance at the side. Even entering there, instead of the lobby, he would stand out. People tended to remember you when you were six foot seven. But he had years of experience blending in, shrinking his frame until it was nothing but a vague memory. A half-assed recollection people would be unable to describe.

He made his way down a side corridor and used the key card he'd swiped from the staff room to let himself into the bowels of the hotel. There were more dark corners here. Better places to secrete away in the shadows where he belonged. Where he could keep his sins to himself.

His boots were soundless along the cement floor as he found his way to the little hideout he'd made for himself. Three nights ago, he'd stationed an empty laundry cart in front of a series of pipes and wires in the back corner of the basement, and no one had moved it since. Not even the hotel security who'd been through the corridor. It was ineptitude that irked him when he should have been grateful for it. It allowed him to do his job with ease.

But it also put Nicolette at risk. Because if he'd done it, who else had as well?

D'Angelo maneuvered his massive body into the tight corner, dropping his backpack at his feet and pulling out the tablet he'd left tucked behind the pipes. He stuffed an earbud into place and swiped the screen to see the two women had already made it inside the suite. They were safe, for now, but as the sand in the invisible hourglass hovering over their heads began to dwindle away, they wouldn't stay that way. A strange anxiety had started to grow inside him lately. More feelings he'd attempted to stuff away, hating the weakness they represented.

His people—his country—were counting on him. The stakes were as high as they were ever going to get. He'd wasted too much time already in trailing the Daisies. At first, it had been to ensure Nicolette was who they suspected she was. Then, it had been to find the assassin who'd mistakenly killed her friend. He needed the man to lead him to the person commanding the anti-royalists. They needed him taken out before they brought her in so there wouldn't be a snake in the grass waiting to strike. The *Cavalieri* had been confident they'd find the traitorous bastard before now, and yet the days had slipped away, and the Judas was still on the loose, still sending men like the one in the alley to finish her before she had a chance to claim what was hers.

Irritation spun through him that he had to force back

down.

His only consolation for having let so much time slip by while trailing the Daisies was in knowing he'd been able to exact justice against those who'd wronged them. He'd gotten revenge in a way the Daisies' security would never have been able to do. Not only because of ties that bound them legally but also morally. D'Angelo didn't have those same constraints. He'd been bred to do anything.

All in service of the crown.

Like his father had before him. And his father before that, going back centuries.

The sound of the shower running could be heard through his earbud. He'd hesitated while installing the cameras in the bathroom three days ago. Was it the wild beast in him or the actual need to have eyes on every part of the suite that had him slipping the camera in place? He'd never know for sure. All he did know was that he had to keep her safe for a few more hours until his plan came together. Until he had her next to him for good.

As he swiped through the camera views, his fingers hovered over the steam in the bathroom. Just the single thought of her bare under the stream was enough to have his entire body tightening. He quickly flipped the screen before he risked seeing her like he had accidentally weeks ago. It had been another hotel, in another city, and he'd switched the camera on without knowing she'd just emerged from the shower. His breath had disappeared. It had been like watching Rhaibele herself descend from the heavens. Nicolette didn't have an ounce of extra flesh on her. She was composed of purely cut lines and defined muscles that traveled the tall length of her, accentuating her small curves. Seeing her that way, invading her privacy, had given him a new reason to hate himself.

He'd been disgusted with his body's instant reaction to her. He shouldn't have craved her. She wasn't his to have or want or even look at as a man would a woman. It was a violation of the oath he'd taken. His duty was to the crown he served, and she was the embodiment of it.

He tightened his jaw and concentrated on the next camera, the one in the living area of the suite. Clarissa Rani was pacing, fingers on her phone, glaring at it. It made his eye twitch, an inner warning he'd learned to listen to. He pulled out his phone, skimming through the screens until he came to the clone of her device. There was a text from Jerome Barry saying he wanted to see them in Monte Carlo.

Surprise filtered in for the second time that night. None of the alarms he'd set around Barry had pinged to notify him of the man's travel. Knowing Barry would be in Europe right as everything came to a head made D'Angelo determined to dig deeper into the man's life. To start over and look for any gaps and holes he might have missed when he'd investigated him previously. Was there any way Barry could be tied to the anti-royalists and San Fiore?

Clarissa looked up as the bedroom door opened, and Nicolette emerged in a pair of tight pajama bottoms and an oversized sweatshirt. Her hair was wrapped in a satin scarf, hiding the shiny black coils underneath it and putting her oval face on display. Her slim nose was set artfully between eyes so dark a brown they looked black at times…like his midnight-blue ones could as well. Her full lips were curved upward at the edges as if she was permanently smiling. Even now, without lipstick, they were tinted a soft red, as if from heated kisses. Sensual. Tempting.

He turned the volume up.

"Jerome wants to see us before we set sail," Clarissa said.

Nicolette's brows went up. "He's in Europe?"

"Conducting a joint training effort with a French Special Forces unit." Clarissa headed for the bedroom. "I'll tell him we can have dinner with him tomorrow night."

Nicolette's smile grew until it settled in D'Angelo's chest like a sunbeam, as if it could burn through the black shadows lingering there and wash away the dark spots on his soul.

An absurd notion. One he pushed aside just like he did the longing that always hit him when he saw her. Longing and at that something more he couldn't name. Something that felt bigger than respect and more like devotion.

There was no room for anything but one-hundred-percent focus right now. He wouldn't make the same mistakes his father had.

After the two women settled in for the night, D'Angelo pulled a laptop from his backpack and opened his file on Barry. He'd investigated the former Green Beret-turned-government-consultant as soon as the police report on Landry Kim's murder had listed him as one of the people at the farmhouse. The man seemed to have an alibi. He'd flown into New York from a joint training exercise he was conducting with the U.S. government and the Ukrainians and had just barely arrived before picking Clarissa up from her hotel and heading to the Swan River Pond farmhouse. The man had supposedly come to Grand Orchard for the same reason Clarissa had—to check on Nicolette due to the stalker messages the band had been receiving.

Jerome and Clarissa had been one of dozens who'd been concerned and watching over the band in those days. Unfortunately, no one had been there to prevent Landry from losing her life.

D'Angelo had seen it firsthand.

He'd seen the blood on her throat and the unseeing eyes.

He'd heard the tormented cries of her sister when she'd found her moments later.

What he hadn't seen was the person who'd done it.

He'd been a handful of minutes too late. In many

ways, it had been his failure more than their detail's because D'Angelo had known what to look for when they hadn't. He'd allowed himself to be persuaded into believing it really was a stalker without the skill or balls to actually follow through on his threat.

But a stalker hadn't been the one to kill Landry.

The feather on the scene, if nothing else, had proven it.

D'Angelo gritted his teeth and drew his mind back to the task at hand. How would Barry being there alter his plans for Monaco? He'd go with them to the hospital if everything went according to D'Angelo's schedule. He wouldn't wait outside the room like her detail. He was in his sixties, but the man was still a trained Green Beret. If he saw D'Angelo, there'd be a commotion, and that was what he couldn't afford. It would draw her bodyguards, and then he'd have to hurt people who were only doing their job. It was the one thing he avoided—harming innocents.

He pulled up the hospital's floor plan. Could he revise the plan this late in the game? Intercept her somewhere else?

His phone vibrated.

COMANDANTE: Where are we?

D'ANGELO: I'll deliver her to you the day after tomorrow.

COMANDANTE: I'd feel better knowing the plan. Knowing when to expect her so we have others in place.

D'Angelo, on the other hand, wouldn't feel better if others knew. He preferred working alone unless he didn't have any other options. The fact that he didn't this time, that he was having to use people in Monaco, was already making his eye twitch. He shouldn't doubt the strength and loyalty of his brotherhood. The *Cavalieri d'Oro* had never been breached.

Except with Dad. He'd never been able to prove it, so he pushed the thought away.

> *D'ANGELO: All that's important is she'll be there well before the deadline.*

He shut off his phone before he could see the *Comandante's* response. He despised the fact he'd continued to botch one aspect of this mission. In never catching Landry's killer, the leader of the anti-royalists remained at large, weaving his threads. It was as if D'Angelo had been hunting a ghost. Someone with almost the same access and resources as the *Cavalieri*.

Which resurrected those doubts he hated.

Instead of following a rabbit he'd spent too many years chasing until his boss, his father's best friend, had pulled him from the black hole, he spent the next few hours doing what he was renowned for within the brotherhood. He broke into secure locations, looking for clues, searching for answers. He was in so deep that Nicolette's phone alarm going off actually surprised him. He'd spent the night digging and getting nowhere. He'd found nothing new on Barry. Just some redacted videos of him conducting trainings in the Middle East.

He slammed the laptop shut and stuffed it into his backpack with one eye trained on the cameras in the suite. Nicolette climbed out of the bed with her long legs bare. She'd lost the pajama bottoms at some point, and the deep bronze of her skin caught and held his gaze. There were parts of her that showcased the Black woman her great-grandfather had given up his crown for, and others that showed off the Native American ancestry she'd inherited from her biological mom, but there was also something that was just uniquely Nicolette. All the pieces of her having come together in a way that could never be replicated. A stunning perfection causing that ache in him to reemerge. The one he could never quite explain.

His time trailing the Daisies had somehow made him soft. Emotional. Malleable.

He packed up, disconnecting everything but the surveillance until the last minute. Until Nicolette left the room, dressed in jeans and an oversized sweater that still couldn't hide the beauty of her curves underneath, with her mom beside her. Whereas Nicolette seemed to shine, Clarissa seemed to fade into the wallpapered hall, blending in.

He yanked the cord from the tablet, adding it to his other equipment in the backpack, and slid from behind the laundry bin. His body was stiff from sitting on the floor all night. It wasn't anything he was unused to, but at thirty-five, it took a greater toll than it had when he was ten years younger. He shouldn't even be in the field anymore. He should be sitting at the table with the other *sergentes,* but he didn't know if he'd ever be able to sit back and just direct the action without taking part in it.

He moved through the hotel's basement, slipping quietly behind the cleaning crew stuffing their carts for the day. No one even looked his way. Sometimes, he wondered if he was actually invisible. If he was as cursed as the people of San Fiore believed the monarchy was.

As he emerged from the employee entrance, the overcast Irish skies loomed above him. Dark thunderclouds blocked the weak sun, and heavy raindrops landed on his face, landing in the heavy beard he'd grown and reminding him to lift his hood. He strode along the building, head down, at a pace he'd perfected over the years. Not hurried enough to draw eyes, but quick enough to let him eat up the sidewalk.

When he arrived near the hotel's entrance, he stepped behind the pillar and watched as Nicolette and Clarissa got into the vehicle heading to the private jet terminal and their flight to Nice. The SUV's door had barely closed before D'Angelo's phone pinged. He glanced down and saw she'd written a text in the Daisies' group chat. A sweet goodbye she didn't know would be the last before her entire world changed.

Because no matter which way the next few days fell, the life she'd been living would be over. She'd either be dead—and him along with her—or she'd no longer be just the quiet guitarist of The Painted Daisies. She'd be much, much more.

Chapter Three

Nikki

LIVING A LIE
Performed by Aly Stiles and Julian Greene

SEVEN DAYS BEFORE

Something deep inside Nikki rejoiced as they returned to the coast of the Ligurian Sea. The ocean felt different here than anywhere else on Earth. Even the air felt different. Golden and shimmering with some hidden magic. Nikki wished her dad had sailed with them here before she'd lost him. Instead, he'd said there was too much to explore nearer to home, teaching her and her mom to sail along the stormier waters of the Pacific or the teal depths of the Caribbean.

As she looked out the hotel window at the marina filled with expensive yachts and sailboats, her shoulders relaxed ever so slightly. One more night and then she'd be on the water again. Her heart leaped in her chest at the thought. Maybe she'd find some peace there. Maybe she'd forget, for just a few days, the burden she'd carry for the rest of her life.

Even as she had the thought, her finger settled on the point of the bird brooch hidden in her pocket, and the full weight of her choices hit her all over again. She could never forget. She could never let the mantle slip.

She rolled her jaw, trying to ease the tension that had

her teeth clamped so tightly together it felt like they'd break. She'd end up with a migraine if she wasn't careful.

"We have time before meeting Jerome. I'm going to work out. Care to join me?" her mom asked as she came into the living area of the suite.

Nikki turned to see her mom was already dressed in yoga pants, a sports bra, and a tight workout tank. She was muscled and strong for her age. The effects of a dozen years of rigorous training that had started with Nikki's dad and continued after his death with Jerome. For Nikki, the workouts had been a part of her life for as long as she could remember. She'd joined her dad's sessions before she'd learned to read.

When she was on tour, it was harder to maintain her strength and skills, but not impossible. The band knew she worked out but respected her request to do so in private. Only a bodyguard or two knew her full strength because her father had embedded into her the need to keep it hidden. *Surprise is your biggest asset. If your enemy doesn't know your true strength, you'll have a better chance of escaping them.*

Before the nightmarish events of the last two years, she'd thought her father's words—his insistence that they be prepared—had been almost doomsdayer-ish. But she'd still loved the time she'd spent with him on the mats. She'd loved the way she had his complete focus when they were practicing, so she'd never rebelled against it. Once he was gone, she and her mom had continued the sessions, partly out of tradition and partly to honor his wishes.

"Give me five minutes to change," Nikki responded.

She shed her casual wear in the bedroom, pulled on workout shorts and a sports bra, and then rejoined her mom in the main area of the suite. They moved the furniture to the side, emptying the space in the middle of the room. They started with a warm-up routine they both knew like the backs of their hands. Choreographed steps that felt like a ballet, requiring balance, dexterity, and strength. Then, they moved on to Krav Maga sequences, brutal punches and kicks to the air using a strength that came from deep inside.

An hour later, they were both sweating, but their breathing was still even.

They'd barely finished the last set, and she'd started to turn away when her mom's fist came at her face. Nikki blocked it on instinct, and they engaged in a strangely fierce battle. One Nikki hadn't faced in months. She ended up on her back with her mom straddling her. She barely blocked the heel of the palm coming at her nose. Her mother grabbed her wrist and came at her with the other hand as Nikki lifted her thighs, dug her heels into the ground, and flipped them. Then, she was pushing her hand toward her mom's face.

Her mother laughed, tension leaving her muscles. "You're stale but still come with surprises." Her mom's gaze settled on Nikki's hand inches from her face, and her eyes narrowed, gripping Nikki's wrist harder. "What's wrong with your finger?"

Nikki moved in a flash, breaking the contact, standing, and pulling the heavy bundle of her hair in the bun at the top of her head tighter.

"Nik?" Her mom lifted herself into a sitting position with her legs crossed and her palms settled into her lap.

"Snagged it on a sharp fret," she said calmly.

"That didn't look like just a snag, Nikki. That looked scarred and broken open again."

"Don't be silly."

"Then let me see it."

"I'm not a teenager, Clarissa. I don't need you hovering over me, waiting to see if I'll break. I'm fine." As soon as the words were out, she regretted them as her mom's concerned face shut down until there were no emotions left. Nikki couldn't remember the last time she'd called her by her name. Certainly not since her dad had died. They'd been a team—friends, even more than just a mother and daughter.

"I see," her mom said, standing and heading toward the bedroom opposite Nikki's in the suite. "We have an hour until we meet Jerome. We're at La Pauletta, so wear something nice."

The door shut, and Nikki let out an exasperated sigh. Her mom was the last person she should have taken her frustration out on, but she also couldn't have her probing deeper. If she did, Nikki knew she'd break. She'd spill every ugly detail burning up her insides, and that would only put her mother at risk.

You can't tell them. You'll risk them all.

The professor's words swirled in her mind all the time. She'd seen the devastation of his office that awful day, and yet she'd still agreed to meet with him. She'd likely led the killer to Landry. For what? A stupid idea that she belonged to some ancient kingdom? Ridiculousness. Fairy tales that would never come true. It was the imagination of the damn romantic child inside her who needed to grow up.

And yet, if it was just a nonsensical notion, then why had they come for her?

Stop it! she yelled silently to her curious brain. "You can't go down that road *ever* again." She said the words out loud, forcing herself to listen.

She hurried into the bedroom. She had an hour to get ready. She needed to concentrate on one thing at a time as she had been doing for years.

Before she got into the shower, she sent a text in the group chat with the band.

NIKKI: Is everyone home?

LEYA: Holden and I are in D.C.

FEE: Asher and I made it to Boston. Adria and Paisley are still mid-flight to LA. How's

Monaco?

NIKKI: Beautiful. Warmer than the East Coast, I'm sure.

LEYA: All of us should have come with you. It's snowing here. I could use the sunshine.

FEE: And give up your first Christmas with Holden's family? You wouldn't have.

Nikki snorted. It was true.

LEYA: You're right. After all he's done to learn our Hindi traditions, I want to celebrate this with him. How are you holding up, Fee? For the first time, you're going to be a mom on Christmas morning.

FEE: Stepmom at twenty-six…seems…unbelievable.

Nikki's eyes drifted toward the door of the suite and the walls separating her and her mom. Her heart sank all over again for snapping at her.

NIKKI: Wren's lucky to have you, Fee. I know because I have a wonderful stepmom too.

FEE: Clarissa is almost too nice.

LEYA: She has to be in order to put up with Ronan's control-freak ways.

FEE: Says the woman engaged to a massive superhero of a control freak.

*LEYA: ***laughing emoji*** Well, sometimes I like him taking command.*

FEE: I bet you do.

NIKKI: As we've now dissolved into sexual innuendos, and I am decidedly left out, I'll say goodbye and go get dressed for dinner.

FEE: We need to hook you up, Nik. It's been too long since you've taken anyone back to your hotel room.

LEYA: How did I not know that Nikki took anyone back to her hotel room?

NIKKI: Because I use discretion, unlike Adria and Fee.

FEE: That just means you've never felt so worked up you couldn't wait.

NIKKI: I'll never be you and Asher, basically disrobing in the middle of a stadium.

FEE: As I've said repeatedly, he'd just asked me to marry him, so it shouldn't count. We should be given a free pass for any PDA that happened that day.

NIKKI: So, if I get engaged, you'll give me a free pass?

*FEE: ***falling off chair laughing GIF****
I'll believe you're engaged when I see it.

Nikki was smiling again as she put the phone down. She loved them. It made every burden and every secret worth it. They were content, and safe, and living full lives. The best kind of fairy tales. Real happily ever afters that they'd earned. She may never get one, but at least they had. She'd do anything to make sure they kept them.

♫ ♫ ♫

Even after Jerome showed up in the suite with flowers, her mom remained withdrawn. Nikki's stomach clenched tightly as they headed out to the restaurant. She knew she needed to apologize, otherwise the next two weeks on the water were going to be anything but relaxing. Her finger found the tiny pin inside the pocket of her dress. The fact there were pockets at all had been the entire reason she'd chosen the gold satin to begin with.

Tucked into a small building not far from Monte Carlo's most famous hotel and casino, La Pauletta was the epitome of exclusive French restaurants. Eighteenth-century furniture, sparkling crystal, and hushed voices. The dim lighting allowed the flickering candles to dance along the thickly brocaded wallpaper. Guests were required to reserve tables several months in advance, no matter how big of a celebrity you were or how many dollars were in your bank account. Which meant Nikki's mom must have booked it as soon as they'd made the plans to go sailing over Christmas break.

As they stepped up to the desk, the maître d' looked them up and down, as if assessing their net worth and the appropriateness of their attire in one fell swoop. Once he'd deemed Nikki's cocktail dress, her mom's burgundy-and-black sheath, and Jerome's charcoal-gray suit suitable, he turned on his highly polished dress heel to lead them to a booth at the back.

After the waiter had come and gone with a flurry of decisions being made about wines and appetizers, Jerome turned his pale-blue gaze on Nikki. Unlike many veterans who'd lost their strength and speed after leaving the service, Jerome was still trim and fit. It wasn't the gray mixed into his buzz-cut hair, or even the wrinkles time had written on his skin, but the experience and loss in his eyes that truly revealed his sixty years.

"Your security has gotten better," he said, glancing toward two of her detail at the front of the restaurant.

"Holden has managed them with an iron fist since the incident in Colombia."

"They were outnumbered in Cadencia. Not much a man can do when it's hundreds to one," Jerome said, and Nikki's eyes widened in surprise at him knowing as much as he did about the incident. He chuckled. "I keep my finger in the pot, Nik. I promised your dad I'd look after you, and I do."

Like always, mention of her dad flooded her with emotions.

"I'm glad you're here and talking security. You can tell Nikki how we need to keep at least one of her detail with us on the boat," her mom said, brushing a finger along the linen napkin on her lap.

"And where will we put them, Mom?" Nikki asked.

Her mom's eyes narrowed. "We can turn the table down, or you and I can bunk together."

Nikki barely held back a frustrated sigh at the repeated conversation she'd had not only with her mom but Holden. With its two staterooms and a dining table that could be turned into a bunk, the *Tangled Melody* was big enough for a hulking bodyguard to go with them, but she wanted to breathe without someone lingering around her twenty-four seven. Someone who might not know how to sail the way she and Mom did. She didn't want to spend her entire two weeks off ensuring they stayed out of the way when things got dicey. She needed this time to honor her father. To remember all the winter-break trips they'd taken as a family.

Back then, they'd sailed on her dad's sixty-foot yacht docked in Marina Del Rey. Now, she added another boat to their family's collection, leaving this one in Europe so they could sail from the Atlantic or the Pacific at any time. It was one of the few splurges she'd allowed herself from the money she'd earned with the band and the surprise inheritance she'd gotten after her father died.

"Unless we're attacked by pirates, there's no way someone can hurt us while we're at sea," she said and turned to Jerome. "My security detail knows our schedule and will have people waiting in each port. We'll be fine."

"I just want to go on record as having said I oppose the idea," her mom insisted.

Nikki didn't reply. Why have this argument yet again in front of Jerome?

"Pirates are relatively unheard of in this part of the Mediterranean, especially if you keep close to the coastline," Jerome agreed.

Mom didn't look happy he'd agreed with Nikki, but no more was said as Jerome shifted the conversation to safer ground. As the courses came and went, they discussed the tour, her mom's work with Ronan at the movie studio, and Jerome's current assignment with the government. It felt comfortable and relaxed…like being with family.

Maybe it was because Christmas was so close that Dad's memory was weighing on her so heavily today, but she wondered what he would have added to the discussion if he was there. Would he have teased her mom about her worries? Would he have harassed Jerome about the gray in his hair? Would he have been surprised that the Daisies had actually made it big?

He'd been nervous about her joining the band before he'd died. He'd always preferred keeping a low profile and had even forbidden Nikki to have any social media accounts. As head of internet security at a major corporation, he'd seen exactly what could go wrong and how your privacy could be invaded. Even now, she hardly used any of the accounts the band's PR folks had created for her.

Nikki and her mom declined dessert, opting for espressos instead, and the waiter pouted, as if they were somehow ruining the experience by bypassing the last course. The man's frown pushed Jerome into ordering the profiteroles the restaurant was renowned for, but when the waiter came back, he carried two plates instead of one.

He placed Jerome's dish in front of him, and then, with relish, placed the second in front of Nikki. "Almond cake for you, Ms. Rani. A gift from a fan. They didn't want to embarrass you but wanted you to know how much they love your music."

The waiter's voice dripped with flattery. Nikki glanced out at the tables, trying to identify the person who would be enthusiastically watching the dessert's arrival and her response to it. She couldn't see any particularly eager eyes, but she still couldn't reject it without offending the unknown person.

"Tell them thank you," she said. She picked up the fork and dug into the cake as if she was going to eat it. The waiter smiled and moved off. There was no way Nikki was taking a single bite of the nut-filled treat for the same reason she hadn't drank a sip of the wine Jerome had ordered. She couldn't afford the migraine trigger, not after the string of them she'd been having.

She looked up to find her mom watching her. Mom sighed and said, "Slide it over here. I'll eat it on the sly so you won't upset them."

Relief filled Nikki, and with Jerome shifting forward to help block the view, her mom ate the dessert instead of her. The plate was almost empty when her mom suddenly clutched her throat, and her eyes went wide.

"Mom?" Nikki leaned forward, grabbing her other hand. "Mom, what's wrong?"

Her mom's mouth opened, but nothing came out. Not even a cough or a gasp. At first, Nikki thought she was choking, but then white foam emerged, coating her lips.

Fear flew through Nikki as she cried again, "Mom!"

Jerome sprang into action, pulling her mom from the booth and laying her on the floor. He checked her pulse, saying, "Clarissa. Stay with us, hon."

Nikki slid to the floor beside her, heart pounding viciously as she grabbed her hand, squeezed, and called out, "Help! Someone help!"

Nikki thought she heard someone calling emergency services, but it was from a tunnel as terrifying images flew through her mind. Another funeral. More death. Losing the one person who'd been her rock for the last nine years.

"Please don't leave me," she begged, a sob escaping her chest.

Her mom's eyes were wide with shock before they rolled back in her head. Her body shook, and more foam escaped her lips. Jerome was bent over, listening for her breath, and then he started chest compressions. Nikki's heart and lungs constricted, tears making her vision blur.

There were shouts and muffled cries as the customers began to freak out. Her bodyguards had sprinted over and were hovering as Jerome continued to work on her mother.

"Please, don't let her die, Jerome!"

She squeezed her mother's hand even harder, her tears falling onto her mom's arm.

She hadn't had a chance to apologize.

She hadn't been able to ask forgiveness.

And then, amongst the heartache and panic, the truth hit.

The dessert had been meant for Nikki.

Chapter Four

D'Angelo

GHOST OF LOVE
Performed by Imelda May

The ambulance arrived ten minutes after the call D'Angelo had placed—well before Clarissa had even started to react. The paramedics administered a dose of naloxone spray and Clarissa started breathing again. Nicolette's face had been a sea of relief, fear, and sadness as she trailed her stepmom to the ambulance surrounded by her bodyguards and Barry. Once the ambulance took off, she was directed into her detail's SUV.

In the chaos of the EMTs arrival, D'Angelo had retreated to the black motorcycle he'd left outside the restaurant, and now, as her SUV swung away from the curb, he slid in behind them. He kept his distance as he maneuvered the bike through the crowded streets. This area of Monte Carlo was busy at night, and the traffic slowed their progress.

As he followed them, Nicolette's large eyes, full of trauma and loss, tormented him. Clarissa wouldn't die. He'd made sure of it. But when he'd put this plan into motion, he hadn't thought about how she'd react to the potential loss of yet another person in her life. He'd only been concerned with ensuring she understood the danger that was coming for her. He'd been solely focused on the end result. Now, the guilt wouldn't leave him alone, and he itched to cut it out and throw it away. To bury it.

He'd been on this assignment too long. Gotten too close.

But he'd finish it because the crown needed him.

He'd finish it and then get the hell away.

He parked the motorcycle on the street near the delivery entrance of the hospital behind the Mini Cooper he'd placed there earlier. He'd rather use the bike again, but he'd have to trust the modified car would have the speed and maneuverability he needed to get through the busy streets quickly.

He raised his hood, drifting in the shadows until he got to the door where the security guard raised crossed fingers to his heart and then his temple in an ancient sign of shared brotherhood. D'Angelo eyed the man with his stomach hanging over his belt and shoulders that hadn't seen a bench press in years and wondered how this man was one of his brothers. The *Cavalieri* prided themselves on strength. Readiness. Honor. This man screamed laziness.

It made D'Angelo cringe inside, but he didn't know if it was his instincts talking to him, or if it was just because he'd had to use more individuals today than he'd had to use in years. There'd been three people at the hospital, two at the marina, and then Langston on the boat in the bay. Langston was the only one of the bunch he trusted unconditionally with Nicolette's life.

He slipped into the building that looked more like a five-star hotel than a hospital, ignoring the stunning views of the ocean. He went directly to the hospital room one of his insiders had marked as being under repair. He shed his black apparel for scrubs, shoving the clothes into his backpack. He double-checked the bandolier under the shirt, ensuring his knives were in easy reach, and then retied his military boots and tucked another two knives there. The boots would give him away if anyone took the time to look at them. Her bodyguards should. They should note any discrepancy, but hopefully, he'd be gone before they even realized they should have paid attention to him.

He pulled a needle filled with midazolam from his backpack, shoving it into the pocket of the scrubs, and suddenly hating the idea of using it to knock her out as much as he'd hated the guilt from the events at the restaurant. He gritted his teeth, tried to push back those emotions into a well of nothingness to focus on the plan, and stepped into the bathroom.

It was a mess of tile and Sheetrock. Earlier, he'd pulled out the sink and mirror, cut a hole between this room and the one next door, and then fixed the bathroom on the other side so the makeshift door was invisible. He'd set up cameras and mics in the adjacent room, giving him complete access to what was happening. He used a tablet to swipe open the video feed, waiting poised by the hidden door for the right moment.

Not even an hour later, the room bustled to life as orderlies and nurses wheeled Clarissa Rani in and set her up in the bed, hooking her to wires and monitors. Even though he'd known she'd live through the fentanyl overdose, he still felt a strange relief at seeing her breathing. He'd calculated the amount carefully. He'd known this would happen, and yet, Nicolette's face full of tears continued to haunt him.

A few minutes later, Nicolette, Barry, and the bodyguards appeared. The bodyguards cleared the room, scanned the empty bathroom with its false wall, and then walked out. Nicolette went to her mother's side, grabbing her hand and sinking onto the chair next to the bed. Her hair had tumbled from its precarious perch atop her head, the curls spiraling about wildly, landing well below shoulders that had been left exposed by the tiny gold dress.

The satin barely covered any of her muscled frame, and it had drawn eyes at the restaurant. People who didn't even know her as a member of The Painted Daisies had watched as she'd glided through the tables with a natural grace and vitality. She always seemed to shimmer with it, but tonight, he'd found himself hating every single one of the looks sent her way. Worse, the desire in their eyes had made him want to tear them apart limb by limb.

More reasons to drop her off in San Fiore and then disappear again into the shadows.

D'Angelo watched as Barry sat across the bed from her.

"She almost died! Because of me!" Nicolette whispered.

"You heard the doctor. She's going to be fine, Nik," Barry said. "This could have just been food poisoning. Let the authorities do their job. The blood tests will tell us more."

She shook her head, not believing him, and D'Angelo was filled with a pride he had no right to. She was smart enough to know this had nothing to do with bad food. She and Barry stared at each other for a long moment, words not being said but communication happening anyway. The man rose from his chair.

"Let me see what else I can find out." He strode out of the room toward the nurses' station, and D'Angelo suddenly wished he'd installed cameras there as well.

His eyes were drawn back to Nicolette when her mom's voice, scratchy and faint, broke through the beeping of the machines. "Nik."

Nicolette leaned forward, brushing hair from Clarissa's eyes and said, "You're okay, Mom. You're going to be okay."

Clarissa stared at her for a long moment. When she spoke, her voice was tired and drained. "You know, I never wanted to be a mom. I'd never liked babies. Never intended to put my body through the trials of pregnancy."

Nicolette's face showed all her emotions. Troubled. Confused. She reached down and squeezed her mom's hands again. "Shh. Just rest."

Clarissa ignored her, continuing, "I never wanted a relationship either. The first time I met your father, he was so cocky and sure in our Krav Maga class that it made me dislike him. But then, he smiled, and it was…unexpected. The first time he took me to your house, you surprised me too. You were nine. I shouldn't have expected you to be a baby, but the fact that you seemed like such a little adult was perplexing. You were a whole person already with your own stunning personality. You had his smile and his eyes, but a hint of something even more. That was the moment things changed for me."

"We wheedled our way into your heart," Nicolette said with a watery smile.

"You did. Sent all my life plans spiraling."

"You were meant to be part of our lives, Mom. We were lucky to have you."

Clarissa closed her eyes as if the words pained her. "I wouldn't have married him, you know. He gave me an ultimatum."

Nicolette's brow raised. "He did?"

"He could feel my hesitancy, I guess. Those years of me being on my own and my desire to keep it that way. He said he couldn't bear the idea of you having and losing another mother figure. He said as much as he loved me, I had to be all in or not in at all."

Nicolette's throat bobbed. "That sounds like Dad. He'd deny himself anything if it meant the people in his life had what they needed."

Barry's laugh outside the room drew Clarissa's attention, and she forced herself up on her elbows, leaning toward her stepdaughter, and lowered her voice. "Listen to me. You need to get out of here. You need to board the *Tangled Melody* tonight and go. Once I'm out of here, I'll meet up with you."

"What?!" Nicolette asked, shock and worry rippling through her. "No, I'm not leaving you."

"We both know that dessert was intended for you, Nikki. You need to get the hell out of here. On the boat, just like you insisted, there'll be no one but you and the sea. Here"—her stepmom waved around the room—"there are thousands."

"This was just an accident," Nikki said, reversing what she'd just told Barry, and D'Angelo cursed silently.

"Go. Use the sat phone to keep in contact. Once I'm released, I'll ditch Jerome, and we'll meet in Vernazza."

The twitching in D'Angelo's eye was back, slamming into him, and his body stilled at her words. Nicolette had the same reaction, eyes going wide. "You can't possibly think Jerome had anything to do with this."

Her mom's gaze darted toward the doorway where Barry was still talking to a nurse. "He wasn't supposed to be in Grand Orchard that day, Nikki. We'd talked about the stalker notes, and I'd told him I was going to check on you, and he said he was stuck in a training exercise. Then, he surprised me by showing up. Even then, even after Landry, I didn't think anything of it. There was no reason to. Not after the years we'd spent as practically family. But then…tonight…"

Nicolette was shaking her head. "He knows I wouldn't eat almond cake, Mom."

"Something hasn't been right with him, Nik. He's been secretive. He used to tell me things… And now…I can't tru—" Clarissa gasped as if in pain, and then her body fell back on the bed and began twitching again.

"Mom!" Nicolette cried and then turned toward the doorway, shouting, "Help!"

Barry and a nurse came running. The nurse pulled out more of the Narcan nasal spray. She shot it into Clarissa's nostrils, and after a few moments, her body grew still.

Barry looked from Nicolette's mom's prone figure to her, eyes concerned. "What happened?"

It wasn't Nicolette who responded but the nurse. "We often have to administer several doses to counter the effects of the fentanyl. It's pretty normal."

Nicolette was watching Barry, eyes wide, and D'Angelo could almost hear the whirl of her thoughts. The fact he was special forces, and someone with skill had killed her friend. The idea that he'd surprised Clarissa that night in Grand Orchard. D'Angelo's mind was spinning with the same thoughts—more doubts about the man.

Nicolette grabbed her tiny handbag from the foot of the bed where it had lain and headed for the door.

"I need… I need some air. I want to change out of this damn dress. I'm going to go to the hotel, but I'll be back."

"I'll come with you," Barry said.

She shook her head. "Will you please stay with her so she isn't alone?"

Barry looked unsure.

"Please. I won't be gone long, and I have my detail," she begged.

Barry still didn't look happy. He shoved his hands into his pockets while glancing out at the bodyguards. There was something in the air that was sending signals to D'Angelo he knew better than to ignore. Instincts that had kept him alive for far too long. There'd been no sign of Barry being connected to the anti-royalists, and yet little things kept pointing back to him. Maybe the man was that good. Maybe he'd planted all the information D'Angelo had found in case anyone came looking.

Finally, Barry gave her a curt nod, and D'Angelo cursed silently as Nicolette twirled around, heading for the door. There was no way to get her out of the hospital now without causing a scene with her bodyguards. He hated deviating from plans he'd made weeks ago and had cost him an entire day to enact. But he had a backup plan. He always had several.

In the room next door, he waited until her team had taken her down the hall toward the elevators. Then, he grabbed his backpack from the gurney he'd intended on using to hide her body and strode toward the back elevators. His mind was already whirling with the secondary plans, including the layout of the streets he could take to beat her back to the hotel and the marina nearby.

In the basement, he jogged past the security guard with another two-fingered salute. He really wanted to take the motorcycle again, but he'd need the Mini Cooper once he had her.

"Where's the girl?" the security guard called after him. "Thought it was going to happen tonight?"

The hair on D'Angelo's neck rose, and he eyed the overweight man once again.

"Perhaps you should worry more about getting to a gym than my plans."

The man made a strangled noise of irritation that D'Angelo ignored as he merged into the darkness outside. Down a block, the Mini Cooper waited for him. He folded his body into the tiny vehicle. His head touched the ceiling, his shoulder was jammed into the door, and his hip pressed against the console, but it was fast and agile.

He shoved the car into gear and merged in with the oncoming traffic. He palmed his phone and pressed a few buttons. When the man on the other end answered, D'Angelo said, "We're a go at the marina."

"Now? She's going out in the middle of the night?"

"Now, Langston."

He hung up, flying through the alleys and side streets that were quieting down for the night as the bars closed and people went home. Another two-fingered salute had the guard at the marina's entrance opening the gate for him. He parked the Mini in the shadows of the gatehouse, got out, ditched the scrubs, and reassembled his black uniform with relief. He leaned his body up against the building, almost disappearing in the shadows.

He pulled the tablet from the backpack and searched the folders until he found the one with the cameras at the hotel. Nicolette and her bodyguards were in the elevator.

He didn't have a plan formulated to take her from her suite, and he cursed himself for it. Instead, he'd have to wait and see if she really did what her mother had asked and took the boat out. Langston was right. Setting out at night solo was not recommended, even for the strongest of sailors. Nicolette was experienced. She'd been on boats since she was a child, but this was different.

Maybe he should have stayed at the hospital.

If she returned, he could put his plan there back into play.

He hated he hadn't been able to predict this.

Hated that one missed step could mean failure for him and, worse, could end up with her dead and his country in ruin. San Fiore had been ruled by the Fiorani family for thousands of years. He'd be damned if it ended on his watch.

Chapter Five

Nikki

THORN IN MY SIDE
Performed by Bon Jovi

The hotel suite was silent, but Nikki's blood was humming furiously inside her veins. Adrenaline spiked from fear and worry but also confusion. She didn't know what to do. Her heart was telling her to stay. To go back to the hospital and make sure her mom fully recovered, and yet Mom's voice and years of listening to her dad telling her to trust her instincts were screaming at her to run.

The memory of her mother convulsing on the restaurant floor and then again at the hospital filled her vision.

Her chest grew tight, and tears threatened.

She looked in the mirror above the desk in the bedroom and found eyes that were haunted and red-rimmed—again. How many times had she cried like this? For her father, and Landry, and each of her friends as they'd faced the worst? How could all of this happen to one family?

Because of you!

The thought came fast and unbidden.

Professor Maynard had told her the same thing, but she'd still tried to deny it. She'd wanted to keep the single shred of doubt she had left that all of this was because of her. She fingered the bird-of-paradise pin in her pocket. She should have had no doubts after Holden had reviewed the evidence that had been gathered on Landry's murder while they'd been enroute to Colombia. The most damning evidence had been the long, blue tail feather from the birds kept by the royal family. San Fiore was the only place on earth you could find the Regina astrapia. But that hadn't been the worst part. The worst had been finding out the knife used to kill Landry was one given only to the Green Berets.

Pain ratcheted through her.

She couldn't believe the man she'd known as an uncle, the man who'd trained her alongside her father and loved her father like a brother, would be behind any of this. They were family. Surely he wouldn't try to kill her?

Her mother had to be wrong. There had to be another explanation.

But Nikki knew, with a sudden sense of clarity, that her mom was right about one thing. She had to leave. Not for herself, but to keep everyone else safe. If she was around, there was a chance others would continue to get hurt. On the *Tangled Melody* she might be injured, especially considering the risks that came with sailing alone, but at least no one else would be resigned to the same fate.

She stripped off the gold dress and stilettos, pulling on jeans, a bright-blue sweatshirt, and her all-weather boat shoes. Her hair had tumbled out of its bun, and she just left it. The long curls would end up a snarled mess that would be a nightmare later, but she didn't have time to fix it. She needed to be gone.

Most of her luggage had already been placed on the boat because they'd planned to leave at dawn, so she had only a few things left at the hotel. She grabbed her messenger bag with the Royal Haze daisy embroidered on it and shoved her charger and her pajamas into it before running into the bathroom and swiping all her toiletries in as well.

Her head was throbbing, but she couldn't afford to use the nasal spray that helped stop the migraines before they got too bad. If she did, she'd get sleepy and, worse, dizzy. She simply slipped all her prescriptions in her bag with the other items. She'd take something once she'd anchored the boat far enough away.

She needed to tell Jerome and her security detail what she was doing, or they'd come looking. But she also needed to put enough space between them that they wouldn't be able to stop her. She'd have to wait until the last minute before divulging her plans—at least until she was aboard the *Tangled Melody* and ready to push off.

She slipped out of the room and into the corridor where two of her detail stood at the ready. They'd come and gone in so many waves Nikki barely knew their names anymore. Another thing she regretted.

"I'm going to sleep on the boat tonight," she said.

The bodyguard didn't even flinch. He just put his finger to his ear and said, "Rani is on the move. We're headed to the marina."

They made their way down into the lobby and then out onto the street. It was easier to walk to the dock from there, so instead of getting into the SUV waiting for her, she turned and headed down the sidewalk.

"Ms. Rani!" the man called, and she just continued.

He and the other guard caught up to her.

Neither said anything, but they relayed their whereabouts to the command post.

Nikki wondered if Holden was getting all this back in D.C., or if he'd actually taken time off to spend a few days with Leya and his family. If he was keeping up on what was happening, she should have already gotten a string of texts or calls from Leya. From all the Daisies. It was strange she hadn't, but she couldn't stop to think about it. Not now.

The security guard at the entrance to the marina eyed them as Nikki used her thumbprint to open the gate. She showed him her identification card, and he nodded her through, but she felt his eyes watching her as she and her bodyguards moved through the maze of slips. The boats ranged from yachts the size of a small cruise ship to much smaller sailing vessels like the *Tangled Melody*.

One of the bodyguards slipped onboard, unlocking the cabin with her keycode and clearing the small space before stepping back out on the dock.

"You're not going back to the hospital tonight?" he asked. His voice was emotionless, and yet somehow, she still heard the reproach in it. How many people would just leave their mother in a foreign hospital after what she'd been through? Guilt washed over her. She should have been used to it by now, should have felt numb to the emotion, and yet every day it struck her with a fresh wound.

She swallowed hard and then answered with a shake of her head, "No, I'm in for the night."

They took up their stance on the dock, and she headed downstairs. She'd have to be quick and quiet to get away before they stopped her. She threw her bag onto the bench seat in the galley and shot off a text to Jerome.

> *NIKKI: I'm leaving. Please stay with Mom until she's better.*
>
> *JEROME: What do you mean you're leaving? You're going out on the water? Now? It isn't safe!*
>
> *NIKKI: Exactly. It isn't safe for anyone with me around. I'm heading out. I have the sat phone. Please call me if anything changes with Mom.*
>
> *JEROME: Nikki, this is ridiculous. You know how dangerous it is to sail by yourself, let alone at night.*

She ignored the text and the one that vibrated in after it, throwing the phone down on top of her messenger bag. She'd call the band and Jerome from the sat phone once she was out at sea.

She eased open the cabin door silently, thankful she paid a small fortune to keep the boat well-maintained and ready for her. She mounted the steps, peeking out over the seats in the cockpit. The two guards had their backs to the boat, facing both ways down the dock. They were talking about something in hushed tones, and she hoped they hadn't already caught wind of what she was doing from Jerome.

She kept herself low and slunk over to the knots tying the *Tangled Melody* to the quay. With experienced hands, she undid them. Then, she eased into the driver's spot at the helm and turned the key. The engine hummed to life, and the two men jerked around. In the dim light shining over the marina, she could see the surprise that littered their faces.

"Just charging the generator," she said, wondering if they knew anything about boats and if they'd see through her lie.

They both looked at her uneasily, but she just ignored them, leaving the engine idling and slipping back down the stairs. She eyed the phone sitting on the seat again.

Was she really doing this? Ditching her security? Leaving everyone?

Her heart banged wildly. Fear and aching loneliness filled her. She was tired. So tired of the remorse and the guilt and the constant waiting for something else to happen.

And it had.

They'd come after her and hurt her mom instead.

Her finger landed on the brooch in her pocket.

If she was really who Professor Maynard thought she was, some heir apparent to an island with the GDP larger than most of Europe, and someone didn't want her claiming it, would she ever be free? It seemed absurd and nightmarish. Her father would have known, and he would have told her.

But…maybe they'd killed him before he could.

That was what Parker Maynard had thought. He'd said her father's shooting wasn't random, even though they had a gang kid in jail for it. The teenager had always denied it, saying he'd been set up. But the gun and her father's wallet had been in his car. His prints had been all over them and the crime scene.

She caught a sob that tried to escape her chest. Her dad and Landry may have been killed by the same people, but surely her mom was wrong about Jerome. She couldn't believe he had anything to do with it. He loved them. They were his family.

She shook her head and moved quietly back up the steps. The bodyguards were relaxed again, and the engine was still humming quietly. She moved into place at the helm and shifted into gear. She always reversed in when she docked so she could head out without having to back into the lane, and tonight that preparation paid off. The boat was moving and had already reached the end of the slip by the time the two men realized it. They ran toward the edge. "Ms. Rani!"

She waved a hand and hollered over the noise of the engine and the breeze that had kicked up. "I decided not to wait until morning. Tell the team I'll check in on the sat phone."

As soon as she was in the lane, she increased the speed. She turned on the driving lights and carefully maneuvered through the bay until the bodyguards were left behind along with the speed buoys.

Instead of feeling relief, she felt a moment of panic and more aching loneliness.

Then, she threw her shoulders back and hit the throttle another notch. But instead of kicking into gear, the engine let out a cough and a sputter before dying completely.

"What the hell?" Nikki said with a frustrated groan.

She pulled a flashlight from the cockpit, eased along the deck until she got to the hatch to the engine compartment, and was just about to go down when a voice called out to her from the dark.

"Ma'am, you can't stop your boat here."

Nikki jerked back, and her flashlight slipped out of her grip. As it hit the wooden planks, it turned off, rolling away. She turned to find an SNSM boat pulled up alongside her. A French Coast Guard turned a spotlight on her. How had she not heard it? Had it been there in the darkness all along, and she hadn't seen it? Her heart banged wildly at the thought of what would have happened if she'd accidentally rammed into them.

"I know. Just having a little engine trouble," she said.

"Do you need us to call a tow?"

Her stomach fell. If she was towed back in, she'd never get away. Jerome and her detail would put the kibosh on it. Holden and the Daisies would try to talk her out of all of it. Worse…she'd burst. The guilt and regret and secrets would boil over, and if they knew, they'd be in danger.

"I don't think so. Let me just take a look at it. I'm sure I can get her going again," she said. She leaned over, feeling around in the darkness for the flashlight, and that was when someone grabbed her from behind.

An enormous arm locked around her waist, and she reacted on instinct. She lowered her stance, gripped the man's forearms, and attempted to flip them both. He countered the movement with his own, locking her legs between thighs that were like vise grips.

Nikki cried out, hope flaring as the officer from the SNSM boat leaped onto the *Tangled Melody*. She struggled against her captor, using the heels of her palms and her feet to inflict damage. But the man holding her was the size of a mountain, and she felt as ineffectual as a flea. To her surprise, instead of helping, the officer turned toward her engine compartment. Her heart fell into her stomach as the realization hit that they were together.

She turned her head and bit into the man's bicep, knowing it was futile to break skin through the sweatshirt he was wearing, but hoping the surprise would give her an advantage. And it did. He grunted, easing his hold ever so slightly.

She let herself go limp and slipped down, almost out of his grasp. She grabbed his hand as she went, wrenching his wrist backward. She wasn't going to go down without a fight. These people… They were the reason she'd lost so much! They'd taken things from her she'd never get back, all for some damn fairy tale that might not even be true. Anger swarmed through her, twisting with the fear and giving her a burst of adrenaline.

She stomped on the top of his foot, wishing for the stilettos she'd abandoned or even her clunky, heeled Doc Martens, anything but the soft-soled boat shoes. His arms loosened even more, and she kicked backward, colliding with a knee, and was satisfied to hear another grunt of pain. She took one step forward before an iron grip surrounded her waist again.

The man in the engine compartment shined his light in their direction and said with a hint of laughter in his voice, "You need some help there?"

They were laughing at her.

They thought this was funny?!

She used every ounce of muscle she had and every bit of knowledge she'd earned training for just this situation—when you were outsized and outmuscled—but none of it worked. The giant who'd captured her had her pulled back up against his chest, arms and legs constrained by his, in less time than it had taken for her to take a shaky breath.

Chapter Six

D'Angelo

MONSTER
Performed by Skillet

D'Angelo had been surprised by her strength. By the knowledge of hand-to-hand combat she seemed to have. Even now, when he thought he had her subdued again, she thrust the heel of her palm backward, barely missing his nose as pure instinct had him jerking his head back. She still managed to hit him in the cheek with enough force he'd have a bruise.

He tightened his hold, dropping his mouth next to her ear. "Stop struggling. I'm not going to hurt you."

"Fuck you!" she said, folding at her waist and attempting to roll him over her back in another practiced move. Who'd trained her? There was nothing in her history that even showed her working out, but it must have been Barry. The Green Beret had spent time with both Paisley Kim and Ronan Hawk. He should have suspected this.

Another thing he'd missed. Another mistake he'd have to shoulder tonight.

He gripped her wrists, crossing her arms over her body in a knot. He knew the pressure on her shoulders would be enormous. Knew he was one tug away from causing her a serious injury. It was the opposite of what he'd been chartered to do. Save her. Protect her at all costs. And here he was, about to dislocate her shoulder.

"I won't hurt you," he repeated.

But his words seemed to have the opposite effect than he'd intended, and she continued to struggle violently. Fuck. He was going to have to use the needle. As he loosened his hold on one wrist to reach into his pocket, she smashed her head backward. If he'd been a normal-sized man, it would have hit him in the chin, but it only barely grazed his chest.

His fingers found the needle in the sweatshirt's pocket, flicked the cap off as she kicked backward, hitting his knee a second time, and then he was pressing the tip into her bicep. She cried out, fighting harder for a moment before the fast-acting sedative had her body slumping into him. He caught her before she fell to the ground.

When he looked over, Langston was smiling, and it made him want to wipe it off.

"Never thought I'd see the day," the man said.

"Get the engine going, and get the hell out of here."

D'Angelo threw Nicolette over his shoulder and headed for the side of the boat. In one large leap, he'd gone from *Tangled Melody* to the SNSM boat Langston had parked in the bay waiting for her.

He placed her on a bench and then turned to the helm. He started the engine, wishing he could head straight to San Fiore, to be rid of her and the emotions wafting through him—pride, respect, that damn ache he always felt looking at her, and a new fire. Fire that had been triggered by simply touching her. But there was no way the small boat they'd requisitioned for this part of the plan would make it to San Fiore. He'd thought, if they'd needed to enact this backup plan, it would have been during the day, and Nicolette and her mom would only stop for a SNSM boat. He should have planned for this scenario as well so he could have taken her straight to the island.

Frustration and anger—all self-directed—flooded

him as he headed back into the marina instead of the open water. He needed to capture the feelings and lock them away, or worst case, funnel them as his father had trained him. There'd been too many fucking variables he'd left untied, all because he'd gotten cocky. He'd been assured of his plan working.

As his irritation eased, his mind started to spin new scenarios, and he realized it might have worked out for the best this way. Everyone in her life would think she'd run of her own accord. He had her sat phone cloned. He could send the needed text messages to keep the truth hidden for a few more days.

Easing the Coast Guard vessel into the marina, he docked in a slip on the opposite side from where she'd left her bodyguards. He doubted they were still there. They'd likely scrambled back to the hotel, but he couldn't take any chances.

Once he'd tied off the boat, he opened a large crate he'd stored there as part of his backup plan, lifted Nicolette, and curled her into it. His heart thudded for a moment as she looked uncomfortably like the woman he'd locked into a coffin a few weeks ago. The only difference being that woman had deserved her imprisonment. This woman…she didn't even understand what was happening to her.

He ground his teeth against the wash of sympathy, lifted the crate onto his shoulder, and stepped onto the dock. He only needed to keep her there for a few moments. Just in case there was anyone to see him carrying a passed-out woman into the parking lot. Without glancing around, he strode at the pace he'd perfected toward the Mini Cooper parked in the shadows of the guardhouse. Making sure they weren't visible to anyone wandering by, he pulled her from the crate and set her into the passenger seat of the car, tilting it back so she was reclined. He'd just gone to shut the door when a voice had him freezing.

"Stop where you're at."

D'Angelo's body tensed. He slowly turned to find a SIG Sauer pointed in his direction. His gaze locked on the security guard's face as his worst nightmares came to life. The *Cavalieri* wasn't free of traitors. He'd known it. Felt it in his core after what had happened to his father and sister, and even though there'd been no proof to be found, even though the *Gran Duca* had insisted they were clean, D'Angelo had still preferred to work by himself. Better to be the lone wolf than be turned on by one of your own pack.

He carefully reached up as if he was going to scratch his neck, and the man's eyes glittered. "Don't move. I've heard enough about you to not trust anything you do. You have two choices. Live or die. But either way, she doesn't make it out of the marina breathing."

"Who paid you to turn on your brothers?" D'Angelo asked, his voice barely traveling across the space.

"Maybe I'm in it for the cause," the man sneered.

"If that were the case, you'd have the insignia," he said, nodding at the man's uniform shirt and the absence of a red lapel pin the man in the alley the night before had on. Those who truly believed in the anti-royalist's movement always had one. The rest were just mercenaries—weasels for hire who only believed in ways to increase their bank accounts.

"Just because I'm not wearing it doesn't mean I don't have one," the man stepped forward. "Move aside."

D'Angelo wanted desperately to use his fists and his knives to get information out of the man. Not only because he needed to know who their leader was but because he was furious at the way the guard had casually thrown away centuries of *Cavalieri* loyalty. But he didn't have the time. He needed to get the hell out before someone saw or heard something they shouldn't. Before her security detail or Barry came looking.

He extended his elbow just enough to reach the first knife tucked into his bandolier, his fingers closing on the hilt. He studied every breath the security guard made, eyeing the careless flick of his wrist holding the gun as the man said, "I will shoot you."

In one flowing movement, D'Angelo had tugged the knife from its sheath and sent it sailing through the night where it plunged into the security guard's eye. The man howled, and his gun clattered to the ground as he reached for the blade lodged in his face. He fell to his knees as D'Angelo reached for his second weapon. In one large bound, he was at the man's side.

"Who paid you?" D'Angelo growled.

"Fuck you," the man gasped. "Forever sixty-five."

D'Angelo cut his carotid arteries and flung the man from him.

He sprinted back to the car and slammed the passenger door shut. He'd just rounded the back of the Mini when a shot rang out. He pulled his Glock from his waistband, whirled around, and returned fire. A second shot came from the opposite direction, and he sent a bullet toward that assailant as well as he reached the driver's side. Two more rounds filled the air with an eerie staccato rhythm he returned. A muffled cry traveled through the darkness as one of his bullets took purchase. Then, he was inside the car, shifting it into gear, and squealing through the lot toward the chain-link fence.

He drove the Mini Cooper straight through it, but as he hit the street, a motorcycle slid in behind him.

His fucking motorcycle. The one he'd left at the hospital.

Anger flared to life, growing inside him like a flame that threatened to burn him up if he didn't douse it. Threatened to put them in more danger because he'd be unable to see beyond it. But, fuck, they were using his personal resources against him. There was no way the safe house was an option now.

The proof of someone in the *Cavalieri* betraying them burned inside him. The demon others called a soul raged. He'd kill them all. He'd end every life of every brother who'd turned their back on centuries of honor and loyalty.

But first, he had to get Nicolette to safety.

He needed to ditch the Mini Cooper.

His mind ran through a thousand different calculations, including street maps, possible locations, and how much money he had on him.

The stoplight in front of him turned yellow, but he didn't slow, steering the car onto the thankfully empty sidewalk. Shots rang out, busting the rear window, and glass rained down around him. He spun the wheel, taking a sudden left and running another red. It was late enough the streets had thinned some, but brakes still screeched, and horns still honked as he flew through the intersection.

The last thing he needed was the police chasing them.

He needed to lose this asshole.

He made two quick turns, aiming for an even less congested street. The motorcycle rode his tail, more bullets riddling the back of the Mini. Damn it. He couldn't risk her getting hit. On his third turn, he spun the car one hundred and eighty degrees, gunning it back toward the motorcycle just as it cleared the corner. Metal crunched against metal, and the driver flew over the hood with a resounding thud.

Punching the accelerator, the tires squealed as he headed back the way they'd come, searching the streets for more vehicles with guns. He'd taken four more turns before he felt safe enough to slow down. Spotting the driveway for a parking garage, he whipped inside, steering through each level, mind logging all the cameras he'd have to hack in order to delete any evidence of tonight's events.

At the top of the garage, he pulled in next to a Volkswagen Golf GTI. It was common enough to go unnoticed but had enough speed he could put his foot into it. He dug in his backpack for his equipment and had a new fob keyed and ready within two minutes. Two minutes too long. They needed to get the hell out of Monte Carlo.

He transferred Nicolette into the new vehicle, buckled her in, and tilted the seat back again before sliding into the driver's seat. At the exit, he paid the "lost ticket" price, adding one more hack to the long list that would keep him up through the night.

He emerged onto the motorway, heading out of Monaco, grateful for the nonexistent border control between it and France.

Nicolette's head slid sideways, and a soft moan escaped her lips that had his breath evaporating for multiple reasons.

He couldn't afford for her to come awake yet. He needed time to get them somewhere safe. To get somewhere he'd have the time to explain while she struggled and fought.

Time he didn't have.

Chapter Seven

Nikki

KARMA

Performed by Taylor Swift

Her mouth was dry, and her head pounded as Nikki woke. Her eyes felt heavy, and they fought opening, as if she'd taken one of her pain pills. She put a hand to her head, trying to orient herself. There was light behind her lids. Weak, natural light as if it was early morning.

The tour… What stop were they on?

Images slowly started to filter in, and as they did, her heart started to pound. The pace picked up with each new memory she reassembled.

Monaco. Her mom! The hospital. The *Tangled Melody*.

She'd been kidnapped!

She forced her eyes open and struggled to sit up. She was on a large bed squeezed into a small room with a severely sloped roof. The bed's frame was wrought iron painted white like the downy comforter on top of her.

She looked down, seeing with relief that, other than her shoes, she was still fully clothed. There was water on the bedside table next to a bottle of ibuprofen. She desperately wanted both but knew better than to touch either.

She rose on shaky legs. She felt weak and lethargic,

like she often did after a migraine, but this was from the needle that had filled her with who knew what. Her bicep was sore from where he'd jammed it into her.

Her breath caught, thinking of the enormous, hulking body of the man who'd taken her from her boat. She'd never gotten a good look at him in the dark while trying to escape. She'd barely been able to register his size as she struggled against him. Waves of fear rolled through her all over again. She had to get out of here.

Remain calm, her father had taught her. *Breathe through the rush.*

She inhaled slowly, closing her eyes, steadying her body, and then letting it out.

Concern for her mom filled in behind the fright. Was she okay? How long would it be before anyone realized Nikki had been taken? Would her mom just think the satellite phone wasn't working on the boat? Would the unspeakable have happened to her in the meantime? Would she be dead like Landry?

Why wasn't she dead already?

Her friends! God, the last thing they needed was another one of them to be taken. How stupid was it—how completely absurd—that they'd all been attacked?

Her eyes went to the tiny window shoved into the peak of the building. It was covered with a thin lace curtain Nikki drew aside. It wasn't the sight of the ocean that surprised her but the ancient stone wall running down to it. A flock of seagulls cried out as they passed by the glass. The sun was just barely cresting over the waves, turning the blue into a sparkle of pink and gray.

She knew this town. She and her mom had stopped here before. Antibes was one of her favorite locations in France. If she could get to a phone, at least she'd be able to tell the authorities where to find her.

She turned toward the door and saw her boat shoes resting at the foot of the bed. She slid them on and got dizzy just from looking down and back up. She had to steady herself using the bed frame before stepping forward again. As she approached the door, the old plank floors creaked, and she froze. Had he heard it?

She stood in that same spot, the pounding of her blood ringing in her ears and making it hard to hear anything else. After several long minutes with no one bursting in, she eased forward again, gently pressing on each floorboard to see if it would make a sound before she put her full weight on it.

The doorknob seemed as ancient as the bed and the building she was in—aged copper spotted with greens and blues. It would be beautiful if it wasn't on the door of the room where she was being held captive.

Her fingers closed around it, turning slowly and fully expecting it to be locked. She was more than a little surprised when it turned silently in her hand. She tugged gently, hoping the hinges wouldn't screech and give her away.

She'd scarcely opened it a couple of inches when she registered a distinctively human shape sitting on the floor in front of it. His back was against the opposite wall, and his long legs were spread wide, planting his booted feet on either side of the doorframe, essentially caging her in. He was enormous. The largest man she'd ever seen. The hood of his sweatshirt was pulled low, covering his forehead and eyes, but his long straight nose was visible, and he had a full mouth embedded into a beard so dark and black it seemed to absorb the light.

She knew him. At least, she knew the image of him and the name he'd given her friends. The pulse she'd tried to slow bounced back to life, hammering against her wrists and her chest like an injured bird trying to escape. She stood motionless. Frozen not only because of who he was but also because he was strangely beautiful.

He didn't budge. Only his chest showed any signs of life as it expanded and retracted below a black sweatshirt. He was asleep. She'd have to cross over his leg to get to the narrow stairwell that was just beyond him. She swallowed hard, taking in every inch of him before she made any moves. His arms were at his sides, and his hands, so large a single one could surround her neck, were resting against the floor. Her stomach flipped when she saw the butt of a gun tucked partially under a massive thigh.

She had to go before he woke.

She eased the door open just enough to slide out and stand between his spread legs. Not trusting herself in her weakened state to stay stable, she put a hand on the doorframe before raising her foot. She'd barely moved it when his hand snaked out and grabbed her ankle.

"No." The one word was deep and guttural. A command he expected to have followed. And it sent chills coursing over her body. She'd never heard a voice that deep in real life.

The warmth of his fingers soaked through her jeans, embedding itself into her skin…her veins…her bones. The heat was almost more overpowering than the physical grip, as if it was branding her in a way she'd never escape.

"What do you want?" she asked and hated that her voice shook. Hated that it sounded tired and unsure when she wanted to sound strong and confident.

Don't let them see your fear. Her father's voice rippled through her as if he was there. As if he was right behind her, training her all over again.

"You," the dark voice traveled through her, and her body reacted as if it had been a sensual word issued by a lover, and she silently cursed herself. "Safe."

He raised his face, and eyes so dark a blue they were almost black met hers. The look in them was fierce and yet somehow tortured, and it hit her in the chest. *He doesn't want to be here…doing this*, she thought and immediately scolded herself. How could she possibly know what this beast of a man thought?

She jerked her foot out of his hold and placed it back down. She was still trapped between his legs, and she eyed his groin and then her soft boat shoes. Could she even strike him before he'd draw the gun?

The only thing you can do once a bullet is let loose is to get out of its way. The key to getting away from a gun is to prevent it from being raised. The lesson returned to her automatically along with the seriousness of her dad's dark-brown eyes as he'd spoken the solemn words.

She'd barely flexed her thigh, preparing to kick him, when he said, "Don't even think about it." He was deadly calm. He picked up the gun, and both it and his hand came to rest over the zipper of his jeans. The bulge underneath seemed to grow, and her eyes darted up to his face again.

His eyes were wary.

"If you want me safe, Angel Carter, then you need to let me go," she demanded, lifting her chin in a defiance she wasn't sure she felt but was determined to fake anyway.

"That's not my name."

She scoffed. "I've seen your picture. Fiadh and the others have already identified you."

He pushed the hood back, and she could finally see his entire face. Her breath evaporated. He was…stunning…in the darkest of ways. A fallen angel. Black hair and black brows with olive skin stretched over bones crafted from stone. A bruise bloomed along his cheek, and she realized, with a start, it was from her striking him on the boat. This man who'd seemed untouchable to her and her friends had been marked…by her.

She shivered.

His gaze drifted down her in a way that would have been sexy if the situation was different. Then, he shifted as if to rise, and she stepped back on instinct, running into the door and causing it to drift open farther.

He slowly came to his feet, wide shoulders taking up the entire hallway as his head grazed the slates of the roof. She had to look up to meet his eyes again. He was almost a foot taller than her five foot eight, making her feel frail and vulnerable when she'd never really felt that way before. Her dad had trained her to be strong, and her mom and Jerome had kept her that way. Even after everything that had happened with Professor Maynard and Landry, she'd never felt weak, only exposed, guilty, and angry. But she knew, with absolute certainty this man, with his massive hands and body, could snap her in two without even breaking a sweat.

For years, he'd been blending into the shadows, drifting in and out of the Daisies' lives, and she wondered how he'd been able to do it just considering his size, let alone the way his entire being demanded you pay attention to his presence. How could anyone not have seen him when he was around?

She had. She'd seen him back in Grand Orchard. She'd thought he was godlike…magical, and she still felt that way. It wasn't just his physical appearance. There was an aura, an energy to him that was impossible to ignore.

She should be terrified—and there was a piece of her that was—a piece of her screaming, "Run!" But there was another part of her, a larger part, that was simply reacting in a primal way to the entirety of him. To the astonishing masculinity and magnificence he presented.

She crossed her arms, and the movement drew his eyes to her chest. They flickered with a darkness—a heat—she thought might just turn her to ash if it was ever allowed to consume her—which was the very last thing she'd ever let happen.

She needed to escape. She needed to remember every skill her dad and Jerome had taught her. She reeled through one move after the other, attempting to find any that would help her with someone his size. What would her mom do if she was here? God…her mom!

"Please, Angel," her voice cracked. "Let me go. I need to check on my mom."

"Again, that isn't my name."

"What is?"

His eyes narrowed. "You haven't earned that yet, *Principessa*."

Her heart pounded at the word. Did he know? His gaze held a truth she couldn't afford. The last time she'd let herself believe in the possibility of that word, her friend had died.

She pushed back the panic growing steadily larger inside her, lifted her chin, and said, "Fine, Kraken, you need to let me go."

His eyes widened in a moment of surprise, and then his lips twisted into what might have been a smile but ended up looking like a cruel snarl.

"Created by Ceto, the Kraken protected the Titans. It's more fitting than you can imagine."

"Because you're protecting Titans by kidnapping innocent females? Am I supposed to offer myself up as a sacrifice?"

His nostrils flared, and white-hot flames leaped in the depths of his gaze as he said, "The only sacrifice will be mine."

Her heart stopped and started again, the pulse in her veins so strong she was certain he could hear it. "That hardly seems logical when you're the one who kidnapped me."

"It's my duty to keep you safe."

She blew out a frustrated breath. "If you wanted me safe, you should have left me on my boat."

"You weren't safe there. Not by yourself or with your mom."

Nikki's throat bobbed. "I need to know how she is."

"They'll release her today or tomorrow. She's recovered."

She stared at him. Was he lying? Or did he really

know somehow?

He took a step toward her, and she backed into the bedroom farther, retreating to the window.

He glanced at the water bottle and pain meds she hadn't touched.

"You should drink."

"And have you drug me again? No thanks."

"It isn't spiked."

She just stared at him.

He shoved his gun into his waistband and strode toward her. She pulled back as far as she could into the window's alcove, and still, his arm brushed against her, causing shivers to rush through her. He twisted the cap off the water bottle, the sound of the seal breaking filling in the silence. "It wasn't open."

"There could be a pinhole somewhere."

His eyes narrowed, and then he took a drink before handing it to her. "I wouldn't drug myself."

"You're twenty times my size. That one little sip would probably do nothing to you."

His lips curled again, and he huffed out what might have been a laugh but sounded more like a grunt that landed somewhere in her belly.

"Who taught you to be this suspicious?"

She almost blurted out her dad and then bit her lip to keep from telling him anything. The less he knew, the better.

"You're dehydrated. You need fluids. I can force it if I need to, but I'd prefer not to." He said it with a deadly calm. It wasn't a threat. It was a fact. He could and would make her drink.

She yanked the bottle from his hand, and the mere touch of skin flared through her, leaving a trail of fire in its wake that was entirely too confusing.

"Fine," she said. She took several large gulps while

he watched.

"More."

She did as she was told, drinking about half the bottle before replacing the cap and holding it up tight against her chest as if somehow a stupid plastic bottle could protect her from him.

His hand reached into the front pocket of the hoodie he had on and pulled out something shiny. When he opened his palm, she saw it was her brooch. She gasped, letting the bottle drop to the ground and reaching for it, but he closed his mammoth fist around it again.

"Where did you get this?"

"Why do you care?"

"Answer me."

When she didn't respond, he moved slightly, eliminating more of the minimal space that had existed between them.

She responded quickly, "It was given to me."

"By whom?"

She didn't answer, eyes locked on the fist where the bird-of-paradise pin was held prisoner even more than she was. She didn't want to do this. She didn't want to let out the secrets she'd kept tightly coiled in her chest for nearly two and a half years. The secrets that had likely ended Landry's life. The ones that threatened her, her mom, and all those she loved. The truths that whispered in her nightmares about her father's death and things no one was supposed to know.

"Did your father give it to you?" he asked.

Her gaze jerked upward to his face. "Wh-what do you know about my dad?"

He searched her face with those midnight orbs. "I know he wasn't killed in a random shooting."

She gasped again, hand going to her stomach, pushing into it, hoping to stop the pain his words caused. Professor Maynard had insinuated the same thing.

"Nicolette, you must tell me where you got it."

Her gaze widened, searching his face. No one called her that. No one. Not her father. Not her friends. It was a name on a birth certificate she'd never heard breathed aloud.

Her teeth clashed together, the top sliding along the bottom, sparking pain through her temples she knew she'd regret and couldn't stop. It was all coming undone. The secrets. The lid she'd tried to shove over them, locking them away with the steel of her willpower. Everything was crumbling.

"If I tell you…they'll come for me," she whispered, fear and regret curling through every syllable.

It hardly seemed possible, but his dark gaze seemed to gentle as he said, "They already have."

Chapter Eight

D'Angelo

NOT RUNNING ANYMORE
Performed by Bon Jovi

D'Angelo watched the expressions travel over her face. She knew something. Maybe not all of it, but enough to be afraid. The fact she had the pin wasn't entirely the proof the Old Houses would demand, but it would be a kick in the face to any doubters. After they saw it, they'd want her blood. He needed to get her to the island, the castle, and the throne room, but after last night's debacle, he wasn't sure who he could trust.

"The only person who's come for me is you," she said, and he had to admire her defiance.

"Landry was killed by the same people who are hunting you now."

It wounded her, his words, and he hated himself for it. But she had to face the truth. She had to come out from hiding and declare who she was before everything he believed in collapsed.

"Why?" she asked, and the single word was full of remorse and torment. Emotions he was acutely familiar with and attempted to keep locked away while doing this job.

"Because your great-grandfather was Prince Dario Alberto Gregorio Fiorani, and you are now the last living heir of the Fiorani monarchy."

She hesitated for a beat too many, which made him realize she'd known more than he'd thought. Finally, she said, "Even if I believed that was true, surely I can't be the only heir. There must be others."

He didn't respond, but he also didn't remove his eyes from her face.

She looked away.

She needed a history lesson, and he wasn't a teacher.

"Drink," he told her. "I'll bring you food, and we'll talk."

He watched as she rubbed her temples with slender fingers. The tips of her index fingers were scabbed and scarred. Was it from her guitar? They looked like small pricks. His heart squeezed tight as the realization hit him. The pin. She'd been hurting herself with the pin. His jaw tightened. He shoved the brooch into his pocket. He wouldn't let her harm herself any more than he'd allow others to hurt her.

He'd gotten through the door when her husky voice called out to him softly, "Please…just let me go."

He'd heard the plea many times in his life while on assignment, from men and women alike. And not once had it ever done anything to the cold muscle that beat in his chest, but those five syllables she'd spoken landed inside him like an arrow, piercing the tough outer layer and causing blood to emerge just as the pin had done to her fingers. He couldn't afford it any more than his anger and fury at the marina the night before.

He had one job.

Ensure she took the throne before midnight on December 31st.

He turned to look at her. Her shoulders were pulled back even as she begged. Her hair a black halo lit up by the window behind her. It was the most awe-inspiring sight he'd ever had. Not the view from the top of the Alps, not the sun as it turned the castle on San Fiore into fire. There was nothing nature had created that could be as stunning as this woman…this queen…standing there, refusing to just go quietly into the night.

"Your life is no longer your own, *Principessa*. It belongs to the people of San Fiore. That is where I will take you. To them."

She inhaled sharply. He shut the door, locking it with an old-fashioned skeleton key before wedging himself into the tiny stairwell and going down two floors to the back of the house. A small kitchen with appliances so old they belonged in a storybook dated the house to the early part of the last century, and it reminded him of simpler times. Of visiting this house as a child with his family and playing in the tiny corridors with Antonella. The townhouse was owned by distant cousins who lived in Marseille but kept it ready for last-minute weekend getaways.

He'd used the place before, but usually with their knowledge. Last night, he'd parked across from it and watched for a long time for any sign of life before stealing inside to ensure it was empty. He couldn't stay here more than a night. The house was tied too closely to his family. But it had gotten them off the streets, and it had given him the time he'd needed to erase as many of the incidents in Monaco from the video feeds as possible.

He quickly made two sandwiches, grateful for the supplies his cousins kept there, before making his way back up the stairs. His body barely fit in the stairwell, but he was still light on his feet, and he didn't make a single noise. As he reached down to unlock the door, he was surprised to see it swing open.

Nicolette let out a startled shriek and backed up into the room. He held his breath in shock. She'd almost escaped. He looked down to find a bobby pin in her hand. Where had she gotten it? It was yet another thing he'd missed. Another failure.

She couldn't afford for him to keep having them.

She couldn't afford to escape, or she'd end up dead.

Frustration brewed inside him. How could he make her see that she needed to trust him?

"Where did you learn to pick locks?" he demanded, stepping forward and using his foot to slam the door shut behind him.

She didn't answer.

He set her plate on the bed before leaning against the door with his body, blocking her exit.

"Eat," he said.

She grabbed the sandwich and then surprised him yet again by approaching him. His body stilled, watching every move and yet unable, unwilling, to stop her approach as curiosity and longing filled him. When she was close enough to touch him, she swapped the sandwich for the one on his plate. His lips tried to twitch into a smile he couldn't remember having let out in…years…maybe even a decade.

She retreated to the bed, sitting cross-legged, facing him, taking a tentative bite. His sandwich was gone in mere seconds. He was used to eating fast and on the go. Food wasn't anything more than fuel to him. Savoring delicacies wasn't for the likes of him.

Left with nothing else to do, he watched Nicolette as she ate with a grace that shouldn't have been possible. Every move of her long fingers, every swipe of her tongue along her lips, even the way she chewed had him craving something only she could provide. As if he could find salvation in a simple touch.

He bit his cheek. Touching her wouldn't save him. Nothing could. Instead, it would cover her in the stench of his sins. The blood on his hands would take her light and dim it. Even if she wasn't his queen, even if the simple idea of touching her wasn't forbidden in his mind, he would never do that to her…to anyone.

His life was his burden and his alone.

As if uncomfortable under his scrutiny, she set the sandwich down. "Did you… Did you kill Landry?"

"No."

"But you were there," she said. "I saw you…that summer…" His eyes narrowed, but he didn't say anything, and she continued. "Holden said you were at the pond. That you had pictures of Landry before Paisley found her."

Her throat bobbing was the only sign she was upset. Once again, he felt an unreasonable sense of pride at her strength. Her ability to rein in her emotions would serve her well. Just like it had him. Until recently. Until she'd been thrust into his life, and he'd been slammed with them repeatedly.

He didn't want to talk about the night at the pond. He didn't want to talk at all. He wanted to drag her out to a boat and take her to San Fiore and be done with all these torturous thoughts. But in order to do those things, he needed her to trust him. So, he told her the simple truth. "I was afraid she was you."

Panic and despair had hit him in the gut when he'd first seen the body. Certain he'd already failed after just having arrived.

A flicker of fear came and went from her face before she said, "But you didn't—"

"No. She was already gone by the time I got there."

She had no reason to believe him, and yet he was almost desperate for her to do so.

"Why did you go to San Fiore last summer?" he asked, partly because he wanted the answer and partly to turn her thoughts from that awful memory. From seeing her friend. He remembered her cry. The grief in it as Jonas had pulled both Paisley and Nicolette into the house. He didn't want her to relive it.

She played with the edge of the sandwich, crumbling it. "I didn't want to go," she said quietly. "I tried to convince my mom not to…"

"It was foolish."

Her eyes whipped up to him.

"If I'd kept fighting her on it, she would have suspected something. After Lan…the professor…he warned me not to tell anyone. I couldn't risk Mom finding out, and we stayed barely a day."

"So, you knew. You already knew what you were to the people when you showed up?"

She rubbed her temples again.

"Knew what? A fairy tale Professor Maynard tried to convince me was true about abdications and disappearances? I didn't know my grandparents or my great-grandparents. My dad never talked about his family. My mom… She died when I was barely three, and she had no family either. It was as if my parents had found one another because of that…as if one lonely soul had been drawn to the other." She came to a complete halt, and he wondered if that was possible. If loneliness could draw you to another person. Was that what he felt when he looked at her? The ache inside him matching some similar feeling in her?

She took a deep breath, and continued, "My dad said the past was better left buried, and I thought… I thought he'd experienced abuse…or just ugliness. I never wanted him to be unhappy, and talking about his childhood made him sad, so I didn't press. I figured he'd tell me when I was older…when he was ready."

"And Clarissa? Does she have family?"

He already knew the answer. Knew everything there was to find on paper about Clarissa Rani, but Nicolette had relaxed some while talking about her family, and he needed that. He needed her calm.

"No. She's alone as well. She'd just moved to California when they met. She'd gotten out of a controlling relationship and didn't want anything more than friendship. But… well, sometimes love has other plans."

He knew she was thinking about her dad again. He

knew that pained expression. It was the one he felt deep inside whenever he thought of his own father.

"So, it was Clarissa's idea to go to San Fiore?" he asked, diverting her again from grief and pain.

She nodded. "She'd heard about the beauty of the island and its architecture but also the flowers and the birds. She promised the entire experience would be worth giving up our stay on Capri."

He suddenly wanted to know what Nicolette had first thought when she'd arrived on the island where he'd grown up running along the sand, through the coves, and up the narrow, curved streets lined with mosaic tiles. Everywhere you turned in the capital, there was marble and gold. The buildings, fountains, and statues of the gods were all dripping with it.

"What did you think of it?" he finally asked, not daring to hope she'd loved it at a mere glance. Not daring to believe the bond she had to it would have weaved its way into her soul.

"It's breathtaking. Like stepping into the past and the future all at the same time."

He felt another wave of pride at her words, but this time it was for his home. For her ability to sense the agelessness of the island. As if it lived in a bubble unaffected by the travesties of the world around it. A haven. Money abounded in San Fiore. There wasn't anyone who was living on the streets or in poverty. It was a Utopian world he would protect from everything and anything.

After the Romans had briefly invaded and then been repelled from the island, San Fiore had retreated from the world. For centuries, they had kept to themselves, never letting any ship dock in its harbor. They'd watched as Europe had been transfigured over and over again, passing hands like currency. Romans to German fiefdoms and beyond. It was only once San Fiore had grown its own military might that it had joined the modern landscape of

Europe. And even then, the Great War had tried to destroy it.

In many ways, they were still trying to escape the shadowy grasp it had laid on them. Most San Fiorians believed the curse uttered by a bitter mother during the war haunted the island and that it was the reason for the early deaths of its kings.

He'd never been a huge believer in the curse, but he knew one simple truth—the one he uttered gruffly, meaning every word. "San Fiore needs her monarch. She needs you."

Chapter Nine

Nikki

INTO THE ECHO
Performed by Bon Jovi

SIX DAYS BEFORE

Nikki's eyes widened at his words. When was the last time she'd been truly needed by anyone? The band had asked her to pick up Landry's guitar parts and her lyrics after her death, and Nikki had done so riddled with guilt. She'd wanted to fix it, fix them, in any way possible. She wouldn't have denied them anything, and yet what she really should have done was stay away. She'd put them all at risk all over again. This man had confirmed Landry had been killed because of her, and now her stepmom had almost been murdered as well.

She shook her head at him. "You realize how absurd that sounds."

"How much did the professor tell you?" he asked.

She fingered the unfinished sandwich again. "I *hate* talking about this." She looked up at him, pain radiating from her. "I hate that I listened, and Landry died."

"It isn't because you listened. It's because you didn't act."

His words landed like a knife in her chest.

"What?"

"If you'd come forward and claimed your throne, the *Cavalieri* would have protected you, and no one would have died."

She climbed out of the bed and stood in front of him, trying not to let him see her shake as fear and remorse and anger welled inside her. She clenched her hands, the bite of her nails in her palms a similar relief as her pin would have been, but not enough. He'd pocketed the brooch, and she wanted it back. She controlled her voice the best she could, raised her chin, and demanded, "Release me. I need to go back to Monaco. My mom and my friends will be worried."

"Your mom received a message from you this morning. You're on your way to Vernazza just as you'd planned," he responded.

Her heart hammered. "How in the hell did you do that?"

"Sat phones can be cloned as easily as cellular phones."

Her mouth dropped open for a moment before she clamped it shut again. "You cloned my phone? You've been listening and reading all my private conversations? How dare you!"

He took a step toward her. His bulk and his height should have been intimidating—was intimidating—but she couldn't let him see it.

"Let's get one thing straight, *Principessa*. I don't serve you. I serve the monarchy, and I will do whatever it takes to protect it."

She moved forward instead of back and jammed a finger into his chest. It didn't budge. Not even the slightest. It was a rock wall behind the sweatshirt.

"I don't want to be your monarch. I don't want anything to do with any of it. I want my friends and family to be safe. I want to play my music and sing in the band, and when I'm not doing that, I want to sail around the world and forget any of the awful things that have happened. I will never take the throne.”

“Then you’ll end a two-thousand-year-old dynasty. You’ll put us into chaos.”

“How? The island was faring fine when I was there without its supposed queen!” She barely got the word out—queen. It felt wrong and yet also right. She hated it.

“If you don’t claim the throne by the end of the year, everything the San Fiorians believe in will end.”

“Like what?” she demanded.

“Tradition. Honor. Faith. All those things are tied to our monarch. Everything that makes us San Fiorian would be thrown away until we become nothing more than just another tourist attraction.”

“So, all I have to do is *not* show up, and all of this”— she waved around at the room—“all the threats, all the nightmares, will go away? No one will care anymore that my DNA may have some kind of royal blood in it?”

He gritted his teeth. “You will show up.”

Just like earlier, his voice held neither promise nor threat. It was a complete fact. He would drag her there, kicking and screaming.

“Even if you force me there, you can’t force me to accept it. Professor Maynard said my great-grandfather abdicated, right? I’ll just do the same. Whoever doesn’t want me to claim the throne can have their way.”

“You would let the people who chose to murder your friend take over our country? You would let evil win?” he asked, and the disgust in his voice twisted something inside her chest. She didn’t like it. Didn’t like that this huge man talking about honor and tradition would look at her as if she was a bug underneath his feet. Didn’t like the feeling of abandoning anything…anyone…to the people who’d come to kill her and murdered Landry instead. But she didn’t owe the San Fiorians anything, whereas she *did* owe the people she loved safety and protection.

When she didn’t respond, his face became a blank

slate. "I need to know where you got the brooch."

Maybe if she told him, he'd leave her alone. Maybe it would prove she had nothing to do with any of this. "Professor Maynard gave it to me."

"And where did he get it?"

Nikki shrugged. "He didn't tell me. He just said it belonged to me and could prove who I was."

"Did he tell you the king passed away in 2015? The same year as your father?"

She nodded. He'd told her their last king had died childless, which was why they were looking for the family of the long-lost prince. After meeting with the professor the first time, she'd gone online to see what she could find out about the island. She'd read through the brief history and the death of its last king, but there'd been no information past that. It was a simple Wikipedia search that had left her with more questions than answers. But after that awful night at the pond, she'd never repeated it. Instead, she'd tried to burn what she'd learned from her mind.

"You never saw the brooch with your father?" he asked.

"No."

"We need to talk to the professor. Has he been in touch with you again?"

"I asked him never to contact me after that night…" Her voice died away, thinking of the farmhouse in Grand Orchard and the horror that had greeted her when she'd been woken from her migraine-induced sleep by Trevor's voice and Paisley's desperation.

"Did you know he disappeared?" he asked.

Her eyes widen. "No." She shook her head. "But I saw a sketch of his brother. Holden said you met with him in Boston."

"You met his brother?" His voice dropped impossibly further, and his heavy black brows furrowed.

"Only once. That same day. I'd gone to Wilson-Jacobs, and the professor's office had been tossed. His brother showed up and demanded he stop looking into all of this."

The man she only knew as Angel, and who'd refused to give her his real name, brushed a hand over his thick beard. The facial hair made him look even more menacing than the sketch artist's rendering she'd seen of him.

There was a note of heavy suspicion in Angel's voice when he said, "He didn't tell me you'd met."

He whipped a phone out of his sweatshirt pocket and sent a text with surprising agility for hands so big on such a small device.

He picked up his empty plate and turned toward the door.

"I have to go to the bathroom," she told him before he could leave. While it was true, she was also hoping to get a better layout of the house and see if she could escape from another room.

He looked surprised, as if the entire notion of her having a human bodily need was shocking to him. He didn't respond. He simply stepped out into the hallway, ducking slightly to get out, and then looked back at her.

"Are you coming or not?"

She followed on hesitant feet. She tried to keep her distance from him as they made their way down the stairwell she'd noticed earlier. It was so small he had to twist his large body sideways to fit, and their arms kept brushing. Every time they did, some strange energy coasted over her, like a static-electric field flickering. She hated it and yet wanted more. It was confusing. As confusing as him and this entire situation.

Instead of going all the way down to the bottom floor, he stopped on the second. The walls there had stucco and wallpaper that looked to be from the 1930s. Old but well cared for. She caught a glance of another room, larger than the one she'd been in, but with a similar wrought-iron bed and white linens. He opened a door and gestured for her to go in. A pedestal sink sat beside an old-fashioned toilet with a tank high up on the wall and a drawstring used to flush it. It was like the bathroom had been stuffed into a closet, which it likely had been. Unfortunately, that meant it had no window.

She turned around to face him as he stepped back, asking, "Any chance of getting a toothbrush?"

"Stay," he said, and she bristled at the command. She wasn't a dog or a two-year-old. He ducked into the bedroom she'd seen and came out with a bag. It was plain black. The kind of toiletry bag a man would use. When he handed it to her, she realized it was one of those kits you get on an airplane. Socks and toothpaste and a tiny brush.

She didn't thank him. Instead, she shut the door in his face.

She faced the mirror and almost gasped. Her hair was a mess. Her eyes were dark and shadowed. She looked like she felt—like she'd just escaped her latest migraine.

She used the toilet, trying to ignore the fact he was likely on the other side of the door, waiting and listening. She eyed the chipped, ceramic bathtub, desperately wishing for a shower so she could scrub away the last twenty-four hours, but she doubted she had that kind of time. The last thing she needed was for him to bust in with her naked.

She washed her face, brushed her teeth, and used the travel-sized deodorant before pulling her hair up into a loose bun with a hairband she found in the bag. When she looked in the mirror again, she didn't look any less haunted, but she at least felt and smelled better.

He knocked on the door, and it made her jump. "Nicolette, we need to leave."

She opened the door, and he took her in from head to toe like he had upstairs—in that way that made her toes curl but her brain revolt.

"Unless you're taking me back to my mom, I'm not

going anywhere with you."

He'd have to leave her here. He'd lock the door, but she'd find a way out. She'd almost escaped the attic room, hadn't she?

He acted as if he hadn't heard her. He simply grabbed her by the elbow and steered her toward the staircase again. "I want to see what Maynard has to say when he sees you."

"Professor Maynard is here? In France?"

"We're meeting his brother."

Nikki couldn't help the shudder that took over her at the thought of the cold-eyed man with the scar. "Why is he here?"

"I'm helping him look for the professor. We followed the trail to Nice, and then it just disappeared. I'm pretty sure he's dead, but Maynard hasn't given up looking."

He said it so matter-of-factly that it chilled her entire insides—the ease of someone being dead—and it brought back everything she knew about this man as Angel Carter. The fact he'd tortured the musician Ziggy Klein after the man had come after Fee. The way he'd saved Leya but then placed Adria's sister in a coffin and would have left her to die. How Claudio had died at the hand of a sniper who no one had been able to find, but her friends suspected was him. This man might say he was there to protect her, to deliver her to an island where she could claim a monarchy she didn't want, but she also had to remember he was a skilled killer. He'd said it himself. He'd do anything for the monarchy…

But it was that last thought that sent a wave of relief rushing through her. He wouldn't hurt her or kill her because he needed her alive and well. Knowing that gave her a sense of power. Power she'd just have to figure out how to use in order to escape.

Chapter Ten

HITMAN STORY
Performed by The Hall Effect

THE SCREWUP: He contacted me. I'm meeting up with him in Cannes.

SAN FIORE 65: We don't need him anymore. Get rid of him.

THE SCREWUP: It'll cost you another two hundred.

SAN FIORE 65: Let me get this straight. I paid you three hundred thousand dollars for a job you botched, a hundred thousand to figure out what Castelli knew, and now you have the audacity to ask for even more?

THE SCREWUP: As we've discussed, you were at fault as much as I was that night. You told me she'd be alone at the farmhouse. And I silenced my brother for you for free. Flesh and blood. I want another two hundred grand in advance. And then I want the three million you promised me when this is over.

SAN FIORE 65: I'll wire a hundred over now, but I want proof of Castelli's death before I send the rest.

THE SCREWUP: Fine.

Five minutes later.

SAN FIORE 65: Do you have eyes on her?

SEGRETI: She's on the boat. I'm just waiting for the storm to hit.

SAN FIORE 65: Are you sure?

SEGRETI: She used the sat phone. She's there. Why?

SAN FIORE 65: Castelli went dark, blocking out even the Cavalieri. I needed to make sure he wasn't with her.

SEGRETI: In nine days, any threat he ever was to us will have vanished.

SAN FIORE 65: I'm not taking chances that he'll pull off a miracle. After today, we won't have to worry about him at all. I'll have one little loose end to tie up, and then you and I will be the only ones left who know the truth.

SEGRETI: Is that a threat?

SAN FIORE 65: Don't be ridiculous.

Chapter Eleven

D'Angelo

IN THE SHADOWS
Performed by The Rasmus

Nicolette had been silent since he'd led her to the Volkswagen he'd stolen the night before. He needed to ditch the vehicle today, but it would get them to Cannes with the new license plates he'd swapped out. Last he'd checked, the car hadn't been reported stolen yet. Even after hacking the surveillance cameras last night, he couldn't be sure someone hadn't already seen some of the footage before he'd deleted it. It was the best he could do under the circumstances with the tools he had left at his disposal now that he couldn't use the *Cavalieri* resources. Every plan he'd carefully crafted had disappeared when the security guard at the marina had held a gun on him.

How many of his brothers had been turned? Disgust and fury filled him. He wanted to put his hands around the necks of every single person who'd betrayed their oaths. But he also needed to package all that anger and shove it away until he was done with this.

"You never wear gloves," Nicolette's voice drew him from the road and his dark thoughts.

"What?"

"Aren't you afraid some authority will match your prints to any of the awful things you've done?"

His chest tightened at the disdain in her voice. He

could easily toss back he'd protected her and her friends with those awful things. That he had blood on his conscience because of her. But she'd never asked for it. Only the crown had demanded it of him. And he'd easily given it without compunction. Without remorse. Until now. Lately, there were moments when some of their voices made their way into his nightmares. A girl alive in a coffin. A man with a bullet to his head when he'd already been in jail.

He pushed those thoughts away and focused on her question. He held up one of his hands, palm up. She glanced at it but didn't take it, so he moved it closer to her face.

"What are you doing?" she demanded.

"Take a look," he said.

She grabbed his wrist, and he instantly regretted the decision as her touch burned through him. The heat and intensity of it traveled up his arm and through his chest as if he'd been hit with a stun gun.

She looked from his palm to his face, eyes wide. "You have no fingerprints."

"None of the *Cavalieri d'Oro* do."

She dropped his hand, turning to stare out the window for a long moment before she looked back at him. "Did it hurt?"

He shrugged. He could barely remember it. He'd had other things that had hurt worse. Stab wounds and gunshot holes. Broken bones. A lifetime of service was written across his skin.

"It had to have hurt," she said quietly.

"All I cared about was the pride in my father's eyes as he saw me initiated into the brotherhood."

"You did this for your father?"

"I did this for the crown. For the centuries of Castellis who've served it."

Her eyes widened slightly, and he realized his

mistake. He'd given her a last name. His jaw clenched. She was dangerous, creeping in under his guard.

"Come on, Kraken, you've already spilled the beans. You might as well tell me your first name."

He didn't respond, concentrating instead on weaving through the Cannes traffic toward the bar they were meeting Maynard at. He parallel-parked in one swift swirl of the wheel and turned off the engine.

She reached for the door handle, and he grabbed her wrist, pulling her back toward him over the console. "We need to reach an agreement."

Her face was an emotionless mask. A beautiful mask. They were so close in the car, it would take nothing but a mere tilt of his head for their lips to brush. Her eyes darted to his mouth, and it hit him in the gut, low and tantalizing, as he realized the desire he felt for her was somehow returned. Bodies reacting to some kind of pheromone in the air, except it wasn't just his groin that was drawn to her. It was that damn ache he had in his soul for something bright and shiny and good.

It took more effort than it had to shoot at his assailants last night for him to pull himself back from the edge and say, "If you run, I'll have to sedate you."

Her eyes flicked up to his, anger sparking in them. "I'm supposed to agree to be your captive so you won't knock me out again?"

"No, because you're in danger, and I can protect you. Whether or not you take the throne, until December 31st, they won't stop coming for you."

"Who exactly is *they*?"

"The anti-royalists." He could say more, but now was neither the place nor the time.

When he didn't continue, she huffed and said, "If you'd left me with my bodyguards, I wouldn't be in this position."

"You would have been on a boat in the middle of the

Mediterranean. An easy target."

She scoffed again. "How would they have found me?"

He looked at her for a second as if he couldn't believe she was asking that question before he growled out, "Your sat phone, or *Tangled Melody*'s navigation system that reports your location, or how about the schedule you left with your detail that would predict the route you'd take to those locations. You'd be a sitting duck in the water."

She struggled against his hold, but there was nowhere for her to go. She could call out for help. She could scream, but he'd have her out of there before the authorities even had time to show up. She knew it too, and it pissed her off enough that the anger emanated from her in waves.

He understood her desire to regain control over her life. Understood but couldn't give it to her. Worse, he used it, playing on it. "What's it going to be, *Principessa*? Tag along and find answers to everything that's been happening to you, or..." He left the rest unsaid, but he never removed his gaze from hers.

She attempted to break free of his hold once more and then let out a frustrated groan.

"Fine," she all but yelled.

He still didn't let her go. Instead, he pulled her wrist so she was forced to lean toward him until their mouths were even closer. "Swear on it. Swear you won't try to run. Swear on the lives of the people you love most."

When she didn't answer, he reached his free hand into the pocket of the hoodie and pulled out a needle. Her eyes went wide.

"Fine, I swear!"

"On?"

"I swear on the lives of the people I love most."

He let her go, and she seemed almost as surprised by that as she'd been by his demands and the needle. He got out of the car and was around the front of it by the time her feet hit the sidewalk. He tugged her hand into his, dwarfing it. Her skin was soft in places and then rough. The calluses from her guitar and the scabs from the brooch had marred her. They'd left visible lines telling the story of her life, just as the ones on his body had. They were alike in this one way, and that simple idea seemed to undo him a little, as if he'd loosened the first button on a collared shirt after wearing it for too long.

Her hand fluttered in his, and it felt bird-like and fragile. She was fragile even when she'd surprised him with her strength. She was still made of flesh and bone that could be broken in multiple ways—ones he knew from experience. And it sent a wave of terror up his back at the thought. He wouldn't allow her to be hurt again. Not physically, mentally, or emotionally.

He was so caught up in those thoughts he almost missed the doorway of a boutique he'd planned on going through.

He cursed himself silently before leading her through the clothing store, darting an eye at the clerk up front, and pressing through the employees-only door at the back. They wound their way through a sea of crates and racks to a side door. With a quick pull of his knife, he undid the alarm on the emergency exit, and then led them into an alley behind the building. The air was cool, the wind bitter, sending the smell of rotten food and urine up over them. She coughed, putting her free arm over her nose as he led her through the dumpsters and refuse until they reached the back door of the restaurant they were meeting Maynard at. It was propped open just as he'd expected—delivery time. Fresh crates of seafood and vegetables were being hauled inside by a couple of the bar's staff.

He waited for the workers to take in another load before he eased in after them on light feet, glad she had her soft boat shoes on instead of the clunky Doc Martens she wore onstage. The dim hallway ended in a swinging door that led into the bar's main room.

The pre-lunch crowd was light with only a handful of people scattered across the restaurant at scuffed wood tables. Maynard was seated near the windows with his back against the wall in a way that gave him a clear line of sight to the entire restaurant and all its entrances. If possible, the man looked even more haggard than the last time D'Angelo had seen him. His hair was oily and long, pulled back in a man bun that didn't suit him and made his face seem even more pointed—like a weasel. A scraggly goatee now partially covered the scar on his jaw. Maynard clocked D'Angelo and Nicolette as soon as they'd emerged from the back. His gaze went to their joined hands, and D'Angelo's eye twitched at the smug look that swam over the man's face.

They slid into the chairs across from him, a waitress appeared, and D'Angelo quickly ordered them two espressos in French. When the woman left, he turned back to Maynard. "Your brother…he found a brooch he believed was tied to the monarchy. Where did he get it?" D'Angelo asked.

The man scowled. "I'm good. Thanks for asking. And, oh, by the way, I found Parker."

D'Angelo's entire being tensed. Maynard went for the pocket of his brown leather jacket, and D'Angelo had his wrist in his grip before the man could reach inside.

"What the fuck, man?" Maynard said. "I'm just taking out my phone."

"Nice and slow," he said.

Maynard shot Nicolette a look. "You finally got *her* here, so now you've become suspicious of me?

D'Angelo didn't respond. He'd always been suspicious of the man, but he'd used him. Used him to find his brother who had the real answers D'Angelo had needed. This man was only a means to an end. As Maynard slowly took his phone from his pocket, the movement gave D'Angelo a look at the butt of a Glock tucked into his waistband. His eye twitched all over again, his senses telling him to get Nicolette the hell out of this man's presence.

But he had questions first.

Maynard swiped the phone open and shuffled through his photos. He set it on the table and slid it in D'Angelo's direction. It was a picture of a man lying in a field. His tweed coat was spread wide with holes torn in the shirt underneath. The carrion birds had gotten to the visible flesh, picking at skin and eyes, but it was the slit across the throat that held his gaze the longest.

Next to him, Nicolette made a pained noise, hand going to her mouth. She jerked, as if to get up, and D'Angelo grabbed her thigh under the table, holding her in place.

"Where did you find him?" he growled.

"A chalet up north. Someone with skill had to have done it because my dad trained my brother and I well." When D'Angelo didn't reply, Maynard turned to Nicolette. "My dad was a SEAL. Taught us from the time we were little how to take care of ourselves. And after he got out, we went into the woods for a couple of years, learning survival techniques. It wouldn't have been easy to sneak up on my brother."

The man's voice held a ring of pride that was puzzling considering the circumstances.

"What was he doing at the chalet?" D'Angelo demanded.

"From what I understand, looking into their archives. They have a history of the secret societies of Europe. The owner told me he asked a lot about a group called The Golden Knights. I forget the foreign name. Ca-va-lay-uh day something. Ever hear of them?"

The man was watching him carefully, and D'Angelo didn't even twitch, but Nicolette adjusted in her seat next to him, and it drew Maynard's gaze back to her again. D'Angelo tightened his grip on her thigh, and she stilled.

The touch was burning him, like sticking his hand in the flame of a candle. It was only his training that prevented him from yanking it away. Retreating like some rookie. Like some child who was unaccustomed to being in the thick of a battle.

Maynard turned toward Nicolette. "I told you and my brother to stay away from this in Grand Orchard. And after your friend died, I told my brother someone else would end up dead if he didn't stop pursuing this. He obviously didn't listen. Maybe you should before something bad happens to you as well, Nikki."

Her body went stiff, and D'Angelo leaned his elbows on the table so he could force his upper body toward Maynard, partially blocking her from the man's view. "Eyes here, Oliver," he said the man's name like he would a curse word, and the man's eyes grew beady. He'd thought he'd had the man pegged. Thought the junkie searching for a high had long ago taken over the military veteran who'd once had grand ideas of being special forces like his daddy but had never cut the psyche eval. But maybe, like so many things in the last few days, D'Angelo's cockiness in his ability to read people had been yet another error.

"Where did he get the brooch?" D'Angelo demanded.

Maynard shrugged. "Don't know. Maybe if I saw it, I'd recognize it. You got it?"

His gaze fell to Nicolette again, and every instinct in D'Angelo was screaming at him to break the man's nose, shove a fist into his eye socket, and be gone.

"No," D'Angelo said instead, his voice belying none of his thoughts. "But he had it back in Grand Orchard. The night Landry Kim died."

A flare of surprise hit Maynard's face.

"If he had it then, he had to have gotten it when he went to LA, investigating her dad's death." Maynard tilted his head toward Nicolette again. "He came back from a meeting with the gas station clerk all wound up. Said he finally had the proof he needed that her dad was Prince Fiorani's grandson and that he'd actually been the intended target that day. It wasn't some robbery gone wrong."

"The man responsible for my dad's death is in prison," Nicolette said quietly.

Maynard laughed, and it was dark and cruel. "Yeah, then why'd the clerk tell my brother he could have sworn the person who killed your dad was white as sin and not the Mexican who's doing time? Said the height was right but the build was all wrong. That's why the D.A. settled for such a shitty plea bargain. The clerk would have been reasonable doubt."

"That man signed a plea bargain because the evidence against him was overwhelming," Nicolette breathed out softly, her voice shaky.

"Sure, sweetheart, go right ahead and tell yourself that."

D'Angelo's hand snaked out, grabbing Maynard's T-shirt collar and twisting. "Don't ever speak to her that way again."

The man jerked out of his grip, eyes darting around the restaurant. "I'm out. You promised to help me find my brother, and you did squat. I had to be the one to find him. I don't need you anymore."

The man rose, heading for the door. He was outside and striding along the sidewalk before D'Angelo could think of a way to stop him without causing unwanted attention. After Nicolette was safely delivered to the throne room in *Castrum Aureum*, he'd find Maynard. He'd find the man and root out the truth one way or another.

He threw some cash on the table, grabbed Nicolette's hand, and then drew her back out the way they'd come. The delivery van was gone, and the alley was silent now, but the stench seemed even more potent. The hair went up on the back of his neck as they passed a dumpster, and he whirled around to find Maynard stepping out from behind it with his Glock pointed at Nicolette.

D'Angelo went to shove her behind him, but before he could, she swung her leg in a roundhouse kick that slammed into Maynard's wrist. The gun went off, the gentle puff of the suppressor barely breaking the air, but when the bullet careened into the dumpster, it was loud enough to draw attention. The man had somehow held on to the weapon, and as he stumbled backward, trying to right himself from the kick, D'Angelo hauled Nicolette behind him. His hand slid down the back of his sweatshirt, fingers landing on the first knife hilt.

"Bitch. That fucking hurt," Maynard said, aiming again, this time at D'Angelo. "Freeze. I know all about those knives you have strapped to your body. I know a lot more about you than you think. It's always the foot soldiers who lose their lives, isn't it? I'm done being the first wave. I'm going to be the one behind the lines, calling the shots."

"If you think anyone will let you lead, you're as delusional as you were when you thought you'd cut it in the special forces," D'Angelo said calmly.

Maynard's face contorted in fury.

"Well, what do we have here!" a voice said, and Maynard's gaze shifted toward the space between the buildings as two more men appeared wearing dark uniforms of the police. The round, ruby gemstone pin on their lapels was a calling card D'Angelo knew all too well. His gut clenched, body tensing, readying for a battle Maynard didn't even know was coming.

Maynard didn't give the two officers a second thought as he shifted the gun toward D'Angelo again, finger slowly depressing, and D'Angelo reacted, flinging his knife into the man's forearm. He howled, sinking to his knees, just as the officers in the alley started firing.

Chapter Twelve

D'Angelo

FEEL INVINCIBLE
Performed by Skillet

In another place and time, D'Angelo would have finished them all. Would have stood his ground and seen all their bodies hit the ground, but he couldn't risk Nicolette getting struck in the crossfire. So, he left Maynard to be finished off by the men who wouldn't want any witnesses and did the one thing he was unused to doing—he ran.

He grabbed Nicolette's hand and sprinted in the opposite direction down the alley. The anti-royalists gave chase, their heavy police shoes banging along the pavement. They never shouted out to halt. They never declared their authority as officers of the law. Fucking Maynard had told someone what he was doing, and the anti-royalists had sent reinforcements to make sure the job got done right.

He dragged Nicolette through the shadows of the buildings at a pace that had even his heartbeat speeding up and caused her to gasp. He tried to stick to the shadows, the places he normally could disappear, but she made it nearly impossible, not only because of her uncontrolled breathing but because she seemed to draw the light to her wherever she was.

An emergency door swung open at the back of a

three-story building. A janitor came out, sloshing the water from his mop cart into the alley, and D'Angelo didn't even hesitate. He pushed past the man, who protested with a curse, and yanked the door shut behind them. The janitor banged on it as D'Angelo took in their surroundings. They were at the base of an emergency stairwell. Concrete steps with a metal railing. He started up, taking the steps two and three at a time, and she did her best to keep up. They'd rounded the first landing when the door below them slammed open. Feet stampeded on the cement, a shot rang out, careening into the brick wall nearby, and his heart lurched. He jerked her away from the rail.

"Stick to the sides!" he growled before drawing his gun and returning fire.

A pained grunt echoed up at them, but as they continued upward, both pairs of footsteps followed. He hadn't done more than hit the man's arm, if he was lucky.

At the top, he shoved his way through the door onto the roof. He assessed the area, noting an oversized compressor for the building's air-conditioning and pushing her behind it. Then, he searched for a way to jam the door handle. There was nothing. Instead, he pointed his gun at the door and as the first man burst through, a bullet found its home dead center. The man's gaze widened for two seconds, and then he fell forward. The second man was a bit smarter, shooting from inside, arm sticking out of the entrance. D'Angelo ran shoulder-first, shoving the heavy metal door shut, and the sickening sound of bones cracking was followed by a sharp cry from the anti-royalist.

D'Angelo yanked the door back open to see the man grasping his arm and starting toward the stairs. There was no way he could let the man live and report back to his boss that he'd seen Nicolette with him. He needed them to believe she was still on her boat in the middle of the Mediterranean Sea.

The man jerked his head toward D'Angelo,

attempting to raise his gun with his non-dominant hand at the same time as D'Angelo raised his. There was a grim acknowledgment that flashed over the man's face the moment he realized he was going to die. D'Angelo's shot rang out, and the man's chest bloomed with blood as he tumbled backward down the staircase.

D'Angelo's jaw clenched tight. More people added to his list. More death and destruction. But better them than her. Better them than the end of the San Fiorian monarchy.

He stormed back onto the roof, fury and irritation crawling through him. Maynard had sold them out either because he wanted the money and didn't have his brother to help him find Nicolette, or because he'd been selling them out since the beginning. He'd barely had a chance to glance at the knife wound on the professor's neck, but his gut told him it would show the same nicked blade mark that had killed Landry and her bodyguard.

As he rounded the air-conditioning unit, he heard another door click shut just as he realized the space where he'd left Nicolette was empty.

For two seconds, shock stalled his feet before he was sprinting toward the second door. True fear radiated through him for the first time since he could remember. He tore open the metal door. He'd left her unattended, and they'd gotten to her. He glanced over the rail and saw the flash of her bright-blue sweatshirt. He listened. No footsteps. Only the sound of her breathing twirled up through the stairwell.

They hadn't gotten to her…she'd run. After she'd promised not to.

His dread bled into annoyance.

How was he going to protect her if she ran?

He bounded down the stairs, jumping over the railing in several locations, and her pace picked up.

As she hit the bottom and pulled at the emergency door, he reached her, slamming it shut and trapping her between his arms. She whirled around, panic traveling over her face. She pounded her fists against his chest.

"Let me go!"

She tried to sweep his leg with her foot, and he pressed his body completely into hers, trapping her wrists in one of his mammoth hands, twisting her legs one over the other so he could secure them with his. The touch burned through him again, lightning zapping through all the places their bodies were aligned. Even with sweat and fear clinging to her, it couldn't hide the sweet scent of her. An aphrodisiac that hinted of citrus blossoms and nut trees. The smell branded him almost as much as her touch, leaving a mark he'd never remove.

"You swore, *Principessa*. You swore on those you loved and broke that oath." He couldn't afford to show her the terror she'd sent through him when she'd run, so he showed the anger instead. He knew what he looked like with his dark eyes flashing and his face grim. He looked like the devil. He looked like your worst nightmare. No wonder she was fucking afraid.

Instead of cowering, she raised her chin and glared at him. "Well, you forced me to swear under duress. And besides, I had my fingers crossed, so it doesn't count."

Her words took a moment to settle in him.

And when they finally landed, it took some of his anger and replaced it with a chuckle. When it escaped his chest, it sounded strange, like a hyena coughing up fur and bones because he was unused to laughing. The garbled sound only made her brows furrow together more, her glare growing.

"You crossed your fingers," he repeated, desperately trying to control the odd-sounding huffs he was emitting. They had to get out of there. They had to disappear before the shots called the real authorities. Before more of the anti-royalists showed up. But as he looked down into her face, unhappy and scowling, his breath left his body. Even like this, grumpy and glowering, she was breathtaking.

The perfect shape of her mouth, permanently tinted a soft red, called to him. A siren's song. A lure that would certainly sink his ship.

The fire leaped in his veins again. Like the strongest alcohol coursing through his body. As he continued to stare, her breath turned even more ragged, while his slowed down. Her dark expression eased, the brown of her eyes turning almost golden as if lit by the flames he felt, threatening to destroy him.

Her body went limp. A question in her gaze that he would never answer.

He brushed a thumb over her lower lip, and the softness hurt almost worse than the fire inside him. His other hand loosened its hold enough for his fingers to slide down and find the pulse reverberating through her wrists. A thudding rhythm his blood seemed to echo.

Her eyes fell to his mouth. She pulled a hand free, swiping at his jaw and the thick beard he'd sworn he was going to shave off, before her finger coasted over his bottom lip just like he'd done to her. His entire being convulsed. His head lowered. Was there any way he could refuse her call?

The womp-womp-womp of the French police car wailed outside the building.

He reached behind her and pushed on the bar, swinging the door open. He tightened his hold on her wrist and led them into a different alley on the opposite side of the building. He leaned in to speak near her ear.

"As you saw, the French police will not protect you from them, *Principessa*. They can't. When we hit the streets, don't stare at them. Glance once and then away. Walk slow but not too slow. Measured steps. Unhurried. As if you're curious but need to get to an appointment."

She didn't respond, but her hand fluttered in his grip, and then she was holding on to it instead of shoving it away.

They rounded the corner of the building, joining a

crowd that had already started to gather. He tugged her toward a gift shop catering to tourists. Three cop cars had parked at all angles in front of the building's doors, and a handful of officers emerged from within them, running toward the entrance of the building they'd just escaped. D'Angelo moved them in the opposite direction.

They walked with a determined stride toward the stores along the main thoroughfare. December was not the primary tourist season, but there were still plenty of people on the sidewalks, drifting in and out of the shops and restaurants, some with cameras, some turned curiously toward the police activity.

He didn't look back, slouching down slightly so his height would be less of a calling card, and continued weaving along the sidewalks. Two men in black suits appeared down the street, the sunlight glinted on the ruby on their lapels, and he ducked into the nearest restaurant. He pulled her toward the back, grateful for the tall-backed booths the café offered. He tucked her into one side, sliding into the other and slouching down so his head wasn't sticking up over the top, but he could see the entrance.

He took in the main counter of the restaurant. There were three workers behind it and a kitchen that bustled to the north of them. There was a small hall directly behind him, but it appeared to lead only to a restroom and not a back entrance. They'd have to go out through the kitchen if they didn't use the front door.

His gaze swung back to the street as a waitress came over to them. She asked what they wanted in French, and he responded without glancing at the menu. Two of the daily specials and two black coffees.

She headed back to the counter.

The men in suits passed the front of the café without breaking stride.

It didn't mean they hadn't seen them. D'Angelo had used the tactic many times himself. Let his prey think he'd missed them. They'd let their guard down, and then he'd come around the back. He shifted in his seat so he had a better view of the kitchen.

"You killed those men." Nicolette's hushed voice drew his eyes. She was rubbing her temples with her long fingers, pushing furiously. He frowned.

He leaned in so his voice was barely audible. "Would you have preferred they killed you?"

Her fingers continued the persistent pressure on her temples. "You don't know who they were. They were dressed like cops…"

"Police announce who they are, *Principessa*. They don't shoot first and ask questions later. Did you see their red lapel pins?"

She shook her head. He reached for the crayon and children's menu at the edge of the table. He drew it for her. The ornate rope around the outside, the gem in the middle. "This is the insignia of the anti-royalists. If you see it on anyone, you know they are not your friend, no matter what they say."

The waitress returned, sliding two quiche Lorraines and coffees toward them. He leaned back, taking in the front door and the kitchen again. He needed to get back to the car and his backpack. It had all his equipment. He needed to scour the cameras on the boulevard and check with the bar and grill's security company for recordings inside or out. He couldn't afford to sit here eating lunch.

In mere seconds, he devoured his quiche and drank the coffee, barely registering the burn on his tongue from the scalding drink.

Nicolette's head leaned back onto the seat, and concern spiked as he noticed how deathly pale she'd gone. Her eyes were closed, fingers still working on her temples.

"What's wrong?" he demanded.

Her eyes fluttered open and then shut. "Besides what I just saw and the race for my life?" she hissed, and he was thankful the noise of the café kept her voice from carrying. "My head hurts. I need my migraine medicine."

Fuck. He knew she got them, knew all about her prescriptions—the nasal spray she used as well as the pills. But he hadn't brought any with him. He hadn't grabbed the bag she'd taken with her to the *Tangled Melody* where she'd probably had some with her.

"Drink the coffee," he told her.

She opened an eye and glared at him.

"The caffeine helps, no?"

She leaned forward, face turning even paler at the sight of the quiche. She pushed it farther away from her, reaching for the cup. She sipped, grimacing, and then put it aside as well.

Out front, the two men in black suits crossed the street and headed into a shop on the other side. He threw money on the table, stood from the booth, and grabbed her hand. She swayed as she rose, and his heart picked up pace more at that small motion than it had pulling the trigger on his Glock.

On the sidewalk, he glanced quickly to the shop across the street and then moved them toward the Volkswagen.

The breeze brought the salty tang of the sea with it, but the bright light of the crisp winter day had her squinting. She stumbled, both hands going to his bicep as if holding on to a lifeline.

"Nicolette?" Concern flooded him. He couldn't protect her from this. He couldn't take the pain even though he would in a heartbeat.

"I'm going to be sick," she said.

Damn it. He couldn't have her throwing up on the street. It would draw eyes they didn't need. He picked up his pace ever so slightly, although he couldn't afford for a mad sprint to draw people's looks either.

"The car is another block," he told her.

She didn't respond. His arm wound around her waist, drawing her closer. He was practically carrying her. A few people glanced in their direction, and his teeth ground tightly together. Finally, the Golf came into sight.

He opened the passenger door and sat her down in it. He'd closed it and gotten around to the driver's side just as she reopened it, leaned over, and threw up.

A bystander jerked away, muttering a curse in French.

He strode back around the car, squatting down beside her. "What do you need?"

"My medicine!" she demanded, frustrated. "Without it, a dark room, ginger ale, and a bed."

From the corner of his eye, he caught movement in the side mirror—the black suits heading in their direction. As he rose, a blunt object jammed into his shoulder blades. The sound of the slide of a gun cocking was followed by a man saying, "Nice and slow, Castelli. Put your hands on the roof."

Nicolette looked up at him, shock and fear registering through the pain on her face.

D'Angelo moved his hands slowly, keeping them in front of his body. He pointed down with a finger at his boot, his gaze following the direction.

Her face was pale as she made a moan and a gagging noise but moved toward his shoes. The sound was a good cover as the man behind him made a disgusted huff. Her fingers reached into his boot, pulling the knife from it. Her hand shook. He shifted ever so slightly, giving her room to see the man behind him. From his peripheral, he saw the two suits getting closer. Twenty meters at most. They had maybe a minute left.

"Let's go. We don't need to do this in the middle of the str—" A groan took over the rest of his words as Nicolette jammed the blade into the man's gut. He stumbled backward, his SIG falling as his hands went to the knife and the wound that was already gushing blood through his dress shirt. He hit the wall behind them, gasping.

A burst of gunfire from the two suits had D'Angelo dropping to the ground before he realized they weren't aiming for him as much as the car's tires. Screams rang out along the street, and chaos took over as bodies ran in all directions. D'Angelo rose, trying to use the door as a shield, reached behind Nikki, and grabbed his backpack. He shouldered it, then pulled her to her feet. More gunshots filled the air, and this time, they were aiming for them.

He sprinted, but she was lagging this time, unable to keep up. Her feet stumbling and tripping. They'd never get away. He dropped to his haunches, flung her over his shoulder, and then burst into his top speed. She protested, slapping at his back, a tortured moan escaping her lips that he could hear over the sounds of people crying and screaming.

He turned the corner just as a guy on a motorcycle stopped at the stop sign. Barely breaking a stride, he shoved the man off his bike, dropped Nicolette to her feet, and caught the motorcycle before it hit the ground. The guy yelled, taking a step toward D'Angelo, but when he saw the gun in his hands, he backed away. D'Angelo sat down, and over Nicolette's shoulders, he saw guns and suits bearing down. He had a single shot left. As he aimed, he growled, "Get on."

For maybe the first time, she followed his direction without hesitation. She slid onto the seat behind him and wrapped her arms around his waist as he hit the accelerator, moving them away from the gunfire directed at them. He weaved through the streets. There were too many witnesses. Too many cameras. They were fucked. The anti-royalists knew the truth. Nicolette Rani was not on her boat. She was with him. And they would send an army to fetch her.

Chapter Thirteen

Nikki

WILD

Performed by Bishop Briggs

Nikki's body was shaking uncontrollably as her stomach churned and her head pounded. White lights flickered in her vision every time she tried to open her eyes. She held on desperately to the man everyone kept calling Castelli as the motorcycle tilted and swayed, adding to her nausea. She pressed her face into his backpack, hoping to block out the light…and the image….

She'd thrust a knife into someone.

Holy shit. Was the man dead? Had she killed him?

Her heart pounded, flooding her veins with a rapid pulse that only caused the pain to grow and the bile to sneak back into her throat.

"I'm going to throw up," she tried to say, but the wind whipped it away. It was too late, anyway. She directed the worst of it off the bike, but it slid over her jeans and her shoes. Her grip loosened at the same time. She would have fallen if one of his giant hands hadn't caught her. The bike lurched sideways. He cursed under his breath in Italian. A language she knew like the back of her hand from years of speaking it with her father and mom.

He barely righted the bike. She closed her eyes,

clutching his sweatshirt again. The almost unbearable pain raged through her frontal lobe and over the top of her head. Tingling, as if her entire head had fallen asleep and was coming awake, absorbed her. And wave after wave of agony made her feel like her forehead was going to explode.

The twists and turns made her stomach swim, but she doubted she had anything left in it. She couldn't open her eyes to see where they were going because the light was as painful as the agony inside.

Finally, the motorcycle stopped moving. In one smooth motion, he was off the bike, but she almost slid to the ground with the loss of him stabilizing her. He caught her around the waist again. She buried her head into his shoulder as he guided her over what felt like dirt, bumpy and softer than the sidewalks they'd been running along.

"Can you stand?" His voice was gentler than she'd ever heard it, and it brought tears to her eyes she didn't understand. She did the best she could as his hands left her body. She whimpered but couldn't get up the energy to open her lids.

Then, he was lifting her, not slinging her over his back as he had earlier but cradling her in his arms like you would a child…or a bride over a threshold. They moved inside, and the sunlight almost disappeared as a cool darkness enveloped them. She shivered, goosebumps trailing over her, and she wasn't sure if it was from the migraine or him or the relief of being in a darker space.

He set her down on the soft cushion of a mattress. She squinted, barely taking in a patchwork quilt with a multitude of colors and the dark mahogany of a sleigh bed before her eyes slammed shut again.

He was sliding off her vomit-ridden shoe, and she tried to protest, but it only came out as a strangled sob. Then, his strong fingers were leaning her back, working the button of her jeans and tugging those from her body as well. In another moment, in another lifetime, the idea of this enormous man removing her clothes might have frightened her, but he'd just spent an entire morning protecting her, shielding her from guns and knives and men…

She couldn't think about it. It made the pain worse. As soon as she was free of the jeans, she wrapped the colorful quilt around her body, drew her knees to her chest, and buried her nose in them. She heard him moving around, not because he was loud, but almost because of the opposite. The barely audible sound of clothes shifting as he moved.

And then, the pain was all she could feel, the pain that sapped her strength. Her mind. Her control over her body. She breathed in and out.

"Nicolette, I found some pain meds. It's just regular ibuprofen."

The only part of her that moved was her hand, palm up. He slid four pills into her hands. It would barely take the edge off, but it would do something. She popped them into her mouth, and then there was a glass pressed into her palm. She swallowed. Water dripped along her mouth and down onto the blanket, but she didn't care. She didn't care about anything but the darkness.

She rocked herself back and forth. The bed sank with his weight. A hand found her back, rubbing circles. Two hands found her shoulders, massaging. But the touch only brought unwanted pain. Unwanted nausea. She could barely grunt out, "Please stop."

The hands went away, but he remained.

It felt like a decade before the pain eased ever so slightly. Enough for the rocking to stop. Enough for her body to demand the sleep it always did after the migraine welled. And finally, she lost consciousness.

♫ ♫ ♫

The room was even darker than it had been when they'd arrived as she woke, but she could make out the shapes of the furniture and a flicker of light from behind thick curtains. Her head was pounding still, but not with the piercing fierceness of earlier. There was a ginger ale and more pain meds on a side table.

She didn't know how long it had been since she'd had the first round. She frankly didn't care. She swallowed the pills with a sip of the soda. Flat. It had been open for a while. It was better that way when she was like this. Flat and sugary with a hint of ginger to ease the nausea.

She was slightly embarrassed he'd seen her this way. At her very weakest. She hated the migraines, but even those emotions felt muffled by the layer of exhaustion clinging to every part of her and compelling her eyes to close again.

A shift in the air had her forcing the lids back open. He was squatted down in front of her. "What can I get you?"

"Nothing more than this."

His eyes were black pools in the dim room as he continued to stare. His hand ran over his beard, tugging at the ends of it, and it made her wonder what his jawline looked like underneath it. In the sketch made of him from Fee's recollection, it had been almost razor sharp.

"Where are we?" she asked.

"A vacation cottage. We won't be able to stay long. A night at most."

She couldn't even summon the energy to nod.

And then, she was asleep again.

♫ ♫ ♫

The second time she came awake, the room was pitch-black. Not even a hint of light. The pain had almost dissipated into a dull throbbing. Just a reminder that it had been there. But the fatigue continued to make her limbs feel heavy and slow.

She used caution as she sat up. Sometimes, if she moved too quickly, the headache would come slamming back into her and send her over the edge for a second round. The comforter fell away, and she looked down at her bare legs. While she'd felt embarrassed by her weakness, she didn't feel a shred of it for her nakedness. After all, this was his fault. He'd taken her from her boat without her meds and tossed her into a sea of stress so deep she could have drowned. Nearly had…except it had been in pain instead of water.

She stood on shaky legs. She needed to find a bathroom.

The soft area rug under her feet turned into the sleek coolness of polished wood. With her hand out, she guided herself to the wall, moving along in the darkness until she found a doorframe and a knob. She pulled it open, and a dim light from somewhere deeper in the cottage showed the hulking body sitting on the floor and leaning on the wall opposite the door again. His legs were spread wide just like earlier, boots resting on either side of the doorframe.

"How are you feeling?" His voice was deep and dark, blending into the night much as his body did. She wondered how long he'd lived in the shadows. Wondered if he ever stayed in the light for more than a few seconds. Wondered how his soul survived the heavy weight of the lives he'd altered…ended…

She'd stabbed someone.

Her hand went to her stomach, her eyes coming away with it as if she expected to see the blood she'd spilled from the man staining her as well. It was almost surprising to see nothing there.

"Nicolette?"

The way he said her name caused a shiver to go up her spine. Heated. Concerned. As if she had his complete and utter focus.

"Bathroom?" she squeaked out.

He rose. The movement was fluid and swift, like all his movements. A great black panther stalking through the jungle, each movement calculated and smooth, not a single one wasted. His hand found her elbow, guiding her down the narrow hall to a second door. She was filled with mixed emotions. Grateful for the support as much as she wanted to shake it off. To scream and rant and hurl accusations his way.

Inside the bathroom, a night-light glowed. Even that small light made her blink and her eyes ache, but it wasn't the blinding pain of earlier. She used the toilet and then eyed the shower. The curtain was mostly transparent with only a few brightly colored flowers layering the vinyl, but there was a little rack of towels nearby and a bottle of shampoo sitting on the tub's shelf. She needed to be clean. From the headache and the vomit and the blood... The men who'd died today.

She shed the remainder of her clothes, turned on the shower, and didn't even wait for it to warm up. She just stepped in, letting the icy water jolt her back to reality and away from the haunted, dreamy landscape of her migraine.

She washed her hair, even though her scalp was painfully tender and tingling still, and scrubbed at her body, trying to wash the entire day away. The image of her hand, the knife, and the blood stuck with her. A little sob escaped her chest.

"Nicolette!"

Damn. He was right on the other side of the door. Hovering. Waiting.

"I'm fine," she said, but the shakiness of her voice belied her words. The handle on the door twisted. "Don't come in!"

He didn't listen. He never did.

The tiny bathroom shrank to the size of a coat closet with him inside it. His gaze flew to her, seeing everything through the clear fabric. He cleared his throat and then lifted his eyes to the ceiling.

"You're feeling better."

"Better is a relative word, but the worst of it has passed," she said. She shut the water off and felt him watching her again as she reached for a towel. She wrapped one around her middle and another around her hair. It would be a mess without the products that tamed the wild curls, but it had been worth it. To at least shake off some of the haze even if she'd never shake off the feeling of her hand as it drove the knife into soft flesh.

She shuddered, inhaling slowly to try and calm the wild beat of her heart. Then, she stepped out of the tub. Her shoulder touched his chest, and he tried to back up, but there was nowhere for him to go. As their eyes locked, the air in the room sparked, tension shifting between them like a live wire trying to find ground.

She was grateful for the thick towel hiding how her breasts reacted to him. To that dark aura that clung to him. To his solemness and the way his gaze settled on her with something akin to reverence. As if he really believed she was his queen.

It had finally sunk in that he wasn't the only one who believed it. Men had died today thinking the same thing. Just like Landry…

She swallowed hard, tearing her eyes from his.

His arms moved, elbows bumping into her as he lifted his sweatshirt from his body. It revealed a black T-shirt underneath that clung to his wide shoulders and gargantuan-sized chest. His bare arms were a chaotic mess of tattoos. Mostly black and white with a shot of color here and there.

"Here," he said, giving the sweatshirt to her. The warmth of it seeped into her cold fingers. "I'll put your things in the washer."

Then, he bent to sweep her clothes from the floor. Because they were standing so close in the tiny space, the motion pushed her backward on already unsteady legs, and she reached out instinctively, dropping his sweatshirt, hands landing in the dark strands of his hair. His head lifted, and another bolt of lightning flew through her as she realized how close his mouth was to her stomach. How, with only a slight shift of his shoulders and head, he could be right where her aching body longed for him to be.

Her fingers convulsed, nails digging into his scalp, and he inhaled sharply.

Then, he was moving away, opening the door, and stepping out with a speed that screamed he was running. From her. From them. From whatever this was that flickered to life whenever he was next to her. She knew she should be afraid of him, but she couldn't be. It wasn't just the fact he'd saved her. It was something else. A pull in her chest that said she could trust him.

Maybe it was all those damn fairy tales again, but she knew he wouldn't hurt her.

Yes, he'd kidnapped her…but he'd done so to protect her.

And after today, she had no doubts that he would.

In the hall, he glanced back and caught her staring.

"Go back to the room. I'll bring you a tray."

It was half beg, half command, and she didn't know if she loved it or hated it.

She just knew that, for now, she'd follow it.

Chapter Fourteen

Nikki

BEAUTIFUL GHOSTS
Performed by Taylor Swift

As soon as he disappeared, Nikki dropped the towel, picked up his hoodie, and shoved her arms into it. It was still warm and had the faint scent of him. A scent that was hard to decipher. Like moonlight on the shore. Salty and musky with a hint of recklessness. Like sin waiting to drown you.

She tugged the sweatshirt down over her hips, suddenly feeling incredibly vulnerable without her underwear. More so than she had with guns pointed at her and men chasing her. Dashing through the streets of Cannes, she'd been afraid, but she'd also felt a sense of safety because he'd stood in front of a gun for her. Now her fear stemmed from the things she saw in his eyes that spoke of a devotion she hadn't earned and from the way her body felt as out of control as her life at the moment.

She pulled the towel from her head, the tight coils springing loose, drifting around her cheeks and her chin. She searched the cabinet by the sink and was relieved to find a small jar of hairbands. She wound the thick mass of curls into two buns, and then returned to the bedroom. She flicked on a lamp, grateful when the low-wattage bulb barely shifted the gloom in the room. She straightened the quilt, tucked her feet underneath the sheets, and leaned up against the headboard. She sipped from the flat ginger ale again. Her stomach felt like it had gone through a boot-camp workout. The exhaustion hit her as soon as she stopped moving, and her eyes drifted closed until she felt his presence at the door. Then, they found his in the gloom.

"Did I kill him?" she asked.

"Hopefully." His deep voice traveled across the room, hitting her in the chest.

She shut her lids against a rush of tears.

He eased into the room farther, sinking on the bed at her side. She could feel him scrutinizing her face as tension and worry wafted off him. When she dared to look at him again, his gaze was on her hand clutching the ginger ale can.

"All I can see is the knife…the blood," she whispered.

He reached up, tugged at a coil of her hair that had already escaped the buns, and twined the strand around his finger, watching as if fascinated by it. His knuckles brushed her cheekbone with the movement, and it lit up her entire being and caused the breath to leave her body.

"If you hadn't stabbed him, he would have killed me and then you," he said calmly, factually, as if death was an everyday occurrence.

"You don't know that," she said, surprised by the grittiness of her voice.

"I do." The solemnness was back. When his eyes locked on hers again, she saw that emotion she'd labeled as reverence once more. She hardly felt worthy of it. She didn't even know what to do with it.

"My name is D'Angelo Castelli," he said softly, the depth of it vibrating all the way to the depths of her. Earlier, he'd told her she hadn't earned his name. The idea that she had—that he was giving it to her now—sent a heady feeling rushing through her.

She searched his face, wondering how to respond,

and then settled on the truth. "Thank you for saving my life."

He let go of her hair and eased back on the bed.

"Are they always this bad? Your migraines?" he asked.

"If I can catch them with my meds, no. But sometimes they're worse. Sometimes they last for days."

His jaw ticked. "And the doctors do nothing?"

For some reason, his irritation made her want to smile. "They do prescribe me medicine, remember?"

"I'll figure out how to get you some tomorrow."

Silence settled down. It should have been awkward. But with the strange energy zapping back and forth between them, it felt oddly comforting.

"Did your father have them also?" he asked softly.

She nodded.

"Most of the royal family have had them. Some believe it's tied to the curse," he said.

Surprise drifted through her at his words. This behemoth of a man didn't seem the type to believe in myths and superstitions. "Curse?"

He moved, shifting so he was leaning up against the headboard next to her, long jean-clad legs spreading out before him, almost touching the footboard even while sitting. He crossed his ankles, the jeans shifting over the military boots, revealing another knife hilt that made her stomach flop.

She sipped at the ginger ale some more, looking at him expectantly, waiting for him to explain. He ran a hand over his beard, and when he started talking, there was a deep cadence in his voice that was almost mesmerizing. Tones and rhythms she could listen to forever. A song where the bass guitar she used to favor would have a starring role.

"For centuries, San Fiore was a closed island. No one off, and no one on. This was because whenever we'd opened the harbor in the past, the visitors turned on us. The Romans tried to make us theirs as well as the French. Our little island isn't just beautiful. We have veins of gold so thick and deep that, even today, after being mined for centuries, they still find it."

"I thought I read about gold being one of the main exports, but it surprised me. You'd think it would all be gone by now on an island your size," she said, recalling the little bit of research she'd done before she'd tried to forget everything and anything about San Fiore.

"Maybe the gods replenish it for us?" He raised a brow, and his lips quirked ever so slightly. "We are more careful with it now. But for centuries, we spread it around like frosting instead of a finite precious metal. It's why you see so much of it on the island. All the statues and fountains are layered with it, even the decorative elements on our homes."

"What has this to do with a curse?" she asked.

"In the eighteen hundreds, the king trained all the men of San Fiore as warriors and then opened the harbor once more, inviting our neighbors to come visit. With each ship that came to shore, the military put on a great show—the might of our soldiers on display. A promise of what we would do if we were attacked."

"Wow," Nikki said. "Did it work?"

He shrugged. "We weren't attacked. Not at first. The king made alliances with other countries, hoping it would protect us from larger forces. Austria-Hungary was one of our allies, but when World War I broke out, we declared ourselves neutral, and this infuriated the empire. They turned on us, sending a small armada of ships to take control of our island and the gold they'd need to fund their war. They were so certain they'd overpower us that their officers had brought their families with them. Their idea was to set them up in our villas and castles and enslave the people of San Fiore. We defeated them, taking the families prisoners. The wives and children were given comfortable rooms in the castle, but they weren't allowed to leave. Unfortunately, one of their general's young sons snuck out and tried to murder our king. He was killed, and his mother cursed the monarchy, saying they were all doomed to die an early death."

Nikki stared at him, surprise shifting through her. "Did it come true? The doomed monarchs?"

"None of our kings have lived past the age of forty-eight."

"Do you believe in it?" Nikki asked.

D'Angelo considered her for a moment. "Lifestyle choices can be blamed for many of them. Car accidents and boating accidents due to a love of speed and danger. But there are many on the island who would insist it's the curse working. Just like they blame it for our kings never having more than one child and for the migraines they've all had ever since."

Nikki's mind whirled. She'd never believed magic was real. Never believed that a fairy godmother would appear and make her a princess, but she had ached for the romance the fantasies spouted. She'd wanted to find her one true love. And maybe, if you believed in such things as soulmates and fate and finding forever with the person who was always supposed to be yours, it wasn't such a leap to believe in a curse that had doomed a monarchy.

"What do people believe will break the curse?" she asked.

"As it was placed on our kings, they believe that only a queen inheriting the throne through blood instead of marriage will be able to break it."

Nikki swallowed as a sudden chill went up her back. Dread filled her, and her mouth went dry as she stumbled out the next question. "I take it there's never been one?"

His gaze held hers. "Not until you."

She wanted to shake off the words, the deep promise of his voice, the whispering voices that seemed to swirl in the night around her, but she couldn't. Instead, her entire body shuddered.

"At first," she started, and her voice was scratchy, so she stopped to clear her throat before continuing. "When Professor Maynard first reached out to me in Grand Orchard that summer, I laughed at him. My dad never talked about his family, but I thought for sure he would have told me something this large…that we were related to royalty. The story the professor told was so…tantalizing…a fairy tale. A king who gave up his throne for the love of his life."

"It was not a proud moment for our country. Prince Dario's request to marry Mathilda was refused by the parliament because she was Black."

"It explained this," Nikki said, pointing to her black hair and the wild curls that were tucked into buns. "And it also gave me…a history. Roots I hadn't even realized I'd been seeking. Maybe I wouldn't have been searching so hard for it if Dad hadn't died when I was only seventeen. Clarissa has been nothing but wonderful. She's the only mom I've known. She is my mom. But there was always a piece of me that…" Nikki faded away.

"Felt like you didn't belong anywhere."

She looked up from worrying the comforter to see his eyes boring into her, as if someone had given him the key to her soul. As if he could see thoughts she'd never shared with anyone. There was a gentleness to his look that his entire being belied. He wasn't built for tenderness. "Yes. Exactly," she breathed out. "And here was a professor, telling me about not only past relatives but an entire country I belonged to. Like I was some sort of Anastasia, being found and returned to her people."

"But then?"

"His office was broken into, and his brother—that man today—showed up to say it was because the professor had basically poked the sleeping bear."

"They were after the reward money."

Her eyes widened, her heart pounding. "What reward?"

"Two million dollars for anyone who had proof of a descendant of Prince Dario."

Her mouth dropped open, and she shook her head as she put down the soda can. "I didn't know."

"Was that the only time you saw his brother?" D'Angelo asked.

"Yes. The professor came by himself that night to the farmhouse. That was when he gave me the brooch and told me everyone I loved was in danger if I said anything. To just forget the entire story. And I believed him because…" Her throat closed again. "Because Lan…"

"When I went looking for the professor to interrogate him, I found Oliver instead," D'Angelo told her. "But I never fully trusted him. He loves his cocaine too much."

"Was it really the professor in that awful picture?" she gulped.

He nodded. "I believe so."

Her eyes grew wide, her pulse still trembling inside her. The silence settled down between them, and something D'Angelo had said in the alley came back to her. "He said his dad was a Navy SEAL and trained him… Did he really try to get into the special forces?"

"Yes."

Her hand played with the edges of the pocket on his sweatshirt, longing for the brooch he still hadn't returned.

"Holden showed us a sketch of him…asked if we knew him. I denied it because I was terrified they'd open this door and someone else would die. My mom…my friends… me."

"No one will hurt you," he said softly.

"But what about the people I love?" Tears clogged her eyes. She shook them away. "The knife that was used to kill Landry. Holden called it… I don't remember the word, but it's a knife only Green Berets are given."

"A Yarborough," D'Angelo said.

She looked into his face, searching for answers.

"Was that one of the units Oliver tried to get into? Do you think he could have been the one to kill Landry?"

His heavy brow furrowed together. "If the anti-royalists promised him a larger reward for killing you in lieu of finding you, yes. I don't think he'd be loyal to anyone."

"But?"

His eyes darkened, concern and worry drifting through them. "The knives are hard to get, but not impossible. They can be found on black-market sites, so he could have found one." He considered her for a moment, and then added, "It might be much simpler than that. There is someone close to you who was an actual Green Beret."

Nikki's heartbeat jumped again, and she shook her head. Her mom had tried to say the same thing. She'd sent Nikki running because of it, but her soul refused to believe it. She couldn't think of any reason for Jerome to have turned on all of them. Not even for money. "No! Jerome was my father's best friend. He's trained me and Mom. He's been there for us through the worst of times."

"He was in Grand Orchard. He's here now."

Her eyes closed against the words so similar to her mom's.

"Where was he when your father was killed?" D'Angelo asked softly.

"Out of the country," she said.

"You know this for sure?"

God, no. She had no way of proving he'd actually been where he'd said. "He was devastated when he heard about Dad. His face… I don't think you can fake that kind of emotion."

"Actors do it every day."

It was true, but she didn't want to believe it. She just wanted it all to be done. Over. Gone. She wanted to return to sailing with her mom and making beautiful songs with her friends. She wanted a life that didn't involve espionage and intrigue and murder.

"What do I do? How do I make it all stop?" she asked, hating the desperate plea in her voice but unable to stop it. She could only hope that, somehow, this man who'd sworn he was there to protect her would be able to make it all go away and allow her to return to a simpler life.

Chapter Fifteen

D'Angelo

THE FIRE INSIDE
Performed by Bon Jovi

D'Angelo felt something inside him ripping at the look in her eyes. Desperate and hopeful, it was somehow even more exposed than when he'd seen the entirety of her in the shower. It was as if she was begging him to navigate through her past, fix all the wrongs, and then clear the way to a future where she didn't have to remember the lives that had been lost for her. He was surprised by the desire inside him to give it to her. A life without the complexities of being a queen who was hunted by her own people.

He gritted his teeth.

His only job was to see her safe and installed on the throne. He didn't owe her anything else. In fact, wanting to give her other things was only opening a door that would lead to devastation. For him. For her. For his people.

But sitting on the bed with her, smelling that natural floral scent of her that even the cheap shampoo she'd used couldn't hide, feeling the electricity drifting back and forth between them…he was almost ready to toss it all off. To serve her instead of the monarchy.

He slid his feet to the ground, putting distance between them, hoping to break the leash she'd somehow hung around his neck when he wasn't looking. A Titan holding the reins of her Kraken. The imagery she'd brought to mind earlier was so apt at the moment. He'd destroy whole cities for her.

"Get some sleep. Tomorrow, we'll make a plan."

"I don't want to be a queen. I'll abdicate just like my great-grandfather," she said, chin raising in defiance, repeating her words from earlier.

"Then everyone who has lost their lives to bring you here will have died for nothing," he said, trying to keep his voice neutral but knowing there was a hint of frustration and disappointment that still coated it. "For over two thousand years, we've had a Fiorani monarch guiding our country. Break the monarchy and you break the people."

"Don't the people think the monarchy is already over? If he died the same year my father did, it's been nine years."

"No. They've been seeking you."

"Not *me*. Some vague person who may be the descendant of a prince who walked away from his people. But what if that person doesn't exist? What if *I* didn't exist? What would happen?"

"If a rightful heir has not ascended to the throne before the deadline, the monarchy ends, and our government reverts to a parliamentary republic."

"So, the prime minister who is already running the country remains in charge, right?"

"Yes."

"Tell me why that's a bad thing."

He remained quiet for a moment. Battista Massi had been prime minister of San Fiore for twenty years. He'd seen their country through the death of a queen and a king. He ran the military and was part of the secret part of the *Cavalieri* only a few knew about, as all prime ministers before him had been. But the truth was, he still had to earn his position through an election every five years.

"Because he needs to be re-elected. Humans will do anything to keep their power."

He shifted uncomfortably at his own words. What would Battista do to keep his position as prime minister? The gray-haired man he'd grown used to reporting to—the man with a ready smile, sparkling gray eyes, and a laugh that made you think of Santa Claus—had been there every step of the way while he searched for Nicolette. Sent him to find the assassin they thought killed Landry on behalf of the anti-royalists. He was one of the good ones, wasn't he?

"That includes a king or a queen, right?" she probed further. "They'd want to keep their power as well."

What would a king do to keep his throne? Kill a barren wife and her bodyguard? His skin crawled. King Sergio had loved Antonella. D'Angelo had seen their love with his own eyes. He'd felt it when they were in the room together, blooming like its own entity. And the king had refused to remarry for years. It wasn't until he'd turned forty and had been reminded of both his obligation to provide an heir to the throne and the limited mortality of the Fiorani monarchs that he'd started to consider it again. He'd died in a boating accident before he could fulfill any of his obligations.

He couldn't afford to show her any of the doubts her simple questions had raised. Instead, he continued his duty by trying to convince her that accepting the throne was the right thing for all of them.

"Our monarchy is not like England's," D'Angelo told her. "Our sovereign has executive powers similar to your president. Prime Minister Massi recently fought against new banking laws allowing known criminals into San Fiore's financial institutions. Without a monarch to veto the bill and force the upper and lower houses back into discussion, it passed. The anti-royalists want to banish more than our monarch. They want to get rid of the seats the Old Houses have inherited in the Parliament.

They want to turn our country into nothing more than one ruled by money and two-faced politicians."

"I don't even get half of what you're talking about. You act like I'd somehow know exactly what to do and what to veto. I'd be clueless."

In his desperate search for the heir to the throne, and his even more desperate attempts to protect her, D'Angelo hadn't stopped to truly consider what exactly it would mean for Nicolette to ascend the throne as a real person. He'd thought of her as some ambiguous creature, breaking curses he wasn't sure he believed in and throwing down her gavel to protect the thing he loved most. He'd thought of her as someone who'd grown up on San Fiore like he had, with a deep love for the people, the land, the religion, and its history. Not an outsider who saw it as a pretty tourist destination.

What would make a queen who'd been raised in another country any better for them than a prime minister who needed to line his pockets to afford his re-election campaign?

His world shook, his faith in what he was doing trembling.

He stormed toward the door, soul growing dark. This was not the time to have a crisis of faith. To doubt everything he'd been raised to believe. To doubt her.

"D'Angelo," her soft voice called to him, and he turned back toward her as if she'd commanded rather than pleaded. As if he didn't have a choice. She sat in the bed, back straight, dark eyes simmering, and he was stunned again by her beauty. By the sheer energy that wafted from her without her even realizing it. They stared at each other for too long. Too many thoughts and desires brewing between them that would never come true. Finally, she let out a shuddery breath and said, "I'm… I'm sorry."

He wanted to demand, *'For what?'* For making the earth below him give out? For not being what his people needed? For saying things that stabbed at his soul? Or for forcing them to quit running while she recovered from a migraine that had terrified him?

For a moment, he'd thought he'd lost her. That she would die from a brain aneurysm as her great-uncle had, and he would be responsible for it as he'd left her medicine on a damn boat. He'd shielded her from the anti-royalists today, but he'd been unable to protect her from her own body.

Would any of it matter?

If she abdicated—if she disavowed her rightful place—everything would fall apart anyway. The anti-royalists would win. Their island would lose two-thousand years of tradition.

He turned and walked out.

In the tiny living area of the cottage, he dug through his backpack and pulled out his equipment. He had work to do. Evidence to find and video footage to monitor. An ache in his chest to force back into submission. He yearned to hear his father's voice once more. To be reminded of their cause. Of the truth. Of the importance of what he was doing.

But he would never again hear his father. The House of Castelli had been cut in half in one fatal day. Feelings D'Angelo hadn't had since his father's death threatened to overtake him. The uselessness he'd felt. The confusion.

He'd almost turned away from everything then. He'd spent months trying to prove what had happened wasn't an accident. It was the *Cavalieri's* leader, his father's friend, who'd saved him. He'd sent D'Angelo on mission after mission where his grief had become his sword until he'd realized that those emotions, the ones his father had told him to channel, were likely the ones that had cost his father and his sister their lives. On the job, D'Angelo had to take any and all emotions and shove them away so he wouldn't be blindsided. So he could see the full three-hundred-and-sixty-degree view. All the possible outcomes. All the holes in the plans. All the weaknesses.

Nicolette was making it impossible. Or maybe the simple fact he'd been nothing but his job for thirteen years was the problem. There was nothing of D'Angelo Castelli outside of the work he did. Maybe the seals on the doors he'd shoved his emotions behind in order to do this for so long were finally cracking. The storm of Nicolette was simply the last wind to blow them loose.

Or maybe she was simply reminding him of what it felt like to be a man instead of a beast.

His jaw ached from clenching it so tight. His chest felt like a vise grip was squeezing it. But he had to do his damn job. And that was to protect her. His fingers flew over his keyboard. He opened the back doors he'd established years ago into the Police Nationale, gendarmerie, and Interpol systems and scrubbed as much of him and Nicolette as he could from their reports. He deleted witness statements and altered others, making the facts conflict. He'd have the authorities chasing their tails for a while at least.

Then, he moved on to footage from the businesses around today's incidents. His hand paused at an ambulance parked in front of the bar where they'd been attacked. When he saw who was sitting on the stretcher, fury and disgust flew through him—Maynard. D'Angelo had been certain the anti-royalists would've eliminated him, but there he was with a bandaged arm and a scowl on his face.

He wanted to kill the man for betraying him…for betraying her. But first, he needed the man caught. They needed to know who'd paid him.

D'Angelo turned on his phone, hiding its real location through a series of IP addresses that would be nearly impossible to trace before he opened his messages. One waited for him from the night before.

COMANDANTE: What happened?

D'ANGELO: There are traitors in the

Cavalieri.

COMANDANTE: Impossible!

He wouldn't argue it. The security guard at the marina had used the sign of the brotherhood and then directed a gun at him and their queen.

D'ANGELO: The professor we sought is dead, and his brother turned on us. The anti-royalists saw the queen with me. She has Prince Dario's royal brooch.

COMANDANTE: Bring her and the brooch to me.

D'ANGELO: They'll be expecting us.

COMANDANTE: We'll be ready. Tell me the time, and we'll have the full force of the brotherhood there to protect her.

D'Angelo's eye twitched. Did he want the full force of the *Cavalieri* there when they didn't know who was truly loyal to them…to her?

D'ANGELO: Weed out the traitors. I need to know who I can truly trust to defend her.

COMANDANTE: We can't afford to spin our wheels waiting. The clock is running down.

D'ANGELO: Find them.

He didn't wait for a response. He disconnected, sending another fake signal spiraling one last time in case anyone was attempting to backtrace him.

He needed to move her. They were still too close to

Cannes.

He needed a new plan even more.

He glanced at the date on his computer screen.

The procession of the Dawn Priestess was in six days. It would provide them cover if they approached the castle as part of it. It would also put them much too close to the deadline for comfort, but he didn't see another option, and he was damn good at finding them. He'd use these six days wisely. He'd use it to uncover the traitors in their midst and convince Nicolette to take her rightful place on the throne.

He wouldn't fail his country. He wouldn't fail her.

Chapter Sixteen

Nikki

BLOOM

Performed by The Paper Kites

When Nikki woke, the room was full of hazy gray light that shifted the furniture into hulking forms instead of black nothingness. She was still worn out. The migraines always left her this way, sometimes for days. But the pain had receded, not even a dull pulsing left. She rolled over on her side to see the door was open. She was suddenly aware of the telltale signs of someone in the kitchen. A pan banging softly. The soft thunk of ceramic on a counter.

She sat up, and the two buns she'd tugged her wet hair into toppled over. She took a moment to rearrange them, and her gaze fell on a pile of clothes on the chair in the room. Her clothes. There was something terribly intimate about the idea of him washing her things. As if it bonded them in some way. Which was silly. They were just clothes.

She removed his sweatshirt with a strange reluctance. The scent and warmth of him had been a comfort. As if she'd been wrapped in his embrace all night. She shouldn't want to be wrapped in anything of his. The man had done violent and vicious things. Not just the day before but in his past. He'd stuffed Adria's sister in a coffin, for heaven's sake. What kind of person was capable of doing that?

And yet, knowing he would go to such lengths…for her…it filled her chest with the weirdest sensation. Almost…sensual. She'd never thought of herself as the kind of woman to fall for the bad boy, the man in the shadows, a murderer—and yet, she was very much attracted to him. It wasn't just a physical lure either. There was something in her soul that responded to his command. She didn't know what it said about her that it was true.

She was drawn to a villain. But then again, she supposed it depended on whose eyes you were looking through whether you saw him as either a villain or a hero. His people would call him the latter. She supposed they were her people as well, but it was hard to get her head wrapped around the concept. She may have had the idea bouncing around in the back of her brain for almost three years, but it didn't make it any easier to accept. Her father had been a prince. She was…a princess? A would-be queen?

She snorted softly to herself. It seemed absurd.

After sliding into her jeans, she looked around for her shoes but didn't see them. She'd feel better having them on after yesterday's debacles—after the number of times they'd had to run for their lives. She shuddered, thinking again of the gunshots and the knives…the one she'd wielded. Was this what her father had been preparing her for? Had he known someday they'd come for her?

She wasn't sure she could handle that idea any more than the one of her being someone's queen.

She used the bathroom, washed up as best she could, and then started down the hall. D'Angelo appeared at the end, filling the entirety of the opening.

"Are you hungry?" he asked.

For days after a migraine, her stomach was iffy, but she needed something. "Is there toast? Something bland?"

He backed out and headed in the direction of the rest of the cottage. She followed. The place was tiny, and she realized she'd been in the only room. For the second night, he must have slept on the floor or a couch—although the floral sofa looked far too small and delicate to have housed him.

The kitchen was even tinier than the living area. There was barely room for him to stand between the cupboards, ancient appliances, and the two-person table shoved up against the wall below a multi-paned window.

He popped two slices of bread into a toaster and then turned back to his plate, which had a sandwich on it.

"There's coffee," he said, waving his head at a single-pod maker in the corner of the crowded counter.

She shook her head. "As much as I'd love caffeine, my stomach wouldn't be able to stand it. Is there any more ginger ale?"

He opened the refrigerator and grabbed a can, popping it open for her. The move was strangely gentlemanly, making her heart squeeze tight. Silence fell between them while he finished his meal in two large bites and then pulled the toast out when it popped up.

"There's no butter, but there's jam."

She nodded and then asked, "Where did you even get all this? The ginger ale isn't exactly a normal staple." When he went to spread the preserves on the toast, she stopped him with her words. "It's easier if I do it. There's only so much I can take the day after."

Stepping farther into the minuscule kitchen caused her shoulder to rub along his arm, and sparks lit her up all over again. As if he'd felt it too, he left the jar on the counter and backed out, sitting in one of the chairs and making it look absurdly doll-like.

"Delivery service. They can leave just about anything on your doorstep these days without ever knowing who they're really bringing it to."

Instead of joining him at the table where their knees would have bumped, she remained standing, eating the toast over the sink.

She didn't know what to do now. She wanted to check in on her mom. She wanted to talk to her friends. She wanted away from all of this. He'd supposedly told her mom she was on her way to Italy, and that was where she wanted to be in reality. He watched her while she ate, and it was as if he could see every thought she was having. As if he somehow knew where her mind and heart had gone. She was about to chastise herself for romanticizing everything about this damn situation when his words proved he'd read enough in her silence.

"Clarissa was released from the hospital yesterday. They don't believe she'll have any long-term side effects from the overdose. She's on her way to Vernazza."

She realized this had nothing to do with him reading her and everything to do with the hacking he'd done. It irritated her that he'd cloned her phones and listened in on private conversations, things she'd said in confidence to those closest to her.

"Where did you even learn how to do all of this cloak-and-dagger stuff?"

He raised a brow as if her word choice had amused him. "I was raised by a *Cavalieri*. Grew up in the brotherhood. Was trained by the best of the best."

"So…you're what, like the Navy SEALs?"

"Better."

She couldn't help the eye roll at his arrogance, but she also believed him. He'd eluded her security detail, the Secret Service, FBI, CIA, Colombian DNI, and more. He'd been a ghost, a mere shadow, in and out of places, including police stations and jails, doing what he wanted and then disappearing again.

"Was it Barry who taught you your moves?" he asked.

"My dad started teaching me from the moment I could practically walk, and later, Jerome joined us. They also put me in classes. Krav Maga was my favorite, but I liked Aikido as well."

"It's a beautiful art form. Dance like."

"Dad thought it was too soft." Her voice clogged, thinking of her father. People said time healed loss, but it had never felt that way to her. She'd grown accustomed to it, like wearing her hair in a certain style, but when she took the pins out, it still hurt. The ache was still there.

When the silence grew too heavy between them, she cleared her throat and asked, "So, what now? You hold me prisoner? Take me to San Fiore against my will?"

That made his glower return, and she instantly missed the almost relaxed look he'd had on his face.

"Now, I keep you safe until I can present you at the castle."

She wanted to roll her eyes a second time, but instead, she lifted her hands and adjusted the bands holding her hair up. It lifted her shirt, and his gaze drifted to her skin between the hem and the waistband of her jeans. Out of everything they'd said and done, that simple move seemed to make him uncomfortable. He shifted in the chair, mammoth arms crossing over that gargantuan chest.

"Why can't we just go now?" she asked. "Get it over with."

"They'll have eyes on the harbor and the shore. We need a distraction and a disguise. On the twenty-eighth, the *Sacerdotesse delle Tombe* start their three-day Transition of the Night Priestess to the Dawn Priestess. The procession kicking it off will be our way in."

Nikki frowned, trying to recall what she'd read about the island's religion and the priestesses who served as guardians of their souls and wielders of justice. She'd purposefully tried to forget most of it, and now she wished she had her phone so she could read it all again. Not because she was going to become their queen, she rushed to insist to herself, but just so she'd know what the hell he was talking about. So she wouldn't feel like a clueless child.

"*Sacerdotesse delle Tombe*? Priestesses of the Tombs, right?" she asked.

"Your Italian is very good," he said.

"Not as good as your French."

"I speak six languages."

"Of course you do," she snorted. "You're basically superhuman. Are you sure these priestesses aren't making their offerings to you?"

One side of his lip did curl upward at that, and it sent dark swirls through her stomach. Heat filled her body as she wondered what those full lips would feel like pressed against hers. What the beard would feel like against her soft skin.

"The human sacrifices left for the Kraken weren't really for him," he said in a voice that might have been a tease but still sounded so serious it was hard to tell. "He was responsible for bringing the sacrifice back to the Titan who controlled him or destroying the city if they refused the god his due."

She felt only the slightest pang of remorse at his referral to the taunt she'd thrown at him when he wouldn't give her his name. He was scary. He had to know that. A large, scary beast of a man. And yet, remembering the tenderness with which he'd cared for her yesterday, it made it hard for her to continue to see him in only that light.

"If the harbor and shore are being watched, how do you expect to get in?"

He shook his head. "There is a secret entrance to the tombs from the sea only the priestesses and the keeper of the tombs are privy to. Once inside the basilica, we can join the procession."

Nikki arched a brow at him. "Because you'll blend in easily as a woman in a robe?"

"I will be disguised as one of the lynx pulling the chariot that brings the Dawn Priestess statue to the temple."

She huffed out a half laugh. "D'Angelo, you could be wearing a clown costume, and you'd still be recognizable."

"I've spent fifteen years blending in. Don't worry about me."

"I'm not," she said with a careless shrug before putting the last piece of toast in her mouth.

She barely had time to realize he'd moved before he was in front of her, thumb smoothing the lines on her forehead. The touch was like being zapped with a stun gun. Low currents fluttered through her, paralyzing her and making her mouth go dry.

"The lines here tell otherwise, *Principessa.*"

She tried to swallow and couldn't. A lump got stuck in her throat. Her eyes watered, and then she was coughing. She leaned forward, forehead colliding with his chest, and one big hand reached around her to rub her back. Once she was finally able to get the toast down, she swiped at her eyes and looked up.

"If you'd tell your body to stop trying to do you in, I'd appreciate it," he said, lips quirking again. "Having the anti-royalists after us is bad enough."

The tease in his words, the absolute absurdity of the entire situation, suddenly hit her, and she couldn't stop herself from laughing. And once she started, she couldn't stop. Every time she thought she'd gotten control, it would bubble out of her again, and the more she laughed, the more his lips lifted upward until there was a full smile on his face. And if he was breathtaking when he was broody and dark, the grin moved him from a dark angel of death into an angel of light with a flaming sword. Not a Kraken but Perseus riding Pegasus to the maiden's rescue.

Before she'd thought about it, her hand had moved, finger tracing the corners of the smile. The heat of it bled into her, and his eyes sparked with a white blaze. The hottest of flames. If his thumb on her forehead had been a stun gun to her body, her touching his mouth and the look he sent her way acted like a defibrillator to her soul, starting a rhythm that whispered of those damn fairy tales she'd convinced herself she couldn't believe in again. It was too dangerous. To her and those she loved.

They both stepped back at the same time, and it left an aching void in her chest, as if the cardiac machine had done its job, but now she was left with a cracked heart to heal.

A car engine outside the cottage had them both jerking their head in the direction of the door. He moved, lithe and fast on his feet, looking out the window. "They drove past to the next cottage," he said before turning to take her in from top to bottom. He frowned at her bare feet. "Your shoes were not salvageable."

"They're boat shoes. They can withstand just about anything."

He shook his head. "I threw them out."

"You threw my shoes away?" she repeated, stunned by his audacity.

He moved into the cottage's small sitting area and shoved a laptop into the backpack he seemed to carry with him everywhere.

"We'll get you a new pair along the way, but we need to go. Now."

"On a motorcycle? Without shoes?"

His jaw ticked. "It isn't ideal, but we can't stay here."

"Why not?"

"It's too close to Cannes. We're not registered guests. If the anti-royalists don't find us, the police will."

She crossed her hands over her chest, trying to display strength as her father had taught her, but D'Angelo didn't even register it. Instead, he just wrapped a hand around her bicep and dragged her out the door.

He'd parked the motorcycle he'd stolen off to the

side of the cottage behind some shrubs, and the gravel path poked at her bare feet. He threw a long leg over the seat, nestling the bike between his thighs in a way that made her pulse thump ridiculously. Dressed all in black, with his broody brows and dark eyes, he was the epitome of everything you were supposed to run from. In high school, she'd had a boyfriend who'd driven a motorcycle, but he'd never looked like this.

He held out a hand, and she stared at it for a long time.

Somehow, she knew accepting it and getting on the back of the bike with him was crossing a line she'd have trouble retreating from. As if she was accepting much more than a hand or a ride. As if she was buying into his plans and the stories he'd told.

As if she really was a queen being led home by a golden knight.

Chapter Seventeen

D'Angelo

LIMITLESS
Performed by Bon Jovi

Relief settled through his veins as Nicolette took his hand and mounted the motorcycle behind him. He passed her the backpack to wear so it would be easier for her to hold on to him. She slid it on without question before wrapping her arms around his waist and settling her thighs on the outside of his. He'd known she was going to do it, had tried to prepare for the sensations that would wind through him, and yet his body still reacted to it. It had been a long time since he'd been this close to a woman. Her touch, her smell, the essence of her surrounding him brought an ache to his groin that begged to be relieved and made it difficult to concentrate on the traffic as he weaved through it.

As it had every moment since he'd first seen Nicolette, his attraction to her frustrated him. She wasn't just some woman he could lose himself in and then leave behind. She was his queen. She should be untouchable. But just like her words last night had reminded him that she wasn't some vague monarch, the feel of her body touching his reminded him of the woman she actually was. What he craved now wasn't just the physical pieces of her. There was something inside him seeking the lonely girl who'd thought she was rootless and lost. Parts of him yearning to show her a place she could belong that had nothing to do with an island that was hers to rule.

And that felt far worse than just wanting to know what she looked like completely bare and moving beneath him.

His thoughts were going to undo him…ruin them both. What he needed to do was concentrate on getting her to safety. But first, he needed to get her some damn shoes.

He spotted a superstation off the freeway and pulled in. He filled the tank using a credit card for one of the false identities he'd established without using *Cavalieri* resources, and then scanned the parking lot for another motorcycle he could swap plates with. He spotted three near the back, and he drove over to them. She got off first, careful to watch the tailpipe in a way that made him realize she'd ridden a bike before. Some strange emotion akin to jealousy filled him at the idea of her touching another man in the way she'd been touching him for the last twenty minutes.

He ground his teeth together, pulled the backpack off her, and dug for his tools. He eyed the cameras on the building. Too far to get a good shot of him, but he took her shoulders and moved her body so she'd block some of his activities.

"Could you stop manhandling me? Just ask."

He grunted out a reply and set to work removing the license plate of one of the bikes he'd parked next to, replacing it with his stolen one.

He pulled a baseball cap out of the backpack and handed it to her.

"Is that a Mary Poppins bag?"

He frowned. "What?"

A single eyebrow rose. "You don't know who Mary Poppins is?"

"The character in the Disney movie?"

"Yes," she said. "You've never seen it?"

He shook his head. He hadn't watched much television growing up. Movies and shows were for normal people with normal lives. He'd been born into the brotherhood and, simultaneously, the sisterhood. Books were encouraged, and video games were offered as a means of increasing hand-eye dexterity, but movies and shows were for those with nothing to do. He'd always had things to do.

When he didn't respond, she lifted her hands and unraveled the buns she'd had her hair assembled in. The wind blew the coils everywhere before she pulled them back into submission, assembling them into a single, low ponytail the hairband could barely contain. Then, she slid the cap on, tugging the tail through the opening at the back.

He pulled the hood of his sweatshirt down over his forehead, and they made their way into the superstation. In addition to several American fast-food chains and a coffee shop, there was a convenience store he directed her to. In the personal hygiene aisle, he threw a few items for himself into the cart and waited while she chose some for herself. Then, he led her to the racks of tourist clothing—T-shirts and sweatshirts with red hearts and the Eiffel Tower. There weren't many options for shoes. She grabbed a pair of Crocs off a hook, and they made their way to the register.

There was a small Christmas tree with corny tourist ornaments at the counter, and the clerk was wearing a Santa hat. The sign on the counter read in French, "Closing early Christmas Eve. Closed on the 25th."

His brain frizzled. Christmas was in two days.

He'd been so focused on getting her to San Fiore, he'd been so lost in the plans for weeks now, he'd completely forgotten. His jaw tightened. The people of San Fiore observed rituals that were closer to the Wiccans and ancient Greeks. They celebrated Yule and the Transition in December, but Nicolette would have been celebrating Christmas if she'd been with her mother, and now she wouldn't be. Instead, she'd be in hiding with him—a brutish beast who couldn't really remember what revelry of any kind felt like. He hadn't been home for any of the traditional rites in years.

As she bent to put the Crocs on, for some reason he couldn't quite fathom, he slid an ornament from the tree and placed it with the small collection of items the clerk rang up and bagged. D'Angelo paid in cash and then led them back out to the motorcycle.

He shoved their purchases into the motorcycle's saddlebag and then lifted his laptop from his backpack. He set it up on the seat of the bike and, in a few quick strokes, had accessed the superstation's security cameras. He could feel her watching him as his hands flew over the keys, bringing up the system's coding, and with a few deft clicks, he wiped out the last half an hour from their recordings before disabling it for another twenty minutes. He slid everything back inside, threw his leg over the seat, and then held the backpack out to Nicolette.

She crossed her arms over her chest and glared at him.

He inhaled deeply. They didn't have time for this. For niceties and etiquette any more than they had time for holidays and celebrations. "Please put this on and get on the bike, *Principessa*."

One side of her lip quirked as she grabbed the straps. "How badly did that hurt?"

He snorted. "Worse than losing my fingerprints."

His words wiped her partial smile away, and he wanted to kick himself.

She got on, he started the bike, and they headed out onto the motorway.

♫ ♫ ♫

Albenga was a city that had a bit of everything. The ocean, an old-town center on the river, a beautiful clock tower, and an aura that was all Italian. He'd first spent time here when he'd gone off-grid after Langston had shared his suspicions about the way D'Angelo's father and sister had died. He hadn't wanted the *Cavalieri* to know he'd come to Italy to poke around. It was also the first time he'd created an identity that no one knew about but him, using resources that had nothing to do with the brotherhood. He'd found nothing back then. Just like he'd found nothing when King Sergio's boat crashed four years later. Either there was never anything to find, or the betrayal within the brotherhood had been there for longer than D'Angelo wanted to believe.

With the tourist season being well behind them on the Italian Riviera, the penthouse in an old villa he'd rented back then was still available on a vacation site. He paid for it using the same card as he'd used at the superstation. It made him itchy. Too many things to tie them together, but he wasn't ready to blow his only other non-*Cavalieri*-created identity yet. It took too much time and money to create them when he was doing it on his own.

He used the code the rental company had given him to let them into the underground parking, found the spot reserved for the penthouse, and reversed into the space for an easy exit if needed. They both slid off, and he led her through the darkened space to the elevator.

"I take it we're not squatting here?" she asked quietly.

He raised a brow. "No."

He would have preferred to use the stairs, but her skin was pale, and the dark shadows under her eyes had grown. She was exhausted. The migraine from the day before was still taking its toll. In the elevator, he eyed the cameras. More work. More places he had to make them disappear from.

The penthouse itself opened with another code. He'd have to change it while they were there. He stepped inside, eyeing the high ceilings, brick walls, and modern glass and steel furniture before turning back to her. "Stay here."

She was accustomed to having her bodyguards clear the rooms for her, and at least in this she didn't argue with him. But by the time he came back from ensuring the spacious two-bedroom, two-bath apartment was empty, she'd moved into the open kitchen, checking out the cabinets.

"This isn't at all what I expected." She waved her hand around the combined kitchen and living space.

He didn't respond. The building was ancient, but it had been renovated, and the owners kept it maintained. It appealed to those who wanted to be in the old town center with its quaint charm but also have modern-day conveniences at their fingertips.

She still had his backpack on, and he crossed the room, closing the distance until the citrus-blossom scent of her filled his nostrils, and the warmth of her seemed to reach out and touch him. She looked up at him, eyes growing wide for a second before his hands landed on the straps of the bag. She shrugged out of it, dark eyes flashing at him as their fingers momentarily slid together, causing that intense awareness to zip between them once more.

He forced himself to step away, turning back to the large island dividing the kitchen from the rest of the open space. He concentrated on setting up his equipment and removing them from every camera he could find on the route to Albenga, in town, and inside the building.

She sat down on one of the barstools, watching his fingers fly across the keys. He knew this because he could feel her gaze rooted to him.

"So, you don't have an invisibility superpower. You're just a really good hacker?"

He paused, looking up at her for a second and then back down at his keys. "It's practically impossible to stay out of the cameras with two people and not draw attention."

"But by yourself, you could have?"

He didn't respond. He could have avoided more of them than he had with her. He'd been focused on speed rather than stealth in trying to get her as far away from Cannes as possible.

She watched him some more, and the longer it went, the more his body started to react to it. Tingling sensations trailed up his back and neck. He was rarely nervous, and yet the tension she raised in him caused an unease to settle deep inside. He liked her staring way too much. Liked being her entire focus.

He looked up, fingers stalling once more, and raised a brow.

She blew out a breath and stood up.

"Bedroom at the back? I'd like to take a nap."

He gave a curt nod and tried to drag his eyes away from her, but they followed her down the hall. Even in those ridiculous gas-station clogs that looked like nothing she should own, she walked with a grace that couldn't be taught. Her bandmate, Adria, might have been a beauty queen in her past, but Nicolette was the real beauty. The real queen. His entire being tightened, and he forced his gaze away from her and back to the computer.

Desiring her made him continue to feel wrong. It wasn't because of his name or where he'd come from. His sister had married the king, and his family was one of the Old Houses. No, this was because of the role he was serving as her protector. It felt like an abuse of power. It felt almost traitorous, and no one in the thousands of years the Castellis had served the crown had ever called them that. He would be glad when he could finally hand her off to others.

A little voice inside him laughed and called him a liar.

He shook his head, shoved those thoughts and feelings behind the door that was still threatening to let loose, and focused on his plans to get her onto the island. He needed to find out if she was as strong of a scuba diver as her file read. Using the underwater cavern below the goddess Rhaibele's statue would get her onto the island undetected, but the rifts and tides between the skerry where the statue was perched and the caves were treacherous. Boats avoided the tiny strip of ocean as if it was a version of the Bermuda Triangle.

He clicked over to a search engine, bringing up places to buy the scuba gear they needed. There was a shop here in town near the Centa River where it spilled into the Ligurian Sea, but he'd be making a large purchase that would remain in the staff's mind, and he didn't want to do so this close to where they were staying. He clicked along the coastline. There was a store farther east he could get in and out of with relative ease, but it would mean leaving her, and that made his entire body convulse.

He turned on one of his phones, bounced the signal off several different satellites, and sent his triangulated signal to a place in London before sending a text to check-in.

D'ANGELO: How are the waters?

LANGSTON: Smooth and clear. No unexpected snags. There is a storm looking to come in on the twenty-fifth that could make for a few days of rough seas. But it isn't anything I haven't been through before.

Out of all the men in the brotherhood, Langston was the closest D'Angelo had to a friend. They'd gone to school together, trained together, and joined the *Cavalieri* together. D'Angelo had attended the man's wedding and had been there for the birth of his son. But he also had to keep in mind that the man had been one of only six people who'd known his plans in Monaco. Unless there were more the *Comandante* had trusted in the main office. The buzzing behind his eyes returned.

He tapped into Nicolette's cloned satellite and cell phones, sending off texts to her mother and friends, copying language she'd used in her prior messages to keep them from suspecting anything was off. If she didn't touch base at all, they'd send out a search party he couldn't afford any more than he could afford the anti-royalists finding them.

He ordered groceries to be delivered, and then his gaze settled on the gift bag he'd spontaneously bought at the gas station. His jaw ticked. She deserved something better than he could provide her on Christmas with the food he'd just bought.

Movement down the hall brought his head up. Furniture being shifted. It had been quiet for several hours while he'd worked, and he'd assumed she was asleep—or rather, he'd hoped she was.

He let his feet guide him to the noise. One of the bedroom doors was cracked open. Soundlessly, he pushed it wider to see she'd shoved the two chairs and a trunk that had been at the foot of the bed to the side of the room. It had opened up a fairly large space between the footboard and the dresser. She was in nothing but underwear and the T-shirt he'd washed the night before. It bared legs so long it was impossible not to stare at them. Impossible not to think about how well they'd fit around his waist on the motorcycle and how well they could cling to him if they were face-to-face with their cores aligned.

He bit his cheek and started to turn away, but then she shifted onto her toes. It was a Muay Thai sequence, one he recognized and had done many times himself, but she made it look like art. The grace with which she normally moved flowed into the steps as well. Thrusts and kicks followed a slow twirl on the balls of her feet. She had the swiftness and agility of a cat that seemed to mesmerize him. It was like watching a ballet but much more enticing to him than any woman in a tutu could be. This had a beautiful fierceness to it. A raw power tugging at that ache deep in his soul he'd been feeling for days.

She'd been trained well.

Her father and Barry had done their job.

He'd felt it when they'd fought on her boat. She was strong and skilled.

He watched for too long, the ache inside him growing like a spring from the earth, threatening to embed itself in him in a permanent way that would cause him to lose all sense of self, drowning him until he was lost in a sea of Nicolette.

Chapter Eighteen

Nikki

PAPER DRAGON
Performed by Dami Im

When she woke from the nap she'd taken, Nikki still felt groggy. She was determined to shake it. She needed to find a way out of the situation she was in, and that meant she needed her wits about her. She had to shake the haze hanging over her so all her faculties were working at maximum capacity.

She needed to work out.

She searched the dresser and closet, hoping someone had left a pair of leggings or sweats, but there was nothing. So, she peeled off her jeans and then moved some of the furniture out of her way, opening a spot between the bed and the dresser. The area rug was soft and thick beneath her. Her toenail polish was chipped and fading, but at least her feet were clean after scrubbing them furiously in the tub before falling asleep.

She started with a combination of Aikido and Muay Thai that brought her comfort at the same time as it made her heart hurt. It felt like a lifetime had come and gone since she'd been practicing in the hotel in Monaco with Mom. D'Angelo might have said her mother was doing well, but she longed to talk to her. To see for herself that she'd recovered.

She did another sequence, moves that felt like home

but also brought back memories of Jerome because he'd taught them to her. He'd moved her feet and arms into the proper formation until she'd perfected them. Then he'd sparred with her, repeating the same arrangement over and over until she could do it fast and with little thought.

As a former Green Beret, she knew he had the skills and the resources to have done everything her mom and D'Angelo had insinuated. But she couldn't believe it. He may have been ten years older than her father, but they'd been best friends since the day he'd tried to recruit Dad into the military after seeing him spar at a Krav Maga gym.

It didn't make any sense for Jerome to be behind any of this. How would he even know she was related to the San Fiorani monarchy? Unless her father had told him. But why would a Green Beret from the U.S. care what happened on a tiny island in the Mediterranean?

D'Angelo had said there was a reward for information on her family. Professor Maynard's brother had obviously been in it for the cash, had likely turned on her for even more. Could that have been what had happened with Jerome as well?

It made her sick. Made her heartbeat stutter in a way that had nothing to do with her workout.

As she twisted her body, the reflection in the mirror across from the door revealed a dark shape leaning into the opening. She twirled to face D'Angelo, and her pulse sped up a notch as their eyes locked. She prided herself on her controlled breathing during her workouts, but now it felt raspy and sharp.

Those midnight eyes trailed down her body slowly, pausing as her breasts rose and fell, lingering over the underwear covering the heat of her, and then carefully examining her bare legs. He'd seen her completely naked in the shower the day before. Seen every single part of her. But this silent scrutiny felt loaded. Expectant.

When his gaze finally found its way back to her face,

the fire in it was enough to scorch her from across the room. She took a step back, reaching for the towel she'd brought out of the bathroom and wiping at nonexistent sweat. She hadn't worked out long enough to earn any.

He stepped into the room, and it immediately felt smaller, as if he absorbed the light and the air both at the same time, making it difficult to breathe and see anything but him. At the edge of the carpet, he leaned down and undid the laces of his boots, slipping out of them before standing again.

She swallowed hard, thinking of all the reasons he could be taking them off. Reasons that shouldn't make her body respond…but did. Finally, she found her voice and was proud when it didn't shake as she asked, "What are you doing?"

He pulled his sweatshirt over his head and tossed it on the bed. It drew her eyes to his mammoth arms and chest and the tattoos spiraling up over the bulging muscles before ducking below the sleeves of his black T-shirt and then reappearing along his neck. A piece of her longed to be able to explore the art. Leisurely. With fingers and lips.

He stepped onto the rug.

"You have some strong moves, but there are holes in your defense."

Her eyes narrowed, chin lifting. "How do you figure?"

"You're here with me, aren't you?"

She huffed out a breath that was half-frustrated, half-humor. "I don't think there's anything I could've done to stop you from taking me."

His lip lifted ever so slightly again, as if he'd forgotten how to smile, but his body was attempting it anyway. For her. Her heart banged wildly at the idea. Of him smiling and laughing while looking down at her with his fiery gaze before reaching out to touch her with that full mouth. She'd be nothing but a melted pool of desire if he ever did.

"Nothing would have stopped *me*, but none of your assailants will ever be me."

"You're so damn cocky," she scoffed. His eyes narrowed at her words, but he didn't respond. "Haven't you ever heard that arrogance leads to a downfall?"

"Only if it isn't earned."

She wished she had the strength to teach him a lesson. Instead, she turned away. She felt him move, not only because she was hyperaware of him whenever he was near but because this was exactly what she did when training. Wait for engagement and return the volley. And she did. Just as his arm moved out to grab her, she ducked, spun, and grabbed his wrist, twisting it backward.

His eyes flickered with something she thought might be pride but definitely wasn't shock. He'd expected it, and he easily countered, freeing himself, sweeping her legs, and then catching her before she fell. She was in his arms, pulled up tight against his chest, and their mouths were way too close. For a beat, they stared, and then she used his wall of muscle as a tool, pushing against it and doing a backward roll out of his arms, dancing beyond his reach.

His mouth twisted again.

"What would you do now?" he demanded.

"Run," she said.

Surprise hit his eyes.

She shrugged. "Run and hope I was faster than the behemoth. I'll never win against someone your size in hand-to-hand."

"But if you break a rib in the right place to puncture an organ, you can disable them."

"That would take a lot of practice and precision, and I'd risk bringing myself too close."

"You have the speed to back away quickly. Let me show you."

And he did, making her repeat the move over and over just like Jerome used to. It was a kick that drove her heel at the exact upward angle into his chest in order to break a rib and potentially send it into a lung. They practiced until she was sweaty and tired, and her eyes were blurring again.

She stepped away from him, rubbing her temples.

"Are you hurting?" he demanded, focused on the swirl of her fingers.

She shook her head. She was, but it wasn't a migraine. "Just habit."

She crossed her arms over her chest, and he watched the move carefully. She'd lost any self-consciousness she'd felt with him while practicing, but now her partially naked state came flying back. She picked up the towel again and headed for the bathroom. "I need some more clothes."

When she turned back, he averted his eyes, but she knew they'd been on her ass.

"Tell me what you need, and I'll have it delivered."

She shook her head. "Nothing ever fits me right if I order it online. I need to try them on."

"No."

She blew out a frustrated breath. "You don't get to keep telling me no. I need clothes. I will go out and get them. You can either figure out how to make that happen, or I'll do it myself."

He stepped closer. "You just want to leave so you can try to escape again."

She couldn't blame him for thinking it. When he'd placed her behind the air-conditioning unit on the roof in Cannes, all she'd been thinking about was escape. From him. From the men shooting. But now, for more reasons than she could count, she felt safer with him than she had in a long time. Safer than she had since the night Landry had died and Professor Maynard had told her *they* would come for her too.

"I won't run. I want this to end. If following your

plan is the only way to make it happen, then I'll stay with you until it's over."

He didn't look like he believed her. He closed the distance again. When his sock-clad feet were all but touching her bare toes, he reached out, twining a lock of her hair that had escaped around one large finger, and her breath caught.

His look was intense as it locked on her. "The shops are closed tonight. I will take you in the morning. But, Nicolette, you must do exactly as I say without question."

Why did those words, said in his deep voice, light her up inside? She'd never been a person interested in playing games with sex. She'd certainly never wanted to be commanded, and yet thoughts of him demanding every move…it made those fires deep in her belly dance once more.

"Fine," she responded. It was way breathier than she wanted, giving away things she didn't want him to see.

He didn't respond, but he stared at her mouth for a long beat before he turned, denying them both any kind of relief from the inferno building between them. He picked up his boots and headed out the door without another word.

♫ ♫ ♫

When she opened the bedroom door the next morning, it was to find him in the same place he'd been every morning—on the floor, feet on either side of the frame, as if he'd turned himself into some kind of human alarm system.

The night before, they'd had a dinner of cold sandwiches he'd made after receiving a grocery delivery. The meal had filled her stomach, but it could hardly be called more than sustenance. He'd swallowed his in seconds, as if he was used to eating on the run, and she guessed, he probably was. Nothing he did seemed to be for pleasure. Not even taking in the comfort of an actual bed. It made her unexpectedly sad. Did his devotion to an ancient monarchy mean only a life of sacrifice? Living in the shadows without any comforts? Like sleeping on a floor night after night?

Just as he'd done that first morning, when she lifted her foot to go by him, he caught her ankle. The only difference today was she wasn't afraid. In fact, she almost would have smiled at his grumpy possession if she wasn't so overwhelmed with sadness for him.

"Don't get your panties in a wad. I'm just getting some breakfast."

He released her, and she stepped over him just as he rose, causing their bodies to tangle, colliding in multiple places. Every time he touched her, the electricity jolting through her was strong enough to almost be painful. They both backed away at the same time, and it did very little to reassure her, knowing he felt the same way. Instead, it made her want to close the distance. To test his resolve and his control. To see if he'd deny himself even more pleasure.

She cursed her terribly foolish thoughts and retreated to the kitchen with him following her. There, he pulled out more bread, lunchmeat, and cheese.

"Don't you ever get tired of eating sandwiches?"

"They're easy to make, easy to eat, and easy to take with me when I need to."

"What was the last meal you actually enjoyed?"

His nostrils flared, eyes darting up as if retrieving some long-forgotten memory. Whatever he'd thought about seemed to irritate him, because his face turned stoic. "Food is just a means to an end. A tool to be used just like my knives, my guns, and my computers."

Sympathy flooded her veins, and he seemed to read it, because his look turned dark.

"Don't."

She huffed. "Don't what?"

"Don't look at me as if I'm someone to be pitied, *Principessa*."

She noticed he used the name when he was irritated with her. Or looking down on her. Or maybe just trying to remind himself of who she was. When he said her full name, the one no one else on this earth had ever called her, that shot pure lust through her veins. The *principessa* just irritated her and made her poke instead of retreat.

"But it is sad. Sure, sometimes, you just need a meal to get you through, but food can also bring the same amount of pleasure as sex. It can be a delight you savor."

His pupils dilated, and his voice was impossibly deeper when he said, "You and I must have very different ideas about sex and pleasure, then."

"I can prove it to you," she said, lifting her chin with the dare.

The blue of his eyes practically disappeared as desire filled his eyes. His jaw flexed. They were both tiny movements that few people would notice, but because she seemed to be so aware of him, so tied to everything he did, she saw and felt and reacted to them as if they were large leaps instead of minuscule ticks.

He slid the sandwich toward her. "Eat."

Then, he swallowed his meal in several large bites.

"I didn't figure a big guy like you to be a chicken," she said as she nibbled at the bread.

He growled, "Excuse me?"

"Pleasure, enjoyment…you're afraid of them."

"No."

She laughed. "Yes, you are. Do you even have sex? Or is that something else the *Cavalieri* has stolen from you?"

He slammed his palms onto the counter on either side of her, leaned forward, and pushed into her space. She swallowed hard as her pulse picked up and her breasts tightened. She glanced down at his lips and then back up.

"Let's get one thing straight," he barked out. "The *Cavalieri* hasn't stolen anything from me. I gave my life willingly. For the monarchy. For *you*."

His tone dipped down at the end of his pretty little speech, the depths of it traveling through her veins again. It was like a hit on a joint. Like a shot of alcohol. Something she could easily see herself craving over and over again.

"I don't want anyone living some half-life for me. Especially not—" She barely bit back the next words before they escaped. The fact she especially didn't want this breathtakingly powerful man to be living a half-life for her. Her eyes dropped to his mouth again. It was beautifully shaped. Arched on the top, full on the bottom. Set amongst his beard and mustache, it stood out even more. Tempting.

As if he read her mind, he withdrew.

Another retreat.

Another thing he was denying himself for a cause she didn't know how to believe in.

All for her.

Chapter Nineteen

D'Angelo

FOR ALL YOU GIVE
Performed by The Paper Kites

FOUR DAYS BEFORE

The words coming from her mouth landed straight in his chest and traveled down the veins to his groin. Pleasure and sex. Denial and sacrifice. He was barely holding on to his control around her. Barely covering the lust behind a wall he'd taught himself to build decades ago—first at the hand of his father, then at the hand of his mentors, and finally due to his family's death. None of his trainers had been cruel. His father had been almost effervescent in expressing his pride and love. But all of them had shaped him into the hulking man he was. The shadow. The beast.

His father had made the mistake of trying to wear both hats, loving father and protector. He'd been in charge of his daughter's security when he shouldn't have been. He'd loved her, been focused on their time together rather than their safety. They'd both died because of it…from enjoying a glass of Nebbiolo juice, a sweet ambrosia some Italians called the nectar of the gods, which had turned deadly with the botulism that had infected it.

No matter how deep D'Angelo dug, he could never prove they'd been poisoned.

The queen had died. The king and the people had mourned.

Life had gone on, leaving D'Angelo's mother and him with nothing but their sacrifices. He couldn't let what his family had believed in—and died for—end because Nicolette was too scared to accept her birthright.

She was one to talk about being afraid. Of being chicken.

He put down the empty plate that had held the sandwich he'd barely tasted. When was the last time he'd truly enjoyed a meal? It pissed him off that she'd put the idea in his head. All her ideas, especially ones like earth-shattering sex with her long legs around his waist and him lost deep inside her.

"We're leaving in ten minutes," he said and then stormed out of the kitchen to take a shower. To ease the pain in his groin before he let the part of him with no brain gain control.

"Anybody ever tell you that you're an ass?" she hollered after him.

"Ten minutes, *Principessa*. If you're not ready, I'll tie you up, go without you, and buy what I think you need."

She snorted. "And what would that be?"

The baggiest, ugliest clothes he could find. And something to put over her mouth so she couldn't continue to spew words that made his entire world crumble at the edges. But he was smart enough to keep all those thoughts to himself.

He took a cold shower, letting the freezing water take the edge off because after gripping himself, he hadn't been able to start or finish. It had felt wrong, jerking off to thoughts of her, with her in the other room and him assigned to protect her.

When he emerged from the second bedroom with the bed he hadn't slept in—and would never sleep in while he stood watch at her door—he didn't know if he was relieved or disappointed that she was waiting for him with those ugly shoes on her feet again. She had the baseball hat on he'd handed her the day before, and her hair was caught in a loose ponytail beneath it instead of the two buns she wore more often than not. The ones that always looked ready to topple over. He wanted them down. Wanted to unravel every coil of her hair just like he wanted to unravel her.

She hardly acknowledged him. Instead, she was focused on the television she'd turned on while waiting for him. On the screen was the prime minister of San Fiore. His gray, almost-white hair made the light gray of his eyes stand out below bushy salt-and-pepper eyebrows, but the smile on his face was soft and charming.

"What are the chances of the monarchy being saved?" an off-screen reporter asked.

A flash of something appeared in the prime minister's eyes that D'Angelo couldn't read.

"Better than they were a month ago," he responded jovially, and a murmur went through the crowd. D'Angelo cursed silently. The man had all but told the anti-royalists they were on their way.

"Wouldn't it be better for you if the Fiorani heir was never found?" another reporter asked.

"Don't be ridiculous. The Fiorani family is San Fiore. Over two thousand years of traditions are built around the monarchy, and I have sworn to uphold it."

"I thought your traditions were built around Rhaibele and her priestesses?" someone else poked.

"One of the most beautiful things about our island is how our religion, our government, and our people work together. It's a delicate dance with three parts twined together—the crown, the priestesses, and the parliament. If we lose any of those pieces, we are no longer San Fiore. We would have to remake ourselves into something new."

"New can be good. Like tearing down an old building instead of wasting time, money, and energy trying to retrofit it. No matter how much you spend, it will always be old and broken, sucking resources that could be better spent on truly entering the modern era," a man with a red gemstone sparkling from his collar said.

The prime minister eyed the man for a long time. "In doing so, you lose the character of the place. The history. The truth."

"The truth is we don't need a king—or a queen—to tell us what's right and wrong. The people should have that role."

D'Angelo's blood chilled and boiled at the same time. Only a handful of people even knew Prince Dario's heir had been located, let alone that the heir was a female.

"But perhaps we need her to break the curse," someone else in the audience shouted.

Chaos broke down over the assembled crowd, and it was the prime minister, slamming his hand into the podium repeatedly, that finally brought silence.

"We have one week left before we must lose hope. I ask the people to join me in praying for the Fiorani family's safe return to the island."

D'Angelo reached over and turned the television off.

Nicolette turned to him, wide-eyed. "What do the people really want? Me or freedom from a monarch?"

"You."

She shook her head. "Has there been a poll? Do you know that for sure? Dragging me there to accept or abdicate without knowing what the people actually want isn't right either. It should be up to the San Fiorians as a whole to decide what happens."

"I'm telling you what the people want. They want our traditions to continue. They want a monarch who will keep us safe from the greed of elected officials. They want you."

She shook her head. "By crowning a queen who knows absolutely nothing about the island or what's best for it?" They were locked in a battle of wills, neither willing to turn away. Finally, she broke, glancing down at her feet and then back. "I need proof. Numbers. I want to know what the people truly want."

He gritted his teeth until they made a loud noise, and his jaw cracked. "That isn't my job, *Principessa*. My job is to make sure you get on the island safely."

"Fine, but I'm not accepting until I get an answer."

His heart lifted ever so slightly at the words because she'd moved from insisting she was going to abdicate to asking for more information. It was no longer a denial of the crown. Maybe he had time to convince her still. He didn't have the data she was asking for, but he'd work on getting it for her.

"Let's go," he said, picking up his backpack and heading for the door. In the elevator, he said, "There are several shops within walking distance. That's as far as we're going, so find what you need quickly so we can get back. Keep your head down, try not to talk, and try not to draw attention to yourself."

"No enjoying the shopping experience. Got it."

He tried not to react to her dig, but the more she insisted he didn't know how to enjoy himself, the more he wanted to show her, to prove to her, just how good he could be at pleasure—at giving it and receiving it. Instead, he simply led her through the lobby and out of the building.

The sun was bright, but the air was cool. Brought in by a brisk breeze, the scent of the sea and the river mixed together as they made their way down the streets of the old town. A Christmas tree stood in the town square decked in red and gold, and the sidewalks were packed with last-minute shoppers. The busy holiday crowd meant it was less likely they'd stand out, but it also meant more people who might recognize her as Nikki Rani, lead guitarist of The Painted Daisies.

His entire being grew tight. Going out was a mistake.

He should have listened to his instincts. The urge to drag her back to the penthouse and just order her a pile of baggy sweats online consumed him.

She stumbled twice in her attempt to keep her head down, and it was with something akin to trepidation that he finally reached out and engulfed her fragile fingers in his mammoth ones. He pulled her closer to him, their sides aligning, and that zap of awareness spiraled through his veins like an intoxicating drug, dulling his senses, narrowing his vision.

He shook it off as they entered the first shop full of casual wear. As she wound her way through the racks, the stack in her arms grew higher and higher—so many clothes she couldn't wear them all in a month.

He bent his head and asked quietly, "What are you doing?"

"I told you. I have to try them on."

Their gazes locked for a second. He sighed, grabbing the entire pile from her arms. Her lips twitched as she turned back to another display. By the time she made her way to the dressing rooms, he could barely see her over the top of the heap. His eye twitched as the attendant led Nicolette into one of the fitting rooms.

While she was ensconced inside it, he made his way to the men's section. With one eye peeled to the fitting room, another at the front door, and his senses taking in every customer and clerk in the store, he grabbed several pairs of black jeans, shirts, and sweatshirts from the shelves. Just enough to get him through the next few days.

It took him less than five minutes to return to the bench in front of the dressing room, but another thirty minutes went by without her emerging. He could hear her and see her feet below the door, taking things on and off in a way that drove him a bit batty. As more minutes ticked by, the voice telling him to get them the hell out of there grew stronger. They'd been in the store too long, drawing too many eyes with his height and her grace.

His eye was spasming by the time she finally came out with only a small collection of hangers and folded garments. His eyebrow raised at the tiny stack, but he didn't say anything as he took them from her, adding them to his items.

As they made their way up front to the checkout stand, her feet stalled at a rack of costume jewelry. Flashy and cheap. Nothing that was good enough for her. She fingered a pin shaped like a daisy. It was similar to the Royal Haze daisy the world knew her as in the band. White petals, yellow center. Fake stones that glittered in the store's light.

She looked up at him and asked softly, "Do you still have the bird brooch?"

"It is a Regina astrapia."

She nodded as if it was a fact she knew, but she didn't say anything else.

"I have it," he told her.

She swallowed, rubbing the tip of one finger over the other and the pinprick scars there.

He darted his eyes around the store to make sure others weren't close enough to hear him before leaning in next to her ear and whispering, "You hurt yourself with it."

"It helped me remember." He got lost for several seconds in the pain and bitter grief that seemed to fill her entire face before she hid it and looked away.

"Remember what?" he demanded.

"All of them. Of what could happen if I said anything. Of the pain I was responsible for causing my friends and the people who loved them."

Her words stabbed at his chest. He wanted to comfort her. Wanted to rip apart the people who'd made her feel this way by taking her loved ones from her. "Punishing yourself won't bring them back."

She swallowed, stepping away from him. "Denying

yourself enjoyment won't prevent the worst from happening either, and yet you do it. We all have our ways of coping."

She turned on her heel and walked toward the counter. He couldn't move. He couldn't even think for too long. He'd never considered the way he lived a punishment. A sacrifice, sure, but he hadn't been holding himself responsible for the things he'd not been around to stop. Had he? His father and sister could no longer enjoy anything. A meal. Sex. Love. But that wasn't the reason he did this, lived this way.

He did this to honor his ancestors and his family's memory, not punish himself for having survived. But just like every conversation they had, just like the dare she'd laid out earlier, these words crumbled the edges of his world and what he knew, causing more and more damage. What would be left of him by the time he handed her over?

Would D'Angelo Castelli no longer exist? Would the beastly shadow who defended the monarchy become something else? Something weak? Something frayed and missing parts?

He couldn't afford it.

He couldn't afford her.

And yet, he had no choice.

So, he followed her to the checkout stand, paid for the dozen items she'd chosen, and then gripped the bags in one hand while leading her out of the store with the other. The touch burned into him, leaving a mark instead of removing them like the acid that had taken his fingerprints. He could only hope this brand wouldn't be visible to the rest of the world and his enemies along with it.

Chapter Twenty

Nikki

...READY FOR IT?
Performed by Taylor Swift

From the first store where she'd gathered a handful of casual outfits and exercise gear, D'Angelo led her down the street to a shoe store and then a lingerie shop. He did nothing to irritate her. He was patient at each location, carrying her things like a boyfriend would and paying with a black card that seemed to have no limit. And yet, she grew more and more frustrated as the morning wore on.

She missed her mom and her friends.

It was flipping Christmas Eve, and she was with this hulking man who barely spoke and wanted to box her into some role she didn't want and his people may not want either. She was on the run, afraid for her life, and he just…acted as if it was nothing.

He'd kept her brooch and not once apologized for taking it.

He'd manhandled her and gotten her shot at.

She wanted to be done with it all. He'd said they couldn't go directly to San Fiore, that he had to sneak her onto the island during some ritualistic procession, but it was just…irritating. Infuriating.

All those emotions seemed to grow and fester as each minute ticked by.

And with it, the anger at what had been taken from her.

The fact he was calm, nonchalant, as if there was nothing wrong, sparked some need to strike out at him. She wanted to punish him, and there was one way she knew she could. It had to do with the fire that burned in his eyes when he looked at her. The way his jaw clamped tight and his hands withdrew whenever they touched her. She had one way to push him and his boundaries to his limit.

She pulled the sexiest bra and panty set she could find off the rack and turned to him. "This?"

His eyes narrowed.

She tossed the black lace set at him, and he barely caught it as his hands were full of her other bags.

She hated being like this. Bratty. Spoiled. Resentful. But she was also tired of being nice. Tired of not having control.

She grabbed another set. This one was bright red with sheer fabric stripes built into the cotton. "How about these?"

Still no response. She tossed those at him as well and moved along, adding several more sets to the growing stack. At an underwear display, she dug through a pile of lace thongs and pressed those into his hands as well. His face was growing darker, and she couldn't help it—she liked it. She wanted it. She wanted to see what would happen when she pushed and pushed and pushed until he exploded.

She went to the sleepwear section. Normally, she slept in sleep shorts and a tank, or leggings and a tee, but today she chose satin and lace nighties that would end mid-thigh and handed them over.

"*Principessa*," he finally grunted out a hushed warning.

She flashed him her best smile. "Problem?"

Then, she whirled around and went to the dressing rooms with him following her. Inside, she lost the jeans and T-shirt she was so tired of wearing she might just burn them and tried on several of the bras. They weren't anything she'd normally wear. She was a plain-Jane, cotton kind of girl, loving comfort far more than sexiness. But when she looked at herself in these, she could see his eyes bursting into flames, and it twisted a deep longing through her that layered over the fury and frustration.

She slid into one of the nighties, pulled back the curtain on the dressing room, and stepped toward him. His mouth twisted tight, and he squinted in disapproval as he searched the store for people watching before returning to look at her.

"What do you think?"

He stood up from the chair, leaving the half dozen bags he'd hauled around for her, and closed the distance between them in two long strides. Their toes were touching, and she had to force her head back to look up into his face, which was grim with warning but also the desire she'd been almost desperate to see.

"I think you need to stop playing whatever game you think you've started before you get burnt in ways you can't imagine."

"Yeah?" she said, forcing the tremor away from her voice. "Who's going to burn me? Not you? That would require you actually enjoying something. To find pleasure in something."

He put his hands on her shoulders and practically shoved her backward into the fitting room, but his feet followed, and his voice lowered until it carved its way through her belly again.

"I will never find pleasure in you. Do you understand?" His head lowered, mouth descending until it was decadently close to hers, and the whiskers of his beard teased her chin. "You are my queen. I am your soldier. That is all that will ever exist between us."

"Bawk-bawk-bawk."

His eyes darkened, and she could have sworn his hand shook as he reached up to the curtain and pulled it between them. "Get changed. We're going home."

She scoffed, still able to sense every piece of him standing on the other side of the velvet drape. "Home. That's a joke."

When she looked at herself in the mirror, she saw a person she didn't recognize. Angry and fiery. Cheeks flushed. She put her palms to her face. What was she thinking? Taunting him? He could break her. Break her in half without even sweating.

But somehow, a piece of her craved it.

Or maybe she just craved being the one to determine what happened next. Maybe it wasn't D'Angelo at all. Maybe any man would do the trick, but she didn't think so. He was the one who'd brought out this wildness in her. He was dangerous. That was what Fee and the others had said, and she believed it. But he was even more so for her because it wasn't just his past or what he'd done or where he was forcing her to go she should be afraid of. It was the feeling deep in her soul that he had the ability to devastate her. To leave her torn from the inside out.

She had to stop playing with fire, and yet, she didn't think she could.

She pulled on the jeans, T-shirt, and ugly Crocs.

Then, she left all the sexy lingerie in the room. She didn't even look at him as she swept her way back through the store. This time, she pulled down basic cotton. Comfort was what she'd always strived for, and that was what she would buy again. She couldn't let him or the anti-royalists or this situation turn her into something she wasn't.

But as she strode toward the checkout counter, she grabbed the red set once more. It was sexy and comfortable, and damnit, she deserved at least that much.

He paid again with his credit card. The girl at the

counter kept glancing at him in a way that turned Nikki's gut. Was it his size? The pure animalistic power of him? Or the way his eyes saw every inch of you? Her rage hadn't dissipated. She was still irritated and on edge, but she was also upset with herself for taking it out on him.

He may have been dragging her toward something she didn't want, but it wasn't really his fault. He was following orders. What had he and the prime minister both said? They were following thousands of years of tradition. What would it be like to have that kind of devotion to something bigger than you? Driving you? Pushing you? Sometimes, it was how she felt about the Daisies, as if she was just one part of something much larger than her. But the band was a mere blip in the sea of time the Fiorani monarchy had existed.

How would it feel to be part of something so ancient and respected? To not only be a part of it, but sitting atop it? Had her father known about it and kept it to himself? He had to have. It had to have been the reason he'd had the brooch and trained her to fight. But he hadn't reached out and grabbed it for himself—for them. Maybe, like her, he'd only been afraid of it destroying the life he'd created for them. It sliced through her chest that he'd never told her. That he'd kept secrets from them.

Just like you, her conscience rang out. Her friends would be upset she'd kept this from them, even knowing it had been for their protection. They would have wanted to shoulder it with her. But she hadn't been able to take the risk. She wasn't one to be taunting anyone about being a chicken.

They were quiet as they headed back the way they'd come, her emotions too strung to do much more than go where he led. But as they approached a bakery displaying its wares in an old, multi-paned window full of confetti and sparkle, she pulled her hand from his, and her feet came to a stop. She didn't wait for him to agree to take her inside. She just ducked into the store and barely heard his whispered curse.

Every year, for as long as Nikki could remember, they'd had gobeletti at Christmas. They'd bought the tiny pie-like treats filled with either bitter orange and chocolate, quince jam, or custard from an Italian bakery in downtown Orange, where you had to order them weeks in advance. Her dad had loved them when he normally wasn't a sweets kind of guy. She wanted this piece of her father with her tomorrow. She needed it even more than at any time since his death because she felt like she was losing pieces of him to questions he could never answer.

There was a line wending its way through the store, and Nikki got into it with the hulking presence of her captor and savior behind her. He leaned down, his mouth close to her ear again as it had been all day, and his breath coasted over her skin, causing goosebumps to emerge all over her body as he said, "No. We are not waiting in line."

She hoped he couldn't see the way his whispered words and the brush of his breath lit her up inside. The way her body practically quivered as if anticipating where those strong lips would go next. She turned her head slightly, and it brought their mouths perilously close. "Yes, we are."

"A dessert is not worth the risk. I will order you something." His gaze settled on the people filling the tiny store.

She gritted her teeth and said quietly, "It's Christmas, damnit. I *will* have something that reminds me of my family."

They glared at each other, and she was half-surprised when he was the one to relent. He grabbed her shoulders and shifted her so she was close to the shelves, and he was blocking her from the view of most of the store and its customers. It softened her anger to him some. He was big and tough and sort of scary, but with her, he showed these moments of tenderness, relenting when every instinct in him was telling him to do otherwise.

Her pulse raced. What would have happened if they'd met under different circumstances? When he was just D'Angelo and not *Cavalieri*, and she was just Nikki and not his supposed queen? Would he have let the blaze burning between them come out? Would he get lost in it?

It took them twenty minutes to reach the counter, and every minute that ticked by, she could feel the tension in him grow, and it wound her up almost as tight. It was with relief that she finally got to order. "I'd like two dozen of the gobeletti, please. A variety."

The woman smiled, grabbing a box and starting to fill it.

Nikki jumped as D'Angelo's voice boomed out, "Not the nuts."

The woman looked back with a start but put the tart back that she'd had in the tongs, moving on. Nikki's mouth watered as she watched the woman add the treats to the box. The irritation of the morning twisted into melancholy. She always missed her father at Christmas, but at least she'd had Clarissa. And sometimes Jerome. Now she had none of them.

The woman wrapped the box with a brilliant red ribbon, and D'Angelo paid once again. He let Nikki take the desserts from the woman's hands, when he hadn't let her carry anything else, and then steered her back outside. They were in the elevator at the apartment building before she thought to ask him about what he'd said at the bakery.

"How did you know?" she asked.

His brows furrowed. "Know what?"

"About the nuts?"

"You rarely eat them. Just as you rarely drink alcohol and especially not wine. They trigger your headaches. It's why I knew you wouldn't eat the almond cake at La Pauletta."

His answer settled over her, and it took her several seconds longer than it should have before what he'd said truly hit her. "Excuse me?"

His jaw ticked. He hadn't meant to tell her. Her pulse

quickened, not at all for the reasons it had at the bakery. A sense of panic overcame her that hadn't really been there since the cottage outside Cannes when he'd taken care of her with such kindness.

"You?! You poisoned my mom!"

He glanced at the cameras and then back to her. "I needed to get you alone."

Her breath left her body. She couldn't believe he'd admitted it.

The elevator doors opened on the top floor, and she burst out, dropping the bakery box and racing for the exit stairwell. The bags he'd carried crashing to the floor was the only sign he'd given chase because his feet were silent, as always, on the tile floor. Before she could push the exit door open, he had her yanked back against his chest. Those mammoth arms and legs pinned her to him. His voice was ominous and sexy all at the same time.

"I told you not to run."

Her body lit up, and still, she struggled. But it was useless. He had her back in the apartment and shoved into her bedroom before she could figure out a way to break away and show him exactly what she'd learned the day before at his hand. He'd taught her how to break a rib. To injure and maim. She wanted to maim him. The need to strike back reemerged until it burst free from her in an incoherent scream of frustration.

He slammed the door, and she heard a key turn in the lock. Then, something large was dragged down the hallway and shoved against the door.

"Let me out!" She banged on the wood.

"Not until you calm down," he said from the other side of the door.

"You could have killed her!"

"No. I knew exactly how much she could take."

A sob burst from her that she hated. She didn't want him to hear her cry. Didn't want him to think she was sad when really she was furious. "Why?! Why would you hurt her?!"

"You needed to understand the lengths the anti-royalists would go to in order to kill you. I needed to use your fear."

"Goddamn you. Let me out!"

"Calm down."

"Otherwise what? You'll tranquilize me again? Poison me?!"

She pounded and kicked the door some more before turning and looking around the room. There was a small window that didn't open, and even if she broke it, they were four floors up. The side of the building had no ledge or terrace. It was a straight drop to the ground. The bathroom was no better. She was trapped.

Back in the room, she took the stained-glass shade off the lamp. The base was made of metal. Heavy and sturdy. She took it to the door and started banging on the doorknob.

"You will hurt yourself," he said, his voice low, and she ignored the concern she heard there.

"So what! According to you, I'll be dead by the end of the month anyway."

"No. I will keep you safe."

"By drugging me? Poisoning me?!"

Silence was her only answer as she continued to smash the knob, using all her strength. It finally bent and twisted, drooping from its hole. She swung the door open only to find herself blocked in by a solid cabinet that had been down the hall just moments before. There was a tiny space left at the top of the doorframe, but it was too small to crawl through.

She pushed on the cabinet. The items inside rattled, but it didn't give. It was heavy and old. An enormous piece of furniture that had been moved by a monster of a man, but even as large as he was, she wasn't sure how

D'Angelo had dragged it without hurting himself. She hated the spark of concern she felt at that thought.

She sank to the floor, resting her back against it, drawing her knees to her chest. She'd thought she felt safe with him. She *had* felt safe with him. Had even let those traitorous thoughts invade her mind that there was something more between them than just lust. Something sweet and tender. Another goddam fairy tale she'd let herself get lost in.

But how on earth could she ever really trust him?

He'd poisoned her mom.

He'd put Adria's sister in a coffin.

He was a beast. Only concerned with one thing. The San Fiore crown.

But…even as she said it, she knew there was more to him than just those dark moments. He'd also saved Leya and Holden when the hate group chasing them had almost caught them, and he'd avenged Fee by retaliating against the man who'd hurt her in order to get to Asher. He'd let Tatiana out of the coffin when Adria had asked.

Which was the true D'Angelo? The monster or the knight in shining armor?

Or was there something that existed in between the two?

A beast that could be tamed with a kiss.

She scoffed at herself. Hated the thoughts. Hated the way her romantic brain still tried to turn his treachery into a fairy tale. She'd started to believe it all. Started to let herself be reeled in once more by words like *principessa* and queen, forgetting the price her loved ones had already paid for it.

For two seconds after listening to the prime minister, she'd thought that if the San Fiorian people really wanted this, if they did a study and the numbers leaned in the direction of the monarchy, that maybe she could do it. *Should* do it. But this was the reminder she'd needed. Her life would never be anything like the make-believe stories of her youth where the long-lost girl became a queen.

Instead, she needed to remember the mantle of penance she'd picked up.

Grief and guilt were hers to carry. Not a golden crown.

Chapter Twenty-one

D'Angelo

HERO
Performed by Skillet

His body was tense in ways he never was, and it was all due to the woman behind a cabinet he'd shoved in front of her door. She had him feeling too damn much. Rage and lust. Exasperation and longing. He wanted to shake her and kiss her and fuck her. And all of that was wrong not only because of their roles but because it risked blinding him as his father had been.

Her silence worried him almost as much as her pounding on the door with whatever she'd found to break the knob. He ended up doing the one thing he'd sworn to himself he wouldn't do while she was with him. He turned on the camera in her room. He'd installed it while she'd slept last night as a precaution, knowing he'd need eyes on her when he left the apartment and went to the dive shop. It had been the only time he'd intended to use it. He'd convinced himself he didn't need cameras while she was under his protection.

He rotated the camera's view until he found her. She was curled up in the fetal position on the floor by the cabinet. Her face was tear-stained, but her eyes were closed, and her breathing was slow and even. She was sleeping. He needed to leave, get what he needed done, and return before she woke.

He made another damn sandwich and left it and a water bottle on the top of the cabinet where she could reach it. Then he stuck a note to the back, letting her know it was there. He threw on his backpack and stepped into the hall. The bakery box was on the floor where she'd dropped it. He'd brought the rest of their things inside but forgotten the treats near the stairwell. His stomach tightened as he opened the carton. The treats were relatively unharmed. He thought of her voice when she'd asked to get them. The sound of longing and sadness that had filtered into his gut. An echo of feelings he'd long since pushed aside.

She missed her family and her friends.

He was the reason she wasn't with her mom for Christmas. For the first time, he wondered if he could have taken them both. But then he rejected the thought. On the run with just her was hard enough.

He placed the desserts inside the apartment, headed for the garage, and zipped out into the traffic on the stolen motorcycle. Making a spur-of-the-moment decision, he pulled the bike over at the clothing store from earlier. It wouldn't fix anything, but maybe when she saw it on Christmas, it would bring some kind of damn comfort. Proof she wasn't alone. Proof his intentions had always been noble. He scoffed at himself, pocketed the purchase, and then headed out of town.

He needed to ditch the motorcycle for a larger vehicle that would haul the dive equipment. A town over, he dropped into an underground parking garage, parked the bike, and searched for a small SUV. He programmed a fob, switched plates, deleted himself from all the video feeds, and then drove one more town farther east where he parked in the tiny lot of the dive shop he'd found online. The owner was just turning the sign to closed, shutting early on Christmas Eve, but D'Angelo knocked on the door to get his attention.

"Please. I have a list. I'll be quick," D'Angelo told him, placing his phone's notes app up against the glass.

The man's eyes glittered at what he saw there. The sale would be a nice little holiday bonus for the store, but it would also make D'Angelo memorable in ways he cursed.

Once the man let him in, he assembled the long list of gear as quickly as possible. He didn't have to linger over the different brands. He knew from years of experience exactly which ones he wanted, and after just a few attempts at suggestions, the owner retreated, allowing D'Angelo to simply pile the equipment on the counter. It was only when he got to the women's wetsuits and fins that he paused. Her file had read that she was an experienced diver, but what would make her the most comfortable when under the water?

He ground his teeth together in annoyance. Comfort didn't matter. They had two dives to get through. A practice run and then the actual dive. She could put up with whatever he bought for such a short period.

The man was humming a Christmas tune as he rang D'Angelo up. "Quite the gift. Your girl is going to be ecstatic."

D'Angelo didn't reply, handing over a wad of cash he'd stashed in his backpack as the man's words rang through his head. *Your girl.*

He cursed to himself at how right those two syllables sounded.

The owner helped him haul the equipment out to the SUV. D'Angelo slid the cover over the items in the trunk, thanked the man, and got behind the wheel just as his phone buzzed. He'd left it on so he could watch over Nicolette, hoping to hell the hack he'd done so it would triangulate off a tower in London would hold.

LANGSTON: Look what I found on her boat.

The image made D'Angelo's blood run cold.

D'ANGELO: Where was it?

LANGSTON: Tucked between the engine and the hull. Someone had to all but remove the engine to get it there. It wasn't a small job.

D'ANGELO: Did you disable it?

LANGSTON: No. Remote detonate with a failsafe.

D'ANGELO: Get off.

LANGSTON: I'm going to anchor far enough offshore that it won't harm anyone and take the dingy into the bay. Storm is brewing tomorrow. My bet? They wanted it to look like an accident when it hits.

D'ANGELO: This had to be someone close to her. Someone who knew their schedule and the boat.

LANGSTON: More than likely.

D'ANGELO: Let me know when you make it ashore.

Only her detail, her mom, and Barry had known the ins and outs of her trip. From what he could tell in monitoring her conversations, not even the other band members had been privy to her full itinerary.

He brought up the camera in her room. She was awake, sitting on the bed with the sandwich and water he'd left her, but there was something in the way she was searching the room with her gaze that made him wary. She was looking for an out. Panic flew through him. He started the engine, pushed the accelerator down, and drove at speeds that risked him being pulled over in a stolen vehicle, but he had to get there before she did something stupid.

When he parked in the underground garage and took two seconds to glance at the camera, it showed her knotting together the bedding. Fuck. He took the stairs instead of the elevator, racing up them at a pace that would leave even him winded. He slammed his way into the apartment, not caring about stealth, only hoping it stopped her. He stalked down the hall, dragged the cabinet far enough away to squeeze into the room, and found her guiltily shoving the knotted sheets under the comforter. He crossed his arms over his chest. "Are you trying to break your neck?"

"Excuse me?" she asked, pure defiance in her voice, chin raised, shoulders back.

She was a queen. A goddamn regal beauty.

"If you go out a window using the bedding, you're going to break a bone at a minimum and your neck at worst."

Her eyes narrowed, sparks flying, as she turned in a circle, checking for the cameras. If she found them, he'd know he was really slipping.

"You're watching me. That's gross and a violation of every code of decency in the book. What would the *Cavalieri* think of you watching your queen?"

"They'd thank me."

"I don't want any of this, Kraken. I want out. I want to go home."

He pulled up his conversation with Langston and shoved the phone at her. "Do you know what this is?"

She swiped it from his hand with an angry huff, looking at the picture. Her brows furrowed together. "No. What the hell is it?"

"A bomb, *Principessa*. On your boat."

The hand holding his phone dropped, and he barely caught it before it crashed to the ground. Unfortunately, it also brought him too close to her. Close enough to see the spark of fear in her eyes and smell the sweet, floral scent that was drugging him, dulling his senses.

"You're wrong."

"I'm rarely wrong—and most definitely not about this. Do you get it yet? There is no going back. There is only forward. Only claiming the throne will protect you. This is your new life!"

She sank onto the bed, face in her hands, as her chest expanded and contracted with the heaviness of her breathing. When she looked up, the terror had grown, making her eyes almost wild.

"Won't they just try to kill me anyway? If I'm gone, there will be no royals left!"

"The clock would start over again. They'd have to wait until the end of the ninth year following your death before the government could revert. They need to end this now before you take the throne and have a child."

His words were meant to reassure her, and yet they did nothing but increase the desperate look on her face, agitation brewing inside along with the fear. She waved her hand as she spoke, "Child?! So, now I'm just supposed to give up everything I love? To what? Screw the first person who comes along so I can get knocked up and have a herd of kids?"

He barely caught the yes that almost burst from his lips. It would only piss her off more. But that was what San Fiore needed—her, taking the throne and then spitting out babies right and left. It might have been archaic, but it was the truth. An heir and a spare were what they needed. Multiple spares.

"And what then?" she demanded when he said nothing. "They come after my children?! I couldn't bring kids into this world knowing they'd be hunted just like I am. What mother would?"

Her words landed in his chest like a crowbar had slammed against it. She was right. And wrong. His primary goal had always been to get her to San Fiore and prove to the world, to his people, there was a rightful heir to the throne. But he'd also sworn to himself he would find not only the leaders of the anti-royalists but every single last member. He needed to end this once and for all so she and any family she had would forever be safe.

He squatted in front of her, bringing their faces to the same level. "I swear on my breath, on my mother, on the blood of every brother and every priestess who shields the crown, if you take the throne, I will find and destroy them. One by one if need be. You will be safe. Your children will be safe."

His voice was lower than it had ever gone in his life as he pledged it to her. He meant it. There would be nothing of him left before he'd ever give up. He'd protect this magnificent woman…their queen. Her and all her children.

Her eyelids fluttered closed and then opened, displaying the tears that swam in them. A solitary drop fell to her cheek. A lone bead that gave away everything she was feeling as she fought to stop the rest from crashing down. She was so damn brave. Strong. Fucking resilient.

His thumb gently wiped the tear away, and the soft warmth of her skin bled into him, holding him hostage. Before he knew what he was doing, he'd cupped her cheek in his palm. She stilled, breath catching, and then, she leaned into it. She didn't close her eyes. She didn't look away. And he saw the fight return to her face just as he saw the dare. The one she'd flashed all day long about pleasure and sin. She moved ever so slightly, turning until her mouth found his palm.

Hot. Wet. Soft.

He bit back a groan.

His entire body tightened, and every damn muscle, including the one in his pants, came to attention, ready to do her bidding even if it meant throwing her on the damn mattress and devouring her.

Her eyes pleaded, begging him for something. A moment of forgetfulness. Release.

Everything he couldn't give.

His phone buzzed, and it jerked him from the trance he'd fallen in.

He stood.

Her mother was calling the sat phone. He had to have her return the call before things got out of hand. Before someone sent a search party to a boat that was set to explode.

"Did you have any maintenance done on the boat recently?"

She shook her head. "No. And my detail was there when the delivery company stocked it for us."

It wouldn't have stopped him.

"You need to call your mom. Tell her the winds are too strong for you to dock in Vernazza tomorrow. Tell her you're heaving-to and riding it out in the open waters."

"She won't approve."

"We can't afford for her to report you missing. We need a couple more days, Nicolette. I'll have someone bring her to the island for you. She'll be safe, and she'll be there by the time you arrive."

"When you say, 'go get her,' do you mean kidnap her like you did me?" Her eyes flashed.

"No. You can send her a message the day after tomorrow. Tell her something went wrong on the boat and that you were towed to San Fiore and are waiting for her."

She didn't respond, and it made his stomach cramp in a way it hadn't since he'd found out about his dad and his sister.

"If I agree, I have conditions," she said softly. He'd promise her just about anything if it meant he could keep her safe. "You can't lie to me again or keep secrets. I need to know everything about this plan of yours. Everything!"

Secrets were the way he'd lived his life. They'd kept him safe. They'd kept her safe. But if telling her everything was the way for her to agree, he'd do it. Easily. Readily. He gave a curt nod.

"And if I have an opinion on any of it, you have to agree to at least consider it."

His lips twitched. She hadn't demanded he agree with her opinion, just listen to it. As if she already knew he wouldn't relinquish control that easily.

"Fine."

She seemed surprised by his easy agreement.

He opened the app with the clone of her satellite phone and handed it to her. "Call your mom."

She took a deep breath, grabbed the phone, and dialed. They went through a normal greeting. How her mom was feeling, how the seas were, and then Nicolette told her about waiting out the storm in open waters. D'Angelo expected an argument from Clarissa. He would never agree to let Nicolette stay out alone in the middle of a storm that was expected to last several days.

"That's probably a good idea," Clarissa replied instead. "I wouldn't like you fighting that tiny harbor and the rocks by yourself in a storm."

"I'm sorry we won't be together for Christmas. Is Jerome still with you?"

"No…" her mom trailed off.

"What's wrong?"

It took several beats before her mom picked up again, lowering her voice. "He disappeared, Nikki. After he took me to the hotel when I was discharged. I asked him… I asked him why he came to Grand Orchard that day. He said he was checking up on you just as I was with all the stalker letters, but he was acting really strange."

D'Angelo's eyes narrowed. He couldn't put his finger on what was wrong, but there was something. His eye was at full spasm again. Every time he'd looked into

Barry, he'd found nothing. But then, he'd made a career out of clandestine work just as D'Angelo had. There was something there though. A trail. A clue. He just needed to find it.

Nicolette squeezed her eyes shut. "I can't believe he'd hurt me, Mom."

"That dessert was meant for you."

"But he had to know I wouldn't eat it."

Silence on the other end. When her mother spoke again, there was something in the tone. Suspicion if not fear. "You're right. So why…" She drifted off and then came back stronger. "I have to go, but I need you to keep me up to date on your location at all times."

"I'll keep in touch." Nicolette swallowed hard as tears rushed back into her eyes. "I'm sorry we'll both be alone, Mom."

"It's just a day, Nikki. We can celebrate it when we're together again."

They signed off with more I love yous that made his chest ache. When was the last time he'd even spoken with his mother let alone given her an I love you?

She handed him the phone, looking at him with a plea in her eyes that almost unraveled him. "Don't let anything happen to her, D'Angelo. Please. She's the only family I have left."

They were alike in that way. It was with a sense of shock that he realized they were alike in many ways. They were both the last of their families, carrying on traditions that were centuries old. They were both fighters. Both used to getting their own way. They would die to keep secrets if it would protect others.

But he vowed, as he had repeatedly since discovering the truth about her, she would not be another Fiorani monarch whose life ended shortly. He would keep her breathing even if he had to take the breaths for her.

Chapter Twenty-two

A STROKE OF LUCK
Performed by Garbage

SAN FIORE 65: We've found them.

SEGRETI: Where?

SAN FIORE 65: Albenga.

SEGRETI: Curious. Why would he take her there?

SAN FIORE 65: Why doesn't matter. They'll be gone by this time tomorrow.

SEGRETI: It will take me longer than that to get there and put a plan in place to ensure it can't be traced back to us.

SAN FIORE 65: I don't need you for this. You just take care of the boat, and I'll take care of them. We'll place her body with the wreckage, or maybe just get rid of it so they'll never recover it. It'll look like the ridiculous San Fiore curse doing its worst once more.

SEGRETI: The curse has served you well.

SAN FIORE 65: Us. Has served us well. And

now the light is coming. The dawn finally and truly taking over the night. The island will be ours.

SEGRETI: Don't get cocky. Castelli won't be so easy to take out.

SAN FIORE 65: He's just a man. A single man. Alone.

SEGRETI: He's not alone. He has her. Don't underestimate either of them.

Chapter Twenty-three

Nikki

ROOM AT THE END OF THE ROAD
Performed by Bon Jovi

The room was gray and dim when she woke on Christmas morning. The bright-blue skies of the day before were hidden behind dark thunderclouds. The storm her mom thought she was riding out in the middle of the Mediterranean was going to shower down on them for a few days before the sun reappeared. She wondered if it was some grand universal metaphor for her life. The dark before the light. The evil before the good.

She rolled her eyes at her stupid thoughts—as ridiculous as princesses and fairy tales.

As ridiculous as the promise she'd made D'Angelo to go with him.

She'd believed the vow he'd given her last night. Heard the promise in each word he'd uttered. He'd protect her. Not only her but any children that came along after her.

That idea made her stomach twist.

She definitely wasn't ready to have children.

Was she truly considering this again? Just hours ago, she'd sworn it off.

Something he'd said earlier came back to her. If she abdicated, if she walked away, she was letting murderers win. Once she was on San Fiore, she could ask for more information. She could ask what the people really wanted. Maybe that was what she truly was meant to do—give the people a voice.

No matter what, D'Angelo was right about at least one thing. She was never going to be the same again. There'd been a cataclysmic shift in her world. An earthquake had erupted along the fault lines defining her life until there was now a huge divide labeled before and after. Bigger even than her father's death or Landry's murder, because after those, she'd still been Nikki Rani. She'd just been a person who'd experienced great loss. Now she was Nicolette Dariana Alberta Rani…or she guessed Fiorani…a queen.

It still felt mostly wrong. A prize that wasn't hers. A reward she definitely hadn't earned. Not when so many had died because of it. But it also felt dishonorable to walk away and have their sacrifices be for nothing.

She let her thoughts torment her some more while she showered and changed into a pair of soft jeans and an even softer sweater. The bright marigold color warmed her skin and shifted her normally dark eyes to a softer shade. Yellow wasn't exactly a Christmas color, but the cheery shade boosted her mood.

Instead of finding D'Angelo propped in front of the door with his feet spread wide, she was surprised to find two small packages in brown paper tied with a red ribbon that looked like the one the clerk at the bakery had tied around the gobeletti box.

Her heart squeezed tight.

He'd gotten her a Christmas present. Not just one, but two.

She didn't know what to think or how to feel about it.

She heard a soft clang coming from the kitchen. D'Angelo was stealthy in most circumstances, a strange stillness to each movement that only added to his shadowy, dangerous aura, and she wondered what he was making that had him shedding his quiet for noise.

She picked up the presents, unsure of what to do. Unwrap them here? Go to him and unwrap them? It would be awkward either way. Especially as she had no gift to give him in return. She would never have thought of getting one for her kidnapper…or her savior… It was hard to decipher which he was. Except, the little voice deep inside her soul was whispering a different truth. A different word to define him.

Another soft bang from the kitchen had her retreating into the bedroom. She set the packages on the bed and stared at them for too long. Finally, she reached out and slowly undid the ribbon on the first one. The wrapping fell away easily to reveal a kitschy snow-globe ornament. The kind they sold to tourists. The words on the bottom were in French, but it was easy to decipher that it said *Merry Christmas from Cannes* or something close to it. Inside the glass was a sailboat near the shore. It was a soft mint color like the *Tangled Melody*. She wondered if he'd thought of it when he'd bought it. Wondered when and why he'd bought it at all.

The second present unraveled as easily as the first. As the strings loosened, unseen ones around her heart tightened, growing tauter as the gift was revealed. There were two brooches inside. The first was the bird-of-paradise pin that had belonged to her father and had seen her through the last two years. Relief filled her as she clutched it to her chest, running a finger along the sharp edges of the beak and tail. She hadn't realized how much she'd truly missed it. Needed it.

Having it back made her feel as if her father was there with her, standing right over her shoulder, humming his favorite Doors song, kissing the top of her head, and telling her it was all going to be okay. God, she wished he truly was there. Wished he could help her navigate these treacherous waters just as he had many times while teaching her to dive, and sail, and fight.

She shoved the brooch into the pocket of her jeans before picking up the second one. It was the daisy pin she'd seen yesterday in the store. He had to have gone back to get it when he'd left her locked in her room. Unless he'd pocketed it at the store. She supposed he'd be good at stealing. All she knew was he hadn't paid for it with the other items they'd purchased. A choked little sob escaped her.

Why would he do this?

She felt him before he spoke, and she turned watery eyes to his looming presence in the doorway.

She shook her head, brows furrowed. "Why?"

He looked away and then back. He didn't respond.

She pocketed the daisy pin along with the brooch, rose, and closed the distance between them. As always, she had to tip her head back to look into his face. Sometimes she forgot just how large he was until she was right next to him.

His gaze turned wary as she went up on her tiptoes and ever so slowly placed a kiss on his cheek. The bristles of his beard tickled her chin and lips. The softness of his skin surprised her. She inhaled the deeply masculine, briny scent of him, and it invaded her veins like hot coffee, spiking her adrenaline at the same time as it soothed. She wobbled as she came down, and his hand reached out to stabilize her, gripping her hip. It remained there as she said softly, "Thank you."

Something smoky and dark filled his eyes, and his normally gravelly voice fell even lower when he spoke. "Merry Christmas, Nicolette."

They stood that way, frozen, for perilously long seconds. Hearts beating out a decadent rhythm, forbidden and tempting, as a beautiful tension drifted back and forth between them. She felt like a little girl, attracted to a flame, knowing it would burn her if she touched it, and yet desperate to keep it close. To know what the bright colors felt like against her skin.

He was the one to step back first.

"Breakfast is ready."

He turned, retreating down the hall, and she followed.

She almost laughed when she saw what waited for her on the kitchen's island. It was essentially the same food they'd been eating for days now—another sandwich. But this one had been made with eggs and sausage. She bit her lip, trying to keep the smile away.

He glowered. "What?"

She shook her head. "Nothing. Thank you."

Every time they'd eaten, he'd done it standing up or on the edge of a seat, as if ready to run at any moment. This morning, he sat on the stool next to her. While she ate slowly, tasting each bite, his food was gone in seconds, but she noticed how he cupped the mug in his large hands and sipped from it as if coffee was the only thing he let himself enjoy.

The bakery box with the gobeletti sat on the counter minus its red ribbon. She pulled it toward her and opened it. The smell hit her in the pit of her stomach with a melancholy so strong she thought she might get lost in it. The sweet crust and fruit smell triggered thoughts of Christmases in California.

A sweet memory of her dad laughing as he and Nikki fought over their favorites took hold. He always left the last one for her. She had a vague, disjointed image of her biological mom, Génesis, and her dad biting into one together. It was a classic romantic shot of two lovers sharing food. She wasn't sure if it was an actual memory or a picture she'd seen. Her mom had been a stunning, black-haired, warm-skinned woman with eyes as dark as Nikki's. She'd died when Nikki was so young it hardly seemed possible for the image in her head to actually be hers. But love did funny things, burning people into your heart, so maybe it was an actual memory.

"You're sad," D'Angelo said softly.

She jerked her eyes from the treat to him. "Not really…just thinking about my parents." His gaze bore into her, reading her thoughts and feelings again. How could someone she knew so little see so much when her mom and her friends who'd known her forever didn't? She swallowed the knot that had formed in her throat. "What do your parents think of you doing…all this?"

A shadow crossed his face, making him look even grimmer than normal. Strange how beautiful the foreboding expression could be. Not savage…but raw. Authentic. She doubted D'Angelo had ever been anything but what she saw in front of her.

"We've all sacrificed for the crown. My mom is the Night Priestess. One of the three High Priestesses of the Tombs. The procession this week transitions the leadership from her to the Dawn Priestess who will hold the role until April. That's when the Mother Priestess takes over until October when the cycle repeats."

"Women can be a priestess and have children?"

"Yes. This isn't a Christian religion requiring abstinence. The priestesses are caretakers of the spirits of the San Fiorian people and also the souls of the kings and queens who have gone before us. They maintain the tombs and our rites, but they're also in charge of the justice system on the island."

"She has an important role, then?" When he didn't respond, she moved on. "And your dad?"

"He died at the same time as Queen Antonella. She was King Sergio's wife…and my sister." The words spun through Nikki like a knife. He'd lost them both? On the same day? Compassion twined with grief filled her as she watched a shadow drift over his face once more. She finally recognized it for what it was. She saw it over and over again when she looked in the mirror—loss and sorrow that would never let you go.

Her breath caught. "I'm so sorry. What happened to them?"

"They drank a juice contaminated with botulism while on a royal visit in northern Italy."

Her sorrow grew for him. To have lost so much. Like all of San Fiore had lost too much. Queens and kings, one after the other. The story D'Angelo had told her about the curse and the short lifespan of the Fiorani monarchs returned to her. Nikki's father had been a prince…and he'd died at forty-five years old. Would that happen to her as well?

Just like moments ago, he read her, and his tone was deadly when he spoke. "I won't let anything happen to you."

She was unable to meet his gaze as emotions threatened to overwhelm her. She wanted to believe him. Wanted to believe there was at least one thing that could shield her from whatever fate had in store for her. But if he did his job, if he stepped between her and whatever was coming, it could mean he'd end up dead, and that idea only increased the unease in her stomach. His family had already given enough. His mother could hardly afford to lose her son on top of her husband and daughter.

"Your family has sacrificed everything," she whispered.

His hand dwarfed her chin, and he tugged it gently, forcing her to look at him.

"And we'd do it all over again."

The warmth of his fingers spread through her, the touch sparkling and sizzling, increasing the ache that grew larger every moment she was near him. She wondered if he realized he was as big of a threat to her as anything outside this room. These emotions…this terrible longing…it felt like it could shatter her soul if she let it.

He withdrew, and she couldn't help rubbing her palm along the place where his hand had been. It felt like he'd branded her. Left a mark. Her heart skipped a beat as she wondered if he could see it.

She turned back to the bakery box.

"I didn't buy you a gift, obviously, but I can give you something today." When she looked over at him, a single brow rose in curiosity. "I'm going to teach you to savor your food. Well…at least these treats."

"Those are desserts."

"Yep. Haven't you ever had dessert for breakfast?" When he just stared, she laughed softly. "No. You probably haven't." He still didn't respond, but she swore his lips twitched. She took out a treat and handed it to him. He eyed it and then popped the entire thing into his mouth, chewed, and swallowed.

She gave out an exasperated huff. "That is not at all how you're supposed to do it. Close your eyes." He didn't, and she rolled her eyes at him. "Just do it, Kraken."

Slowly, watching her all the while, he let his lids drop.

She took another tart from the box, broke it in half, and lifted it to his nose. "First, just smell it." When his lids started to open, she took her other hand and pushed it over his eyes. "Don't cheat. Smell."

His body went completely still at her touch, but after a long moment, he did as she asked, inhaling deeply.

"What do you smell?"

"Citrus. Fig. Sugar." His voice was gravelly.

"Good. Do those scents remind you of anything? Transport you to some long-forgotten memory?"

"Banquets in the Great Hall of *Castrum Aureum*."

"Were you there often?"

"As my mother was a priestess and my father was *Cavalieri,* we were at all the celebrations. It was why my sister knew the king so well and how they fell in love."

She didn't want him to think about the people he'd lost. She wanted him to experience pleasure from the treat and remember it for this single beautiful moment that wasn't tied to the grief of his past. She rubbed just the crust on his lips.

He jerked back, and she chuckled.

"Don't be a baby. It isn't going to bite you. Lick your lips."

He hesitated again, but then he swiped at the hint of crumbs. She hadn't thought this through, because being so focused on his mouth and his tongue brought sensual images to mind of places on her body where she'd love for them to land. Of other ways they could find pleasure in the simplest of sensations.

Her voice was breathy when she asked, "What do you taste?"

He tried to open his eyes again, and his thick lashes fluttered against her palm like a butterfly kiss. Every fiber in her being lit up.

"Same. Fig. Citrus. Sugar. But also butter."

"What feelings does the taste evoke?" His throat bobbed, and his hands that were crossed over his chest gripped his biceps so hard the tips turned white, as if he was fighting for control. A decadent thrill coursed through her in knowing this experience was as torturous for him as it was for her. When he said nothing, she used her foot to kick against his shin and prompted, "Come on, Kraken."

"Joy."

The single syllable was a heady aphrodisiac, sending tingles over her body from head to toe.

"Open your mouth." He did, and she placed a small portion of the treat on his tongue. "Don't swallow. Just...explore it."

She sounded completely wrong. She sounded like she was in the throes of an orgasm, and damn if it didn't feel that way. Watching him close his mouth, knowing his tongue was trailing along the bits of the pastry in ways she wanted it to explore her...it was insanely erotic. Maybe the most sensual experience she'd ever had. She'd never be able to eat gobeletti again without this memory taking over all the others she'd ever had with her family.

"Okay, swallow, and then tell me what you feel, and taste, and remember."

She watched his throat move, the long, strong column bobbing. Eyelids fluttered again, but she didn't let up until, in one fast, smooth motion, he'd grabbed both her wrists, pulling them away. The dark abyss of the ocean took her in, and far from being cold, it was ablaze with heat.

"Tell me." Her whispered words were almost a beg.

"You. That's all I can smell and taste and feel." The words tore from somewhere deep inside him. Pained admissions that seemed to cost him everything and added further to the sensations flooding her.

She leaned her body forward and placed her lips on his.

And the world seemed to explode.

Lights. Colors. Sounds. All blending into this life-shattering experience she'd never be able to repeat.

Chapter Twenty-four

D'Angelo

THE RESISTANCE
Performed by Skillet

He'd tried to stop her. Tried to stop himself. This was what came of savoring something. Of enjoying things that weren't yours. You ended up taking what didn't belong to you. But as soon as those beautiful lips touched his, something shattered inside him.

He let out a pained groan, and then he was devouring her.

Screw the baked goods. She was a treat that was meant to be cherished. Unwound. Broken open. And he did just that, thrusting his tongue into that pretty mouth. Licking into her. Tasting every sumptuous corner.

She whimpered. A delightful sound that would forever be embedded into his mind and soul. He let go of her wrists only to land on her waist and drag her from her stool onto his lap. Her hands went to the back of his neck, nails biting into the skin. Pain he deserved for kissing her.

But he couldn't stop.

The dam had cracked.

He was lost. Drowning in a sea of Nicolette.

She pressed her breasts into his chest, and his entire body burned at the touch, going up in flames as his fingers dug deeper into the lush swell of her hips, and his mouth commandeered hers as if it belonged to him and him alone.

His conscience was screaming at him.

His brain was ranting and raving.

But his body was rejoicing.

She fit into him like a glove. Like notched pieces rejoining. She was perfect in his arms. Perfect against his oversized body. Perfect against his lips.

He slid one palm under the golden sweater she had on. The heat of it scorched him and flooded him with comfort all at the same time. Like finding his way home and finally being able to sleep in his own bed. He wanted to feel every inch of her. He wanted his tongue on every curve and valley. He ached from deep inside him to explore every ounce of her as he had the gobeletti.

A sound broke through the haze of passion and sin that had overcome him. A blaring he couldn't ignore. An alarm.

He tore himself away from her. Her lids were shut, her chest was heaving, and her mouth was red from the fierceness of his kiss. She was always stunning—always beautiful—but like this, she was an undefinable splendor. When her lashes opened to reveal her eyes, the desire in them almost had him going back in.

But the alarm was still sounding. Not just the one from his phone, but the one deep inside his soul that chastised him for losing control. For touching something that was not ever supposed to be touched by his darkness. By the monster who'd destroyed as much as he'd saved.

He all but shoved her back onto the stool next to him and reached for the blaring device. What he saw made his entire being tighten, throwing the lust into a bucket of ice water.

In the lobby were four men in black suits. The cut of their jackets did nothing to hide the guns underneath them. Even if he hadn't seen the man who stepped up to join them, he would have known their collars held redgemmed lapel pins. But Maynard's scraggily goatee and scowl on his face told him all he needed to know.

"Get your shoes."

"What?"

"Now. Get your shoes."

She ran down the hall as he grabbed his backpack. The men were already in the elevator. He didn't have time to make sure he had everything. Fuck. Whatever he already had would have to do.

She was back, sliding into lace-up boots that weren't yet tied.

He double-checked the knives strapped to his back and the gun at his waist.

"Do you have the brooch?" he demanded.

She nodded, and he grabbed her hand and drew her into the corridor outside the apartment, heading for the stairwell. When she started to go down, he dragged her up instead. Behind them, the elevator dinged in the background.

He slowed their steps only enough to try and hide their sounds. He punched a code into the door at the top, and they emerged onto the building's terrace. An oasis had been built there, looking over the towers in the square. He jogged past the lap pool and the elegant patio furniture, not stopping until he reached the edge. The next rooftop was an easy jump for him.

"Can you make it?"

Her eyes widened, fear flooding them. "You want me to jump?"

"Can you make it?" he demanded.

She paled.

"Fuck."

He looked around but saw nothing to help them on this side. The roof of the other building, however, was going through some kind of renovation. Construction debris littered the surface along with a ladder.

It wouldn't take the anti-royalists long to realize where they'd gone.

"Don't move," he demanded.

He took several steps back, burst into a run, and then easily leaped from one roof to the next. She gave a small cry as he landed. A cry they couldn't afford.

He grabbed the ladder, slammed it shut, and then went back to the edge. He slid it toward her on the opposite roof. "Grab it."

Her hands shook as she did as he told her. She set it on the ledge. It was a ludicrously shaky bridge, but it would have to do. "I'll hold it steady, but you have to crawl across."

Her head shook. "I… I don't think I can…" She looked down to the alley between the buildings. Four stories. She'd definitely break something.

"Listen to me, *Principessa*. You can and you will do this. Don't make me carry you across."

Her chin went up, and she put her hands on the rungs, pulling herself up onto it. The ladder bowed, and D'Angelo's heart almost gave out. She inched forward, eyes darting toward the ground.

"Don't look down."

She was halfway when the door behind her burst open.

"Hold on tight," he said. She'd barely gripped the ladder when he hauled it toward him. She bobbled, foot sliding off, a leg. His stomach lurched, and his hands had just landed on her wrists as the ladder fell. He dragged her up over the side and into his chest as the metal crashed below them. The sound was as loud and violent as two cars colliding.

A garbled sob escaped her, but he didn't have the time to soothe her. The first gunshot breezed past them, ringing through the air like a church bell. He returned fire, barely registering the hate he saw in Maynard's eyes as he pulled Nicolette down low and headed for the door that led inside. Her feet stumbled, and he righted her. He'd put her on his back if he had to, but it would be easier if she could keep up.

He thanked the stars when the door wasn't locked, and they pounded their way down the stairs. Three days ago, he'd chased her down a similar set while fear had bloomed inside him that she'd get away. Now his fear was that they wouldn't.

They burst into the lobby with enough noise and speed it startled a small group waiting there. He couldn't do anything about them. He couldn't delete this memory from their mind any more than he could delete the taste of her from his mouth.

He'd never fucked up like this. He never made mistakes, and yet this day…this week had been filled with them.

The streets were nearly empty due to the holiday. It made them stand out in all those ways he hated. As soon as they cleared the building, gunfire emanated from the rooftop. He hauled her back against the brick, ducking into the shadows, and then down another alley. He was fucking grateful he'd moved the car last night. Something deep inside him hadn't liked having all their eggs in one basket…one building. A gut instinct he almost always listened to. Except when it came to touching her…kissing her.

Shit. Get your mind on the job, D.

He weaved them through a maze of streets, purposefully taking wrong turns before doubling back to the SUV. Relief hit him when the vehicle came into sight without any anti-royalists standing over it. He popped the locks, and she climbed into the passenger seat without comment. He pulled his laptop out. "Get down," he said, and she did, squeezing herself low in the seat, head bent toward the dash and the floor.

He just needed a minute. One minute to make them disappear.

But when he opened the computer, his heart stopped.

There was a hole in the screen.

He looked down at the backpack and saw the matching hole in it.

Fuck.

He threw them both into the back seat, started the car, and merged onto the street. She moved to sit back up, and his hand landed on the back of her head. "Keep down."

They'd be looking for two people. If he could keep her out of sight, it might slow them down in identifying them from any camera feeds. But they would find them eventually. They'd know what vehicle they were in. They'd hunt them down just as he would have done if their roles were reversed.

What he wanted to do was cross the bridge over the Cenna, head to the marina, and get her the hell out of Italy, but they'd likely look at those cameras first. Instead, he drove north, keeping them just above the speed limit. Once they were far enough inland, he'd circle back around.

"Was that Oliver Maynard with them?" she asked from her crouched position.

His jaw ticked, wishing he'd let his knife land in the man's heart instead of his arm. He didn't respond. He didn't need to. But he swore he was going to end the man. End all of them. They'd feel the same fear she'd felt today before they died.

It took twenty minutes for them to get to Porgli and head back toward the ocean, but it felt much longer as he continued to scan his rearview mirror for anything suspicious. When the rain started, it felt like an omen, coming down in steady sheets that made it difficult to see the road and required him to slow down even more.

Without his computer, he couldn't remove them

from the cameras, so they needed to ditch the car. As they drove, he scoured the lanes for a vehicle that would work. Finally, he found it—a car parked along a stone wall outside a gate, hidden from the view of the house and the people it belonged to. He parked and dug through the ruined backpack, realizing the device he used to rekey fobs wasn't there. He cursed silently. He'd have to do it the hard way.

"Is that… Is that a bullet hole?" Her voice was shaky as she eyed his backpack and the ruined computer. "Are you hit? Are you hurt?"

Panic emerged in her voice as her eyes trailed over him.

"No."

He stepped out into the pouring rain and was instantly drenched. He jogged over to a tree and broke a thin limb off. He palmed a knife from his back and used it as a wedge between the glass and the door. Then, he used the narrow limb to push down on the automatic lock button. It took way longer than he wanted it to, but they were in.

When he looked at Nicolette in the passenger seat of the SUV, she was shivering. The storm was a cool one for the Mediterranean, but it wasn't enough for her to be shaking that badly. Adrenaline and fear had kicked in, and he could only hope it wouldn't trigger another migraine. They didn't have time for it. They needed to move.

He opened the door and knelt at her side. "Nicolette, I need your help. We need to move the equipment quickly."

She nodded instantly, but her eyes were glassy. As she tried to get out of the car, she almost tripped over her undone laces. No wonder she'd been stumbling all over the place as they'd run. He stopped her from moving, taking a moment to tighten and tie the boots for her. When he looked up, her eyes flickered with something he couldn't take the time to name. Gratitude. Tenderness.

Things he absolutely didn't deserve and hadn't earned.

Especially not now.

Water ran down his face in rivulets, and the rain drenched her in mere seconds. He needed to get them safe and dry. He moved to the back of the SUV and started transferring all the equipment into the trunk and back seat of the tiny car. He swapped license plates yet again, left the fob for the SUV on the driver's seat, and hotwired the new car. He had them back on the road in less than ten minutes.

She was shivering even more now with her damp clothes sticking to her and the long spirals of black clinging to her face and neck. He turned the heater up, frustrated that they were back to where they'd started without the clothes, food, and supplies he'd let them risk discovery to obtain. They were actually in worse shape because he didn't have half his gear now.

He kicked himself because he was certain it was their shopping spree that had given them up. They'd been seen somehow. Or someone had discovered his hidden accounts.

That made his blood run cold.

"Where are we going?" she asked over chattering teeth. "Why do we need the dive equipment?"

"The marina. Our way onto San Fiore without them seeing you is through the tombs. There's a secret entrance in the caverns below the island only accessible by water."

"S-so we're going now?"

He shook his head. "No. The channel we need to pass through is full of riptides and fast currents, and they'll be worse in the storm. I need to know you can handle yourself before I take you in. We'll do a practice dive tomorrow."

"I have my divemaster certificate. My dad made sure I knew what I was doing," she retorted, irritation flaring, chin raising.

He didn't respond. He needed to see it for himself before he took her into the dark catacombs below the water.

When they got to the marina, he eyed the sleeping boats. Not many people would have been out on Christmas to begin with, and the storm would put off the few who might have tried. The docks were empty.

He eyed the cameras near the gates. He'd have to disable them manually.

He took his gun from his waistband and set it on the center console.

"Do you know how to use this?" he asked.

Her eyes widened, and she shook her head. He shifted the safety off, slid the hammer back to load a round, and then set it back down. "The safety is off. It's ready to go. Point and aim, but hold it fairly tight as it'll have a strong kickback."

"Where are you going?"

"To disable those cameras and find a boat that will work for us. I'll be gone ten minutes at the most."

Her face paled.

"They won't find us this quickly now that we switched vehicles. I'll be back in ten minutes."

She swallowed, her hand resting on the gun's grip.

"Don't shoot me when I come back," he said, half-teasing and half-serious.

She looked indignant. "I won't."

He got out of the car, and the rain immediately added another layer to his already soaked clothes. He slipped behind the cameras at the gate, glanced around quickly, used one hand to lift himself up on the chain-link fence, and then cut the signal with his knife. It was crude. It left evidence and a trail the authorities and the anti-royalists could follow, but it was all he could do for now.

He broke the gate's lock and jogged down the line of slips, eyeing and easily dismissing the first row. The boats were all small sailing and fishing vessels that wouldn't be able to handle the storm or the distance. Two rows over, the bigger boats were docked. He slowed, taking in each one, looking for signs it had been sitting for a while. He needed one that wouldn't be reported missing right away.

Finally, he found what he was looking for. He leaped onto the deck of an Armaud racing boat. It was fast and lean. One similar to it had broken the record in the *Conquistar de la Atlántica* cup a few years ago, crossing from New York to Spain in less than fifty-three hours. If the boat could take that kind of beating, he was sure it could take whatever winds and waves that came at them. He took the handful of steps down to the cabin door, used his knife to unlock it, and then stepped inside. It had the smell of disuse. Not quite moldy, but a dank that didn't fit with the rich designs. The single, king-sized bed shoved into the hull made his jaw tighten.

In one of the drawers in the minuscule galley, he found what he'd hoped to find—spare keys. It amazed him how trusting people were. How lax they were in their security. This boat cost more than most people made in years, if not their lifetime, and yet someone had left the keys just sitting there.

He jogged up the steps, jumped onto the wharf, and made his way down at a slower pace. He kept his hood pulled tight over his face, hoping he'd appear a mere shadow in the darkness of the storm.

He approached the car from behind, knocking on the glass. She lifted the gun in his direction but, thankfully, didn't shoot. He opened her door, grabbed the gun from her, and stuffed it into his waistband at the back.

They grabbed all the equipment they could, leaving only the air tanks behind.

She followed him through the gate and down to the slip where the Armaud racing yacht was docked. They dropped everything into the cabin, and he handed her the gun again.

"There was a gas station down the road that was open. I'm going to grab whatever food I can find."

He didn't want to leave her without a thousand cameras around the boat so he'd know she was safe, but he didn't have a choice unless he wanted her to starve. He'd feel better if she wasn't sitting in the car while he went inside. He'd move faster this way, and it would be easier to blend in without her in that damn golden sweater that shimmered like the sun even on this wet day.

She didn't respond. She just sat on the bench seat in the galley. She rubbed her temples and shivered.

"Nicolette?" he asked.

She glanced up. "I-I'm okay."

"Is it a migraine?"

She shook her head. "No."

"I'll be back. Twenty minutes at the most."

She stared at him for a moment and then gave the slightest of nods. His heart clenched. His body grew tighter as he thought of all the ways he'd failed her. Not only her but also her friends. Women had died and been injured while he'd spun his wheels, seeking the proof of who she was, and sought the leader of the anti-royalists.

He wouldn't fail her now.

He couldn't. Because if he did, he'd lose pieces of his soul he hadn't even known existed that had been dragged into the light with one damn kiss. But it was those bright, new, shiny parts that terrified him more than the blood and shadows that hung over him, because he was suddenly worried he would sacrifice everything to keep them…to keep her.

Chapter Twenty-five

Nikki

RIVER
Performed by Bishop Briggs

For a few minutes after D'Angelo had left, she'd just sat there. Stunned. Cold. Heart still beating as wildly as it had when she'd almost fallen over the edge of a building. The sound of the ladder colliding with the ground rang through her head just as much as the gunshots had.

He'd almost been shot.

She'd almost died.

Her body felt like it was quivering from the inside out.

She had to get out of these wet clothes.

The boat wasn't intended for overnights. It was a day cruiser, so it was designed loft-style with a bed in the hull, a galley with a sink and refrigerator but no stove, a long bench seat with a small table, and a tiny latrine. While the interior of the boat was minimalist, the materials used were luxurious. High-end leathers, titanium, and even hints of platinum. She was pretty sure she'd heard these boats went for millions—more than some yachts twice its size.

Near the bed, there was a wardrobe cabinet, and when she opened it, she found several pairs of ginormous sweats along with a couple of men's swim trunks. She glanced at the cabin door before struggling to get out of the drenched jeans and sweater clinging to her frame. They landed with a soggy slap on the waxed wood. The sexy red bra and underwear set she'd put on this morning to boost her spirits were just as wet, and she barely hesitated before removing them as well. Then she pulled on the sweats that seemed to have the smell of the ocean entrenched in them. The top went almost to her knees, and even after rolling the waist several times, the bottoms still wouldn't stay up. She searched around in more drawers, found a spare rope, and wrapped it around her waist. It would have to do.

She took the bird-of-paradise and daisy pins from her jeans and slid them into the sweatshirt's pocket. Her heart did a funny clench when she thought of the snow-globe ornament she'd left behind at the apartment. That and all the clothes they'd bought the day before. What a waste. They were back to where they'd started. A single pair of everything.

There were towels in an open shelving unit next to the small latrine that she used to wring out her hair. She turned back to the galley, exploring the handful of cupboards. They revealed fishing gear, a worn ukulele, some bottles of water, and enough alcohol to get really drunk. If she wasn't so afraid of ending up with another migraine, she would have cracked open the vodka and taken a swig just to calm her nerves, to hopefully stop the shaking and shivering.

She stilled when she heard movement on the dock outside the boat. She moved cautiously to the steps, peeking her head out. D'Angelo was striding down the quay, looking more beastly than ever in the rain that still hadn't let up. His black hood shadowed his face, and his hands were full. He was carrying the four air tanks they'd left behind, and several grocery bags hung over his forearms. Even with the load he was carrying, his stride was easy and light, as if it was nothing. He leaped onto the deck of the boat with as much power and grace as he'd leaped from one roof to the other, like that damn superhero she'd called him and her bandmates always teased Leya's fiancé, Holden, about being. But D'Angelo was even more of one because he had the darkness in him that most superheroes struggled with.

He glared at her beneath his hood, and she shifted back to allow him into the cabin. He glanced over her makeshift outfit with his jaw ticking and his lips drawn in a straight, unhappy line. It caused her gaze to linger on his mouth. The kiss they'd shared at the apartment had been…life-altering. Never in her life had she felt the intensity she'd experienced in that kiss. When he'd pulled her onto his lap and gone at her like a man starved, only one thought had been in her head—the desire to feed him. Feed his soul. Feed his passion. Give him everything he'd been denying himself.

It made her feel unhinged. She didn't even know him, and what she did know should have scared the hell out of her, should have had her running to escape. And yet, when she'd had every opportunity to do so while he'd been gone just now, she hadn't. Because deep inside her beat a strange and unexpected truth. About him. About her. About them.

"The water is going to be rough, but I'm taking us out. Stay down here," he commanded.

She suddenly regretted changing into dry clothes. "You'll need help."

"Stay here, *Principessa*."

She huffed but didn't have the energy to fight him. Not with her body still shaking and fighting exhaustion that seemed to bleed through her limbs. Not with her head pounding and threatening to merge into another mighty migraine. She rubbed her temples, and his gaze lingered there.

"I bought some ibuprofen. I looked for some over-the-counter migraine medicine, but the gas station didn't have any."

He didn't wait for her response. He just headed back up the steps. The line of engines in the transom of the boat grumbled to life, deep and throaty just like D'Angelo himself, and she almost laughed because the yacht fit him perfectly. Black with gold stripes, panther-like and fast. Graceful and powerful. She briefly wondered how he'd gotten it started before recalling how quickly he'd stolen the car earlier.

As the yacht backed out of the slip and began idling through the marina, she turned back to the bags he'd dropped on the galley floor. She dumped out the contents, finding the pain medicine and taking a handful of them dry before putting the bread and boxed foods he'd bought into the cabinets. The refrigerator was small, but there was room for the packaged salami and cheese he'd picked up. More sandwiches. In her entire twenty-six years, she'd never had a sandwich for Christmas dinner.

Thoughts of the gobeletti they'd left at the apartment burned through her chest.

The yacht picked up speed, and as it hit the first large swell, she stumbled to the side, barely catching herself on the sink.

She loved being on the water and was never seasick, but being in a stuffy cabin wasn't her first choice. She sat at the table, attempting to ride out the beating the boat took as it fought the weather and the ocean. As the minutes ticked by, she eventually lay down on the bench seat, knowing the bed would be more comfortable but reluctant to go there. Reluctant to have him find her there.

Even as rough as it was, being on the ocean had a way of soothing her. She closed her eyes, letting the movements of the yacht slow her heartbeat back to a more normal rhythm as the shaking inside her receded along with the mainland. She didn't know how far he was going out, but she suspected it would be closer to San Fiore than the Italian coast.

Eventually, the boat slowed before coming to a complete stop, engines cutting. She heard the whine of the automated anchor dropping and wondered briefly if he was throwing out a second to keep them from swinging wildly in the winds. It would be a rough night being batted about, and she almost laughed, realizing the lie she'd told her mom the day before was actually true. She was now out in open waters, waiting for the storm to pass.

A storm that felt much bigger than the clouds over them.

Even bigger than the men chasing her.

Because inside her, a new war was waging. This one had everything to do with him.

It shouldn't have been surprising that D'Angelo moved as stealthily on a boat in military boots as he did everywhere else, and yet it was. The only reason she knew he'd joined her was because of the rush of cold air and wind that blew into the cabin, sending the scent of him over the space. She didn't move other than turning her head to the side and opening her eyes to watch him.

The cabin shriveled to the size of a shoebox with him in it. He was still dripping wet. He had to be cold, but he seemed like a blazing fire to her. One that would scorch her and leave a scar. One telling her to run the other way, and yet there was nowhere for her to go. She'd had her chance and chosen to stay.

A rush of heat flooded her veins with those thoughts, and she had to force it aside in order to speak. Her voice sounded wrong. Throaty and sexy. Husky like Landry's had once been. "There's another pair of sweats in the wardrobe."

He didn't say anything, just grabbed a towel off the shelf and stepped toward the bed and the cabinet with the clothes. He pulled his sopping wet sweatshirt over his head and the T-shirt below it as well, and her breath caught.

He was stunning. Chiseled muscles that flexed with the simple movement of tossing his wet clothes aside. His arms, chest, and shoulders weren't just defined. They were built in a way you only saw on bodybuilders or maybe MMA fighters. And every inch of skin was covered with tattoos. They danced over his biceps and shoulders, twining around his neck and disappearing over his back. Black and white with random shots of color graced his chest and led down over the eight-pack he boasted to his narrow waist and the band of his black jeans.

She should have looked away, but she was held in some kind of thrall.

When he popped the button on his jeans and his giant-sized fingers slid the zipper down, the sound filled the quiet of the cabin and caused her eyes to jerk up to his. They were dark in the dim lighting, almost black when they were actually a magnificent blue, a color that spoke of the dawn sneaking into the night.

His hands stilled on the waistband of his pants, and while his face showed not a single emotion, his eyes were screaming at her, daring her to keep looking and begging her to look away all at the same time.

He'd seen her naked in the shower. Watching him now was fair, wasn't it? She could even the score. He turned, giving her his back as he bent to undo the laces on his boots, toeing them off and then sliding out of the sodden jeans with much more ease and grace than she had hers. His back rippled, and the large Regina astrapia bird etched into his skin moved with it. The long, vibrant blue tail feather curved down around his waist and over his hip.

When nothing remained of his clothes, her mouth went dry, and her pulse, which had finally slowed, bounded back into action. He was magnificent. Carved and colored like an artist's rendering of a Titan rather than a Kraken. He was not a monster. He was a god. Vicious and cruel when he needed to be. Kind and generous when it served his purpose.

She ached to touch him. To warm her body with the flame of his.

To forget everything that was happening for a few short hours while she lay wrapped in the embrace of a man who'd promised to never let anyone hurt her.

He reached for the sweats, and once the dry clothes landed fully on his body, the trance she'd been held in was completely broken. She barely held back a laugh. The sweats that drowned her like a lost kitten barely covered him. His ankles and calves were showing as well as his wrists and forearms. The cotton was spread so tight over the rest of him it threatened to burst. But when he turned toward her again, the bit of humor she'd found disappeared because the tight gray sweats outlined the bulging pieces of him he'd kept hidden by turning his back.

Her eyes flew to his face where a small twitch of his lips told her the joke was now on her. The dare she'd laid down by not looking away had backfired. She flushed, twisting her head to scrutinize the ceiling.

The wind howling around them buffeted the boat, and the waves slammed into the fiberglass side. D'Angelo took a step sideways to counter the movement. She sat up on the bench seat, leaving room for him next to her at the small table. He hesitated.

"I promise not to bite," she said. His jaw ticked, but his eyes dropped to her mouth before looking away again.

The air was thick between them, flashing with the same electricity that was in the storm. At any moment, she expected to be struck, and she wondered if she'd survive it. She'd felt the same intensity in their savage kiss at the apartment. A tornado had blown through her soul, destroying what was there and leaving her with only bits to try and rebuild.

"I don't regret it." She was surprised to hear herself say it. Would he even know what she meant?

"It was a mistake," he responded, proving he did. It tore at her gut…or maybe her soul…but she also knew he was lying. It hadn't been a mistake. It hadn't been an accident. She'd done it on purpose, and instead of pushing her away, he'd hauled her onto his lap and taken control.

"It didn't feel like one."

His teeth clamped so tight she could hear them grind together. His knuckles were white again, digging into his biceps as they had earlier. Some feral part of her loved that she was the reason for it. Rejoiced that this man, who was calm while bullets flew around them, was having a hard time restraining himself now.

Maybe it was the disastrous situation she found herself in, or maybe it was just the way he looked at her in that way no one else ever had, but she wanted him as she'd never wanted anyone. She needed to feel what it was like to have all his strength, and focus, and control centered on her body.

"Stop," he growled.

She quirked a half smile in his direction. "Stop what? I'm sitting here doing nothing."

"Stop thinking what you're thinking."

"You're a mind reader now?" she tossed back. "Tell me what I'm thinking."

He moved swiftly, hands clenching the sides of the tiny table, leaning across it until their faces were so close she could have easily joined their mouths again. "You're thinking about the kiss and what it felt like to be in my arms with your pretty little ass tucked up against my groin. How your breasts felt smashed against my chest, and how it tasted when my tongue was inside you."

"Sounds like you're thinking about it way more than I am."

He ignored her comment, but his eyes fell to her lips as he said with a deep, dark threat in his voice. "I promise you. It won't happen again."

"Are you promising yourself or me?"

He grunted out his annoyance at her comment, and she couldn't help the smile that appeared as it turned his face from a frown to an all-out glower, and a giggle escaped her. She hadn't giggled since she was twelve. She covered her mouth, trying to stop it, but another burst out.

"Nothing is funny about this situation, *Principessa.*"

"You're right," she said between chuckles, desperately trying to get ahold of herself. It was the second time the seriousness of the moment had sent waves of laughter through her, but she couldn't help the reaction.

He backed up, and she wished she'd taken her chance when he'd been close. Wished she'd kissed him again just to prove she could and that in this one thing—her desire for him—he didn't have a say. Those thoughts made the laughter dry up, leaving behind only a great longing. Because he might not be able to control her desire, but he could and would control everything else...including if they ever just gave in and got lost in the feelings that swam between them.

Chapter Twenty-six

D'Angelo

AWAKE AND ALIVE
Performed by Skillet

His body was wound tight from the tension in the cabin. Every fiber of his being wanted to strip them both of the ludicrous sweats and pick up where they'd left off before his phone had sounded at the apartment. He wanted what she was offering…but he refused to take it. He couldn't, not if he expected to resurrect the dam she'd broken inside him. He had to build the wall stronger and higher than ever before because if he didn't, he'd fail. And he was done failing.

He needed a distraction from her body, and her soul, and the dares she didn't think twice about throwing his way. Because if he took her, it wouldn't be for a few hours, or a night, or some time defined by humanity. It would be for eternity. Infinity.

An infinity that wasn't going to happen.

What he had to do, what had to be his focus, was untangling the net that had been tossed around them. Instead of others being caught in a web he had woven, he felt like they were stuck in someone else's. A spider lurked in the dark, wrapping them in silk they hadn't felt or seen until it was too late. Not only had the *Cavalieri* been betrayed, but it was someone who'd known him well enough to track him even when he wasn't using their resources. When he was using accounts and traces he'd hidden and told no one.

It made his head and heart hurt. It made him think of his father and the betrayal D'Angelo and Langston had always believed had existed.

Langston…

He didn't want to believe it was his friend, but he would dig anyway. He'd find the truth either way.

But first, he'd use this opportunity to make sure she really knew as much as she claimed about scuba diving. He hauled the equipment over to the table where she sat. Then, he quizzed her about the different regulators, the computer, buoyancy, atmospheric pressure, and hand signals. She crossed her arms over her chest and rolled her eyes but snapped out the answers quickly without even having to consider them.

"Why didn't you get a rebreather instead of a standard tank?" she asked. "They'd last longer."

"I couldn't be sure you knew how to use one, and we aren't going to be under that long," he replied as he moved the gear back into a neat pile on the floor, assembling what he could and lining it up so they could pull it all on fast, if needed. He turned back to her, asking, "Have you ever cave dived?"

"No."

He gritted his teeth. "We won't have time to practice, so you'll need to stay close and be confident in my signals. The riptides in front of the entrance aren't the only dangers. There are a couple of turns you can get snagged on if you're not careful."

"How come no one knows about this secret entrance?"

"The gold miners found the cave by accident in the early fifteenth century, but as it led to the sea and not gold, it was closed off. The *Cavalieri*'s Keeper of the Tombs and the high priestesses decided to utilize it as an escape route for our king, in case of an attack on the island that we couldn't defend. They found an offset chamber and explored it using diving bells. They even stored one near the entrance to the cave for our monarch to use, if needed. Knowledge of the cave and its route to the ocean has been passed down only from the high priestesses and the *Cavalieri*'s keeper to their successors."

"You're a keeper, then?" she asked.

His eye twitched. He rubbed a hand over the short strands he was unaccustomed to on his head. For years he'd worn it almost completely shaved, but over the last two years, he'd grown it longer, trying to blend in rather than standing out in the United States. "No. My father was."

"And he passed the information along to you?"

"My mother and father both."

"If they did, who's to say more keepers and priestesses haven't passed it along to their kids and friends and lovers? Who knows how many people actually know about the entrance?" she said with a huff.

He hated that she was right, but it was still their best option.

"It's a better option than landing on shore and being shot at."

Her face paled. "The whole thing is preposterous. So, I get on the island, you disguise me in some ancient procession, and I end up at the castle. Then what? How do you plan to keep the guns at bay then?"

His stomach flipped and turned. A week ago, he would have told her that once she was at the castle, there would be dozens of *Cavalieri* on hand to shield her. But with the brotherhood broken, he couldn't promise her that anymore.

"Once you've accepted the throne, and I've handpicked the men to watch over you, no one will get close to you. I swear it."

"Can't I just show up anywhere and say who I am? I

mean, from Italy or Spain or the top of the Eiffel Tower?"

"The rules say you must be in the throne room on San Fiore when you take the oath. And the Old Houses of parliament will need to see the brooch, validate its authenticity, and take a DNA sample."

"DNA? That will take forever."

"Rapid DNA takes less than two hours. It isn't a complete genetic profile, but it can identify an individual and tie them to relatives, including aunts and uncles. We have King Sergio's DNA on file. We even have Prince Dario's from a hair sample found on his crown before he walked away in 1940. As your great-grandfather, you'd have similar markers. Your relationship to the monarchy can be validated with a rapid test first and then a full genetic test, which will still only take a few days."

She pulled the bird-of-paradise pin from the pocket of the sweats, running her fingers along all the points of the beak, feathers, and tail. "How will they know if this is the real deal?"

"There's a mark on the largest stone in the bird's chest. You can't see it without a jeweler's tool. Only two brooches like it were ever made. They went to the king and his heir. The brooch you have…it should have been left with King Caspian to be handed down to his child, but Prince Dario disappeared with it before it could be locked in the treasury."

She rubbed her temples again.

"Did you take the pain meds?" he demanded.

She nodded. "Yes, but this isn't because of a migraine. My brain hurts from keeping up with your gobbledygook. I barely read about some of these people once upon a time. I hardly know who they all are and what you're saying really means. How could I ever declare myself San Fiore's queen?"

"Gobbledygook?" he asked, raising a brow, unable to keep back the small smirk at the word.

"It means nonsense."

His lip twitched even more. "Yes, I could infer the meaning, *Principessa*. I've just never heard an adult use it."

"You keep calling me that. Which am I really? Princess or queen?"

"Both. Until you accept the oath, you are a princess. You will be asked to accept the duty of guarding the lives and souls of your people, and once you do so, you will become queen."

"Will there be a coronation ceremony? Like what King Charles had?"

"There will be a formal coronation held at the basilica, but it won't happen until they've had time to invite the appropriate dignitaries and celebrities. The swearing-in this week will be small and private, held within the throne room with the members of the parliament and representatives of the Old Houses."

"Old Houses?"

"The families who have existed on the island for as long as we have existed. They have seats in the parliament like the nobility in England."

As he watched, her finger landed on the tip of the pin's clasp, pushing ever so slightly. He reached across the table and settled his palm atop it. "No."

She stilled completely, staring at his hand atop hers for a long time before slowly bringing her eyes to his face.

"I'm not ready for any of this. Even with everything that's happened, it's still hard to believe, and..."

She trailed off, and he prompted, "And?"

She took a large breath. "And listening to Professor Maynard say these same things got Landry killed. I promised... I promised I wouldn't be the reason anyone else lost their life for some fairy tale."

"This isn't a fairy tale. This is the truth. This is your birthright. But it's also what got your friend killed."

"But who...who actually did it? I want them held

accountable. I want to give Paisley and her family some justice.”

“The knife is the answer. My gut says the person to actually have wielded it was either Maynard or Barry.”

She shook her head in denial. “We’ve been through this. Why would Jerome hurt me?”

“For the same reason the professor wanted to unveil you. Money.”

She swallowed hard. “Jerome has never lived big. He has a cottage in Long Beach. He surfs and trains and travels the world. He doesn’t have any other family. We are his family.”

The burning sensation in his eyes returned. He was still missing something. He knew it, but he couldn’t put his finger on it. There was a piece of the puzzle hidden from view, and until he found it, the spider would continue to lurk, and D’Angelo wouldn’t be at ease.

♫ ♫ ♫

D’Angelo spent the afternoon hooking up his phone to a portable satellite access unit someone had installed on the boat. Then, he did what he always did—bounced the signal around satellites and locations through backend coding. He was limited on what he could do using just his phone, but he was able to delete their arrival at the marina from the video surveillance and any images of him from the gas station.

Then, he handed her the phone. “You need to call your mom and your friends. If they don’t hear from you on Christmas, they’ll get worried.”

He only half listened while she talked with her friends. Inane conversations, but all of them coated with love and caring, the teasing in the tones as much as the actual words showcasing it. However, when she called her mom, he couldn’t help but be drawn into it fully.

“I miss you,” Nicolette said.

"I miss you too. I wish…" her mother's voice trailed away.

"Wish what?"

"Maybe your dad was right all along. Maybe we should have stayed away from Europe and just stuck to the Caribbean."

Nicolette's eyes filled, and she brushed at them. "Did Dad ever tell you why he didn't want to come?"

"You know Renato, always an enigma."

"You thought he was keeping secrets?" Surprise washed over Nicolette's face.

"Didn't you?"

Her dark coils danced as she shook her head. "No."

"You never once wondered about all the trainings and extreme privacy?"

Her throat bobbed. "No. It was just Dad. He'd always been that way for as long as I could remember."

Quiet settled down between them for a moment. "You've always been that way. Trusting all the souls around you to show only their true faces. It was one of the things that drew me to you. Your innocence. Your complete faith in the goodness of people. But look what happened, Nik. Someone tried to kill you with almond cake. Even if it wasn't Jerome, it was someone."

"It wasn't Jerome," Nicolette insisted, and she met D'Angelo's eyes at the same time. She was trying to convince him as much as her mother.

They moved on to other topics. Memories of Christmas and sailing adventures, but by the time they hung up, Nicolette looked somehow sadder than when she'd started, and it tore a bit at his soul.

When she started to hand him the phone, he shook his head and said, "Call Barry as well."

"What?"

"We need to keep our suspicions of him under wraps.

He would expect a call, right?"

She nodded with troubled eyes but did as he asked. Barry picked up on the third ring. "Nikki! Merry Christmas."

"Merry Christmas, Jerome. Mom says you left. Did you have work?"

His response was delayed a beat so small D'Angelo was sure hardly anyone would catch it. "I had to get back to the training site. So, you're with your mom? How is she?"

"I got stuck out in the storm, but I talked to her. She seems to be doing okay."

Silence settled down between them before he responded. "I'm worried about you, kiddo. Worried that you went out on your own. Worried about why someone would try to hurt you. Do you know what this is all about?"

D'Angelo shook his head, and her throat bobbed. He could tell lying to Barry cost her something. "It couldn't have been meant for me."

His voice lowered. "They haven't solved Landry's murder, Nik. You look like her. Is there any chance they thought she was you?"

Pain traveled across her expressive face. "I... I don't know."

"I have a job to finish, but then I'm going to look into it more."

D'Angelo frowned, and Nicolette rushed out, "Holden and the team are investigating, Jerome. I don't want you... I just..."

"I promised your father I'd look out for you and Clarissa. I intend to keep that promise."

"We've already lost so much." Her voice was desolate.

"Hey now. Since when does the student worry about the teacher? I'll be okay. I always am." When she didn't respond, he continued, "I gotta go, Nik, but know this…I love you, and I promise to look after you."

She told him she loved him back and hung up, pushing the phone toward D'Angelo with doubts and fear on her face he wanted to soothe away.

He swiped through the phone's screens, routed its signal to a different satellite, and placed another call. Maybe someone else would be able to find things he hadn't. He doubted it, but he had to be sure he wasn't missing something. That the blinders he could feel settling along his peripheral vision the longer he was with her weren't blocking him from seeing the truth.

When the line was picked up, D'Angelo said, "I need you to look into Jerome Barry."

Nicolette inhaled sharply at his words, but he ignored them.

"Hello to you as well, Castelli. Where are you? Where is the *principessa*?" Beneath the *Comandante's* normally charming voice, annoyance brewed.

"She's safe. We'll be there soon."

"I need to have men ready for your arrival. Give me something."

"Have you found out who sold us out in Monaco?"

The *Comandante* was silent for a beat just like Barry had been, and his senses went haywire. "The man you killed at the marina has a brother in the parliament who has made several anti-royalist comments. We're investigating."

"This isn't a random attack. They've found us repeatedly. Someone is leaking them information. *My* information. You need to clean things up on your end before we arrive," he growled into the phone.

"I don't take commands from you. It's the other way around. Remember that." There wasn't a thread of charm left. Instead, his voice was steely in a way that grated on D'Angelo.

"The only person I truly work for is the crown."

He hung up without waiting for a response, wishing he'd called from the deck where she hadn't had to listen. Wishing there wasn't a tug somewhere in the pit of his stomach that said he'd lied. That he no longer worked for the monarchy.

"Who was that?" Nicolette asked.

He was glad she'd only been able to hear his side of the conversation. That had been bad enough. "The *Comandante*."

"Do you really… Do you really think someone you trust is working with the anti-royalists?" Her voice was wary, shaky, and he cursed himself again for making the call next to her.

"I promise I'll keep you safe."

"That isn't what I asked."

Her gaze held his, and he was overwhelmed again with pride that he had no right to. She was brave and resilient. She was everything his people needed. Two days ago, he wouldn't have answered her. But he'd promised not to keep secrets from her, and he tried as best he could to honor that. "Yes. There's someone close to me helping whoever is in charge. May even be the leader of the anti-royalists."

It made his stomach twist with fury and frustration. Normally, he was good at seeing all the pieces and pulling them together. He needed to find these loose threads and knot them before everything unraveled. He turned back to the phone, pulling up the internet again. He'd always found the answers he needed when he dug long enough. *Except with Dad.* But this wouldn't be like then. It couldn't be. There was more at stake than ever before.

He pulled up what he knew on Barry first and then moved on to Langston. Nothing in his friend's life gave away any red flags. His family had served the crown as long as D'Angelo's had. They were one of the Old Houses. He had to trust his gut. He had to trust the man who'd come to him first about his father.

He put his search of Langston aside and moved on to the *Cavalieri* he'd interacted with in Monaco. The chain had to be there. The dots were waiting to be connected. He grew more and more enraged when he found several large deposits into the bank accounts of both the security guard at the marina and the one at the hospital. Money that went back to the Caymans and then a Swiss account. Those he couldn't hack because the Swiss knew what they were doing. They had criminal masterminds who ensured their systems were protected.

The man at the marina was dead, and the hospital security guard would be soon. He promised it to himself. For her. For his brotherhood. For the crown. He just needed to get Nicolette to the castle, and then, he'd make every last person who'd betrayed them pay.

He looked up from his phone to see Nicolette had unearthed a worn pack of cards and was playing solitaire. It had been hours since they'd eaten. She needed food. They both did.

He rose to make sandwiches, and she joined him. His anger turned into regret as they sat down at the table with the same meal they'd shared for days now. A meal that wasn't good enough for her, especially not on a holiday she cherished. Watching her eat it after he'd swallowed his in two bites brought back the gobeletti and the taste, not of it but of her, that he'd gotten. He'd told her it smelled and tasted and felt like joy, and it had. Like almost nothing in his life ever had before.

The storm outside continued to rage, ravaging the sides of the boat, tossing them back and forth. Most people would have spent the entire time hurling in the bathroom, but her stomach seemed as steady as his. She was made for the sea. A long history of it built into her DNA.

She'd returned to the deck of cards after dinner. He watched her fingers as they moved through the pile quickly and easily.

He didn't realize he'd let out a little grunt when she won the game once more until she raised a brow and asked, "What?"

"There's no strategy to that game. Only luck," he responded.

"It's solitaire. What do you expect?"

"Queen of Italy at least has some skill to it," he said.

She raised a brow. "You're making that up, the name of the game, right?"

He felt his lips twitch with a rare smile that he'd almost forgotten was an expression. "It's a real game." He grabbed the deck of cards from her hand. "Is there a second deck?"

She rose from the table, the sweats she'd tied around her body with a rope barely hanging on. The way they hid every curve should have made him happy. Should have made him want her less, but instead, it made his fingers itch to remove them to reveal the true shape of her underneath.

She came back to the table with a second deck. He shuffled, set up the tableau, and talked her through the steps. She caught on quick, and they finished the hand in minutes.

"Much more satisfying," he said.

She rolled her eyes at him. "Sometimes you need a brainless activity to while away the time. Solitaire is good for that. This game"—she waved to the new tableau he'd set up—"you can't really go through the motions as mindlessly."

He started moving cards, and she joined in. After a moment, she withdrew her hands and let him take over. "My guess…" she said, "you've never done a single brainless activity in your life."

He didn't respond.

"You said you were raised to be a *Cavalieri*. What does that mean? Did you go to a secret school? What about college?"

A surprised huff of laughter left his body. "This isn't *Harry Potter*. I went to primary and secondary school on San Fiore. I attended St. Andrew's for college."

"Wow. Isn't that, like, the hardest university in the U.K. to get into?"

He shrugged.

"So, you're not only a superhero, you're a genius superhero."

His hands stilled, and he met her gaze. "Make no mistake, Nicolette, I am not a hero. You called me a Kraken. It's more fitting. I do what must be done, and I show no mercy while doing it."

She leaned onto the table, chin in her hand. "Like with Ziggy Klein. But what did slicing his collarbone open like he'd sliced Fee's do for you? How was that something that had to be done for the *Cavalieri* and San Fiore?"

He stopped the game, sweeping all the cards into a neat pile, and then stood. He folded his hands under his armpits so he wouldn't stare at them. Sometimes, he imagined he could see all the blood he'd spilled there. He didn't regret it. Not in the way the majority of the world would, and he'd do it all again in a heartbeat. But she was also right. He'd done more than what his job entailed. He'd gotten justice for the Daisies in a way the authorities, tied by rules and etiquette and morals, wouldn't have been able to achieve. Somewhere deep down in his subconscious he buried as much as he could, he sometimes wondered if his afterlife would be a fiery hell because of the sins he'd committed.

"You should get some sleep," he said. "The next few days will be taxing, and we don't need your exhaustion to trigger a migraine."

She didn't move. She just stared at him across the table. "See, right there. Getting things done but expressing concern. You're a whole set of dichotomies I can't figure out. You act like you're some brute enforcer following someone else's lead, but you cared enough about my friends to ensure they were safe. Your words earlier, to your boss…you said the only person you served was the crown, but I believe you follow your conscience."

He ignored her and the truth of her words, trying desperately to remember he wasn't a saint. He was the devil. A beast. The man with blood covering his hands because he'd done the unthinkable. "Go to bed, Nicolette."

She turned to look at the single bed tucked into the bow of the boat. It was big enough for both of them, but he wouldn't be joining her there no matter how his chest and loins and fucking soul longed to do so. Because if he joined her there, he'd take every inch she'd offered earlier. And he wouldn't be able to hand it back. He'd want to keep it forever. But in doing so, the shadow of him would bleed all over her, dousing her in his sins, taking her to hell with him. Even if he hadn't been sent to retrieve and protect her, he wouldn't do that. Not to her. So, he'd sleep—as he had every day since he'd picked her up—on the floor outside her door, or in this case on the floor of the boat. It was where all beasts belonged. Standing guard.

Chapter Twenty-seven

Nikki

YOUR ARMS FEEL LIKE HOME
Performed by 3 Doors Down

What Nikki loved most about being on a boat was being on deck, feeling the breeze and the sun, and the peace that came from watching the seemingly endless expanse of the ocean trail out around you. She wasn't a big fisherman, but she would and could do it if she needed something to pass the time. Normally, she was so busy during the day, manning the sails and studying the wind, she didn't have much time to be bored. Whenever she'd sailed with her parents and then with her mom, they'd stop whenever the mood struck them to eat or swim or dive. The pace had always been slow and almost lethargic. If the seas were calm, she'd train at the bow, the sway of the deck adding to the difficulty of balancing and keeping things interesting.

It was always a peaceful way to exist, even if only for a handful of days. It required you to see and appreciate the simplest of things most people didn't even pay attention to as they hustled from their jobs to their homes and back again. Like sunsets and sunrises. Like the moon as it glowed bright and beautiful amongst the stars, whispering about the circle of life and the power of the cosmos.

What she didn't like about being on a boat was being stuck in a cabin. The storm that raged all day had required her to stay inside, and she'd ended up feeling caged. When the night passed with D'Angelo's enormous body on the floor and her on the bed, and the rain still hadn't let up, she felt even more trapped.

But while they ate another meal of sandwiches the next morning, the pounding of the waves on the boat eased, and the pitter-patter on the deck all but disappeared.

D'Angelo checked his phone.

"We have about an hour or two before everything kicks up again. Get ready for our dive."

She raised a brow. "Even with the winds having died down, it isn't really safe to go in. Visibility will be shit."

"The channel between the skerry and the entrance will be just as rough. I need to know you can make it before I take you."

"I thought you said there wasn't another option for getting on the island, so does it actually matter? Why risk it today?"

He grabbed his wetsuit. "Get ready," he commanded and then stepped out of the cabin, giving her an unexpected moment of privacy. She blew out a frustrated breath but shed the oversized sweats and redressed in the red bra and underwear set. It was still damp and cold, but since she didn't have a swimsuit and had no intention of putting the wetsuit over her naked body and ending up sore and chaffed in sensitive places, it would have to do. The wetsuit he'd bought her fit perfectly. It didn't surprise her anymore what he knew about her. Either he found them out from whatever facts he'd gathered, or he read them from her mind like he really was the damn superhero she'd called him.

She was just zipping up the back when he came back into the cabin. He glanced over her and then looked away, grabbing two of the tanks they'd brought and some of the equipment. She picked up the rest and followed him onto the deck.

The sun was trying valiantly to break through the dark clouds, and it sent soft shafts of white light onto the ocean's surface, turning the waves into flickering diamonds. The waters in the Mediterranean were a vivid blue when they were calm, a color hard to capture and even harder to find anywhere else, but with the storm churning them up, they took on a darker hue, thick and grainy.

After being in the cabin for so long, the salt air was like a hit of coffee or a zip of adrenaline. It filled her veins and her soul with energy. The only thing that ever came close to this feeling was when she was onstage, playing her guitar and singing with her friends. Some people felt small when they looked around the expanse of the sea, but for her, it gave her peace. Confidence in knowing she was a part of something much bigger. One piece in the billions of strands making up the intricate web of life on this planet.

Knowing she could impact people by what she did onstage had always felt important. Helping people feel seen and giving them an outlet for their emotions was a beautiful gift. Music was about more than cultural trends slipping in and out of the decades. It spoke to the very fabric of the listener's life. Pain and ecstasy. Love and loss. Fears and celebrations. She felt blessed to be a part of it.

But now, the idea that she might be a queen who could impact even more people, in an even greater, more real, more direct way…that tugged at something deep inside her. It wasn't just the fairy tale that had attracted her when Professor Maynard had told her she might be a missing monarch. It had been much more than the Cinderella idea of gowns and crowns and finding a prince. It had been the idea that she could actually do something…anything…to change even one corner of the world just a bit more.

As if her life might actually have value.

As if she wouldn't just be a breath that had come and

gone, forgotten by the next inhale that came along.

D'Angelo stepped in front of her, blocking her view of the sun and the sea, searching her face, reading her mood that was hardly bright and cheery.

"What's wrong?"

She shook her head, unsure what to say, a sense of alarm hitting her as she realized she was really doing all of this—considering becoming a queen. But she had to know if it was what the people really wanted first.

"I'm fine," she said, grabbing the straps he held. She focused on securing the tanks, checking the regulators, and organizing the belt with her tools, including a knife and an underwater lamp. He gave her a dive watch she wrapped around her wrist that she could use to monitor her tanks and her location.

He scrutinized everything she did as if expecting her to have lied about her confidence with the equipment. Sure, it wasn't her personal gear, but she knew her way around it almost as well as she knew how to play guitar.

When they were both outfitted and ready, he gave the signal that he would go in first. He wanted her to follow in one minute. Then, he threw his leg over the side onto the step next to the line of beefy motors and slipped into the water. Everywhere she'd seen D'Angelo, he'd dwarfed the space, but in this one place, with only the sky and the sea surrounding him, he looked small—a mere speck—and it sent a shock through her. A realization that he was actually human and not the Kraken they'd both claimed him to be, or even the god she'd imagined.

She followed him into the water. It was cold. The wetsuit might keep her slightly warmer than if she was diving in only a swimsuit, but it wouldn't keep the chill completely at bay. She forced herself to breathe normally, adjusting her buoyancy until she could drop down several meters. As she'd suspected, the visibility sucked. Sand and dirt had been twirled up by the storm, and it was like looking through an hourglass as it shifted. A touch at her elbow had her twisting to take in D'Angelo.

He had his light on and directed them downward. To where, she had no idea because they were too far from land to be able to dive to the bottom. Unlike being on top of the water, watching the world from the boat, under here she felt a bit lost with nothing to ground herself. The silence was almost oppressive. While she'd earned her rescue diver and divemaster certificates in open water, it was never her favorite place to dive. She preferred being able to zip around the formations and wildlife of the sea floor, with sunshine drifting through the waters. This was…unsettling.

She fought back a wave of panic, focusing on the light that came from D'Angelo's lamp. If she didn't have her dive watch with its compass and a geolocator, it would have been easy to get turned around. D'Angelo touched her elbow again, and they moved in a different direction, the ocean surging around them, and she felt the unexpected pull of a rip current on her fins.

Before she'd really registered it, she was caught in it, and it yanked her away from him. At first, she fought it, but all it did was buffet her harder, spinning her around and almost tipping her head over fin. She caught herself, adjusting to the forceful pull of the tide and letting herself be taken a few feet to where the underwater current slowed. Once it loosened its hold, she swam out of it, angling herself away and swimming back the way she'd come.

When she found D'Angelo, he was just treading water with his lamp, watching where she'd been. He didn't look worried or surprised by the fact she'd been caught in the rip tide, and it angered her. He'd known it was there and hadn't warned her. It had been another test. Frustration welled through her. He used his signals, pointing east, but she ignored him. Instead, she concentrated on rising to the surface at just the right feet per minute. He tugged again at her elbow, pointing down, but she shook him off.

He followed, and even dim lighting with a mask on, she could tell he wasn't happy. Angry, even. But so was she. She was tired of being tested and tormented. Of being chased and shot at. Of having no control over anything that was happening to her. She'd thought they'd moved past this. She'd told him she needed no more secrets, and she'd thought he'd agreed. He'd even told her the truth last night about someone close to him giving him away, and yet, here he was, doing it all over again. Keeping things to himself.

His fingers closed on her bicep, and she pulled her knees to her chest and used her feet to shove at his stomach with her fins. The move took him by surprise, and he let go. She swam up again, keeping an eye out for him and kicking out whenever he came close.

When she broke the surface, he was right behind her.

She swam as fast as she could toward the boat, which was anchored closer than she'd thought it would be. She pulled herself up onto the step and over the side into the boat. She discarded her mask and the rest of the gear as fast as she could. He was right behind her, his mask already hanging from his fingers as he stalked toward her.

"We weren't done."

"I was!" she bit back at him.

She removed her fins and all but threw them toward him.

"*Principessa.*" It was aggravating how the warning in his tone was strangely enthralling. Stupid that it made her want to poke at it, tempt him further, anger him just to see what he would do. That singular thought pissed her off even more. How many times would she trust him only to be proven that he would always hold something back? Her mom was right. She believed in people too damn much.

It had gotten Landry killed. It had nearly gotten her killed.

The sun had been swept behind the clouds again,

changing the world from one of sparkling diamonds to gray haze. She knew she'd be cold if she took the wetsuit off, but she had to get out of it before he attempted to throw her back in the water.

She reached behind her back, unzipped it, and tugged the thick fabric from her arms, sliding it down until it hit her hips. When she looked back up, she could almost imagine the smoke swirling from his ears like a cartoon villain.

"That little current you encountered won't be anything compared to the ones in front of the cave," he growled.

"You should have told me to expect it," she tossed and then sat on the bench to pull the wetsuit completely off her. "I promised to stay only if you promised to tell me everything. No more secrets. No more lies!"

"I wouldn't have let anything happen to you, but I needed to know how you'd react." He tore his fins from his feet and tossed the equipment from his back down onto the deck where hers was piled.

When he turned back to her, she was standing there in nothing but her red underwear set, shivering, nipples hard, feeling vulnerable and furious all at the same time. She fisted her hands at her waist, glaring up at him.

"You didn't keep your end of the bargain!" she stormed at him. "I'm done. Take me back to land. I'll call my detail and my mom to come and get me. I'm going home."

She twirled toward the cabin, and he easily caught her by the waist, pulling her back against his enormous body clad still in the now icy wetsuit.

He turned them so they were facing south and he could point over her shoulder at a speck of land in the far distance. A mere blip that could be mistaken for another storm cloud it was so far away.

"That is your home now."

"Fuck you," she said, struggling. His grip tightened

more, and she flung her head back, hoping to hit at least part of his face, and was rewarded with a grunt when she collided with his chin. She grabbed his bicep and attempted to somersault out of his arms like she had the other day, but he was prepared for it this time. Before she knew it, she was pinned on her back on the deck, with his full weight on top of her.

Their faces were inches apart, and his voice was deep and dark when he said, "You have a right to be angry."

"Thanks for giving me permission, asshole. Now get off me."

"At this moment, you feel out of control. And down there"—his gaze flicked to the side of the boat and the ocean beyond it—"I made you feel more so. But it's not in the calm where we find our strength, Nicolette. It's in the chaos."

Her anger flickered at his words as her body started to burn everywhere they touched. She'd wanted this yesterday. Wanted every single inch of this mammoth man to be covering her. And now that he was there, it took her frustration and sent it in a different direction.

She bucked her hips and was rewarded with the feel of him beneath the suit, long and hard. His eyes narrowed. He didn't say the warning this time, but she felt it in the way his shoulders tensed and his lips narrowed. Could feel it in the way he caught his breath and held on to it.

She strained in his hold until she could move her head up enough to capture and bite his full bottom lip. He stilled but didn't pull away. She sucked it into her mouth, and his breath left his body in a single woosh, coasting over her face. She took advantage of it, sliding her tongue inside, holding the inner recesses hostage the way he was holding her.

For a single moment, he continued to restrain himself, and then his entire being quivered and shook. His hold loosened, and his lips latched on to hers. The hunger she'd felt in him yesterday, the one she'd craved to feed, was back. It washed over them stronger than the waves that slammed into the boat as the storm picked back up.

She wiggled her arms free, digging fingers into his shoulders as he focused wholly on exploring her mouth, driving into it with a savagery that left her breathless and had her gasping. He took each huff of air and made it his. The kiss went on for what felt like a lifetime, each of them battling for control, each one of them needing the other to submit. And for a moment, she thought she would be the one to completely surrender and let the taste and touch of him break her in half and forge her into something new.

But screw that. She'd given up enough control already. So, she took charge, finding the zipper on his wetsuit, sliding it down, and tucking her hands underneath it. The skin on the wide expanse of his back was cool, and damp, and yet blazing. His body shuddered under her touch. His wet mouth glided over the side of her face to the soft spot at the corner of her ear and jaw, nibbling and licking.

A moan escaped her.

"Fucking joy, Nicolette. That's all I can taste and smell and see." The words tore from him. A pained and tortured growl that lit her up more.

Her hips rocked against him again of their own accord, her legs spreading wide to surround his waist, joining their cores farther. She tugged harder at the back of his wetsuit, wanting him free of the neoprene, wanting nothing but their skin touching.

He stilled, mouth leaving her skin, eyes finding hers.

"Damn it. Don't stop," she demanded.

His forehead landed on her chest. He was breathing harder than she'd seen him do even when jumping rooftops and running from bullets. He drew himself up and away, causing the heels of her feet to hit the polished wood of the deck. He looked down at her from his vast height, eyes closing as if the sight of her was painful. She imagined she looked like a mess—the red bra and underwear with its sheer strips wet and even more see-through, hair a disaster, chest heaving, and body aching. The absence of his warmth made her impossibly colder.

"Go get dressed."

"No. Maybe I'll just stay here, like this…" She dragged her hand down between her breasts to the tiny piece of cloth covering her core. "All day."

His eyes turned dark and steely as he watched her fingers twirl.

"Screwing me isn't going to make you feel any better, *Principessa.* I can guarantee it will make you feel worse."

Her eyes flashed. "Why's that, Kraken?"

His jaw ticked, and his fists clenched. "Because I would take every ounce of control you so desperately want and rip it away. I'd claim you, and there would never be a chance of escape again. But I can't. I won't."

"Why not?"

"Because you aren't mine to take. You don't belong to me."

"I belong to all the San Fiore people, according to you. Aren't you one of them?"

Her hands stopped, and something akin to relief traveled quickly over his face before disappearing. She leaned up, first on her elbows and then slowly getting to her feet. He watched every move with a hint of wariness.

She traveled the two steps it took to bring them toe to toe again.

"Maybe before I give myself over to a life where I will never again have a complete say over what happens to me, I need to have my say in this. Maybe giving in to the way my body feels when it's touching yours is giving me the ounce of control I crave. Because letting go can require as much strength as holding back, D'Angelo. Haven't you learned that yet?"

Then, she did what he'd wanted. She left him. She

went down below and threw aside the wet underwear to pull back on the enormous sweats, tying them with the rope. She pulled out a water bottle and drank almost the entire thing. Her body was shaking. From the cold. From the dive. From the way she craved the man up top.

When she chanced looking out the door, it was to see him at the side of the boat dressed in just the too-small sweatpants, feet spread wide, arms across his bare chest, staring out at the sea. The rain had started again, the dark skies opening back up. And still, he stood there. His bowed head was the only indication he felt the water as it sluiced off him. He looked like Atlas holding up the entire planet.

Paisley had written a song for the band recently. It wasn't on *The Legacy* album. It had been her way of teasing them about what she had planned for the next one, hoping to tempt them all into signing on again with RMI for a fourth go-round. The song had been about the beauty of pain, which had seemed oxymoronic and confusing to Nikki at the time, but now, looking at this man who'd given his entire life for a cause they might lose, for something bigger than himself...his denial felt like that. A painful, tortured magnificence.

She went to the cabinet where she'd seen the worn ukulele and pulled it out.

She strummed, trying to recall the words Paisley had shared and then gave up. Instead, she made up her own. The notes and her voice traveled up and out into the clouds as she sang about a Titan commanding the sea and the skies, destroying one small human princess with the desire she felt for him that he denied. It was a taunt again. One she didn't even feel bad for throwing down. D'Angelo's back rolled, carved muscles rippling in an insanely sensual way, and he twisted to look toward where she stood, framed in the cabin's doorway.

He stalked across the deck to her, placing both hands on the top of the frame. She had a perfect view of every tattoo and every line of his chest and abs, including the dark, pebbled nipples she ached to kiss. A warm stream of lust sank into her veins, weighing her down. She lost her voice, but her fingers still worked. She played the notes on repeat, the beat still echoing the words she'd flung his way.

"You're wrong, Nicolette," he said, voice low, gravelly, and sinful. She arched a brow, and he continued, "I'm not the Titan. I'm still the Kraken you first called me. The monster with a golden leash around its neck barely restraining it. I've told you what will happen if you set it free. You won't be the same. You won't have a chance to run. There will never be an escape."

His words were dark and menacing, but they were also stunningly sexy. Possessive. She'd belonged to a family, she'd belonged to a band, and now he insisted she belonged to an island of people she didn't know. But what she craved, what she'd been wanting since her friends had started to fall one by one to love, was to be bound to another human in the way her bandmates were. To have a man look at her as their men did them. As if there wasn't anything else in the world. As if the sun and moon rose and set and spun only because they existed.

She wouldn't get that from an entire country of people.

She couldn't even get it from the rabid fans who screamed their names, because those fans belonged to all of them.

This…this one magnificent human putting her at the center of his universe and never letting her go…it was exactly what she yearned for. The damn fairy tale she couldn't shake.

Chapter Twenty-eight

D'Angelo

BY MY SIDE

Performed by The Paper Kites w/ Rosie Carney

Everything about what he was doing was wrong. He knew it and couldn't stop himself anyway. He'd barely had the willpower to get off her on the deck moments ago. The song, the damn words about the Titan denying the princess and destroying her even as he tried to save her, had sunk into his chest with a raw pain.

Maybe by denying her this, he was somehow breaking them both.

Or maybe he really was just a monster determined to claim her, even knowing it would leave a shadow she'd never be able to remove. Because he couldn't touch her and then stand by and watch as anyone else did. It wouldn't just be a princess being sacrificed to the Kraken, but the other way around as well.

Which was why he should put an end to this little game before it was too late.

It's already too late, his conscience screamed.

She slowly lowered the ukulele to the floor, stepped toward him, and let her hands land on his waist. He flinched, not from the cold but from the achingly exquisite sensation of human touch. Of *her* touch. Her fingers slid over the ink and muscles along his rib cage, gliding upward to brush over his pebbled tips.

Then, her tongue followed the path of her fingers, and he almost lost it right there.

His hold on the doorframe tightened until it was almost painful. Until the fiberglass groaned in protest.

Her warm mouth continued it's journey up, up, up to his collarbone, his neck, hovering over the pulse pounding in his neck. She sank her teeth in like some damn vampire. Her chest was now pressed into his, but she'd put on the stupid sweats again, hiding everything she'd shown him moments before in a red bra and panty set he would have burned in his memory for the rest of his life.

She stood on her tiptoes, continuing her stormy embrace. The underside of his jaw received an open-mouthed kiss, the hard line of his chin a dozen more, and then her soft mouth was on his. The anger and frustration she'd kissed him with on the deck were gone. This was pure seduction. Pure desire. Pure need.

He groaned, dropping his hands, one settling at her waist and the other tangling in her thick mass of curls. He used his hold on the strands to pull her head backward, scouring her face with his eyes, waiting for the hesitation to return. Waiting for any sign she wasn't fully on board with what they were about to do. All he saw was a fire that would consume him.

He lowered his head, mouth brushing against hers softly, loving the way it made her breath hitch.

"I'm not kidding, Nicolette. There is no turning back from this."

He wouldn't survive having her and giving her away. He had no right to her, hated that the darkness he'd lived in for over a decade would bleed all over her, but he wouldn't be able to taste the joy of her and then give it to someone else.

"Show me why I'll never want to," she said, her husky voice dropping until it landed in his groin, and he became so hard it was painful. Beauty in pain. That was what the song had been about as much as the Titan, the

Kraken, and the princess.

He let his lips settle on hers, a simple slide of mouths, a promise he was embedding into her soul. And then, he took control of it all, plunging into the sweet, wet interior, lapping at it. Proving to her that this was the only tongue she'd ever want inside her again.

She moaned.

His body tightened even more.

He let go of her hair and picked her up by the waist. Her legs and arms surrounded him, and he took the handful of steps toward the bed where she'd lain alone, tossing and turning the night before. He'd listened to every movement. Tormented by it. Wanting to comfort her and knowing it was impossible and wrong.

And yet here he was, laying her down on it with a singular intention.

He tugged the sweatshirt up over her head and tossed it aside. Her breasts were delightfully full, tipped upward as if leaning toward the sun. He found one with his tongue and his teeth, the other with his hand. She whimpered and arched, and he fucking loved it. Loved it more than he could remember loving anything in a lifetime.

His hand slid down her flat stomach, playing with the knotted rope at her waist. When it proved more stubborn than he expected, his gaze met hers, and she smirked. For two seconds, he took her mouth again, wiping away that look and bringing back only the heat. Then he dragged his tongue down the length of her, forcing the knot, pulling it and the sweatpants away from her long legs. He'd seen her naked in the shower, watched as she'd taken those long fingers of hers and sent them over her body with soap and water, and now all he wanted was to follow those paths with his own.

He dragged his nose and chin up her inner thigh, and her chest heaved, gasps turning raspy. Her fingers found his hair, gripping and tightening. Dark eyes begging him. When his mouth landed on her heat, her hips bucked. He slid his hands underneath, squeezing her cheeks while he devoured her, finding every single spot that made her needier, hungrier, and more desperate.

"D'Angelo," she chanted his name like a song. Rocking, taking what she wanted as much as his fingers and mouth were giving what she needed. Her eyes fluttered closed, and he watched as her release took control of her body, much as the undertow had beneath the sea, but this time, she easily gave in to the wave of pleasure. Her entire being convulsed and shook, and he continued his devotion until her body went lax, and her gaze returned to his.

He kissed his way up her body until his lips found hers once more and the length of him was cocooned in the warmth between her legs.

She was the one to break away, gasping for air and then piercing him with her words and her look. "Do it again, D'Angelo. Make me feel that way all over again…but without these." She tugged at the waistband biting into his skin. "With all of you inside me."

He groaned, resting his forehead for a moment on her chest. Trying to calm the flames running through him. Wanting to take it slow so it would last while simultaneously needing to thrust into her fast and fierce. He shed the sweatpants and returned to her, elbows propping him up above her and one hand brushing away the hair that had fallen over her cheek. As he leaned down to take her mouth once more, reality hit him.

He fucking wasn't prepared. He prided himself on being ready for every single thing in his life, but this… He hadn't been prepared for her. Not this way.

He pulled back with a groan. "I don't have protection," he told her. Her eyes flickered with something like regret. "But it doesn't matter. I'll take you over the edge, *Stellina*. Over and over."

"I'm clean. I've never let anyone in me without a condom," she said as her hands cupped his face, and her fingers brushed back and forth over his cheeks and beard.

The breath left his body at the idea of going bare inside her. The simple thought was more exquisite agony. "I'm clean," he said softly. "I'm tested regularly for my job. But are you on birth control?"

Her legs moved, surrounding his waist, locking behind him, and it brought their cores together more intimately. His dick reacted, bobbing, rubbing, seeking entrance as if it had a mind of its own.

"No. Anything with hormones messes with my migraines, and I wasn't active enough to want something semi-permanent put in."

She leaned up to kiss him. Mouth hot and needy. Demanding something he wasn't sure she really understood.

"I need you. Inside me. I need that more than anything else in my life right now. I want to know this was my choice. You. Me. Screwing ourselves into oblivion on this bed."

Her hips rocked into him.

"*Principessa*," he gritted as the movement almost launched him into her.

"Be careful," she said, watching his reaction to her words. "Pull out. Just don't leave me without having filled me."

He shouldn't agree to the beg, and yet he didn't move away either. He wanted to savor her as she'd had him savor the gobeletti. The smells. The taste. The heart-wrenching joy as her lips journeyed over his neck and his chin and his jaw. He let the feel of her beneath him leak into every part of his soul. It wasn't enough, coming this far and not finishing, but his duty would always be to protect her first.

"No," he finally allowed himself to breathe out.

"No?" Her eyes jerked back to his, nails biting into his shoulders. She squeezed him with her thighs again, and his dick twitched once more.

"Do you think you can't do it? Do you not have enough strength to deny yourself at that last moment?" she taunted.

"Don't dare me. Think about the consequences."

She closed her eyes, and a bitter laugh left her body. When she opened them again, there was both a sadness and a resolve in them that tore at his heart and soul. "The consequences? I'd be well on my way to giving San Fiore exactly what they want, wouldn't I? A handful of babies to fill their castle with."

He forced himself away from her, rolling onto his back and staring up at the ceiling. He wanted her. Wanted to be in her, skin on skin. Wanted to let go inside her. Worse, the idea of her flat stomach turning round with his baby inside her…fuck, it did all kinds of things to his heart. It would prove to the world she was his.

He threw his arm over his eyes.

How had he ended up here?

Taunts and dares. A taste of delirium she'd given him that he wanted to continue to get lost in.

There was movement next to him, and then she was atop him, straddling him, her dark heat dangerously close to his hard-on. She pulled his arm from his face, bringing his palm to her mouth. She kissed it first and then licked it. He groaned, hands coasting over her perfect breasts, flicking the tips, massaging and twisting until her lids fluttered as a breathy whimper escaped her mouth.

"Give in. Give in and let me make you mine," she whispered.

He'd thought he'd been created to do as the crown needed, but maybe what he'd really been built for was to follow where she led.

He pulled her hips up, and disappointment drifted over that perfect face. Then, he slid her down on top of his hard length. She gasped, grabbing on to his shoulders, sinking farther until she bottomed out with a delightful, strangled noise that made his chest swell.

It felt like heaven. Like coming into port after months away.

As if this was the only goddamn thing he was put on this earth to do.

Be the one beneath her.

Be the one giving her pleasure and joy and a boatload of babies.

Wrong or right no longer mattered.

Instead, he gave in, hoping she was right. Hoping that, in doing so, they'd both find a strength they hadn't had when they'd been apart.

He lifted his hips, and everything disappeared except the way their skin glided together. The way the scent of her, strong and flowery, filled the air. The way her body moved above his, soft and full and dancing. When he thought he might not last a moment longer, he rolled them over and slammed back into her. She moaned, a delightfully sensual sound that almost cost him his last thread of restraint.

She met each lunge with her own force, her core ricocheting off the bed and into him. The noises in the room a magnificent song, and the feel of their bodies moving together a rhythm he couldn't escape.

"Nicolette," he urged.

"So close. So close," she singsonged.

He sucked a finger and then reached down, dragging it over her, and she went off like a gun, convulsing, pulsing, writhing beneath him as her throat made another gurgling noise full of pleasure. He lasted only through her last quivers before he had to withdraw and spill all over her.

In that singular moment, the only thing he hated was that he hadn't been able to stay deep inside her. But when he looked down and saw the trail of him all over her, it eased the ache at having pulled out. Because this… It was a visual claiming he wouldn't have had otherwise.

His hand landed on her heart, feeling the desperate pounding of it against his palm. Her eyes were dark and sexy, but a smile formed on her face. She reached up, touching his lips, and he realized, with a start, that he was smiling too.

She'd already broken the dam inside him. He'd tried to rebuild it, but it had been a hopeless task. He was hers, and as much as he knew the world would hate it, she was his. The world would just have to get used to it.

Chapter Twenty-nine

Nikki

LIVING DANGEROUSLY
Performed by Dami Im

"Don't move. Let me get a towel," D'Angelo said, shifting away from her.

She felt the loss of his warmth immediately, shivering in the cold air of the boat.

She closed her eyes. *What had she done?*

She'd thrown caution to the wind. She'd taunted the beast.

And yet, she realized with a sudden huff of laughter, she didn't regret it. Not an ounce. She'd do it again. She'd been desperate for him. To have this choice be hers. To make this singular decision. As if she knew once they arrived on the shores of San Fiore, nothing would ever be hers to decide again.

He came from the bathroom with a damp towel, and he cleaned her up with a tenderness that lodged in her throat. When he returned to the bed, he lay on his side and pulled her into him. She looked up into his eyes and realized that this close, his pupils were surrounded by a ring of deep teal that bled quickly into the midnight.

She closed her eyes against the image of him because there was a message in his emotions and the words he wasn't saying that she didn't want to hear. He'd turned solemn again. The brief and glorious smile that had taken over his face had disappeared.

He was beautiful and strong, and she shouldn't have the feelings for him that she did after a handful of days. The emotions flowing through her were wild and untamed but sure. It had happened this way with Asher and Fee as well as Leya and Holden. Mere days on the run, in hiding, and they'd somehow formed an unbreakable bond. She hadn't understood it even though she'd longed to experience it.

D'Angelo had told her there was no turning back. No escape.

But maybe it was simply the intensity of the situation they were in. Maybe she'd wanted to be loved by a man so badly that she'd turned it into something more in her mind. Leya used to say people confused passion for more all the time. Just the thought of these enormous feelings she had for him fading caused her more fear than accepting a throne she knew nothing about. And yet, she had to be realistic. They'd fought and argued more than they'd had any other kind of conversation. They'd fallen into bed in a lust-filled craving that felt like so much more, but in a month, would it feel the same? Would she still see forever in his eyes? Feel the ties binding them together? Or would it fade with the desire?

His hand on her stomach moved in small circles. A gentle caress.

"Nicolette." His deep voice stoked the fires that had momentarily found release, drawing them back to life. How could she feel hungry for him all over again? So soon? When they'd barely stopped moving together?

She opened her eyes and saw his brows were drawn together. She wanted his smile back. The one that had seemed to fill the boat with a warm glow. She wanted to know how to make him smile more than he frowned. How to bring the joy and pleasure he'd denied himself back into his life every day, every hour, every minute.

When he didn't say anything more, she raised a brow

at him, prompting him to finish his thought. His jaw ticked as he battled with whatever it was he had to say, and she tried not to let it panic her.

She rolled slightly, kissing the spot above his heart where a small flower, almost daisy-like, was tattooed. She threw an arm and a leg over his side, drawing them together again, chest to chest. "What's wrong?"

His throat bobbed, and his gaze was so intense it was almost frightening. Finally, he grunted the words out. "It's your choice."

"What is?" She frowned.

"You don't have to go to San Fiore. You can wait it out anywhere. Once midnight comes and goes on the thirty-first, you'll be free."

Her stomach clenched tight, and she was surprised to find tears hitting her eyes.

"You swore to bring me to San Fiore or die trying."

His eyes turned hooded and thoughtful, teeth grinding more. "I did… Things have changed."

"Because we had sex."

His eyes narrowed as if he didn't like her claiming that what they'd done was mere sex. It hadn't felt that way to her. It had felt like she'd leaped over the cataclysmic fault line dividing her life, landing on the other side.

"Because you deserve a life that you choose."

It was too much. Her heart filled so much it might explode. She'd craved what her friends had, someone who would put her at the center of their world, and now he was there, in front of her, giving up everything, an entire lifetime of beliefs, to ensure she got what she wanted. But just like with her friends, these feelings weren't one-sided. She wanted D'Angelo to fulfill his life's work…achieve the things he was destined to do, as well.

Her father had to have known about the monarchy. He'd prepared her to defend herself, and yet he hadn't prepared her to accept it. Maybe he'd never imagined her having to do so, or maybe he'd thought he'd have time to tell her later. If he was here, right now, what would he do? Would he turn away from duty because of a century's-old sin waged against his grandfather? Or would he step into the role and make sure those kinds of decisions, those prejudices, those mistakes never happened again?

She searched D'Angelo's face. "Do you truly believe, in the depths of your soul, the monarchy is what the people of San Fiore need?"

He closed his eyes as if her question pained him, but when he opened them, there was nothing but certainty there. "I do."

She took in a deep breath, slowly letting it out. "Do you promise to be with me through it all? Every moment? Helping guide me through all the decisions I'll have to make, even if this"—she flicked a finger between them—"doesn't last?"

His eyes narrowed, teeth grinding again as if he didn't like her insinuation that what they had might flicker and fade.

"I'm not leaving your side, Nicolette."

Relief coasted through her so great her body quivered with it.

"Then, we'll go to San Fiore."

He stared for a long moment and then pulled her into him tighter, kissing the top of her head. She could hear his heart pounding. Feel its rhythm against her cheek. Erratic and wild in a way she'd never imagined he could be until today. Until he'd given up his control and handed it to her. Now, she would take hers and give it back to him of her own free will. It wasn't being dragged from her. It wasn't being stolen and caged. In a month, when she was overwhelmed by the decision she'd made today, she'd have no one to blame but herself.

He'd given her an out, and she'd rejected it.

She didn't know what it meant for the band. For the simple life she'd envisioned for herself when she wasn't with them. But it felt right.

♫ ♫ ♫

They made love all over again, slower and yet with the same ferocity beneath it that had left them both breathless. Then, he'd made her yet another sandwich. When she'd taunted him again about the lack of pleasure in his food, he'd tossed her onto the bed and showed her the pleasure he really cared about.

Every time they touched, Nikki felt like the invisible strings binding them together drew tighter. She knew it was absurd that the handful of hours they'd spent in each other's company should have turned into something this large, into feelings that would never go away, but they had. But it also bugged her that she knew relatively nothing about him, even when she knew the most important things.

Splayed across his chest with his hands working small circles into her back, she moved to prop herself up on her elbows and look into his face.

"Tell me something about you."

His lip twitched. "Something?"

"Did you always want to be part of the *Cavalieri*?"

"Yes."

She waited, and when he said nothing else, she huffed. "That's it?"

He rolled them so he was on top, caging her, eyes boring into her. "This is who I am. Who my father was. My grandfather and his grandfather before him. As children, Atonella and I played with imaginary swords and defended the basilica and the castle grounds. It has always been my life."

"You and your sister were close?"

"She was six years older than me, but yes." A flicker of something flashed through his eyes. Sadness. Pain. But it disappeared before she was sure it had ever been there.

"Sometimes, I think the rips inside me from losing my dad and Landry will never heal. They'll always ooze and bleed and hurt."

He stared for a long moment and then kissed her, as if he could take away the agony and replace it with other emotions instead. Emotions she didn't dare name but yearned to keep close.

"What about your biological mom?" he asked, finger twining in a strand of her hair until it was wrapped tight and he could caress her jaw.

"I don't really remember her other than pictures and stories. My dad was the one who was there for every nightmare and every illness. My childhood memories are full of sailing with him and diving with him and playing air guitar to classic rock songs. Jerome used to tease us that Clarissa appeared like magic. One day, she wasn't there, and the next, she was. I was nine when she and my dad first got together, but it felt like she'd always been in our lives. She just fit. She made my dad…lighter…as if the burdens of the world weren't solely on his shoulders."

She realized it was how D'Angelo made her feel as well. As if the guilt of Landry's death and the enormity of what she was doing weren't quite as heavy when she didn't have to go through it alone.

She leaned up and kissed him. Soft. Tender. A promise.

But the sweetness of it turned into scorching flames with the soft flick of a tongue, and they lost themselves all over again in the slide of skin and hands and mouths.

No matter what happened, she knew, deep in her soul, she'd never be the same again.

♫ ♫ ♫

"Nicolette." A whispered voice and a soft kiss on her cheek dragged her from a deep sleep. D'Angelo's beard tickled her jaw just as it had tickled her breasts, her thighs,

271

her core repeatedly all afternoon and late into the night.

Her lids flickered open, a smile taking over her face as his dark eyes and sharply defined features came into focus. He was sitting on the edge of the bed next to her in those ridiculous sweatpants, his muscled torso still bare. But instead of it being the magnificence of him that had her heart picking up pace, it was the worry drawing his brows together.

"What's wrong?" she demanded, sitting up.

His gaze fell over her naked body, and then back to her eyes.

"The bomb went off on the *Tangled Melody*."

Her mouth dropped open. "Oh my God. My mom. My friends." She scrambled out of the bed. "They'll think I'm dead."

Her heart banged tightly, and she flew into the galley, turning and twisting around, searching for the satellite unit and the phone he'd had her use on Christmas.

He grabbed her around the waist, bringing her back into his chest. His arms wrapped around her, and instead of feeling confining as it had even a day ago, it felt…like comfort.

"They don't know," he insisted.

She turned in his embrace. "How can you be sure? Someone will report a boat exploding!"

"There was no one close by. The man I had on board…he's been keeping an eye on it. It will be found, but it will take a day at least for the authorities to decide whose boat it was."

Nikki shook her head. "My mom has been tracking it. She'll know something is wrong when it goes dark."

D'Angelo's face turned thoughtful.

"I'll send Langston to her. He'll tell her the truth and bring her to the island—just as we planned."

"Let me text her!"

D'Angelo shook his head. "We can't risk it if they're monitoring her phone. They know you aren't dead, Nicolette. They saw you with me in Albenga. But they still blew up the boat. Until I know why and how they intend to use that to their advantage, we need to let them believe they've succeeded, and that we don't know what they did."

Nikki swallowed. Grief filled her at the idea of any of her family or friends thinking the worst had happened to her. The pain they'd all felt over Landry… God, she couldn't imagine putting them through that. She'd already nearly destroyed Paisley's life once.

"I have to tell them, as soon as possible. I can't let them think…"

"One day, Nicolette. We will get you on the island today. Tomorrow, once you're in the castle and secure, you can call them."

She put her forehead against his bare chest, and a shiver ran down her spine.

It had been easy, lost in the passion the day before, to forget the seriousness of her situation. Of the threat looming just outside of range, waiting for her to show her face. She'd told him she'd go to San Fiore, and she would, but it didn't mean she wasn't afraid of what would happen once she got there.

He put his large hand under her chin and drew her face up, searching her eyes.

"I'm not leaving your side. No one will hurt you."

She heard the promise—the sworn oath embedded in each syllable. This time, it was all for her and not for the crown or his people.

She took a deep breath. "The sooner we do this, the better."

He gave a curt nod. "Breakfast, then we'll get on our way."

She huffed out a half laugh. "By breakfast, you mean

yet another sandwich? If I never eat a sandwich again, it'll be too soon."

His lips twitched. "You just have to learn to savor them, *Principessa*. Enjoy each bite."

She stared at him for a moment as his tease settled through her. A joke. D'Angelo had actually attempted a joke.

"They'll never be gobeletti."

His eyes turned dark, lids dropping, gaze settling on her mouth. "No. Nothing will."

Then, he was kissing her with all the fierceness and, conversely, the tenderness of the day before. As if he was claiming her and loving her and leading her all at the same time. And she reveled in every single moment of it. She wished they could live in this bubble for a few more days. For a week at least. Until they had a chance to see if these emotions were true or a mirage built by the intensity of their lives.

She thought she knew the truth of them.

But what if she was wrong?

Her entire insides clenched tight again.

He'd promised he wouldn't leave her even if whatever this was between them faded. For now, that was going to have to be enough.

♫ ♫ ♫

The stormy skies were mixed with sunshine as the sun drifted in and out of the clouds. It was how Nikki felt. A mix of happiness and darkness. Fear and hope. She hadn't stayed below deck today. She was next to D'Angelo as he navigated the boat at breathtaking speeds across the choppy seas.

As they approached San Fiore, the small skerry with the statue of Rhaibele came into view. The rocky outcrop was only large enough to hold the hundred-foot goddess. The statue was carved from marble. Her heart-shaped face was stunning perfection with a straight nose, large eyes, and high cheekbones. On her shoulder, a Regina astrapia perched with its tail feather carved from blue stones sweeping down to her elbow. Long strands of the goddess's hair spiraled from a crown made of gold flowers, past her shoulders, and over her breasts encased in a diaphanous gown. The material was a semi-translucent glass showing off her stone curves underneath. The dress pooled at her bare feet where a lion, a panther, and a giant lynx lay tangled together, half asleep and half on alert.

She'd been terrified about coming to the island when her mom had suggested it last year. Afraid she'd poke awake whatever evil had been responsible for Landry's death, but she'd also been scared if she protested too strongly, her mom would suspect something. She'd been worried the guilt and torment and secrets she kept would come flooding out. So, she'd given a careless shrug, pretending she'd never heard of San Fiore and didn't care whether they came or not.

When they'd arrived and Nikki had seen the statue, it had called to her, as if the goddess was whispering ideas about where she really belonged, and it had frightened her a bit more. The professor's whispered words about *THEM* coming for her had returned in a rush.

But once she'd stepped foot on the wharf, everything had faded away, and she'd been enthralled. Some people suggested San Fiore was the Atlantis the academics sought, and Nikki thought they might just be right. It seemed an enchanted mirage, as if you had to step through a secret veil to get to it. In the only city on the island, the homes and businesses were built up from the sandy shores onto cliffs that overlooked the Ligurian Sea. They were made of stones accented with gold that shimmered in the sunshine. Carved archways laden with orchids and trailing vines gave off heavenly scents. In every intersection, statues or fountains looked over streets made not of cobblestone but of colorful mosaic tiles that cars weren't allowed on.

Outside the city was a haven of greenery and trees that sloped from graceful hillsides down to white-sand beaches. The handful of small villages scattered around the island were as beautifully crafted as the capital city. The flower farms the island was partially known for filled the air with an exotic mix of aromas and colors.

The island was a magical place.

It had felt wealthy and luxurious. A true fairy tale. A haven.

And now… Now Nikki was going to tie herself to it in a way she'd never be able to undo, and it somehow turned the fairy tale into a dark and terrifying one because at the center of it was the knowledge that not all the people who lived there wanted her to be their queen. Some of them wanted her dead. Some of them had sent an assassin after her, and that assassin had killed her friend.

The bitter pain of her guilt waged war inside her.

Her throat bobbed as D'Angelo slowed the boat, drifting closer to the rocky outcrop with the statue. There was a channel between the skerry and the main island. It was only fifty or so feet across, but the waters heaved like a whirlpool, crashing up onto the statue and the mainland in sparkling white swells.

"Won't someone become suspicious if we leave the boat here?" she asked as her heart began to pound at an indecently fast pace.

"My friend from the boat, Langston, is coming to retrieve it."

"You trust him?" she asked.

He stared at her for a moment. "Yes."

She fidgeted with the brooch, not poking it into her skin but running her fingers over it, and he read it for the nervousness it was.

"Have you changed your mind?" he asked.

Her tormented heart flipped over. Three days ago, he

would have all but tossed her in a bag and dragged her onto the island, kicking and screaming, but in his question now, she heard the truth. He'd let her run if she wanted to. He'd let her run, and he'd come with her.

She shook her head. "No…just nervous."

He leaned in and placed a kiss on her forehead. Soft and sensual. Loving…

God, the emotions were there no matter how much she tried to deny them or how absurd it was when she barely knew him. She'd do this. For him. For the people he believed needed her. And maybe, somehow, she'd get justice for Landry, because even if her killer had won that battle, Nikki wouldn't let them win the war.

Chapter Thirty

D'Angelo

EVEN THOUGH OUR LOVE IS DOOMED
Performed by Garbage

ONE DAY BEFORE

Normally, when he was putting a plan into action, a calm descended over him as the steps he'd rehearsed in his mind hundreds of times finally moved together. But with the feel and scent of her still embedded into him, with his emotions now tied to hers instead of being funneled into action, it was her nervousness that bled into him as they prepped the dive gear.

His jaw ticked. Everything would be fine.

The sun peeked through the storm clouds just as they'd jumped off the boat, but as they sank farther below the surface, the light grew dimmer, and rocky formations loomed. At first, as always when he hit the water, it seemed as if the sounds became muted. His breathing in the regulator and the clearing of his ears took over until he became accustomed to those sounds, and the noise of the ocean filled in. The waves crashing. The swirl of the fish as they went by. Too bad human vocal cords couldn't transmit underwater as well.

He switched on his lamp, and a silvery swarm of fish scattered in front of them. At thirty meters, it was dark but not like it had been the day before with the storm churning. He pointed in the direction of the island, and she swam almost shoulder to shoulder with him as they passed Rhaibele. Just beyond the statue, the underwater streams began pulling at them, going in several different directions all at once. The entrance to the cave was at the vortex where the different currents came together, turning into a whirlpool that could catch you and keep you if you weren't careful.

Yesterday, he'd watched as she fought the rip current before she'd given herself over to it. He'd known where it would end, known exactly how far it would take her, and yet, letting her be swept away had been one of the most difficult things he'd ever done. Every fiber in his being had ached to go after her, protect her, keep her safe.

And now…after having spent the last twenty hours tangled together, he wasn't sure he'd be able to stop himself from going after her, even knowing she'd be okay. It was as if those pieces of the soul he hadn't been sure he owned and she'd brought to life had glued themselves to her. As if, somewhere out in the universe, they were no longer two souls but one.

It was ludicrous. Maudlin. Thoughts he'd never had and never wanted.

He reached out and caught her gloved hand, drawing her closer to him, taking a moment to sign if she was okay. She nodded and gave him a thumbs-up, and yet, for some reason, he had an uncomfortable feeling in his gut. The twitching in his eye was back—or rather, it had never left. It infuriated him that he was having to bring her to San Fiore without having uncovered who was pulling the strings of the anti-royalists.

He passed her the light so he could take her hand and still have another available to grab onto the cave opening when he needed to. As the current grabbed hold, he let it take them into it like she'd let it the day before. It drew them toward the opening and the whirlpool at a pace that was almost unnerving, even to him. If you didn't know it was there, you'd miss the entrance. It was barely a crack in the rocks, tough for a man his size to fit through. As the current threw them toward the outcropping, he let his hand trail over it until he felt and latched on to the crevice.

Her body kept going, and for a moment, he felt a wave of panic, but his grip tightened at the same time as hers did, and he was able to pull them both into the fissure where the current all but dissipated. He tugged her to his chest, looking into her mask where her eyes were a bit wild. He cupped her cheeks, gloved hands sliding along the exposed skin. Her eyes fluttered closed and then opened again. He could swear he could hear her heartbeat along with his own traveling through the water. A stuttered echo of a rhythm crying out, *'You go. I'll follow,'* on repeat. He was no longer sure who was truly leading and who was following, but for now, he was chartered to get her through the cavern and into the tombs, and he would.

He reluctantly let her go, turning and taking them farther into the narrow tunnel. Two meters in and the sunlight all but disappeared. He took the lamp from her again. They had to go sideways in several spots, using the rocks and the kicking of their fins to propel them through the narrow passage. Whenever a split came, he took the right path until they were deep under the island. They passed several openings where the sea water bubbled upward, trying to drag them with it, and he used his might to propel them forward. Finally, the tunnel grew so thin that the rocks snagged at the dry packs on their waists and tried to poke holes in their wetsuits.

Her hand tightened on his, and he looked back to see more panic in her eyes. He drew her into him, placing his mask up against hers once more, trying to give her the calm he normally had and was struggling with himself. He saw her take a deep breath, and then she motioned forward again.

Brave. She was braver than he'd ever expected her to be when he'd first started following her. He'd given her an out, not once but twice now, and she'd stayed the course. She was facing huge unknowns…people trying to kill her, a dark underwater cave you could easily get lost in, and a monarchy she knew nothing about…and yet she hadn't run screaming into the night.

He gave her a sign. Two minutes. The tunnel would open soon, and they would be out of the abyss.

She nodded again.

He turned back, sliding them carefully through the sharp outcroppings.

And then, finally, the darkness broke, and the walls fell away on either side of them as they emerged into a large cavern. It was like swimming inside a water tower. The ocean itself was deep here, the bottom of the cave far below, but above the water was a rounded stone ceiling with electric lights casting blue shadows over the entire space and turning the water a multitude of shades of midnight.

Just as he'd maneuvered them both through the tiny opening and into the cavern, a sharp slice to his bicep had him dropping her hand and twirling around. A diver had been waiting for them! The man was large and bulky, almost the same size as D'Angelo. He lunged at them, the knife he'd used coming at him once again, and D'Angelo blocked it with a jarring slam of bone against bone. He grabbed the diver's bicep, wrenching the knife from him.

The assailant attacked again with a second knife D'Angelo barely ducked under. He barreled into the man's chest, pushing him farther away from Nicolette until they slammed into the wall. Their tanks clanked with a sickening thud that reverberated through his body. His alarm went off on his dive computer. The tank wouldn't take another hit. He used one hand to hold on to the man's neck and reached for the attacker's regulator hose, squeezing it tight. The man's eyes went wide beneath the mask, and he kicked and stabbed, the knife slicing once again into D'Angelo's arm. Blood swirled in the water, thick ribbons that looked like a lava lamp had exploded.

Nicolette came in from the right, ramming the lamp into the man's skull and his head crashed into the rock. D'Angelo used the distraction to drive the man's wrist into the wall with a crack that caused the knife to drop into the depths below. The diver landed a punch to D'Angelo's face, knocking his mask askew. Water began to fill it, and he instinctively held his breath. He could hold it for several minutes, but it meant he needed to end this quickly so they could surface.

The man got in another punch, loosening D'Angelo's hold, and he used the brief advantage to try and reach Nicolette. D'Angelo yanked at the man's regulator hose again. He pulled with a viciousness that came from anger and desperation. Not only had the man attempted to hurt her, but someone had given away the secret of the tombs. There were more conspirators in the midst than he'd ever imagined.

It sickened and enraged him.

He wrapped the hose around the man's throat, tightening until it was a noose the man would never escape. He kicked and struggled, but D'Angelo's hold was unbreakable. The fury his father had told him to channel and he'd tried to hide fueled him now. He found Nicolette's eyes in the dark waters. She was frightened, but she hadn't swum away. Instead, she had the lamp raised as if she were ready to strike the diver again. D'Angelo motioned with his head upward, and they began to ascend with him dragging the man and hoping he could keep him alive long enough to talk.

They came up in a pool with stalactites dripping salt water and glimmering in the false blue lights. D'Angelo inhaled the damp air as he dragged the man toward the single stone ledge that existed in the cave. He rolled himself and the man onto it, keeping his grip tight as the man kicked and struggled against him.

D'Angelo searched the water for Nicolette until she surfaced, hands clinging to the ledge. She pulled her mask off just as he tossed his to the ground and ripped the assailant's from his face. He pinned the man beneath him, loosening the regulator hose ever so slightly, and the man gasped.

"Tell me who sent you!" D'Angelo demanded.

"Fuck you!" The man gasped.

D'Angelo tightened his grip, and the man's eyes bugged.

"Tell me who gave away the secret of the tombs!" His voice was a roar that bounced around the cavern, echoing and rebounding.

The man's eyes landed on Nicolette struggling to pull herself up out of the water.

"You're bleeding!" Panic was in her voice, but he couldn't turn. He couldn't let up his hold on the man.

"Tell me, or you'll die!"

"Death will come to us all," the man wheezed, scrabbling with one hand against D'Angelo's hold while his other went for the dry bag attached to his waist. D'Angelo couldn't let go of the man's throat, but he moved his knee, attempting to hold his arm down. He was just a hair too late, and their attacker pulled out a gun from the bag. He swung it wildly in Nicolette's direction.

"Get down!" D'Angelo yelled as the gun exploded, the ring deafening against the cavern walls. His heart skipped a beat, breath leaving his body as he looked toward the water's edge. Nicolette reemerged, spurting, and he turned to the man with renewed anger.

He pushed down harder on the man's throat, feeling the hyoid bone bending and cracking. The man choked one last garbled breath, "Forever sixty-five."

And then, he was gone.

"Fuck!" D'Angelo roared as he thrust the man away from him. More blood on his hands. More death. More destruction.

He sprang toward the water's edge and dragged Nicolette up.

"Leave the equipment," he grunted, undoing his buckles and letting the diving gear drop to the ground. She was shaking, shivering like a newborn kitten, but she'd already proved she had the fierceness of a lion, of Rhaibele herself. She removed her gear, dropping it next to his.

He opened his dry bag, reclaiming his bandolier of knives, sliding it over his shoulder so the row of them hung at his back. A practiced move that had them in place in less than fifteen seconds. He picked up the man's gun from where it had fallen and then turned back to Nicolette.

"You're bleeding," she said again, worry in her eyes as her fingers trailed along his bicep. He looked down at his right arm and the two slices the man had succeeded in getting in. The wounds were dripping blood and stung like hell, but they weren't interfering with his movement. They couldn't be deep.

"We need to go."

He turned toward the two steps that led from the small outcrop along the water to a thick iron gate planted into the stone. He dipped to put his eye in front of the retinal scanner, and a computer screen emerged from the rock. He punched in a code, and the lock on the gate popped with a clang.

He reached out, tangling his fingers with hers, relief filling him as their bodies connected again. He wanted to kiss her, wanted to pull her to his chest and revel in the fact they were both still alive, but he had to get them out of there. He pulled her into the narrow tunnel beyond the gate. The rock was smooth and cold on his bare feet, the stone slippery and wet as a slow trickle of water ran along the floor toward the water.

He looked up at the cameras that were hidden in the boulders.

Someone should have seen what was going on. The tunnel should have been clamoring with footsteps, and yet all he could hear was their ragged breathing and the water lapping along the walls behind them.

They'd taken barely two steps when she dragged at him, pulling him to a stop.

He turned back to her, scanning her body, making sure she wasn't injured. Her eyes flashed in the dim light. "You're hurt." Her voice was shaky and full of emotions he couldn't take the time to name. "We need to stop the bleeding."

"We'll be in the basilica in minutes. I'll get it taken care of once we're there."

She looked back out past the gates to the dead body they'd left behind, swallowed, and then turned to him. "What if there's more waiting for us there?"

Every part of him tightened in fury and protest at that thought. His mom was there, waiting above the catacombs and the tombs of the kings. His mom and the other priestesses she trusted with her life. He had to believe they were safe there. But someone had given away the secrets of the tombs, and that betrayal stung deeper, doing more damage than the knife had to his skin. Rage filled him again, embedding into his bones in ways he wasn't sure he'd ever be able to let go of.

He'd promised to keep her safe. He'd promised he wouldn't let anyone near her, and yet repeatedly, they'd been taken by surprise. The man's dying words were swirling through D'Angelo with a new suspicion he hated to name.

He needed his computer. His equipment. He needed his hacking skills and the limited resources he had outside of the *Cavalieri*. The only way he was going to get that was by going up into the basilica and using the items he'd left with his mother.

He turned the gun over in his hand, making sure the safety was still off and that there was another round in the chamber, and then handed it to her. She looked at him with frightened eyes, swallowed hard, and then curled her fingers around the grip.

He wrapped her in a brief embrace, bringing her close, inhaling the salty scent of the ocean that was trying to drown out her natural aura. He placed a kiss on her temple. It grounded him. They were here. She was safe. He would continue to chip away at the waves of soldiers the anti-royalists sent as they got more desperate with the hours tipping closer to the deadline, and she got closer to the castle.

When he drew back, he looked at the gun in her hand. "Don't shoot me. Don't shoot anyone unless they come at you first."

With wide eyes, she nodded.

Then, he grabbed her hand and eased them forward down the passageway.

The tunnel ended at a set of steep steps that would lead them into the belly of the tombs. They wound their way up farther and farther. The lights glimmered off veins of fool's gold that lined the walls. The pyrite was often twined with real gold in the mines on the island. One claiming the other as if the two belonged together. One practically worthless, the other priceless. He ground his teeth at the irony of it. Of the way he was twined with the most important thing the island had seen in several decades. A century. The one and only person who could take the throne. The one who might also be able to break the curse hanging over them.

He'd never truly believed in the curse, and yet…

He shook his head free of the thoughts as they rounded the last two steps, and he finally heard the soft scuff of footsteps. When they got to the top, a woman dressed in a white robe with a gold rope tied around the middle of it stood there. The hood of the robe was thrown back to reveal hair that had once been as black as his own but was now streaked with white and eyes the same midnight blue. Her face was drawn tight, eyes narrowed and worried.

"D'Angelo!" She threw her arms around him,

squeezing him tight before stepping back. She reached for his face, cupping his cheeks, and the wrinkles by her eyes creased in concern. Then, she glanced behind him.

He tugged Nicolette forward. "Mom, meet Princess Nicolette Dariana Alberta Fiorani. Nicolette, meet the Night Priestess, Alessia Castelli."

The two women didn't say anything, simply eyeing the other as if they weren't sure either was real. His mom turned her gaze back to him and demanded, "Want to tell me why you're crawling up through the tombs, leaving a dead man behind for me to take care of?"

"Want to tell me why no one was monitoring the cameras to know he was down there to begin with?" he hurled back.

"Can we please get you somewhere so you won't bleed out?" Nicolette's voice was sure and steady when, moments ago, it had been shaky and scared. This woman… The way she pulled herself together… It was noble and majestic, and it flipped his heart over in his chest all over again.

His mom's eyes fell to his arm and the blood that was congealing over the tear in his wetsuit. She turned on her sneaker-clad feet and headed up through the last of the tunnels into the catacombs. Only his mother's steps made noise as they entered the tombs and passed the silent crypts of San Fiore's kings and queens.

Next to him, Nicolette's feet stuttered as she took it in, and for the first time in years, he saw the catacombs with new eyes. He'd grown up here. He'd played hide-and-seek with Antonella amongst the dead kings. It had just been an extension of his home. All fifty-eight of the kings and queens of San Fiore rested here. Their crypts were made of carved marble with elaborate golden reliefs that depicted an event in the king's or queen's reign they were most known for.

The number pricked at something at the back of his brain, and the attacker's words swam through him again.

He'd have to talk to his mom about it. He needed to talk to the *Gran Duca* as well. He should be able to trust the man with his life. His father had trusted him, but his father had died. It made his chest ache.

It was all screwed up. A mess of knots he had to unwind before it was too late.

A wooden door appeared, engraved with scenes of the goddesses and gods of the sea as well as a host of mythical creatures. It was so large it could handle three of D'Angelo standing atop each other. It led them out of the catacombs and up into the basilica that had been built around an ancient temple. The home of the priestesses was crafted of white marble and gold that swathed every room. Large pillars older than the ones at the Parthenon glimmered and shone from thousands of years of care by the people of San Fiore.

When his mom started to lead them through the prayer hall with its piles of Egyptian rugs laid out on the floor and where he knew a few people would still be lingering after morning prayers, he halted her with a hand and shook his head. Her eyes narrowed, but she ducked into a small door he had to bow his head to go through.

She led them through another labyrinth of twisting corridors. Finally, they ended up in the great room where daily meetings were held and where the priestesses cooked, ate, and ran the business of the basilica. This time of year, the room was full of the smell of Yule. Pine-scented logs and branches that didn't normally belong on the island were brought in special and were decorated with white twinkle lights and an abundance of winter flowers. The scent of clove, cinnamon, and cardamom hung heavily in the air, triggering memories of all the seasons and Transitions he'd celebrated in the past.

Thankfully, the room was empty. The rest of the priestesses were out and about at their normal duties either in the temple, taking care of the gardens, or at their own homes and businesses. He followed his mom straight to the enormous kitchen the staff used to cook meals for the priestesses and their families. She waved a hand at one of the stools at an island almost the size of the yacht they'd abandoned this morning while she went into a pantry and came out with a first aid kit.

D'Angelo finally let go of Nicolette, removing the gun from her hand and stashing it into the bag at his waist. Then, he unzipped the wetsuit, pulling it down over his arms, gritting his teeth at the sting of pain. He let the suit settle at his waist before sitting on one of the stools.

"Talk," his mother said as she eyed the two knife wounds with a raised brow.

She reached into the kit, pulling out antiseptic, a needle, and thread.

He darted his eyes around the room, searching for the cameras he knew by heart, and then landed on Nicolette, shivering now as they both continued to drip water along the marble floors. Her eyes were wide as she took in the room. She raised her fingers to rub at her temples, and his stomach flipped.

"Nicolette?" he called, and her gaze found his. Nervous and uncomfortable.

He pulled her into him with his good arm, and she sank against him, burying her forehead into the crook of his neck for a second before taking a large breath and then looking back up.

"I'm okay," she said softly.

When he turned his gaze back to his mother, curiosity and wariness filled her eyes.

Nicolette had convinced him that letting go was a strength instead of a weakness, but remorse flew over D'Angelo because he knew it wasn't true. He'd been weak. He'd taken what wasn't his. He'd tortured men for less. But Rhaibele help him, he had no desire to undo it. Instead, he wanted nothing more than to take her to a secure room and lose himself inside her all over again. To prove to both of them they were alive and well and that they could face anything that was thrown at them if they did it together.

Chapter Thirty-one

Nikki

THE WAY I DO
Performed by Bishop Briggs

Nikki felt like she'd entered an alternate universe. Or maybe like she'd been shoved back in time a thousand years or more. The basilica itself was a monolith of ancient times. Draped in large pillars trimmed in gold and gems and shimmering colors. After being in the quiet of the diving gear in the dark waters, after the fight that had ended in a man losing his life, she felt discombobulated. As if, at any second, she'd tip over and slide back into the sea.

D'Angelo's mom was looking at them with curious eyes. Eyes that were so much like his that even if he hadn't said she was his mother, she would have known they were close relations. She had the same black hair as his, but hers was littered with gray and white stripes that her choppy bob seemed only to accentuate. She looked much older than him, more like a grandmother than a mom. Wrinkles creased her forehead and settled around her mouth, but there was an energy about her that seemed to belie her age.

As Nikki watched, his mother deftly sewed him up with the skill of a doctor. It surprised her as much as it made her stomach turn. He'd been attacked. They'd been attacked. The man had tried to shoot her…and now he was dead. D'Angelo had killed him just as he'd killed the men on the roof in Cannes. Her gaze settled on his enormous hands. Ones that had brought her to the peaks of pleasure the night before…and now had taken the breath from another human.

She didn't know how to feel about that.

About any of it.

She'd been nervous and afraid before they'd stepped off the boat.

Now, it was all amplified.

"Someone was waiting for us. Why wasn't the cavern being watched?" he demanded, as if he was the boss rather than her being his mother. Alessia didn't seem to like it. She arched a brow in his direction in a move that was so like him it almost made Nikki smile.

"The servers went down yesterday. When they came back up, we'd lost some of the cameras. We were just working on it when you set off the stair alarm. Rey got those cameras back up just minutes before I went down."

"Rey saw us, then?" he asked, eyes darting to the ceiling again. "Who else is in the control room?"

His mother frowned. "Just her."

"No one else can know, Mom. I have a plan, but we have to keep the knowledge of Nicolette's arrival on the island absolutely secret until I can get her into the castle tomorrow."

"She's really Dario's heir?"

"Yes."

Alessia tied off the knot and closed the first aid kit, turning to face Nikki and really taking her in.

"Let's find you some dry clothes, and then you can give me the full story."

They left the huge room with its Yule decorations and the smell of the holidays behind them, ducking into another set of tunnels. Nikki would never find her way out of them. She'd gotten lost the minute they came out of the tombs.

Alessia entered a small bedroom. It was sparsely but luxuriously furnished with a double bed covered in thick linens. An antique wardrobe stood in the corner. From there, Alessia pulled out leggings, a long-sleeved T-shirt, and a robe similar to the one she had on, all in the purest of white.

She handed them to Nikki and then waved at a door across the hall.

"The bathroom is in there."

Nikki opened the door and looked back at D'Angelo, nervous again.

"If you're done before me, lock yourself in the bedroom. I'll come back for you," he said, certainty and promise in every word.

She took in a deep breath and then shut the door behind her.

The bathroom had the same simple elegance as the bedroom. Old stones, a gilded mirror, and a porcelain tub and toilet that looked like they were from another era. She shed the wetsuit and red underwear set and then stepped into the separate shower. She scrubbed and scraped the lemon-scented soap all over her skin, cleaned her hair with someone else's lemon-and-coconut-scented shampoo, but she couldn't seem to wash away what had happened. The fear she'd felt when she'd seen the blood spiraling through the water after the man had attacked D'Angelo… The relief and horror she'd felt when she'd realized the man was dead…

God…her entire body shook, and she sank to the floor, bringing her knees to her chest and burying her face in them. What the hell was she doing here? On the boat with D'Angelo yesterday, it had seemed simple—even easy. Come to the castle, claim some vague birthright, and put an end to all the murder and loss that had been following her since she'd first met Professor Maynard.

But coming up through the catacombs…seeing the crypts lined along the walls and carved with the names of the kings and queens of San Fiore…there was no way that could be her. No way.

What in the hell did she know about being a queen? About the island at all, really, beyond a few damn Wikipedia searches and what D'Angelo had told her?

There was no way she could do this.

Her breath was uneven. Her vision grew spotty, white lights flashing.

Crap. The last thing she needed was a migraine.

She pushed on her temples and tried to calm herself.

A knock on the door. "Nicolette?" His voice traveled through the room. Deep. Soothing. Strong. Tears flooded her eyes at the sound of it, and she wasn't sure why. As a little girl, whenever she'd been hurt, she'd been fine until her dad showed up. And then, she'd lose it, crying into his arms. And maybe this was the same thing. Release. Knowing you were safe.

The knock came again, stronger. "*Stellina*?"

"I'm almost done," she called out. Her voice gave her away. Shaky. Insecure. The last thing anyone would ever want in a queen.

She stood up and turned off the water, grabbing a towel from the rack and drying herself off before she pulled on the clothes Alessia had handed to her. She tried to towel dry the wild corkscrews that would shrink and shrivel and frizz but that she'd had no product or hairbands to tame since they'd left the apartment on Christmas. As she fingered through the strands, she could almost feel D'Angelo's impatience on the other side of the door. If she didn't show herself soon, he'd break it down.

She inhaled, taking in the way her eyes looked, startled and scared like a deer caught in the headlights, and her jaw ticked. She couldn't let *THEM* see her fear. Hadn't her dad and Jerome told her that over and over again during training?

Thoughts of Jerome only made her feel sick all over again.

But the lessons she'd learned were still there.

She straightened her shoulders, stiffened her spine, and turned back to the dive suit and the dry bag D'Angelo had given her. Inside it were the two brooches she'd managed to snag when they'd fled. The robes had no pockets, so she pinned the daisy to her chest and clutched the other in her hand. Then, she moved to the door with a confidence she would fake until she could feel it for real. When she opened it, he was reaching for the handle, face grim and brows furrowed.

She stared at him, stunned. He'd shaved his beard! The sharp lines of his jaw were suddenly clear as day, shifting him into a different man—the one from the sketches instead of the bearded man she'd come to trust and adore. It was as if he'd suddenly become a different version of himself, as if the alternate universe they'd walked into had taken him from her. It was ridiculous because, unlike her in strange robes, he was in his normal uniform. Black pants, black shirt, black military boots.

"How come you get to dress normal, and I'm in this?" she asked, flinging her hand toward the thick white robe that matched the one his mother had worn.

"I keep some things here."

"This is your home?" she asked, surprised.

"No. We have a house down the way, but the *Cavalieri* have their training grounds here, so I have a locker. I had Mom retrieve a few things for me. We need to limit the places we go even here at the basilica. Too many cameras. Too many eyes."

He led her back down the hall, opening another door. This room looked like a small conference room you'd expect to see in an office building. There was even a television screen hung from the wall and a phone set in the middle of the table. It surprised her more than anything else she'd seen since they'd emerged from the tunnel.

Alessia was already there, sitting in front of an open laptop. Next to her was another woman in similar white robes with vibrant mahogany hair and startling green eyes. She had an aura about her that exuded power and an agelessness that made it impossible to determine even what decade she belonged to.

The second woman rose and stepped toward them at the door, closing the distance and invading Nikki's space in a way that made her want to jerk back into D'Angelo. She forced herself to hold her ground. "You have the Fiorani nose," the woman said.

The woman put her hand out, palm opened, fingers wide, but she never actually touched Nikki. She closed her eyes and seemed to feel the air around her. Then, she stepped back and smiled. "Welcome home, my queen."

A chill ran up Nikki's spine. Not from fear but from the overwhelming significance of those four words. Her heart skipped a beat, and she pushed her finger into the bird-of-paradise's beak. Not breaking the skin. Just enough pressure to ground her.

D'Angelo's hand landed on her shoulder, and that added another layer of calm to her as the heat of him bled into her. He'd promised he'd be with her every step of the way, and she'd believed him.

The woman stepped back, waving them to the chairs at the table.

"I'm Rey Magellini. I am the Mother Priestess of the Tombs."

Nikki didn't know how to respond. Nice to meet you? Given the circumstances, it didn't feel right, so she said nothing. She just took the seat D'Angelo held for her. The two women watched them with eyes that noticed everything, including the way his hand lingered on her shoulder and the way he took the chair next to her, drawing it close enough their elbows collided.

"Hand me the computer, Mom. I need to shut down

the cameras in this corridor."

"I've already done it," she said. "The servers going down will help as a cover story. I took down a few more random locations so the night crew won't suspect anything. They'll be instructed to leave it for Rey and me to handle tomorrow after the procession is over."

Nikki felt D'Angelo's wariness. She wondered if this man would ever trust anything anyone else did without seeing it done for himself. But just as she thought it, he surprised her by telling the two women everything. He told them about an attack at the marina in Monaco she'd been too drugged to know about, Maynard and the men in Cannes, how Maynard had found them again in Albenga, the explosion on her boat, the man in the underwater tunnels, and even his idea to get her into the castle using the procession.

Both women's jaws were tight, and their eyes glowered.

"The brothers and sisters of the tombs have not been betrayed in centuries." Rey's voice was barely controlled anger. "I will not stand for this to happen on my watch. On Luther's watch."

Nikki didn't have any idea who Luther was, but the afront in her voice was clear. She was as furious as D'Angelo had been. She whipped out a phone and started typing.

"I need some time with a computer. The men in Monaco…I have proof they were paid off. Once I know who I can trust, I'll send someone to retrieve the guard at the hospital."

"And hope he hasn't already disappeared," his mother said dryly.

"Have either of you heard the phrase, 'forever sixty-five,' before?"

Both women shook their heads, but his mom was distracted with something on the laptop, and Rey was typing away on her phone. She wasn't sure either of them had really registered his words.

Alessia shoved the computer in his direction. "Is this the boat you arrived on?"

D'Angelo looked at the screen. It showed the back of the Rhaibele statue, and anchored off to the side was the boat they'd spent two nights on. His jaw ticked.

"Yes. Langston should have been there by now to retrieve it."

The women exchanged a look.

"What?" he demanded.

"Langston is dead. They found him stabbed to death in an alley in Vernazza early this morning."

D'Angelo's face darkened, and she swore she could feel grief wafting off him. Her heart flipped over, and her stomach lurched. Another person killed. This time someone D'Angelo had trusted. The bodies were piling up around her. As if it wasn't horrible enough the man had lost his life, it also meant he hadn't retrieved her mom. Hadn't told her that Nikki was alive and not to worry.

"Oh my God...my mom!" She turned anguished eyes to D'Angelo.

"We don't know that he didn't talk to her first."

"You said he'd bring her here. That she'd be safe!"

D'Angelo pulled the phone she'd watched him stow with his bazillion knives in his dry bag this morning from his pocket. He turned it on, paired it with the laptop, and in a few keystrokes, was swiping through screens of her and her mom's cloned devices.

"There's nothing here, Nicolette. If she thought you were dead, she would be calling people. She'd be talking with your detail and the band. There's nothing."

"Then, where is she?"

His hands flew over the keys again and then stopped. "The last place it pinged was the ferry building in La Spezza." A few more strokes and he'd accessed the cameras in a building that looked like a train station.

"There. She bought a ticket on the twelve o'clock ferry. She's on her way here. Langston must have gotten to her before he was killed."

Relief flew through Nikki.

"I'll go meet her at the wharf," Alessia said, rising.

"Wait," D'Angelo said, stopping her with her hand on the door. "What are you going to say? Where are you going to take her? You can't exactly tell anyone who she really is."

His mother raised a brow at him. "D'Angelo, I've been protecting this kingdom decades longer than you. Give me some credit. After I've explained the situation to her in private, we'll tell everyone she's an academic here to witness the Transition. This will give her a reason to be at the castle as a guest. She'll be there when Nikki arrives tomorrow."

Tears filled Nikki's eyes again. Relief. Fear. Agony that more people were losing their lives for something she wasn't even sure she believed in. But then her gaze landed on D'Angelo. He'd dedicated his entire life to his homeland as had the women in this room. She may not understand any of this enough to fully believe in it, but she felt the strength of his convictions. The power of it radiated from him. She'd let his faith be her guiding light until the day came when she could actually accept it herself.

Chapter Thirty-two

SOMETIMES
Performed by Garbage

SEGRETI: The bomb detonated as planned, but Castelli's minion showed up at the hotel. He knew the truth about her not being on board. I took care of him, but I'm unsure who else they told.

SAN FIORE 65: As long as the authorities are still investigating, we have time to plant the body in the water.

SEGRETI: You have to find them first.

SAN FIORE 65: The beast has already said he'll have her on the island soon.

SEGRETI: I'm arriving today. Bring her to me when she shows up.

SAN FIORE 65: Why? So, you can do nothing like you have for years?

SEGRETI: Don't try to finish this without me.

SAN FIORE 65: Don't be ridiculous. We're in it together. Just make sure you're ready to do what needs to be done this time.

SEGRETI: Everything is in place. We even have an unexpected fall guy. I told you all along that our patience would pay off.

SAN FIORE 65: I've been patient for over thirty years.

SEGRETI: And now we'll reap the rewards.

Chapter Thirty-three

D'Angelo

WITHOUT YOUR LOVE

Performed by The Paper Kites w/ Julia Stone

His mother and Rey left to investigate things quietly on their end and get ready for the procession, leaving them in the conference room with his mother's computer and work to be done. His heart was heavy. Langston was dead. His wife a widow. His four-year-old son would never know his father. D'Angelo's jaw ticked. Fury. Disgust. Frustration welling. How had he become so damn ineffectual? When had he stopped seeing all the moving pieces? Had he ever?

He needed to take care of days' worth of footage to try and hide them. He needed to investigate Langston's death and then tear into the lives of every single member of the *Cavalieri d'Oro*. He also had a call to make to the *Comandante* that neither of them was going to like.

But before he did any of that, he needed to reassure Nicolette.

She was squeezing the bird-of-paradise brooch tightly in her fist. She'd been calm, cool, and collected with his mom and Rey. Her back had been ramrod straight, and her expression blank…except when she'd been worried her stepmom thought she was dead. But he felt the tension in her. The worry. The fear. He felt it just like he'd felt her nervousness on the boat—as if it was his.

He swiveled his chair to the side, grabbed the arm of hers, and turned it to face him. It tangled their legs together, bringing back the awareness that drifted through them at every single touch. She rubbed her temples, and he brushed her hands away with his, taking over. Slow, strong circles.

"You've trusted me," he said, a knot forming in his throat. "And I've failed you."

Her hands settled on his thighs. "I'm here. I'm alive."

She was, but no one should have come this close to her. It ate at him.

"Let me ask you something," she said when he didn't reply. "Let's just pretend you weren't around for any of this. The first thing that would have happened… I would have been on *Tangled Melody*, and when it exploded, I would have died."

That thought tore through him like a strike of lightning.

"And then, in Cannes, even if Oliver Maynard hadn't succeeded in killing me, how many people could have gotten me out of that gun show and race through the streets without me ending up wounded or worse? Do you believe my detail could have done it? Because I don't. Maybe Holden. Maybe Marco or Trevor, but none of them are on my detail. They're watching over Leya and Paisley and Jonas with enough love to make them almost invincible."

"Nicolette—"

She put her fingers over his lips, shaking her head. "No, D'Angelo. I don't trust any of them like I trust you. If I'm supposed to be here, on San Fiore, taking the crown and making it mine, then you are supposed to be here with me at my side. You're the only one who can."

His eyes narrowed as emotions welled through him. As if reading his thoughts, she took his hand and put it palm open on his chest before covering it with both of hers.

"I know you feel it in here. Just as I do. San Fiore doesn't need *just* me. She needs both of us. The man who loved the island first, and the woman who supposedly can break a century's-old curse."

He had her on his lap in one smooth motion with his mouth on hers. Taking, taking, taking what shouldn't be his, and yet, just like she'd said, she was. As if San Fiore and Rhaibele had planned it this way all along. Every press of his lips was a promise, an oath, a brand he kept repeating. One that marked them both as it had every time they'd kissed. Her hands tangled with his hair, nails digging into his scalp. His body hardened, remembering exactly how it had felt when she'd done the same with him inside her. Remembering the way she'd cried out his name and come apart. Every vein in him demanded they be joined that way again, and hers agreed, rocking into him, hips thrusting together.

He parted the robe tied with a simple corded rope and skimmed the leggings and T-shirt underneath that clung to her curves. Below the shirt was nothing but skin and rosy tips that were already pebbled for him. Every touch was a flame. He'd almost lost his life today. She'd almost lost hers. He needed desperately to be reminded of what it felt like to be completely alive. He wanted to unzip his pants and pull aside the cotton covering her and bury himself so deep she'd never forget this moment when they'd come out of the catacombs, having cheated the Grim Reaper one more time.

But they were in a conference room in the basilica where his mom or Rey could come storming in at any moment. And while he had no doubts that they'd already figured out the way it was between him and Nicolette, he wouldn't give them a firsthand seat to it.

He slowed their kiss, dragging his hand from her skin, retying the robe, and finally resting his forehead on hers.

"Later, I'll show you how much your trust in me means."

Her lips quirked upward. "Promise?"

He leaned down and nipped at her lips before releasing them. "I solemnly swear to make you see stars."

A smile took over her face so large and so bright she became a star herself. His star…*stellina*. "I'll hold you to it. But for now, I need you to do me another favor."

"Anything."

"I need to learn as much as I can about San Fiore's history in a day. I have a lot to do before I'll deserve the crown someone's going to slide on my head."

It made his lips twitch but also filled him with a sense of pride. She wanted this. She wanted to be a part of his home. To do more than just take her spot. She wanted to *earn* it. Not many people would look at it that way. They'd see the dollars and prestige and forget the people. It made him love her just a bit more.

His breath left his body as he realized what he'd thought.

He loved her.

It shouldn't have been a surprise when he'd been talking about souls joined together and claiming her forever, and yet the word did slide through him in a startling way. But it was also right. It was as simple as it sounded and yet incredibly complicated, but it didn't change the truth—he loved her.

♫ ♫ ♫

As Nikki ducked her head into a San Fiorian history book, he did what he was most comfortable doing, sliding behind the scenes into computer code—changing, deleting, confusing. Then, he pulled up the reports on Langston's death with a heart that screamed at the injustice of it. The murder had happened early this morning, and the authorities were being tight-lipped. When he read the hacked report and saw it involved a slit neck, his entire being revolted. He thought of the

Yarborough knife with its chipped edge that had killed Landry and the wound on Maynard's brother's neck. It was the same person, and he highly suspected it was Oliver Maynard himself.

With a heavy weight on his shoulder, he placed the call he'd been dreading for so many different reasons. Because every time he did, his eye spasmed. Because there were holes and failures in everything he was doing these days after over a decade of nothing but success behind him.

The phone was picked up after one ring. "Make it quick, I'm going into a press conference."

"We'll be in the castle after the procession tomorrow."

"You're already on the island?" the *Comandante's* voice got quieter as if he'd turned away from the other people D'Angelo could hear in the background.

"As I said, we'll be there after the procession."

A door closed, and there was silence in the background, yet Battista Massi's voice still dropped even more. "I can't plan for her protection if I don't know where you're at."

"Have you arrested the guard's brother? The one in the parliament? Have you even found out if he's the leader or if others are pulling his strings?"

"I can't just accuse him without proof. We're building a case," the prime minister said scornfully.

D'Angelo barely stopped himself from growling out that the man waiting for them in the secret entrance to the tombs was proof and they didn't have time to build a case. But if he did, it would give away their location.

"Langston is dead. How did the anti-royalists even know where he'd be?"

There was a slight hesitation before Massi replied, "They must have followed the mother."

D'Angelo tapped his computer screen, bringing up

the cameras in Vernazza he'd already scanned around the crime scene. It was close to the hotel where Nicolette's stepmom had been, but not too close. It could have been a mugging gone wrong, but the small town wasn't known for it, and Langston had more than enough skills to have warded off the average street thug. The wound itself was the real clue.

"I don't have time for this, Castelli. Tell me where you're at. We don't need you going all lone wolf on this. We need her surrounded by all three branches of the *Cavalieri.*"

D'Angelo didn't respond. He simply hung up.

An uneasiness coasted through him. If the anti-royalists were following Clarissa, would they use her as bait? D'Angelo swiped through camera after camera until he finally picked up her stepmom leaving the hotel earlier. He lost her several times in between video feeds but caught up with her again as she entered the ferry building in La Spezia as he'd seen earlier. Instead of following her inside as he had previously, he let the outside video run a few seconds longer. His pulse picked up pace when he saw what he'd been hoping he wouldn't. Jerome Barry. The man had on a decent disguise—straw hat, white button-down, khakis, and a vivid apron with the name of one of San Fiore's largest flower farms on it. He had an empty sample case in his hands. No one would think twice about him as he got on the ferry, looking like one of them, blending in.

Inside, Barry approached the ticket counter and then got onto the ferry after Nicolette's mom. He remained far back in the crowd, staying away from her instead of joining her as a dear friend would.

D'Angelo's fingers tightened around the screen of the laptop until it popped in protest. He was their friend. A man Nicolette and Clarissa had trusted with their lives. More betrayal. Not only in the brotherhood, that had been free of it for centuries, but deeply personal ones.

He looked over to Nicolette, curled in a chair, book

on her lap, absently playing with the strands of her hair. He'd heard the despair in her voice when he'd broached the subject of Barry before. He didn't want it to be true, because he couldn't stand the thought of being the one to cause her pain by giving her the proof that a man she loved like an uncle was the villain of her story.

And yet what proof did he actually have? The man's actions screamed suspicious, but maybe he was following Clarissa in order to see who was coming after her? That night at Swan River Pond, Barry surely would have known Landry wasn't Nicolette. He'd watched her grow from a child into a woman.

But in the dark…trying to get in and out quickly…things could go wrong.

A Green Beret didn't make those kinds of mistakes.

D'Angelo didn't have all the answers, and the ones he did have didn't fit, and that frustrated him even more. He'd promised to tell her the truth. No more lies. No more secrets, but he couldn't tell her this. Not until he had more information. It caused the pressure building inside him to ratchet up a notch. It would explode if he didn't fix it soon.

He punched through a few more screens until he was bringing up the cameras at the marina where the ferry docked. He saw his mom greet Clarissa Rani. They had a hushed discussion and then set off at a brisk pace up the winding streets to the castle on top of the hill. He waited again, letting the video run, and found Barry once more. The man blended into the crowd. His crate and apron were gone, and in his hand, he now had a camera. Nothing more than a tourist, hiding behind sunglasses and a baseball hat.

At the main thoroughfare, Barry disappeared.

Damn.

He tapped into the *Cavalieri di reali's* online notice board and inserted a wanted-for-questioning post with a note to notify only the *Gran Duca* or Massi themselves if he was found. He left three images of Barry. One from his military days in his Green Beret uniform, and the two from today in different disguises. One of the brothers would find him—or they'd already picked him up because they were in on it with him.

An annoyed breath left his body.

"What's wrong?" Nicolette was watching him from her spot in the corner.

He didn't respond, and she unwound from her chair, crossing the room on long legs in the robes of the sisterhood, looking somehow right and wrong in them at the same time. She dropped a hand to his face, running over the smooth expanse of his jaw.

"It's strange to see you without the beard."

"Good or bad strange?"

"Neither. Just different." Her finger ran over the scar on his chin. "Where did you get this?"

He huffed out a slight chuckle, and it made her lips turn upward. His arm went around her waist, tugging her until she was standing between his legs, and his hands were running over her hips.

"When I was fourteen, my father got me a job working at the aviary with the Regina astrapia. It wasn't a fun job. It was clean-up duty and gardening mostly. I was bored, and I wasn't always careful. One day, as I slipped out, I left the gate open too long, and one of the birds flew out with me. I chased it down, and it wasn't happy when my paws landed on it. Let's just say its beak did a number on me."

She raised a brow, and her smile grew wider.

"That is not at all what I expected to hear."

"What did you expect?"

"Well…" Her smile fell. "You've lived a pretty…intense life."

His smile disappeared also. He had other scars. Ones on his back and shoulders and rib cage. Some from accidents while training. Some from fights in the dark of the night with men like Ziggy Klein.

His hands settled on her waist, looking up into her eyes and wondering if she could see all the layers of blood on him. Around him. The violence he'd dealt all in the name of the crown. When he'd started in the *Cavalieri,* he'd been part of the military branch as a street enforcer. His job had been to ensure those who didn't belong found their way off the island and didn't come back. It had been mostly small-time smugglers and mafia who'd tried to find a foothold. But even then, he'd had blood on him.

"The things I've done…" His throat closed, and he was unable to complete the sentence. But she still understood it.

"I don't for a second believe that a single one of them wasn't justified."

He rested his forehead on her stomach, and her hands tangled in his hair, soothing him when he should have been the one soothing her. He'd rarely regretted his actions before. But then, he'd always shoved any emotions behind his job and his duty. Not hiding, but keeping them at bay. He'd known if he opened the door and let them in, if he allowed himself to feel, it wouldn't just be the good that would sneak in, but the guilt and remorse.

"D'Angelo." Her voice was pained, as if she could feel the conflict in him. When he raised his head and met her gaze, it almost stole his breath. There was nothing there but admiration. Empathy. Caring. And something else he wasn't sure he could afford to name. "We both move forward from here. New lives where only the light shines."

He gritted his teeth. Could he survive in the light? Or had he been created to live in the shadows? Would being with him draw her into the darkness with him?

There was a knock on the door, and his mom emerged. Her eyes glanced back and forth between the two of them before landing on Nicolette. "Your mother is at the castle. She's been apprised of the situation. She'll meet us in the throne room tomorrow."

"How did she…take it?" Nicolette asked.

"She laughed at first, thinking it was a joke, and then grew serious. She asked if you wanted this, and I said that was a question she could ask you in person tomorrow."

He felt Nicolette tense under his hands.

His mom looked at him. "I'd like to go over a few things with you."

He wanted to tell her that whatever she had to say she could say in front of Nicolette, but then he thought of Jerome Barry and knew there were still things he didn't want her to hear—not until he had all the answers.

He pushed himself up from the chair, and she stepped back.

Looking down, he brushed a curl from her face.

"I'll be right back."

Her eyes darted between his mom and him, and then she nodded.

As he stepped out of the room, his mom directed him down the hall and around the corner. His gut churned, knowing what she was going to say, knowing he wasn't going to be able to give her what she wanted, no matter how much it caused her pain. His family had been down this road before. They'd lost more than any family should have at the feet of the crown.

But he wouldn't give her up. He couldn't. It made him a traitorous bastard, but if he had to choose between his role in the *Cavalieri* and Nicolette, there was only one choice he'd make.

Chapter Thirty-four

Nikki

WHAT DO YOU GOT
Performed by Bon Jovi

D'Angelo and Alessia had looked so serious when they left that it pulled at all the worries coiled deep inside her. But it also irritated her they still felt the need to keep things from her. If she was going to be their queen, shouldn't she know everything? He'd promised her there'd be no secrets, and here he was, right back at having them. Even after everything they'd been through. Everything they'd done to each other last night.

She debated for several seconds and then went to the door. She opened it as quietly as possible, tilting her head and listening for the sounds of footsteps. Instead, she heard the murmur of D'Angelo's deep voice. She moved quietly toward it. Down several feet the corridor turned, and she stopped as soon as their voices became clear around the bend.

"Do you know what you're doing?" his mom asked, concern dripping through her voice as she spoke to him in Italian.

He hesitated when normally D'Angelo was not a man to do so. He was decisive, precise, sure. But he responded in Italian as well. "Yes. And no."

"I watched your sister fall in love with Sergio…watched and did nothing to stop it even when I knew what would happen. Knew she'd lose him and any child she gave birth to way too early because the curse wouldn't end with them. I ached for the pain that would cause her, thinking I knew what it would be like, but I knew nothing," Alessia's voice cracked. "Losing the love of my life…losing a child. There is no agony like it on this earth. No stab wound. No physical condition can cause the same pain."

Nikki knew Italian well, but every so often, a word would mess with her. She thought she understood the train of their conversation, and her heart tore for Alessia because she was painfully aware of what it felt like to lose people you loved.

"She can break the curse," D'Angelo's voice said softly.

Alessia scoffed. "And suddenly you're a curse believer?"

"I believe in her."

Silence settled between them. "Do you remember how she has to break it?"

"With the blood of her most cherished love."

Nicolette's entire body froze, thinking she misheard. Chills ran up her spine. They had to be wrong, right? He'd said nothing about it when they'd talked about the curse before. Her hand on the brooch found the back, and the sharp point scratched along her skin. She didn't believe in curses and paranormal…did she? But she'd promised herself she wouldn't be the reason anyone she loved got hurt again. What would happen if it was D'Angelo? The idea squeezed her heart until she almost cried out. She barely caught herself, fingers to her lips.

"You're making a huge assumption, Mom."

"I have eyes. I can see the way she looks at you. I know that look. Whatever happened between the two of you…the bond has already been forged."

"Even if I believed in the curse, she's already paid the price with her father's death and her friend's murder.

She's already lost those she loved, just as we have. It could be as simple as that."

"D'Angelo… There will be nothing left of me but a shell if I lose you to this cause as well."

Nikki heard the scrape of another pair of footsteps, and then, a new voice said, "You're needed at the doors." Nikki retreated, sure they'd all hear her. Not because of the way her sock-clad feet trailed over the stone, but because of how loud her heart was banging in her chest.

Inside the conference room, she bowed her head, looking at the blood that had emerged from her fingertips. "No one is losing their life again for me," she swore to the silent room. Then, she looked up at the ceiling, toward the sky she couldn't see, and the universe that was spinning out there with its fates and gods and whatever it was that everyone believed in. "Do you hear me? No one! Take me if you must, but no one else!"

Silence was the only answer.

Silence followed by the deep resonant echo of a gong from somewhere inside the basilica. The clock on the wall read five o'clock. According to the texts she'd been reading all day, the basilica closed its doors with the sunset and would open again with the sunrise. The night and dawn priestesses took turns in prayers that closed out and started each day.

Nikki's family had never been religious, and yet, the way the San Fiore sisterhood celebrated the earth, the seasons, and the skies, it pricked at something ancient and old resting inside her. She wanted to know more. Wanted to know about Rhaibele, the mother goddess. She could and would learn everything there was to know about this island, its people, and its government.

What she wouldn't do—what she absolutely refused to do—was allow a handful of words spewed at the time of the Great War to cost her another person.

♫ ♫ ♫

They'd had dinner in the conference room so none of the other priestesses would see them. She'd gone back and forth on whether to talk to D'Angelo about overhearing the conversation with his mother, her frustration with him for keeping one more thing from her, and her own fears of more people ending up dead because of her. If she had to lose her most cherished loves—D'Angelo, her mom, her band—it would kill her. But if she told him she'd heard, it would be admitting she'd eavesdropped, and that seemed wrong as well. The pain in his mother's voice hadn't been for her ears. It'd been for a beloved son. So, instead, she did the only other thing she could—learn more about this island she was inheriting.

That sent more goosebumps over her spine. Was she really doing this? Could she do this? What in the hell did she know about running a country…being a queen? She went back and forth between feeling ridiculous and knowing this was the answer—at least for D'Angelo. This is what he needed her to do. And that settled her some.

His mom and Rey came after dinner and walked her through the steps she would be required to perform as part of the procession. For most of the time, she'd just be walking, but after they reached the temple on the castle grounds, there was a dance-like rite. The steps were simple and easy to remember. But the meaning behind them was poignant. The transition between night and day. The importance of both shadow and light.

It drew her eyes to D'Angelo, and he looked up just as she stifled a yawn.

They hadn't gotten much sleep the night before, lost in each other instead. And the day had been a strenuous one. Her body was exhausted, which wasn't good for her migraines, but she was also wired.

D'Angelo walked her to the door of the room where Alessia had gotten the robes for her. As she stepped inside, she eyed the bed. It seemed too small for D'Angelo. His feet would hang off the bottom, and his entire being would fill the mattress, but when he tried to leave her there alone, she slid her hand into his and tugged him into the room with her.

Her stomach was full of worms ready to eat her up from the inside out as she thought about the procession, the risk to those around her, and standing before a group of people and declaring she was their queen. She was pretty sure there was no way she was going to sleep, but she could forget it all for a few more moments by losing herself in him.

When she shed the clothes Alessia had given her, his eyes turned hooded and dark, and his fists clenched at his sides. She took them, spreading the fingers wide, and placed them on her body.

"Tomorrow, my entire life is changing. You said it before. I'll no longer be Nikki Rani. But tonight, for a few more hours, I get to be her. And I need this. I need you to remind me who she is. To burn me up from the inside out. To let me get lost in you before I get lost in a new world."

"You'll never be lost, Nicolette. You're too damn strong. Too brave. You'll always find your way. The truth of it is buried deep inside you already."

Her heart fluttered at his beautiful words. Her eyes fluttered closed, and then she opened them. "The only truth I need tonight…is you."

He stared at her for a long moment and then shed his clothes and led her to the bed where he brought her down on top of him. He let her set the pace, and it was a wild one, driven by a craving she didn't think she'd ever fully satisfy. When she could feel the end approaching, he rolled them over and took her to the edge where they went off together. It was an earth-shattering, cataclysmic joining. Hearts and souls twined, blending in with the stars he'd promised her.

This was the fairy tale. The one she'd ached to have and longed to keep.

She closed her eyes, letting the peace of him and that moment take over, letting the strength of his arm around her and the beat of his heart beneath her ear soothe her.

And the next thing she knew, light was peeking in the window, and she was alone.

There was a breakfast tray on the side table and an elaborate robe made of a sheer white material threaded with silver and gold hanging from the wardrobe. All the priestesses in the procession today would wear similar ones. The Dawn Priestess would be at the head, followed by six more priestesses and then six men wearing enormous headdresses that resembled lynx. They would pull a chariot with the ancient statue of the Dawn Priestess that had been on San Fiore for thousands of years.

That feeling of having stepped into another world, another universe, another timeline came back to her. Even having read briefly about the island before and having delved further into its history yesterday, it was hard to imagine participating in a rite this old.

She rose, examining the skintight white mini-skirt and a white tank top she was supposed to wear below the semi-transparent gown. They were made of soft, stretchy cotton that showed all her curves, and she was grateful someone had found a pair of underwear and a bra in the right size to go with them.

Whoever had delivered the clothing had also provided her with some hygiene items and a variety of hair ties. It allowed her to pull her mass of curls back into a low ponytail she could tuck beneath the hood of the robe. The hood draped low over her brows and curled inward so only her nose and mouth were visible. Without any pockets, she pinned both the bird-of-paradise and daisy brooches to the inside waistband of the skirt. They dug into her skin somewhat, but they grounded her in much the way the brooch did when she had it pressed to her fingers.

A knock on the door was followed by D'Angelo opening it, and her mouth fell open.

He looked like a Roman gladiator. The defined

contours of his bare biceps and chest were on display, only partially covered by a large over-the-shoulder bandolier like the one he normally wore stuffed with knives, except this one was made of worn leather instead of black nylon. The strap ended near his waist where a skirt of pleated leather hid a loin cloth of white threaded with silver and gold like her robe. His incredibly wide thighs and muscled calves were bare, and his feet were clad in sandals that wound up to stop just below his knees. On his right arm was a manica of gold and silver that went from his shoulder to below his elbow. He hadn't put the helmet on yet. It was tucked under his arm, but the teeth of a lynx snarled in the elaborate face of the headdress. Where the ears should have been, two long plumes of the Regina astrapia tail feathers sat.

"Wow," she breathed out.

He grimaced. "I never wanted to pull a chariot."

"Wouldn't it be considered an honor?"

He looked at her with dark eyes glimmering as he took in her body in the sheer robes. "Yes. And more often than not, it is a *Cavalieri* who is chosen."

"But you prefer to be invisible. To not be seen." He didn't respond, and she closed the distance between them, placing her hands on his chest. "You promised to be at my side every step of the way. You can't be next to me and standing in the shadows at the same time. It doesn't work that way."

"I've been in the shadows for a reason, Nicolette. My darkness…" His throat bobbed. "I don't want it to dim your light."

"Landry died because of me. Her bodyguard. Professor Maynard. Believe me, I have my own things weighing me down. We all do."

"It hasn't stopped you from shining. You're so bright, sometimes it's hard to look at you." His jaw ticked. His hand cupped her cheek, and his voice grew even gruffer than normal as he said, "I took what didn't belong to me, but damned if I can find a way to give it back.”

“You didn’t take anything. I gave myself to you, and you gave yourself to me. There was no plundering. No stealing,” she said. “The only way I’ll survive this is if we do it side by side. Not one of us in the light and the other in the shadows. Whatever happens, we get through it together.”

His Adam’s apple bobbed up and down, and he leaned in to place a kiss on her forehead. But he didn’t agree with her, and it caused fear and worry to squirm through her. His mother’s words in the corridor the day before came back to her. She wouldn’t lose him. She couldn’t. But she also didn’t want any more deaths on her conscience.

“We can’t do anything about the souls that have already been lost,” she said. “But we can do everything we can to not add to them. To not be the reason more people die, whether they’re loved ones or enemies.”

He stared at her for a long time as if truly hearing her request. She didn’t want more deaths on her conscience. She believed he needed to be free of the weight of it as well. He had enough of them dragging him back into the underworld he’d lived in for too long. After what felt like an eternity, he gave her a curt nod. He didn’t say he agreed, but she felt the promise in his gaze. No one had to die.

He held out his arm without the manica. She took an unsteady breath and placed her hand on the inner curve of his elbow, and without another word, they made their way through the tangle of corridors to the prayer hall.

The huge doors of the basilica were open, and bright white rays of sunshine spread through them much like they had peeked from behind the clouds the day before. It added a hazy mirage-like quality to the procession waiting outside, another waking dream she was living. The priestesses and the lynx stood at the ready in front of a chariot made of gold and decorated with the bright-blue and purple flowers of San Fiore. Inside it was the marble statue of the Dawn Priestess, carved to be perpetually young and beautiful. Behind the chariot, a small gathering of female flutists had gathered and a single male with a snare drum.

"Only the priestesses in line know who you are," D'Angelo said quietly. "You'll be in the middle row. Follow their lead."

Everything about the ceremony today was supposed to be subdued and quiet, and yet her heart was pounding like it had the very first time she'd ever walked onstage with her band in a sold-out stadium. That very first time, she'd been overcome with fear. She'd thought she would forget how to play her guitar or forget the chords or that her voice would sound like a tortured cat instead of a professional singer. But as soon as they'd started the first verse, she'd lost the nervousness and found the joy in the music again.

Here, she wasn't walking onto a stage with thousands of hours of practice behind her. Here, she was walking from one unknown into the next. The nervousness she felt was accompanied by something in her stomach that she could only name as dread.

Alessia's words the day before were still haunting her thoughts. *She has to lose her most cherished love.*

Her feet seemed to turn to stone, this last step the hardest one to take. As soon as she joined the procession, there would be no turning back.

She'd become Nicolette Fiorani. Queen.

Her flesh broke out in more goosebumps. She suddenly ached to talk to her friends. Her mom. Anyone who could tell her she was dreaming or that she'd lost all common sense. Someone to tell her to run.

She looked up at D'Angelo, and his eyes held devotion. Love. Pride.

It was the pride that did her in. She hadn't truly seen it in anyone's eyes in a very long time. Her mom had been there along the way, offered congratulations when the band had won awards, gone platinum, or sold out their tour. Jerome had clapped her on the back when she'd put him in the kill position. But pride… She wasn't sure she'd seen it since her dad had looked at her that way.

Her chest nearly exploded with the pressure inside it.

"I'm falling in love with you," she said. The words slipped out at the most inappropriate moment, and she wanted to slap a hand to her mouth and take them back.

He startled, eyes turning guarded as he looked down the steps to where the small crowd of people waited for them. And he didn't say it back. In fact, there was a hint of panic that flew over his face for a moment. Her stomach spun, and her heart fell. But then she reminded herself of where they were. It had hardly been what he'd expected her to say as they entered the last stage of this dangerous game.

She huffed out a breath directed at herself, and then said, "Sorry. Shitty timing. But it's true."

One large hand landed on top of hers. He squeezed softly. "It's only shitty timing because I can't kiss you right now in front of my mother and the rest of our sisters and brothers." The low growl of his voice rumbled through her chest, and the heaviness inside her lightened an infinitesimal amount.

Her gaze went to his mouth and then up to his eyes.

"Tonight, then. We'll kiss each other and bring the stars down to earth like we did last night," she said softly.

He let out a little groan. "Nicolette, you do realize I'm wearing a loin cloth and nothing else? You keep saying things like that, and I'm going to be showing a lot more than just my chest and hairy legs."

She couldn't help the laugh that burst from her.

It drew eyes. Eyes they didn't want. And she quickly looked down at her gold-sandaled feet.

"Go get in line, *Principessa*."

It had been so long since he'd called her that it almost

came as a shock. But it was also a reminder of why they were there. He squeezed her hand one more time and then let go. She slipped her hand from his arm and traveled down the large marble steps to join the others on the mosaic-tiled road.

The young woman next to Nikki took her in from head to toe, eyes wide, and it made her shift uncomfortably. The fact some of the priestesses knew who she was only made the nervousness and the ball of dread in her stomach grow.

The music started, and so did they. A slow march that felt like a magical dance. They would walk down from the basilica to the marina and then back up the winding streets to the castle. In all, it would take less than half an hour. As soon as they stepped out the gates, a sea of people appeared, lining the streets. Young and old, waving flags of San Fiore, throwing orchid petals, and humming along to the music the flutists played as the tiny snare drum tapped out a beat that matched their footsteps.

She wanted to take them all in. To scour their faces. Learn everything there was to know about these people. The ones who wanted a queen and the ones who didn't. But instead, she kept her head down, the hood pulled tight, hiding who she was.

The crash of the sea along the shore joined with the noise of the instruments and the humming of the crowd. But no words were spoken, not even by those lining the street. It was strangely quiet. Solemn. Reverent. Only the screech of seagulls broke through the sound of the flutes.

She'd read last night that over the next few days, there'd be plays and songs and another much larger ceremony at the temple before the Night Priestess's statue was covered with a black veil and removed from the temple, leaving only the Dawn Priestess. Those events would be filled with voices and music and devotions, but today remained a quiet offering.

Ever since her mom had been poisoned, she'd felt like she'd been living a dream. The unseasonably heavy air, the quiet of the music and the crowd…it all just added to it. Surely, she'd wake up in her hotel room in Monaco and be able to laugh with her friends about it. Fee would think it uproariously funny that she'd thought she was a queen when it was Adria who'd been the real one—a beauty queen, but still a queen.

Her chest constricted. What the hell was she doing?

The streets from the marina were steep, but it was the sight of the castle coming into view rather than any exertion that had her pulse picking up. When they came to a halt at the white gates of *Castrum Aureum Lumen*, she closed her eyes. *Wake up, Nikki,* she said silently. But her heart wasn't in it. Because if she lost this, she'd lose D'Angelo too, and she couldn't bear that. In a matter of days, he'd become essential to her existence.

The two soldiers at the gate were dressed similarly to D'Angelo, except their helmets were designed like a bird's head. They bowed to the Dawn Priestess and then swung the gates open. The march continued into the gardens, twining over more mosaic tiles and ending at a circular temple. The Greek-style columns held up a carved roof with reliefs outlined in gold. The wide expanse of the pillars had been hung with vines and flowers. The scent was heavy in the air as Nikki turned with the other five priestesses to begin the motions of the rite. They brought their hands up in the air and then down in a wide arc, feet dancing a little two-step before they swept apart like the Red Sea, dipping their heads as the men with the chariot lifted the statue out and carried her through their parted path. The youthful image of the Dawn Priestess was placed beside the wise and wrinkled Night Priestess's statue carved out of black marble.

D'Angelo's mom emerged from behind the statue, dressed in black robes threaded with silver. The real-life Dawn Priestess joined her. The two locked arms, bowing to the left, to the right, flinging their arms to the sky, and then turning to accept more of the sisterhood who'd silently moved forward with crates of flowers and paper lanterns that would be released into the water just before dawn at the end of the Transition.

Applause broke out as the hundreds of people who'd filed in behind the musicians celebrated the arrival of the dawn. A cheer went up. Laughter and talking crashed through the quiet, an almost jarring contradiction to the somber silence of before.

It set Nikki's nerves rattling just as D'Angelo appeared at her side.

"Let's go," he said quietly, scanning their surroundings and slipping his hand into hers. As he led her out of the temple into the garden, her pulse picked up. An old wooden door engraved with pictures of the goddesses and hung with large iron hinges appeared in the outer wall that ran around the castle. Two guards stood in front of it in the midnight-blue uniforms of the palace guard's branch of the *Cavalieri.*

They crossed their rifles in front of the door. "No admittance this way. Access to the banquet hall is through the main door."

D'Angelo removed his helmet, crossing fingers to his heart and then his temple. One of the men let out a startled breath. "Castelli?" The guard's eyes dropped to Nikki, and she knew he understood the importance of her being there the moment his gaze landed on her. Hope and surprise littered the man's face. He turned, putting his eye on a retinal scanner in the side of the frame, and the door creaked open.

His partner grunted in disapproval. "What the hell?"

"Secret mission," the first man responded. There was a small beat before the second man pulled a knife from his belt and, in a smooth movement, planted it directly in the first man's back. An anguished cry escaped him and the man fell to the ground writhing. A gasp escaped Nikki's throat, and D'Angelo shifted in front of her, drawing one of his own knives and flinging it through the air until it lodged in the other man's shoulder.

He howled, reaching for it, and D'Angelo moved in a flash, shoving the man's head into the wall and knocking him out. He landed next to the first man on the ground, blood spewing from them both, and bile filled Nikki's throat. She'd sworn no one would die again, and now there were two men, wounded, blood pouring from them.

Adrenaline pumped through her body, her fight-or-flight instincts making her want to do both at the same time and causing her feet to turn to cement blocks. D'Angelo tugged at her, and still, she stared, frozen, at the ugly sight in front of her.

"Nicolette!" his voice was low and determined.

When she didn't reply, he lifted her by the waist over the two bodies, setting her down in a dimly lit passage inside the battlement walls. He slammed the door shut behind them, and the sound echoed down the stone corridor. Slender crenels that had once allowed archers to defend the keep cast hazy rectangles of sunshine along the floors and walls, amplifying the dreamlike feel she'd had for days.

But now it felt twisted. Nightmarish. Her skin crawled. Something was wrong. Something burning at the back of her mind and deep inside her gut. She wanted to hold him steady. To stop D'Angelo from going forward...to stop them both. But then, he tugged at her hand again, and they were running, racing along the narrow passage.

As they neared a door leading into the corner tower, it swung open, and three men appeared from behind it. These men had guns in their hands and the red lapel pin of the anti-royalists. A shot rang out, and D'Angelo twisted, shoving her backward into a crevice they'd passed. It was so small she barely fit, and he had to wedge himself into it, but it revealed stairs. Each step was so tall it required even her long legs to stretch in order to mount them.

The pounding of their sandals on the stone was loud, and the rush of feet below them proved their enemies were right behind them. Doors slammed. Shouts and shots echoed from below, and blood pounded in her veins as it sounded like a war had broken out in the keep. Shouts and brutal cries that only added to the dark fear crawling through her.

They rounded the last corner of the steps to find their way blocked by a door. D'Angelo angled her to the side, using his eyes and his palm to unlock it. When he pushed the door open and she stepped out, her breath caught. They were at the top of the parapet, the notched, rectangular crenellations the only thing between them and the sky and sea. The side of the castle fell away, ending where the tides crashed below them, the deep aquamarine pools turning white as they slammed against the cliff.

"Go," he said, pointing toward the next tower and another door.

They'd just reached it when it was thrown open to reveal two more men in suits. At first, D'Angelo's hand slid up to his bandolier, reaching for a knife, but he pulled back. Instead of using his weapon, he dropped low, tackling the first man to come through with his shoulder and causing him to fall back into the other. He pummeled the man's face, blood splattering across them and the stones. When the second man tried to get in his own punch, Nikki stepped forward, determined to help D'Angelo just as the crash of the door behind them had her whirling back around.

One of the anti-royalists from below was there, breathing heavily, blood dripping down his face. She lowered her center of gravity, and as he came close, she swept at his leg. He jumped over it, landing close enough to grab her arm. She twisted out of his hold. The narrow parapet and the dramatic fall on either side had her heart lunging into her throat as it whizzed past her eyes. The man shot a fist out, and she used the moves she'd practiced her entire life to counter it.

Behind her, she heard the grunts and cries of the men D'Angelo was fighting with fists instead of knives.

Because of her. Because she'd said she couldn't handle more souls hanging on either of them. She didn't regret it, and yet she did. Because what if, in not using his weapons, worse happened?

She raised up on the ball of her foot and landed a kick to the man's sternum, wishing she was in her heavy boots instead of golden sandals. But she'd hit him with enough force the man's eyes went wide, gasping for breath. Four more anti-royalists burst out from behind him, and on their heels were Alessia, Rey, and two of the lynx who'd pulled the chariot. A battle roared around them. Savage hits. Bone and skin colliding.

Her assailant pulled a knife, and she struck at his arm with her foot sending the knife sailing. He staggered, but reached out at the last minute to catch her ankle. She jerked back, but it put her off balance enough he was able to shove her against the parapet with his shoulder and hips, pinning her to it. She drove her hand into his sternum, but he didn't let go, grabbing her neck and forcing her backward over the wall until all she could see was the outside of the castle and the ocean far below it. She'd never survive if he pushed her over.

She slid her nails into his wrist, she thrust her knee into his groin, and as he let up an infinitesimal amount, she was able to twist her face from his grip and saw D'Angelo landing one final, punishing punch to a man's face before letting him drop. He took a step toward Nikki just as another man emerged from the door at his back.

"Behind you!" she screamed.

He spun, fists raised toward the new attacker, and hadn't quite stabilized as the man at his feet reached up and jerked D'Angelo's leg backward. Every part of her froze in horror as D'Angelo wobbled, reaching for the top of the wall to balance himself. He didn't have a chance to regain control before the new attacker landed a powerful kick to his chest.

Every part of her soul cried out, and the word, "No!" tore from the depths of her as he slid along the top of the wall. The anti-royalist swept D'Angelo's lower body up and over while he scrabbled for a hold on the stone. One enormous hand reached for a notched groove, but he missed, and then D'Angelo disappeared over the side.

Nikki screamed his name, elbowing the man in front of her in the face, and when he staggered back, she followed it with a roundhouse to his stomach that sent him staggering. A desperate ache like a knife dragging from her heart into her stomach filled her as she fled toward the spot where D'Angelo had gone over, hoping impossibly that he'd held on to something. Anything.

She was yanked backward by the anti-royalist grabbing her by the waist. She kicked at him again just as Alessia and Rey arrived at her side, knives drawn. From the doors of both towers, a host of palace guards poured forth. The anti-royalists, seeing they were outnumbered, dropped their knives and their fists, expressions dark.

Nikki screamed D'Angelo's name again, racing for where she'd last seen him with Alessia at her side.

The castle wall was empty.

He wasn't there.

He was gone.

Something tore through her soul. A slash that showed no blood but carved just as painfully through every nerve ending. A sob escaped her throat at the same time as a tormented one came from his mother. Garbled pain that got lost in a fierce wind that appeared out of nowhere, whipping against the parapet with a force so strong Nikki was compelled to take a step back. Even though there were people and noise all around her, muttered curses and growls as the anti-royalists were taken into custody, she couldn't hear any of it. All she could hear was the beat of a heart as if it was fading away before a deathly silence took over.

Another distressed cry escaped her.

A tortured howl that sounded like a wounded animal.

Bitter. Agonized. Feral.

Wild and feral.

He was gone.

Chapter Thirty-five

Nikki

BIGGER THAN THE WHOLE SKY
Performed by Taylor Swift

THAT DAY

Nikki's hand clutched the stone so hard it was painful. Her body screaming from the inside out. Every piece of her railing at the goddesses and the universe. She'd demanded they take her before they took anyone else…took him…and they hadn't listened.

She has to lose her most cherished love.

No! She refused to accept it even while, inside, she was shattering. A desperate plea rebounded over and over in her brain for it not to be true. He couldn't be gone.

Next to her, she felt Alessia whirl around while Nikki was locked into place, waiting for him to reappear, agony rippling through her like never before.

Alessia's panicked voice behind her cried out, "D'Angelo went over! Send the divers!"

Hope beat through the agony. Was there a way? Was it possible? Nikki forced her body to turn, eyes landing on the way Alessia was tugging on the lapel of a man's suit. A man Nikki knew only because she'd seen him on the television. Battista Massi's brows were drawn together in anger or confusion, she wasn't sure which. His hair, which had almost lost its battle with gray and now was mostly white, was slicked back, accentuating a face strangely smooth for a man who could easily be her grandfather.

He pulled Alessia's hands from his chest, straightened his suit, and then turned to the guards standing around. "You heard her. Tell the men to launch the rescue sub." His voice had the same charming lilt to it that it had on the TV, but today it grated along Nikki's ruined nerves. It was wrong. Everything was wrong.

D'Angelo couldn't be gone. Not now. Not when they'd just found their way to each other. Not when he'd promised to always be at her side. To step into the light with her. The reality slammed into her. Guilt and horror. She'd asked him not to kill anyone. To add no more souls to the weight that they already bore, but if he'd used his knives instead of his fists, would the man have been dead and D'Angelo been saved?

A sob got stuck in her throat, and shudders wracked her body.

Had she cost him his life by asking him to be something he wasn't?

More priestesses appeared on the parapet accompanied by a man in the same black outfit D'Angelo usually favored. One so similar that Nikki's entire being convulsed harder. A guttural sound escaped her along with another sob. She bent at the waist, and Alessia stepped toward her in time to stop Nikki from landing on her knees. D'Angelo's mother drew her close, holding her against her.

The man in black crossed in front of Nikki to join the prime minister. They talked in a hushed tone, eyeing her carefully. They were silently judging her and her tears and the mess she knew she appeared, but she couldn't find it in her to care.

Rey stepped forward, arm sliding through Nikki's opposite one until she had a priestess on either arm. Rey leaned in and said softly, "You need to pull yourself together."

Nikki's entire being revolted. Just minutes ago, she'd told D'Angelo they'd face everything side by side, but they hadn't faced the leap that had taken him away from her together. She hadn't gone over with him. He'd faced death alone.

That brought more tears. Fast and furious. She'd failed him here on this wall, and she'd fail him yet again going forward because she couldn't do this without him. Not on her own.

He'd been wrong about her. She wasn't brave. She wasn't even strong.

He was supposed to be here!

"You're sure this is her?" the man in black directed the question at the priestesses.

It was Rey who answered, "Yes."

The prime minister's jaw ticked, and then he grunted, "What a fucking mess."

"I suggest we get off this wall and into the throne room," the man in black said quietly.

Alessia had become silent—stoic and stiff next to her—but she reached for Nikki's hand and led her toward the tower door. Nikki could barely see where she was going through the tears. Alessia went first, guiding her down the steep steps while Rey followed them to the ground floor of the battlement. They emerged from the slim passage into a courtyard just beyond it.

The garden was full of light and color and sounds. Birds twittered in the trees, the sun filtered through the branches, and above them, not a single cloud cluttered the sky. And yet Nikki felt like everything was turning black. Death hanging its dark veil over them as she was taken into the castle keep.

Another set of stairs appeared, these ornate and beautiful, carved and gilded. Then, they were in a room that was as bright as the day outside. Three large chandeliers dripped crystals of light from ceilings so tall it was hard to see the paintings on the roof. Rhaibele was in her chariot, lions pulling her across the ocean waves as all sorts of sea life and sea people reached up to touch the golden wheels. A raised dais at one end of the room held two giant chairs in gold and blue velvet that even D'Angelo would have looked small on.

Half the group from the battlement had taken the anti-royalists away in zip ties while the other half had followed them inside the castle. Guards and priestesses mingled, speaking in hushed voices. The prime minister turned to one of the men and said, quietly, "Inform the carillonneur to ring the bell, and then go to the banquet hall where the members of the Old Houses and the parliament are gathered for the feast. Tell them our queen has arrived."

The man's eyes turned enormous as his gaze settled on Nikki.

She knew she looked nothing like the queen they'd expected. Tears of anguish rolled down her cheeks. She could barely stand. Her robe was torn, and her hair was askew from the fight on the parapet.

"Nikki!" a voice cried out, and she turned to find her mom running across the golden marble floors. And then she was wrapped in an embrace she knew well. Soft and hard. Calm and sturdy. The one that had held her up after she'd first lost her dad and then her friend. But this time, Nikki wasn't sure she'd ever find her feet again. Not after losing the one person she'd been put on this earth to find. Not after having a mere taste of what it could be like for her fairy tale to have come true.

She hugged her mom back and sobbed in her neck. "He's g-gone… He's gone."

"Dear Rhaibele," Massi cursed behind her. "They were together?"

It was Alessia's voice that answered, shaky and bitter

as she uttered a single syllable, "Yes."

A bell rang out from somewhere on the grounds—chime after chime—and a wave went through the room. Startled gasps. Movement. People turned and stared.

It was Rey who touched Nikki's shoulder and leaned in again, talking as softly as before, cajoling almost, a plea in her tone. "He devoted his life to finding you. He sacrificed everything, including himself. If you loved him, you need to honor what he did by pulling yourself together and facing your people."

Nikki hated her at that moment for stating the truth. The callousness of it. She wanted to curl up in a ball with her mom rubbing her back. She wanted to drown herself in the loss that bled inside her like an open wound.

"Nicolette." Nikki looked up from her mom's shoulder at the name only D'Angelo had ever called her. Alessia's face was drawn with pain but also filled with determination. "Rey speaks the truth. We owe him this."

She thought of D'Angelo's face this morning. The pride and devotion that had been there. The depth of belief she'd heard in his voice when he'd told her she'd never be lost. She wanted desperately not to fail him—not again. He'd given up everything for her. She'd promised herself to ensure his dreams were reached. His destiny fulfilled. If that meant her accepting hers, then she had to do it. Her back went straight, and she pulled away from her mother.

Their eyes met, and Nikki was surprised by the intrigued look she saw on her mom's face, as if she was a curiosity. If her own mother saw her that way, what would it be like when others looked at her? Her friends? Her fans? The entire damn world? How would she face it without him? She didn't know. She didn't have a clue, but all she could do was take it as her mom had taught her to take everything—a second, a moment, an hour at a time until you'd moved through the worst of it.

The man in black stepped forward, bending in a bow,

before rising again to say, "My name is Luther Magellini. I am the *Gran Duca* of the *Cavalieri,* and while we have failed you today, I promise we will not again. I won't rest until every last anti-royalist has been found and put away."

There was something honorable about the man and his movements. She thought she heard truth in his words, but she also wasn't sure she could believe them. Not only because she'd barely escaped today, and D'Angelo had lost his life while fighting alone at her side, but because D'Angelo had said there was a traitor in their midst. It could be any of them, including this man who led them.

"How did they know we were coming?" she demanded.

Luther's eyes narrowed, taking in the room. "I'm not sure. There was only a handful of us who knew you were arriving today."

Nikki wiped at her tears. She had to save them for later. She had to ensure these people knew she wouldn't rest until those responsible for betraying them, for betraying D'Angelo, were gone. The men who'd ordered her family's assassination from afar, who'd taken her father and her friend from her, would be punished. They would all pay the price. Even if she had to do it with her bare hands as he had. She'd been wrong to tell him not to kill. The evil had to be stopped. There was no other way.

"I want them found. I want them found and destroyed," she commanded. Her voice carried through the room just as it would on a stage, and the murmur of voices that had grown to an almost resounding buzz disappeared into silence.

The man bowed again. "You have my word on it."

"You have the brooch?" the prime minister stepped forward to ask.

With a heart so heavy she knew it would cause her to sink to the bottom of the sea if she was in it, Nikki drew her robe aside and unpinned the Regina astrapia. When

Massi reached for it, she closed her hand around it. "No. It won't leave my sight."

His eyes flickered with something—grudging respect or maybe irritation that some unknown slip of a woman was setting the rules. But only this pin and the blood coursing through her veins would be able to prove the claim D'Angelo had insisted was true. She wouldn't give it up.

"Bring the jeweler here," Luther said, and Massi's jaw ticked.

A rush of people arrived at the door. Men and women in designer suits and floral dresses, as if they'd been about to attend a garden party. Some were as old as Prime Minister Massi and some were closer to her age. What they had in common was the aura of wealth and confidence that sprang from them. It was in the way they walked and dressed, and when they spoke, their cultured voices showed it even more.

Nikki was more than used to being onstage with her friends and having hundreds of thousands of eyes turned on them, but this… The way they inspected her was as if she was a bug under a microscope being dissected, bit by bit. Her shoulders grew tauter, her spine straighter. She used the energy of the agony carving its way through her to keep her going. Used the loss to fuel her forward.

The whispers grew even louder. Another white-haired man stepped forward, his eyes a startling green that shone below heavy brows and thousands of wrinkles. He bowed at the waist as Luther had—a curt, formal movement. Then, he drew himself up and looked her in the eye. "I'm Cosimo Bianchi, and on behalf of the Old Houses of San Fiore, I welcome you. As you can imagine, we will need proof of your heritage before we proceed."

"The jeweler is on his way," Luther announced.

"And the doctor?" The man looked from Nikki to the prime minister.

"Of course."

A round, gold-leaf table was brought into the room, and Nikki was directed toward it. A blue velvet cloth was placed on the marble top, and she set the bird-of-paradise brooch onto it, hating having it out of her hold even when it was still within easy reach. Another murmur went through the room as if everyone gathered hadn't really expected her to be able to produce it.

A new bustle at the door revealed a large man with a worn, brown-leather bag in his hand. He approached the little crowd at the table. He barely glanced at Nikki before his eye fastened on the brooch. He produced a jeweler's loupe, and as he picked the pin up to examine it, he asked, "Where did you get this?"

Nikki's back bristled at the doubt she heard there. "My father. He died with it on him."

She heard a surprised gasp from her mom and turned to see that Clarissa's eyes were wide with shock. "But how?"

"The clerk at the store…he took it. A professor who was the first to tell me about all of this"—Nikki glanced at the throne room—"got it back from him."

Before her mom could respond, the jeweler grunted, "So, it lost chain of custody."

He never broke from his scrutiny of the brooch, scouring the front, the back, and then setting it down.

"Well?" Massi demanded.

"It is authentic," the man announced.

"You're sure?" Cosimo asked.

The jeweler shot him a look. "The secret of the brooches has been passed down to each crown jeweler for hundreds of years, and last I checked, that was now me."

More people poured into the room until it felt stifling. Bodies shifted into each other as everyone shuffled to get a look at Nikki. All the while, her heart was cracking open, bleeding out on the floor, and they didn't know it. She shut her eyes briefly before opening them to find Alessia watching her. D'Angelo's mom's eyes were watery but firm, and Nikki's teeth ground together. This woman had lost her entire family for the monarchy, and yet she still stood. She wasn't lying crushed in pieces even though she'd told D'Angelo the day before there'd be nothing left of her if she lost him too. If Alessia could do this, Nikki could as well. They'd get through it together. Somehow.

A doctor arrived, and while the crowd watched, he swabbed her cheek, not once but four times, for DNA. He put each swab into a different sealed container, telling her and the room that a quick match would be in by the end of the day. A full match in two. They'd be sent to independent labs on the island and in Italy. Only the doctor and the senior *Cavalieri* would know where the samples had gone. They'd have proof of her lineage well before December thirty-first.

But Nikki already knew the truth in her veins. She'd felt it when she'd seen Rhaibele's statue for the first time. She'd known it at the bottom of her soul when D'Angelo had reiterated what the professor had told her. She'd felt it for over two years while clutching the bird-of-paradise pin in her hand.

Another man in black approached the *Gran Duca*, whispering in his ear. Luther's eyes found Nikki's, journeyed to Alessia's, and then he stepped closer to them. "The divers can't find his body. They'll continue to look." Hope, stupid and useless, filled her veins as it had briefly on the parapet. Maybe he'd survived? But the man's next words crushed it all over again. "The rip current is strong at the base of the cliff. It likely already took him out to sea. We'll find him and bring him home. We'll honor him as he deserves for the sacrifices he made on behalf of San Fiore."

"What's this?" Cosimo asked.

"D'Angelo Castelli was lost in a fight on the battlement," Luther said, and another startled murmur went through the people near enough to hear him say it.

Eyes landed on Alessia. Even Nikki could feel the empathy and sympathy welling through the room for her. The woman had lost everything for her people. Nikki's throat closed, her temples began to pulse, and white lights flickered in front of her eyes.

No. She couldn't go down with a migraine. Not today.

She rubbed her forehead, and her mom's eyes narrowed at the movement. "Perhaps we can get Nikki to a room where she can change and rest."

The prime minister's eyes settled on her. "Of course."

He looked at the crowd, raised his voice, and said, "Please, return to the banquet. Enjoy the Transition feast. We will notify everyone once we have received the DNA results."

He put a hand on Nikki's elbow and started to direct her out of the room, but she pulled away, turning back to the table and palming the brooch. The back of the pin found her fingertip in a way that brought comfort and pain all at the same time. She flashed on the memory of D'Angelo's hands stopping her from pricking herself. He'd said he wouldn't let her do it anymore…but he wasn't there. He'd broken the most important promise he'd made her—to be at her side.

They'd failed each other.

As the prime minister led her into the hall, they were followed by a small entourage. It included Rey, Alessia, her mom, the *Gran Duca*, and half a dozen men in the black uniform that still hurt her to see.

They moved down an enormous hall where priceless paintings lined gilded walls from floor to ceiling and mingled with equally large mirrors. It reminded Nikki of Adria's family's mansion in Colombia. The Rojas's home had been designed after Versailles, but this castle was older than either estate by several hundred years. The thought of Adria made her ache to talk to her friend. To talk to all the Daisies. To have their comfort and their friendship at her side once more.

But would they want to be there? When she told them the truth about her secrets—about Landry—would they hate her? It lodged another knot in her throat. More tears threatened to pour from her eyes, and only the pain of the brooch and the calm of D'Angelo's mother were enough to prevent her from screaming and crying and howling at the sky.

They wound around another landing of the grand staircase before stepping into a hall with half a dozen chandeliers shining down on them. One golden hall blended into the next until, finally, a set of white doors were thrown open, and Nikki was ushered into a large suite.

It was filled with the same, lush royal blues of the thrones in the room downstairs as well as the gold that appeared everywhere on San Fiore. But here, the precious metal was twined with silver and aged copper as well. The sitting room held several scroll-backed sofas and tufted chaises surrounded by white and glass tables overflowing with vases full of flowers. Tall windows covered in lace and brocade were open, letting in the breeze and the sunshine that continued to feel like a false mirage to Nikki's broken heart.

Beyond the sitting room, two more doors opened to a bedroom. A king-sized bed, even D'Angelo would have fit on with space to share, stood on a platform. A canopy of pale blue embroidered with thousands of colorful birds was held up by bedposts carved with vines and trees.

Everything was bright and beautiful, but all it did was remind her of why she was in the room and what she'd lost to get there. Nikki's eyes watered, and lights shimmered in her vision again. Pain sliced through her head, as harsh and sharp as always, and yet it was still less than the ache in her heart and soul.

"She needs to lie down in the dark and quiet," her mom said, turning to the others. "Otherwise, the migraine will take full hold."

Someone drew all the drapes. The room turned blessedly darker. The chandelier in the sitting room was shut off. Alessia was at her side, squeezing her hand, and she leaned in to whisper. "I'm leaving to take care of a few things, but I promise I'll be back by the time you wake. Don't leave the room until I'm here."

As Alessia turned to leave, Nikki tried to say something—anything—but the pain spiked through her forehead, and her eyes blurred. Her mom led her to the bed, but when Nikki looked at it, she doubted she could sleep in it. The enormity of doing so felt too big…too real. She turned back to the others who'd followed them, wondering if this was going to be the way her life was forever now—if there'd always be a sea of people right behind her, but never the one she wanted most.

"Isn't there a smaller room? A smaller bed?" she asked.

No one responded at first. Her mom was the one to step forward. "Just rest, Nikki."

She did as she was told, sitting on the edge of the silk comforter, drawing off the priestess's sandals, and then lying down. Someone handed her a glass of water and some pain medicine. She swallowed both. And suddenly, for the first time in her life, she was almost grateful for a migraine, because it would pull her down into its dark depths and force her into its oblivion. She'd sleep, for maybe hours, and be able to forget what she'd lost and what had happened to her life.

Chapter Thirty-six

Nikki

SOUND OF SILENCE
Performed by Dami Im

She came awake to hushed voices in the dark of an unfamiliar room. The smell of the ocean and flowers filled it, and slowly, everything came back to her. Their time on the run. The basilica. The parapet where she'd lost him. She barely held in a sob, forcing herself to remain quiet, to listen to what was happening around her.

The rustle of clothing and bags finally drew her attention.

A set of doors on the far side of the bedroom revealed a closet. A light was on, and there were several people inside it, unpacking what looked like dozens of shopping bags. Her mom drifted by the closet's opening with something on a hanger in her hands.

Nikki sat up, and the bedroom spun slightly. Her eyes felt gritty and sore. Every part of her being seemed to hurt, and yet she also felt slightly numb. Lost. Alone. She curled her knees into her chest on the edge of the bed, wishing for D'Angelo. Wishing away the last week… The last two years… Wishing her father was alive to explain himself. She ached for something real instead of this damn dream she'd been living for the last week.

She wanted her friends. The band.

She uncoiled her legs and stood shakily. The

migraine hadn't developed into a full-blown rager. She'd caught it in time, but she needed water and food and more meds. She wondered how long she'd been asleep. She'd just taken a step toward the closet when a soft hand on her elbow stopped her.

She let out a little squeak, but it wasn't loud enough to draw her mom's attention. Nikki swirled, raising her arms to fight off a hit that never came. Alessia was there. No longer in the robes of the priestesses, she wore black slacks and a green button-down, looking more like an everyday person than she had since Nikki had met her. More like a mother when, before, she'd just been a part of the mirage.

"You can't trust anyone, Nicolette," she said softly. Nikki scoured her face and saw the signs of tears. Her eyes were red-rimmed, dark shadows beneath the lashes. She looked like she'd aged decades in a matter of hours. She'd lost everything, and yet she was here with Nikki.

"I know," Nikki said equally as quiet, a mere whisper in the air.

Alessia shook her head, turning to look into the closet and the small group filling it with clothes Nikki had never seen. "No. You don't understand. No one."

Nikki's eyes followed Alessia's to see she was looking at her mother.

"My mom? What the hell? Why would you even say that?"

Before she could answer, her stepmom saw them. She dropped the clothes in her hand and came out of the closet. "You're awake! How's your head?"

She glanced at Alessia and then back to Nikki, a small V burrowing between her brows as she pushed her glasses up on her nose.

"Better, but it's still lingering at the back. It wouldn't take much for it to bloom again."

"I'll send someone for some more painkillers. We have your prescription coming as well."

"What are you doing?" Nikki asked, glancing back at the closet.

Clarissa gave a soft laugh. "We can't have a queen without a wardrobe. We've pulled together some things for you."

Nikki stepped toward the doorway of the closet, wincing at the light. On the shelves and hangers were dozens of clothes.

"A few things?" she said sarcastically.

Her mom turned to Alessia. "Thank you for watching over her. I'm sure we can handle it from here."

"Mom!" Nikki said, surprised at the high-handed tone in her mother's voice. She returned to Alessia, putting her hand through her arm and drawing her close. "This is D'Angelo's mom. I—" She swallowed hard before continuing. "We need to be near each other right now."

Her mom's hand fidgeted with the arm of her glasses. "So, it's true. You fell for your kidnapper?"

"He wasn't a kidnapper," Alessia growled.

"He took my daughter from her boat and kept her against her will. What do you call that?"

"Her protector. He gave his life to get her here." Pain rippled through Alessia's voice, and Nikki squeezed her arm tighter.

Her mom ignored Alessia's tortured response, looking Nikki over again. "You're going to need to shower and change. There are people waiting to meet you."

Nikki's eyes went wide. When they'd lost her dad, her mom had gotten them through with days full of structured routines. Tasks that had to be completed, but at night, Nikki had found her many times with a drink in her hand and a distant look on her face. Grief she didn't show during the day. And now, when Nikki's entire life was rotating out of control, she was doing what she did best, adding that same structure. Only this time, Nikki wasn't sure she could handle it. How did you grieve for something that had barely started and yet had felt like it was her entire future? It had felt much more real than being a queen to people she didn't even know.

"I'm not going anywhere today, Mom. I can't. I need to make sure this headache is gone. I want to talk to my friends. I want to—"

"Get lost in the sorrow. I know. We both know what it's like, don't we? But just like when we lost your father, I won't let you fall apart this time either. You have even more people counting on you now."

"She has mere hours before her world is turned inside out. Let her be for the night. There is no one and nothing that will not be here in the morning," Alessia said, coming to her rescue.

Something felt off again, like it had when D'Angelo had pulled her into the castle wall, as if something dreadful was going to happen, and Nikki felt a wave of panic at it. That horrible feeling had been followed by losing the man she loved. The man who hadn't had a chance to say it back. What were her instincts trying to tell her now? How much more could she possibly lose besides herself?

Her mom's face flickered with irritation. If Nikki had ever gone against her mom's wishes when her dad had died, would she have seen the same annoyance? Or was this something new? Did it have something to do with a castle and an island she was somehow supposed to rule?

Her stomach lurched with a wave of nausea so strong she knew she was going to vomit. She scrambled for the door next to the closet, hoping she'd find a bathroom, and was relieved when it was.

She locked the door behind her, left the lights off, and ran what felt like a half a mile to the water closet where a toilet could be seen in the dim light of the semi-translucent windows. She landed on her knees in front of it. All that came out was acid and spit. She'd been too nervous to eat the breakfast at the basilica, and maybe that was a blessing now.

She sat back against the cool marble wall, knees to her chest, forehead leaning on them. The last time she'd had a migraine, D'Angelo had taken care of her. He'd exhibited a gentleness she would never have expected from the beast of a man. Except, he wasn't a beast. He may have done things people would call monstrous, but she understood them now. The honor that drove him. The inner need for justice to be handed down to those who wounded others. She wanted the same. She wanted to avenge him. To avenge Landry. To make all of those responsible pay.

Tears fell down her face. Drop by drop.

She pulled herself up, shed the priestess's clothes, and stepped into the shower.

It was cold for mere seconds, the iciness making her shiver but bringing back some clarity. Then, it was followed by heat. She washed her body with soap that smelled of lemon. The same scents that had filled the bathroom at the basilica. Scents of islands and flowers that reminded her of sailing with her dad in the Caribbean.

Was she destined to always lose the most important people in her life?

She has to lose her most cherished love, Alessia's voice echoed through her mind.

The pain was almost unbearable as it wielded its way through her.

Was the curse broken now? Was that how it worked? What should come after that? She knew, deep in her soul, there would never be another man who could fill her the way D'Angelo had. And yet, the crown would demand children.

The thought made her gag again.

She was jumping miles ahead. Her mom was right. One task. One hour. One day at a time. It was all she could do.

She wrapped herself in a soft towel, surprised to find a host of products in the bathroom cabinets that she loved. Her mom had done so much in so little time. Nikki's hair almost sighed with relief as she slid the conditioning oil and curl shaper into it. She'd been days without it. The frizz was almost unmanageable, but she wished she was back at any of the places she'd been without it because it would mean she'd have D'Angelo with her.

Her eyes closed against more tears, the hurt unbearable.

She forced herself to move, to keep putting one foot in front of the other.

When she came out of the bathroom, Alessia was sitting in a wingback near the door, and her mom was at the desk, talking into an old-fashioned phone. Nikki ignored them both, entering the closet and trying not to wince at the brightness. She found a dimmer switch on the wall and lowered the lights. Then, she looked through the stacks on the shelves and came up with a pair of lounge pants and a camisole top. Both were fancier than she was used to wearing to bed, but they would do.

Her mom was still at the desk, and the two older women seemed to be in some wordless standoff when Nikki reappeared.

"Can I use your phone? I need to call the band," Nikki asked her mom.

"We have one arriving for you tomorrow. The castle security will sync it for you," she said as she rose and pulled her smartphone from the pocket of her dress pants.

"How do you… How did you do all this so quickly?" Nikki asked, a furrow to her brows.

Her mom had the grace to look momentarily chagrinned. "Once Alessia explained things to me at the wharf yesterday and brought me here, the prime minister and I had a meeting. We knew you'd have nothing when you arrived, so we started the wheels in motion."

Nikki took the phone that was offered. Alessia was already rising from her chair and leaving the room in order to give her some privacy, but her mom stayed. She wouldn't have left at all if Nikki hadn't asked her to leave, and when she did, she looked unhappy about it. Something nasty twisted in Nikki's gut all over again. Since Clarissa had entered her life, she'd been nothing but kind. A good mom. She'd talked with Nikki about boys and sex and how to stay safe. She'd gone shopping with her for award-show dresses and sailed around the world with her. They'd never had any enormous rifts, not even in her teen years.

But somehow, all of this, Nikki being a queen, had already altered them both.

It felt like another loss Nikki wasn't sure she could take. Another hit that would leave nothing but dust behind. Would that happen with the band as well? They had a tour to finish. One that was as much to honor Landry as it was to continue to show the world what The Painted Daisies were made of.

Even if they didn't hate her after this. Even if they wanted her to stay, how could she be a queen and a rock star?

Would *they* even let her?

Her jaw tightened, and instead of finding the point of the bird-of-paradise brooch, she juggled the daisy and bird pin, rotating them over each other repeatedly.

She typed in Adria's number first, hitting the video call button. It rang a few times before she picked up. When Adria's bright-blue eyes came onto the screen, Nikki felt a relief she hadn't felt in days.

"Clarissa? Oh, hi, Nik! You finally get signal again? How's the Mediterranean? Wait. Where are you?"

Nikki looked behind her and saw the canopied bed in the background.

"It's sort of a long story. Can you do me a favor? Can you start a group call? I don't have my phone."

Adria's eyes narrowed. "Have you been crying?"

Nikki's eyes fluttered shut.

"*Dios*," her friend said. "I'm going to hang up and start a call in the group chat. I'll add Clarissa's phone in."

The call came back within seconds, and one by one, her friends picked up until the five of them were together again—virtually, but still together. Her chest swam with emotions as she realized just how much she needed them, and yet wasn't sure where to start or what to say. Her heart snagged painfully at the thought of telling them the truth. That she was responsible for what had happened to them…to the Kims…the loss… She rushed the words out before she could prevent herself from saying them.

"I know who killed Landry."

Silence for a beat. It was Leya who spoke first, her thick brows bending together. "Hang on. I'm getting Holden."

"Nik, what the feck is going on?" Fiadh asked.

Leya and Holden appeared together, squished into a single screen.

"Holden, do you remember when you told us about the feather that was found where Landry died?"

He nodded. "Regina astrapia. The island of San Fiore has an aviary full of them."

"That's where I am now…on San Fiore."

Holden's face turned grim. "You were supposed to be in Vernazza tomorrow. The detail is waiting for you there."

"You can send them here instead…but you'll have to have them work with the palace guard, the *Cavalieri*."

A chorus of confused comments and demands rushed over each other.

"Angel Carter…he works for the *Cavalieri*, doesn't he?" Holden asked over the top of the female voices, eyes boring into her.

Nikki's eyes filled with tears. "He did. He… His real name was D'Angelo Castelli."

Holden's jaw ticked. "Was?"

"H-he…he died today."

Her voice cracked, and a single tear fell. One that couldn't be stopped and was followed by a rush of more. Through choked cries, she told them the entire story. Professor Maynard and the brooch from back in Grand Orchard, her mom's poisoning, and D'Angelo taking her. Holden cursed but held his tongue as she repeated everything that had happened and everything she knew to be true. They listened with only surprised interjections here and there as shock rolled off their faces.

And when it was over, there was nothing but silence once again.

"We're coming to you," Paisley finally said, determination in her voice that sounded so much like Landry used to when she took charge that it sliced through Nikki's heart. Guilt and grief and loneliness. "We'll fly from California to D.C. and pick up Fee and Leya, then we'll be on our way."

Everyone was nodding and agreeing, and the relief that filled Nikki at the thought of them coming to her was so overwhelming another sob broke free of her chest. But the relief was followed by remorse.

"Little Bit…I…" She couldn't even say the words. Landry was dead because of her.

Paisley was shaking her head, her own tears welling. "Don't. We'll talk when we're together."

Holden stepped off the screen for a moment, leaving just the five of them in silence. They were coming. They should hate her. They should be furious with her. Maybe they just didn't understand. Because of her, their entire world had been altered…and it might be again.

"I don't know what any of this m-means. For us…for the b-band," Nikki choked out with a heavy heart. More damn loss.

"We'll figure it out, Nik," Paisley said softly. "Together. We never have to go through anything alone again, remember? We promised each other that after Fee."

"We're on our way, Nikki," Fiadh said. "But I can promise, I won't be curtseying to you." Fee flashed her famous smile, the tease landing home as her friend had intended. It brought a small huff of a laugh from Nikki's lips, and she was grateful all over again for them.

Holden stepped back onto the screen. "The detail is on its way to you. The first few will be coming by helicopter, the rest by boat. I'm working on getting the jet fueled now."

"Th-thank you."

"Do you trust the people there with you now, Nikki?" Holden asked.

She glanced at the closed door. Alessia had insisted she could trust none of them. D'Angelo had known there was a leak somewhere. When she looked back, Holden's gaze was dark, and she didn't have to utter a word because she knew he saw the truth of it in her face, but she responded anyway, "No. The only one I trusted was D'Angelo."

He didn't like her answer. Didn't like that the man who'd broken past every single one of their defenses and wrought his own kind of justice had been the man she'd handed herself over to. But he didn't know D'Angelo. Didn't know what she did. Hadn't lived with him twenty-four seven for the most intense days of her entire existence and felt the love pouring from him.

"We'll be there as soon as we can," he said grimly.

They hung up in a rush of I love yous, the need to pack and be on their way motivating them all. The quiet when they were all gone felt like a sledgehammer, but she'd only be alone for a few more hours. They'd be here before she knew it.

She wouldn't have the man she loved. She wouldn't have the man she trusted most, but she'd have her friends.

She wouldn't be alone. Then, she panicked. What if they came, and something bad happened again? What if, by selfishly bringing them to her, they got hurt as well?

The blood pounded through her at a vicious pace.

But it was too late. There was no way they'd turn back now, even if she told Holden there was too much danger for them to be here. They'd force their way onto the island if they had to swim to do it.

She went to the window and drew the drape aside. The view was of the city below the castle, falling away to the ocean. The sun had set, and the colors were all muted when the island was usually full of it. "You took him…" she whispered to the universe. "I begged you not to, and you took him anyway. You can't take any more from me. I demand that be the end of it."

Then, she let the curtain fall and headed to the enormous bed in a room that was as foreign to her as this world she'd stepped into.

Nikki

IF YOU SAY SO
Performed by Lea Michele

ONE DAY AFTER

She was exhausted and had red-rimmed eyes the next morning, but she had no chance to tell the world to leave her alone. Instead, strangers opened her drapes and brought her breakfast as Alessia and her mom joined her once more. A simple navy dress was chosen for her by unseen hands along with low-heeled sandals. A team of people were sent to do her hair and makeup as if she was going to end up onstage, but everything they did was muted and natural whereas the band's makeup artists always made her look dark and stormy.

Nikki wanted the dark and stormy.

"The fast DNA came back," her mother told her as she came out of the bedroom. "It's clear you're related to the Fiorani family."

A tangled web of emotions hit her at those words. Despair and relief.

She didn't have a chance to even consider it, as an entire calendar of events was presented to her by a tall, skinny woman named Cerise who announced she was Nikki's assistant. Just like that, some unseen person had hired someone to help her without ever consulting her.

Her old therapist had told her to let her feelings out, to speak them, and once again, she knew how wrong his words had been. Just like back then, if she opened her mouth, she'd be screaming at the top of her lungs for days. It was only in burying them, hiding them, tucking them away, she'd fool them all into thinking she was holding it together.

So, she didn't say anything about Cerise or the schedule that took her to the temple and placed her on a chair on a raised dais to watch the plays, poetry, and songs for day two of the Transition. People stared, the murmurs through the crowd almost audible, but between the Reinard team who'd shown up and the palace guard, no one dared approach her—at least, not until lunch.

In a dining room that sat four dozen, she was presented to members of the Old Houses. Men and women and children who all ogled her and asked questions about her father and then, politely, the band. It was a sea of people whose names she'd never remember. Her mom was charming in a way Nikki had never seen her before. The reserved woman she'd been seemed to have bloomed into a vivacious flower, and she stepped in for Nikki whenever she lost her voice.

When she was finally allowed to escape, she was taken back to her room and dropped off like a child at her parents' doorstep. Cerise handed her a stack of papers. "I realized I should have prepared you better for lunch. Here are some bio sheets on members of the Old Houses and the parliament. Many of them will be here for dinner again tonight. If you need more information on any of them, let me know. I've scheduled you two hours of downtime, and then the team will be back to prepare you for the evening events."

The door closed behind her in blessed silence.

Her mom wasn't there, but Alessia had remained. They'd left the half-dozen men outside her door. Men who'd actually tasted her food before she'd been allowed to eat it. She felt like she was living in some historical romance or maybe an old-school spy movie come to life.

Nikki sat down in one of the chaises, head resting on the back, eyes closed.

"What do you need?" Alessia asked.

Her eyes opened, and she took in D'Angelo's mother, and sorrow swarmed through her. "Who was it today that performed your Night Priestess duties?"

Alessia's jaw shifted, and she looked away and then back. "Each of the high priestesses has a successor who can step in when needed."

"I'm sorry…you sh—"

"Should be here. This is what my son would want."

Grief swarmed through Nikki, like bees swarming, waiting to sting and bite and poison her heart until it stopped beating.

"How do you do it?" Nikki asked her. "You're so strong…"

"As are you."

They stared at each other for a long moment.

"Change into something comfortable. I have something to show you."

Nikki was so tired she almost refused, but she owed Alessia this. Anything. Nikki had cost the woman her son. It was the least she could do.

She was glad to be rid of the blue dress that had felt nothing like her, but when she looked in the closet for jeans, there were none to be found. Instead, she chose a pair of wide-legged, white linen pants and a black crop top she partnered with a pair of canvas shoes that made her long for her Doc Martens.

When they left the royal suite, they were followed by the crowd of security, demanding to know where they were headed.

"The aviary," Alessia responded, and it set the men off in a flurry of activity.

The walk through the gardens was quiet except for the clap of the dozen pairs of feet on the tiles and the twitter of birds. The humidity of the day before had dissipated, and in its wake was a cool breeze that ruffled the vivid foliage and colorful blooms.

The path ended at a tall, chain-link fence. The gate was opened by one of the security guards, and Alessia and Nikki ducked past them. The greenery inside deepened, tree branches covering the cage top. A bird fluttered past, startling Nikki. She let out a little squeak, and to her surprise, Alessia laughed softly.

The bird landed on a branch nearby, and Nikki held her breath. It was a Regina astrapia. The bird's head was a stunning mix of teal and royal blue except for its black beak with its dangerous point. The feathers below the aqua band at its neck were a shiny onyx that seemed to change from black to deep purple to midnight in the sunlight filtering through the branches of the trees. The tail feather was at least eighteen inches long, dipping far below the bird's sharp talons. The deep blue of it reminded Nikki of D'Angelo's eyes.

"He told me the scar on his chin was from one of the birds," Nikki said quietly.

Alessia's lips twitched, eyes squinting slightly. "He hated working here. But it was a good lesson for him. Not only that everyone has to clean up shit sometimes, but that, in the silence, you can learn a lot."

Nikki smiled softly.

"I'm not prepared—for any of this," she told Alessia. "I read a damn textbook at the basilica, but that doesn't really tell me what I need to know."

"And what's that?"

Nikki's head tilted. "Who to trust… How to be a queen… How to be someone deserving of this role that's been handed to me… He promised he'd be at my side, guiding me through it." Her voice cracked on the last few syllables.

"It isn't the same. But I'm here. We'll figure it out. I promise."

Nikki wasn't sure she believed in promises anymore. So few had ever lasted.

They walked farther into the trees, the breeze dying away and the heavy scent of flowers coating the air.

"Wouldn't it have been easier, with far less loss and upheaval, to just let the monarchy go?" Nikki asked.

Alessia seemed to consider her question. "The United States has its three branches in order to ensure checks and balances. On San Fiore, it is the same. We have the parliament, the crown, and the priestesses."

"You have a useless queen who knows nothing."

"Who will learn," Alessia said confidently. She pulled Nikki to a stop, hand going to her cheek. "I've lost my husband, my daughter, and now my son to the monarchy, Nicolette. And each of them would say the same thing. Their losses were acceptable if you can keep the balance on our island for a bit longer."

Nikki's throat bobbed as Alessia's eyes filled with unshed tears.

The woman turned and led Nikki farther into the aviary. There, they found a bunch of baby astrapias in nests guarded by several adults of the species. These adults' heads and bodies were black, lacking the color of the other bird she'd seen. These only had a band of teal wrapped around their chests and much shorter, less brilliant tails.

"Unlike other birds of paradise, the females of the Regina astrapia are the ones with the colorful plumage. These are all males. They guard the babies while the females are out hunting and gathering. Also, unlike other birds of their species, these live better in flocks rather than small pairings. There is always one female who is the leader."

Nikki swallowed hard, understanding the parallel Alessia was trying to draw but uncomfortable with it.

"When the leader dies, for some reason, the males all squabble amongst themselves until a new female finally takes over." Alessia looked from the birds to Nikki. "San Fiore has had males squabbling over it for too long, Nicolette. It's long past time for our queen to emerge."

Chills coasted over Nikki's skin that had nothing to do with the breeze.

"What if the queen was trained to be a flightless chicken and not a Regina astrapia?"

"Nature will take over. She'll find her wings."

They watched as one of the females came swooping in, a wiggling insect in her beak. She dropped it among the babies, and the male birds all stepped back. She was graceful and sure. Confident. Nikki longed for the bird's natural instincts to find their way into her skin and bones.

Alessia turned back the way they came, and Nikki followed her.

"Can I ask a question?" Alessia's voice was hesitant.

"Of course."

"Your stepmom… Did she know about all of this?"

Nikki's feet stutter-stepped. "I don't believe so. I'm pretty sure my dad did, but he didn't tell anyone. Why do you ask?"

"I just got the feeling…she was surprised but not amazed when I told her what was going on. And she's…"

"Swooped in and taken everything in hand?" Nikki said with a small smile.

Alessia nodded.

"That's Mom for you. From the day my dad first introduced me to her, she's brought order to our lives. Schedules and control. My dad was messy. Not unclean, but very disorganized, and after she moved in, our house was nothing but neat. It's what makes her excel as an executive assistant. She easily sees how things need to be put together and doesn't hesitate to do it."

"She's very good at it."

They didn't say anything else on the topic, but Nikki's mind prickled again, something worrying her that she wasn't sure she could name.

Back in the castle, Alessia left her alone inside her room with the guards standing outside. It was the first time she'd been that way in literally days. And while she should have been reveling in it, the silence became too much.

She texted the Daisies on her new smartphone that had been provided this morning just as her mom had said. Her content from her old one had been transferred over. It was almost as if she'd lost nothing when the opposite was true.

Not being able to sit and do nothing without falling into waves of tears, she picked up the stack of papers Cerise had left. There were dozens of them. Each one showed how the person was tied to the Old Houses, their birth dates, education, jobs outside of parliament if they had any, spouses, and children. An entire life narrowed down to a page. It even included hobbies and known food preferences as well as talking points she could use when faced with each of them.

It was strange, reading about someone's entire life in that way.

The last page was the prime minister's bio. He was unmarried and had no children. He'd gone to university in Italy and been stationed at the embassy in Rome before returning to San Fiore. He'd dedicated his life to the island, telling anyone who asked that the people here were his family. That they were the only children he'd ever need. Born in 1965, he was now the sixty-fifth prime minister of San Fiore. She'd skimmed past those details and down to his hobbies of gardening and snorkeling. Then, her eyes journeyed back up, resting on the numbers. Her heart forgot to beat for what felt like an eternity, and then a gasp of air escaped her chest.

If she hadn't been found and sworn in by midnight on the thirty-first, Battista Massi would take over the aspects of the monarchy that were left behind. The two branches would merge into one under his leadership. The parliamentary republic would mean he'd have the majority of the power…

And power made people hungry for more.

Was he behind this?

How could she find out?

The door of the suite opened, and she dropped the papers as if they were burning her. The team from earlier had returned—makeup and hair and Cerise. But not her mom.

They shuffled her into the bedroom, chose a cocktail dress of vibrant teal that matched the head of the Regina astrapia. It had a boatneck that landed high on her collarbones before drifting away into sheer sleeves. It fit her tight on the bodice and swung away at her hips to land mid-thigh. Semi-formal instead of formal. A dinner with members of parliament and not a royal ball. Although, they were all a twitter about what she would wear the day after tomorrow when she was sworn in and then later in the summer when there would be a coronation ball.

Nikki sat quietly, listening to them ramble as her mind spun with possibilities. How would she prove or disprove her theory? Who could she tell? If the prime minister was responsible, she would make sure he saw the gates of hell. She would find the strength. She would somehow manifest D'Angelo's own dark shadow to avenge him.

She hardly paid attention as the hairdresser piled her hair on her head, securing it with a diamond clip that sparkled in the light of the dressing room. Loose curls danced around her cheeks, and a few tendrils trailed down her neck. It was only when they offered her trays of old and expensive looking jewelry that she came back from her thoughts.

She declined the jewelry. Instead, she pinned the bird-of-paradise and daisy brooches to the dress. If anyone doubted her, even after the initial DNA had come back, the royal pin would be a reminder. She was a Fiorani. Her great-grandfather had walked these halls, had grown up on the island. She wished she'd been here with him. That he could tell her all the things she needed to know and give her some reassurance that she could somehow accomplish the dangerous tasks ahead of her. Instead, she'd attempt to gather strength and calm from the pin D'Angelo had bought her.

When the door of the suite opened, both her mom and Alessia arrived inside. They both wore black dresses. Her mother's was demure, covering her from neck to floor, but Alessia's was bold and sexy. Even though she was wrinkled and her hair showed the gray of her years, her body didn't reflect it. She was shaped and toned. In fact, both women were fit and strong.

"All I'm saying is that you should go back to the basilica. To your family. They can help you with funeral arrangements and help you grieve."

Nikki's heart plummeted at her mom's words. "Did they… Did they find his body?"

Alessia's eyes were pained when she found Nikki's. She shook her head, and it was stupid relief that filled Nikki again. She knew better. She knew he hadn't made it through the fall, but without a body, she could hope. She could let the little niggle at the back of her head exist. It was ludicrous. It was only going to hurt more when he never returned, but she couldn't help it.

Her phone buzzed, and she looked down at the incoming text in the group chat.

> *ADRIA: We've landed in Nice. We'll be there in just a couple of hours. How are you doing?*

> *FEE: You can't ask her that, Ads. She's a mess, of course. Just hold it together a little longer, Nik. Then you can lean on us and*

break down all you want.

She smiled.

LEYA: Stop bickering over her. It's the last thing she needs.

MOM: Nikki is stronger than any of you think. She has a dinner to attend, but she'll see you when you get here.

Nikki was startled by her mom responding for her, startled to see her in the chat until she remembered she'd had Adria add her to it yesterday in order to hold the group video call with her mom's phone.

When she looked up, her mom was putting her phone away in a small clutch.

"You look lovely," she said, crossing over and kissing Nikki on the cheek. "But do you think two brooches are necessary?"

Her fingers fluttered over the edges of the costume jewelry. "D'Angelo gave it to me."

Her mom's lips thinned out, unhappily, but when Nikki's eyes met Alessia's, they had flooded with tears. Shouldn't it be the opposite? Shouldn't Alessia have pursed lips, angry Nikki was the reason her son was dead? And shouldn't her mom be sad for her that she'd lost someone important to her?

Everything was wrong. Everything was a mess. Nothing felt like the truth. It was as if the dream she'd been living since D'Angelo had taken her was continuing. That alternate universe she'd stepped into had become a dark underworld full of demons, and ghosts, and people who weren't themselves and yet were.

Just like her.

She was somehow still Nikki and yet someone different too.

She wasn't sure which version hurt the most. But all the versions of her—from the romantic little girl who'd lost a dad, to the tormented rock star, all the way to the fumbling, fledgling queen—burned for one thing. They all wanted to see those who'd taken D'Angelo destroyed, no matter the price.

Chapter Thirty-eight

D'Angelo

KING

Performed by The Hall Effect

It was the pain that forced him awake first. That and a nagging feeling he'd forgotten to do something. Left something undone. He attempted to move, and spirals of agony lurched through his left shoulder and arm. When he reached out to massage them both, his fingers and palms screamed at him. They felt raw, as if there was nothing left but muscle and bone without skin like when he'd had his fingerprints removed.

His eyes blinked open but found more darkness in the space around him. A chill filled the air along with a breeze. It smelled like damp earth and salt water. A repeated dripping sound penetrated the silence.

Memories slowly funneled in. Ones he shouldn't have of Nicolette moving beneath him. Naked, face full of desire and love.

He sat, and his entire body protested.

The castle wall. The men.

Fuck.

He'd gone over.

"Take it slow and easy," a voice in the darkness said—a voice he tried to assemble with a name but struggled to do so.

A flame flickered, and a lantern was lit.

They were in a tunnel. One of the many that had been left behind by the old mines.

A web of them crisscrossed the island. Not just above the water, but below, like the ones he and Nicolette had arrived in.

From the shadows, a man in black stepped out. Luther. The *Gran Duca*.

D'Angelo looked down at his body. His left arm was in a sling, plastered to his chest. His hands were wrapped in gauze. He remembered dragging them along the castle wall and then the cliffs as he'd tumbled head over ass on the way down, desperate to find purchase, to find anything that would slow his descent into the water and rocks at the bottom. He'd barely caught some, but none had been able to stop him.

Nicolette's voice screaming his name had landed in his chest, along with his failure, right before the water had slammed into him and knocked the breath from his lungs.

"Nicolette?!" he demanded. His voice was rough and scratchy, barely an echo in the dark, making him more of a shadow than ever before.

"Alive. Well. Installed in the castle. The brooch and her fast DNA have proven her to be exactly who you suspected."

Relief and fear pummeled him at the same time, and he tried to move again. He wasn't in the gladiator outfit he'd been in on the castle wall. He was in the uniform of the palace guard, the *Cavalieri di Reali* branch of the knights. Midnight-blue pants so dark they looked black in this light and a double-breasted jacket with buttons of turquoise.

"Why the fuck am I here?" He tried to stand, but he was unsteady and had to use his hand against the rock to keep from falling. His palm screamed at the touch.

"To hide you. They think you're dead, and I chose to keep it that way."

D'Angelo's eyes jerked to the man who'd led the *Cavalieri* for two decades, who'd been his father's best friend, an uncle. A man who'd trained him. Teased him. Anger welled within him along with a searing sense of betrayal. "You're the traitor."

Luther's eyes narrowed. "No. But I can see how you might think so."

"Rey told you everything. About Nicolette and how we'd be arriving at the castle."

"Yes, my wife told me, but not so I could betray you. So I could protect you."

D'Angelo laughed darkly.

"Tell me who you suspect," Luther demanded, handing him a bottle of water he pulled from a backpack much like the one D'Angelo had been hauling around for years. One the *Cavalieri* had trained him to keep loaded with everything he could possibly need to defend and disappear.

D'Angelo leaned up against the rock, drinking the water and watching the shadows as the lantern sent flickering tendrils of light along the walls. It was the stuff nightmares were made of. Like an opening to hell. Like the one that waited for him in his sleep.

"If I knew, they'd be dead," he finally responded, barely glancing at the other man.

"And you've not ruled me out yet."

D'Angelo gestured around the cave, and every motion hurt. He fucking didn't care. He had to get back to her. He'd climb that damn wall he'd tumbled down if he needed to, but he was going to be at her side.

"You've been out for a day. The rescue sub found you in the water. They thought you were dead, but once I realized you were alive, I had you brought here. There are only three of us who know you made it out of the ocean."

The barely leashed anger he'd felt since waking and finding Luther grew into a blazing inferno as the realization hit him. "You're using her to bait them."

Luther nodded. "They'll make a move, confident you aren't there to protect her."

"Take me to her."

"This is a better plan, D," Luther responded, and the nickname stung. Only his father and Luther had ever called him it. Never his mom or his sister. It had been a sign of brotherhood. Of men he respected and who loved him. Who'd taught him everything he knew and also how to survive the greatest of losses.

"Tell me everything that's happened in the last week," Luther demanded.

D'Angelo's eyes narrowed. "You should already know. I sent it all through the *Comandante*."

Luther's arms, muscled and strong even in his early fifties, crossed over his chest, and his face turned grimmer in the darkness. "As soon as Rey told me what the man who attacked you in the tombs said, I suspected. It's why I was kept in the dark about your moves. Probably many of the moves you've made in the last few years. You were too close, and he didn't want me to find out as well."

D'Angelo's chest tightened. He hadn't listened to the doubts. He'd kept them to himself until he could prove or disprove it, and it had cost them dearly. He'd placed himself and Nicolette at greater risk because he'd thought he was smarter, faster, stronger than anyone who'd come at them, and it had all backfired. He'd been a lone wolf for too long, forgetting there was a pack that could hungrily back him up. Forgetting that, sometimes, the only way to survive was with the pack at your side.

He could blame it on the betrayals at the marina and in Albenga, but the truth was, he'd worked alone whenever and however he could for much longer than that. He'd hated using the *Cavalieri* contacts in Monaco. He'd built a life where he kept his lips tight and as much knowledge as he could to himself.

He'd preferred it that way. He'd thought he was

protecting her, and the *Cavalieri,* and people he cared about, but really, he'd just been protecting himself.

Luther bent and picked up the lantern from the ground. "Come on. There's someone I want you to meet. Someone with a very interesting story to tell."

"Who?" D'Angelo asked, falling into step behind his leader as every bone and muscle in his body protested.

"Jerome Barry."

Chapter Thirty-nine

Nikki

ROLLING IN THE DEEP
Performed by Adele

The chair at the head of the table was empty, just as it had been at lunch. Cerise had explained it was in honor of King Sergio. It would remain that way until Nikki was sworn in as queen. Across from her was the prime minister, and next to her was the leader of the prime minister's rival party. The same man who'd greeted her the day before on behalf of the Old Houses—Cosimo Bianchi.

She was surrounded by people she didn't know, just as she had been earlier.

Her mom and Alessia were farther down the table.

She was in a crowded room, and yet she felt incredibly alone. She was nervous, and it had much more to do with her suspicions than the fact she sat at a table full of strangers.

She was doing her best to keep the anger and distrust she felt underneath a cool façade. She didn't want to tip the prime minister off and start something before she knew how to end it. She wasn't sure how Battista Massi could have found out their secrets enough to betray them. He still had to have someone in the *Cavalieri* working for him because it felt unlikely that D'Angelo would have mentioned anything to anyone outside the brotherhood.

"Your Highness," Cosimo said, and it took her a beat too long to realize he was talking to her. She didn't think she'd ever get used to being called that. "Is it true Castelli was working for the *Cavalieri*? You see, most of us thought he'd thrown off a century's worth of traditions after his father died and gone his own way."

"Cosimo," the prime minister growled a warning, and the older man just waved him off.

Nikki frowned as confusion added to the butterflies flitting through her. "That's what he said, but why would no one know?"

Cosimo chuckled. "Ah. It's true, then. You've proven it for me."

"This is hardly the time," Massi grunted.

"What did I prove?" she asked.

"The *Cavalieri* has three branches instead of two. They have the very visible palace guards known as the *Cavalieri di reali*, and our small military force known as the *Cavalieri del fiore santo*, but there have always been rumors of a secret branch—the *Cavalieri d'Oro*."

"The Golden Knights," Nikki said softly. That was the group Holden had said he was researching for its ties to Angel Carter. The one Professor Maynard had been trying to find information on as well.

"It explains the black hole in the *Cavalieri* funds I've been complaining about for the last five years, Prime Minister," Cosimo retorted, and in his words, Nikki heard the steel of a long-held feud. These men had been fighting for years, and Nikki had inadvertently given one power over the other. This was exactly why she wasn't qualified to be their queen. She didn't understand any of it—the politics, the economy, their culture, or their religion.

"Don't be ridiculous," Battista grunted out dismissively, the grunt a contradiction to his naturally cheerful-sounding voice.

Cosimo turned to her, nudged her arm gently with his elbow, and winked. "As *Comandante* of the military, our prime minister here would know all about the secret organization and be able to funnel the money into it. I've demanded transparency, and he's insisted I'm an old foddering fool, losing my mind."

Nikki's breath got caught in her throat, and she tried valiantly not to show any of the emotions warring inside her. Fury. Fear. Redemption. D'Angelo had been working with a man he called the *Comandante*. She'd read in the text book that the prime minister had a role in the military, but she hadn't read that title anywhere. Maybe because the book had been in English instead of Italian? She pulled her brows together, pretending naivety. Pretending she was nothing more than an innocuous rock star. "I'm completely in the dark, *Signor* Bianchi. Are you saying the prime minister is also in charge of the military?"

"Centuries-old tradition. I suppose it's much like your United States president being Commander in Chief, except our *Comandante* has a much more active role. Don't you, Massi?"

Nikki fought the desire to stand, point her finger at the prime minister, and declare him a traitor. They'd all think she'd lost her damn mind. Her eyes traveled down the table to where Alessia was seated, and much as her son always seemed to feel her eyes on him, his mother turned to catch her stare. Her brows drew together, head tilting as if asking *what*. A servant approached her and whispered something in her ear. Alessia stilled completely and then nodded.

Nikki watched as she rose from her chair, making her way around the enormous table. She placed a cool hand on Nikki's shoulder, leaning in to say softly, "I'm so sorry. I've been called back to the basilica for an emergency. But I will check in with you again before you go to sleep."

Her eyes bore into Nikki, as if trying to tell her something, but Nikki was at a loss as to what. Alessia's hand moved slightly, grazing the daisy pin before pulling back. Nikki didn't understand… What was she trying to tell her?

"Thank you for staying with me for so long. I know you must have things to…just please take care of you. He would have wanted that," Nikki said, confusion drawing her brows together.

Alessia's eyes fluttered closed and then open again, and then she simply nodded and left.

When Nikki turned back around, the prime minister was watching Alessia exit with a thoughtful expression on his face. He looked over his shoulders, signaling to one of the palace guards at the windows. When the man joined him, he whispered something to the guard. The man nodded and left, and Nikki's heart sped up. She didn't have Alessia's phone number to warn her. Hell, she didn't even have her phone. She'd left it, at her mom's request, in the suite. She couldn't leave now to go get it, and she'd have little chance after dinner either, as she was expected in the banquet hall to visit with the guests.

But she knew she needed to tell Alessia her suspicions. She needed help to prove it.

She itched to get up and leave, to run from the room and find what they needed, but instead, she was forced to sit through course after course as her anxiety grew—for Alessia and for herself. If Battista was really in charge of the anti-royalists, he wouldn't stop. Not yet. Not until she was dead.

It was with relief that the dessert was finally cleared, and she was allowed to rise and head toward the door. Her guards led her down the golden halls to another gigantic room. Much like the throne room, this one was lit with chandeliers and elaborate paintings above the mosaic tile floor. The walls here were painted with scenes depicting the three Transitions. The people in them wore togas and sandals, but the men pulling the chariots looked incredibly like D'Angelo had yesterday. It stabbed at her heart, tearing into muscles that felt bloody and bruised.

She buried it to focus on the anger. To find a way to

prove Battista was the traitor and get revenge for D'Angelo, her father, and Landry. All the people who'd died fighting for this cause. She turned away from the paintings to the fourth wall where a raised stage held a small string quartet playing lilting music. It was soft and beautiful. It should have evoked serenity and peace, and yet, all Nikki could feel and see were the shadows lurking. And these shadows were nothing like D'Angelo. There was no honor in them like he'd brought to the darkness. No justice. Only self-serving malevolence.

Tonight, unlike this afternoon, Cerise stayed at Nikki's side, introducing each person as they approached, and she was grateful for it. The stack of bio sheets was a blur in her mind, only one standing out. The one she needed to understand the most. Her eyes drifted to the prime minister. He was laughing, the sound jovial, almost like Santa Claus, except he was not the rounded, full-bellied Santa the kids in the U.S. celebrated. Instead, he was long, and tall, and thin. An anti-Santa.

Another hour went by before a chime rang out, and like wind-up toys who'd reached the end of their spring, the people left all at the same time. Like a concert coming to an end, the audience knew they weren't going to get an encore and all filed out together.

Soon, it was just her guards, Cerise, her mom, and the prime minister left.

Cerise stepped forward and said, "I'm just going to go check on the band's arrival for you."

As her assistant left the room, Nikki turned to do the same, but the prime minister stopped her with a hand to her elbow. The touch sent an automatic wave of revulsion through her, stunning in its force. "Your Highness, if I could have a moment of your time. I'd like to discuss Cosimo and the *Cavalieri.* There is danger to all of us if he's allowed to proceed with his ignorant claims."

Indecision warred within her. There was no way she should meet with him alone, and yet how else was she to gather proof? She could almost hear D'Angelo's voice telling her not to go with him. He'd hate it. But then, he'd also have a plan. That was what she needed as well. So, instead of going with him and attempting to scratch his eyes out or slamming her heel into his rib cage and up into his lungs, she said, "Can it wait until tomorrow? It's been a very tiring day."

"Tomorrow will be full of Transition activities, the swearing-in, and knowing you, you'll want to spend any other available moments with the band," her mom said.

Danger signs were zipping through her chest. As if suddenly sensing her worry, her mother put her arm through Nikki's—the first touch she'd had from her all day. "I'll come with you."

There was no way she wanted to put her mom in the line of fire, but if there was anyone she could trust to know her way around a fight other than her detail, it would be her mom. So, Nikki allowed herself to be drawn from the banquet hall and down a corridor into a less-ornate wing of the castle.

Her pulse banged wildly when her Reinard security was asked to remain at the end of the hall as the palace guards took over the last few steps to the prime minister's office. They cleared the room and then took up their posts outside.

The room was a mix of cherrywoods and teak. The side walls were lined with floor-to-ceiling bookshelves, and—as everywhere on San Fiore—gold highlighted all the furniture. Deep-red brocade fabrics lined the chairs and the curtains on the tall windows behind the oversized desk. It was elegant, and yet dark. Almost oppressive.

Battista had entered the room first, so he was already behind his desk with a drawer pulled out by the time the door shut behind her. He pushed something inside, and a portion of the bookshelves opened. Nikki barely had time to register what was happening when a body came tumbling out, landing on the floor at her feet with a thud.

She gasped, jumping back just as a second body

emerged from the opening. Her entire being convulsed with anger, fear, and disgust as Oliver Maynard stepped into the room. Her fists went up automatically, and he eyed them with a sneer. His greasy hair was pulled back in a ponytail, and his goatee looked even more ragged. In his hands, a knife twirled. The notched wooden handle had a long cord tied to the end, and as he flipped the weapon, the rope caught on the tip—or rather, what was left of the tip. It was broken off, leaving the edge ragged. Her lungs forgot to breathe as the words about the weapon that had killed Landry swirled in her head—how it was marred and would be distinguishable.

She'd suspected it before, but now she knew with a clarity that couldn't be shaken this man had killed her friend. Nikki took a step toward him as fury flew through her, and Oliver's beady eyes flickered with interest, as if he couldn't wait to see what she'd do. But a groan from the body that had hit the ground drew her eyes.

It took her several seconds to realize the face that had been pummeled into a bloody mess was Jerome's. He was tied and bound with a gag in his mouth. Her heart skipped a beat, worry coursing through her as she fell at his side, scrambling with the bindings. "Jerome! Oh my God, are you okay?"

"You'll need to keep your voice down, Your Highness," Battista's charmingly cheerful voice said. She jerked her eyes to him, and the blood drained from her face as she took in the pistol in his hands.

"Why…why have you hurt him?"

"Me? Why I stopped the man who killed your friend, killed you, and who I killed in return."

A lump formed in her throat that continued to make it hard to breathe. D'Angelo had thought Jerome might have been the one hired to kill Landry. She'd known it couldn't be true, but others would believe it. Jerome would be blamed when it was really Oliver all along.

As her mind reeled, trying to catch up with what the

prime minister had said, his other words finally landed home. *Killed you.* Past tense. Not tried to kill you. Not as if he'd stopped it…but as if it was going to happen. A foregone fact. Nikki slowly rose to her feet, stepping between her mom and the man with the gun.

The anger that had been brewing in her all day bubbled to the surface, causing her body to shake. D'Angelo and the rest of the *Cavalieri* had trusted this man, and he'd turned on them. He'd hired the weasel in front of her to do his dirty work, and Oliver had made a mistake and killed Landry instead.

"Mom. Run."

She'd throw herself in front of the bullet before it took her mom. She would not allow anyone else she loved to die for her or for this crown!

Her mom squeezed her shoulder from behind.

"I wish you hadn't come, Nikki. I wish you'd told D'Angelo you wouldn't take the throne," she said quietly, anguish in her voice.

Nikki did as well. Wished when he'd given her an out on the boat, she'd taken it. She could have had him with her right now. No one else would have died. She wouldn't let her mom be yet another one. The pain was too great already. Two lifetimes' worth of pain collapsed in on itself.

As her mom made to move around her, Nikki reached for her. "Damn it, no. Get behind me. Go."

But her mom didn't stop. She pulled away and walked past Oliver, who didn't even budge, and straight up to the desk while Nikki's heart banged in her chest, and terror locked her feet in place. The gun in Battista's hand didn't move to follow her mom, even as she rounded the corner. Even when she stood beside him.

Confusion bled through her.

"I tried to save you, Nikki."

Her mom's mouth had moved. Words had come out.

Words that registered somewhere in her brain, but it was her heart that actually listened, tearing in half, bleeding as reality came crashing in.

"These look ridiculous, Brita." She watched in horrified shock as the prime minister reached up and took the glasses from her mom's face and tossed them on the desk.

"Who the hell are you?" Nikki breathed out, the anguish and pain mixing with anger.

Battista's face twisted into a wry grin. "Those were my exact words the first time I met her at university. Brilliant and smart. As determined as I was to have the power no one thought we deserved."

Nikki's heart was banging violently in her chest, the wild rush of blood making her dizzy. She thought she might lose every ounce of the rich food she'd just eaten. And yet, she couldn't move.

"Why?" It was a tortured cry she hated herself for. More weakness her father had told her never to show. "You said you loved me—us!"

The burn of salty tears filled her eyes, and she fought against them just as she willed her feet to move, but they didn't. Instead, her brain reeled through dozens of tender moments she'd shared with her mom. Laughing with her over stupid shows… Shopping with her… Dancing to songs in the kitchen… Training together… Clarissa had fed her chicken soup when she could barely swallow. Those seconds, those memories, were filled with love. She'd loved her mom. Those bittersweet memories struck home, and she could no longer stop the tears as they rained down her cheeks.

"I didn't lie. I loved you more than I ever expected to. I told you I didn't ever want to be a mom, and yet the role fit me, suited me," Nikki scoffed, and her mom's eyes narrowed. "This is all your father's fault! He forced my hand when he told me he was coming to San Fiore after Sergio died. That his father had made him promise to not let the Fiorani reign end. If only he hadn't known. If only he hadn't told me he was coming, then he'd still be alive. None of this would have happened."

"You knew everything?! God…Dad?"

"That was a pretty neat piece of work." It was Oliver who said it, and Nikki took a step back as he took one toward her.

"Would have been neater if she'd done as I'd asked and killed them both," Battista snipped. He looked at her stepmom. "I knew you were too attached."

Her mom shrugged casually, as if everything happening was nothing. "You and I both know there's usually a way to get everything you want. I wanted her to live. If his brother"—she shot a disgusted look at Oliver—"and Castelli hadn't gotten their hooks into her, she would've gotten past the thirty-first and been none the wiser. We could have come here on vacation, and you and I could've picked up as we'd always planned."

"The risk was always too great to keep her alive, Brita," the prime minister's voice was scolding, and Nikki saw her stepmom bristle at it.

"Risky was hiring him." Her mom tossed another scowl in Oliver's direction.

"At least I've proven I had it in me to do the job, no matter how close they were to me," Oliver said. "I killed my brother. You couldn't even kill one girl who wasn't even related to you. That's why I'm here at all."

"Don't forget how bad you fucked up. You didn't even kill the right person that night in New York. Landry and Nikki look nothing alike," her mom hissed. "You almost led them to us."

"Enough!" Battista slammed his fist down on the desk. "None of it matters now. We have our scapegoat. As soon as you saw Jerome on the ferry, it was easy to see how it would all play out. Oliver will plant the knife in his pocket to incriminate him in the Kim girl's death. The money trail you created will lead to Castelli and the

Cavalieri d'Oro. No one will be in our way, and we'll have everything we wanted."

The words slammed their way into her heart. They were going to blame Jerome and D'Angelo for all of this? No. There was no way she was going to let them collar the people she loved with this. No way she'd ever leave this earth with those two honorable men's names being dragged through the mud.

She had to think. She had to find a way out.

Chapter Forty

Nikki

GOODBYE

Performed by Secondhand Serenade

She couldn't face them all at the same time and win. There were three of them with a gun already pointed in her direction. It was the worst-case scenario in her dad's eyes. But she also couldn't do what she'd told D'Angelo she would if faced with an opponent who outmatched her—she couldn't run because Jerome was there. He was alive. She'd seen the movement of his chest up and down. She had to find a way out of this for both of them, even though he'd never want her to stay. Just like D'Angelo, Jerome would tell her to get the hell out. But she couldn't.

As if he was right beside her, she could hear her dad again and feel his palm pressing against her chest. *This will give you more strength than any training ever can. Men have lifted cars off children because of it. It won't fail you when you need it most. Your heart will be the thing that saves you.*

Would it be enough? The desperate need to save the people she loved?

She'd never thought she'd have to find out.

"We'll need some bruises on you. People will have expected you to put up a good fight," Battista said, drawing her eyes for a second just as Oliver swung at her with first a fist and then the knife. She blocked both on instinct before stepping out of her sandals and then twirling in place to kick at his wrist. The knife went flying, landing near Jerome's battered body, and her mom—Clarissa, Brita, whoever the hell she was—huffed.

"I told you he wouldn't be able to take her." Clarissa's voice was detached and calm in a way that sent chills up Nikki's spine. She'd always thought the emotionless façade was her way of hiding her grief, but maybe…maybe she really was just coldhearted and cruel.

"Fuck you," Oliver threw out at her stepmom, lunging again for Nikki. She let him get close. She let him wrench her arm behind her, the pain jolting all the way through her shoulder. Just as he dragged her closer, she slammed her hand into his nose. The crack was audible, blood gushed, and he snarled out, "Goddamn it, bitch."

She didn't give him a moment to recover. Instead, she drove the edge of her hand in his throat. He gasped, reaching for his neck. She wanted this man dead. There was no remorse that came with that thought. Only rage and desperation. Maybe the guilt would come later, but this man had killed Landry. He'd killed his own brother. He'd tried to kill her. D'Angelo was gone because of all of them! Fury ran through her veins, and before Oliver could react, she'd kicked his kneecap, and when he bent to grab it, she shoved her fingers into his eyeballs.

He screamed, and she didn't let up. She twisted her body, using every skill she'd been taught to hit him repeatedly in every soft spot she could. With another howl, he turned to run, and she followed. She grabbed his hair and slammed his forehead into the bookshelf. Without another sound, he crumpled to the ground.

"Well, hell," Battista said, and it sounded like there was a hint of grudging respect mixed in with his annoyance.

"I told you not to underestimate her. Any of them."

Nikki turned to face them. She watched as her mom

unzipped the long black dress she'd been wearing to reveal workout gear. Nikki's throat bobbed. Too many memories filled her. Training with all of them. Jerome and her dad… Her mom… It hurt too much. All of it. She thought her heart was going to burst as pain blended in with the rage.

"They will have expected me to fight as well. I'll need a few bruises too." Clarissa stepped around the desk, and Nikki raised her arms in a defensive posture. The woman she'd thought of as her mom laughed softly. "Do you really think you can win, Nikki? Do you think I don't know every move before you even make it?"

"Just don't get in the way when I have to pull the trigger," Battista said, and Clarissa stopped, eyes narrowing.

"Don't you dare point that thing at me. You'll regret it."

He huffed out a laugh—that jovial one that made Nikki sick. "After over thirty years, you still don't trust me?"

Nikki stepped forward again, eyeing the door and thinking of the Reinard team that was just down the hall. Why hadn't they heard? Why weren't they here? If only she could get to them. Something brushed at her ankle, and she glanced down to see Jerome's eye lids fluttering. He was alive! In his hand was the knife that had fallen from Oliver's grip.

But in that brief moment, she'd made the mistake of taking her eyes off Clarissa. The woman moved in a graceful flurry, kicking out at Nikki. She barely responded in time to keep the foot from breaking her nose. Nikki lowered her body, twisting out of reach. The problem was, Clarissa was right. She knew Nikki too well, but Nikki knew her as well. They'd spent hundreds of hours like this rotating between offense and defense, and just like in training, now Clarissa countered each action, strong and sure.

Nikki inhaled, ready to scream and hopefully bring the guards, and Clarissa's fist collided with her jaw. Nikki took three steps back, head ringing, more tears springing to her eyes as pain went through her. She countered, and Clarissa batted her fist away. They swept around the room, using chairs and tables to gain height advantages and then flinging them to the side as weapons.

Liquid hit Nikki's cheeks, and she realized she was crying again. She hated it. Hated all of this. Hated fighting the mom she'd loved. Hated that power and money had brought them to this moment. Hated that D'Angelo and Landry and so many more had lost their lives for this. Thoughts of D'Angelo were what she needed. Not only because they fueled her, allowing her to hold off another vicious assault, but to remember the single lesson he'd given her.

She let Clarissa draw closer, dropped her body ever so slightly, and then she used her heel as D'Angelo had taught her, upward with a precise kick that would break a rib and puncture a lung...or a heart. Maybe it was misplaced years of loving the person in front of her, but she pulled back at the last minute, not using her full force. Her foot still collided, she heard the break of bones, and she saw Clarissa's face contort in pain, but she wasn't dead. Nikki hadn't killed her. Clarissa clutched her side, spinning to put a chair between them.

"New moves. Smart. But you shouldn't have pulled back," Clarissa gasped, her breathing shallow and pained.

Battista rounded the desk with his gun pointed in Nikki's direction. "Enough. Back up, Brita."

While she and her mom had been fighting, Jerome had used the knife to cut his ties, and as the prime minister got closer, Jerome swept the man's legs out from under him.

The gun discharged, and plaster rained down from the ceiling.

As Battista hit the ground, the gun went tumbling,

and Clarissa lunged for it.

Nikki was too far away to stop her, but as Clarissa bent to pick it up, a large shadow emerged from the bookshelf opening, and a boot-clad foot landed in her already broken ribs, sending her sailing to the ground. She screamed in pain, rolling to escape, and another booted foot sank down on her lower back, pinning her in place.

Nikki's entire being vibrated as the reality of what she was seeing hit her in waves.

"D'Angelo!" Her tortured sob drew his eyes. They were full of grief and remorse and love, emotions that mirrored her own. She took a stumbling step toward him.

The prime minister made a move, and Jerome landed a blow to the man's windpipe. Battista coughed and snarled as he rolled away, trying to escape, but all the bodies emerging behind D'Angelo made it impossible.

Alessia, Luther, and half a dozen other men all dressed in the dark midnight of the palace guard secured the room. Three of them pulled Jerome and Battista apart, and two more took D'Angelo's spot, holding down Clarissa.

And then, Nikki was in his embrace. Relief, and horror, and so much joy washed over her as D'Angelo's mouth crashed into hers. The pain and sorrow gave way to hope and love as she kissed him back fiercely. Every emotion winging through her was savage and raw. Too many, too much all at once. Good and bad. Sad and happy. She ripped her lips from his, hands finding his face, touching him to make sure she wasn't dreaming. "You're alive! God… You're alive!" And then she was kissing him again, wrapping her arms around his neck and holding on for dear life. She was never letting him go. Not ever.

He pulled her tight up against him, and she felt his entire body convulse, shaking like a wet cat in a windstorm. His eyes were dark and tortured, his voice gritty as he said, "I thought I was too late. The gunshot…"

Then, his mouth landed on hers once more, devouring her.

The Reinard guards, who'd heard the shot, shoved their way into the room, hauling behind them the palace guards who'd been at the door, bound with zip ties. It was chaos for a few moments with guns raised and loud voices while Nikki tried to explain she wasn't in any more danger.

Once tempers had cooled and weapons were put away, Nikki pulled herself from D'Angelo to run to Jerome. He was sitting in a wingback chair with two of the good *Cavalieri* hovering near him. She stepped between the soldiers and him to make sure they understood he wasn't in on it with her stepmom and Battista.

"He's not with them. He's with me!"

D'Angelo was at her side in two long strides. "We know, Nicolette. We know. They're here to make sure he stays safe. That he's taken care of."

She turned confused eyes from D'Angelo to Jerome. She touched her friend's face gently. "What happened? How are you here?"

It was Luther who spoke. "He followed you, and we held him for questioning. Once we let him go, they"— Luther glanced toward where the prime minister and Clarissa had been zip-tied—"took the bait."

Battista was growling and demanding a lawyer, but Clarissa was staring at Nikki with a weird mix of respect and love and hate that Nikki would never understand no matter how long she lived.

"You knew?" Nikki whirled around to face D'Angelo, heart screaming, tears flowing again. "Y-you knew about Mom?"

His eyes filled with unshed tears. Tears for her. And it almost shattered her all over again. He shook his head. "No, Nicolette. I didn't know."

"But you suspected?" The anguish in her was huge.

"I suspected Barry, but once Luther brought me to him, we understood what was really happening."

Nikki stormed toward her mom. "We loved you. All of us. Dad. Jerome. Me. God… How evil do you have to be to turn your back on that kind of love?"

"You'll never understand, Nikki, because you never grew up without power. You were always granted it. You were the center of everyone's universe, whereas I was the person shoved in a closet until I was needed."

Nikki stared at her. "What are you saying?"

"How do you think I learned to be so invisible, so plain, so out of sight? It was forced on me from a childhood where if you were seen, you were punished. I escaped. I escaped and made a life where I swore I'd be the one with all the power. Battista…he was a miracle. A godsend. A gift from the universe when I found him at university."

"What would you have done if Dad hadn't known? If he'd never said he was coming to San Fiore?" Nikki demanded because she couldn't help the tortured *what-ifs* that were swirling through her head and heart.

Clarissa met Nikki's gaze with a cold one. "When the clock ran out of time, I was going to fake my death. We had cosmetic surgeons set up to change my appearance. But once I realized he knew, the plan changed. It was better because it meant I was going to get to keep you and myself. I do love you."

Nikki's heart pounded with anger but also a deep sadness. She wasn't sure who she felt worse for in this moment—Clarissa or herself. "That isn't love… That's so fucked up… Love isn't taking. It isn't power. It's sacrifice and giving in."

Clarissa shrugged, pain creasing her face at the small movement. "You'll see. You'll learn." She glanced at D'Angelo. "Everything in this life is about power. It's the way we're built as humans. It's natural selection, after all. Only the winners survive."

Nikki was shaking her head as Luther stepped up between her and her mom. D'Angelo wrapped an arm around her waist, tugging her back into his chest.

"We need to take her to jail, Your Highness."

Her throat bobbed as she watched her mom, the woman she'd loved and cherished, being hauled out by multiple guards. The prime minister was behind her, making a scene, shoving his body around and screaming about lawyers and parliament and the fall of San Fiore.

A gurney had been brought in, and they were loading Oliver on it.

Nikki's stomach flipped. "Is he… Is he dead?"

Alessia looked up from where she was handcuffing Oliver to the gurney. "No. But he's probably going to wish he was."

Everything in her warred with that response—the piece of her that still wished he'd died, and the piece of her that was glad not to have someone's life hovering on her soul. She'd told D'Angelo they already had too many, but she'd wanted him dead. She'd wanted revenge for what he'd taken from her. She wasn't sure which was right anymore.

Then, she realized it didn't matter. All that mattered was that D'Angelo was here. They were both here. She squeezed his arm, and she heard him inhale sharply. When she looked down, she realized for the first time that his hands were wrapped in bandages.

She grabbed his wrist and whirled in his arms, bringing his hand up with her. Panic flew through her. How bad was he injured? How bad did it have to be for the Kraken, the god she'd seen him as, to have a sling on one arm and feel pain with the merest of pressure? "What is all this? What happened to you?"

"Souvenirs from trying to break my fall down a stone wall." His lips twisted up as if he was going to grin.

It was her turn to inhale sharply, the memory of the heights from which he'd fallen crashing over her. God, they were so damn lucky he was alive.

"That's not funny," she said.

His almost smile disappeared, and he said quietly, "You're right. Not one damn thing about any of this has been funny."

The knuckles of his wrapped hand grazed her jaw where Clarissa had landed her hit. It hadn't hurt until this moment, until the adrenaline started to leave and the reality of what had happened started to settle in. She'd have a bruise. Many of them. But the physical marks couldn't come close to the ones she felt on the inside. Those she wasn't sure would ever mend. They might bleed for an eternity.

Chapter Forty-one

D'Angelo

THE JOKER AND THE QUEEN
Performed by Ed Sheeran w/ Taylor Swift

D'Angelo's body had been full of agonizing pain since coming awake in the cave. Moving took enormous effort. But when Luther had brought him to where they were holding Barry, and he'd explained how his suspicions about Clarissa had been growing and intensifying, the internal pain had grown at a pace that eclipsed the physical ones.

Because D'Angelo had known. He'd known what this would do to her.

And now he could hear it in her tortured voice…the ultimate betrayal. It ripped through him worse than any bullet, grazing his heart, letting it bleed alongside hers.

He wrapped her with his good arm, drawing her body up tight against his. He bent his head, dipping to talk in her ear, trying to find a soothing tone when his entire being was rippling with fury on her behalf.

"Come away, Nicolette."

He wasn't done wreaking vengeance. There were more people to hunt down. More retaliation to seek. But right now, right in this moment, she needed him more than justice. And so, he'd leave his mom and Luther in charge until he could find the rest. For now, he'd just be with her.

She didn't protest as he pulled her from the study.

His mom shot him a look, the same mix of relief and love and fury he'd seen when she'd first shown up at Luther's tonight. He couldn't imagine what she'd gone through. But he'd forever be grateful she'd held herself together in order to be at Nicolette's side, and he promised he'd never put her through this again. Once justice was served, he'd find a way to pull himself from the line of attack.

With every bone and muscle in his body screaming, he held Nicolette up as the emotions of the night finally fell down upon her, and her body convulsed with sobs wracking her. At the landing that led to the royal chambers, a flurry of noise and voices had him placing Nicolette behind him and turning to face the stampede of feet. And then, there was her band, the men who loved them, and the sea of security Holden Kent commanded.

"Where is she?!" It was Fiadh who demanded it of him, her mahogany corkscrew curls flying about a face red with fury.

Nicolette emerged from where he'd hidden her and went flying at her friend. "Oh, Jesus, Mary, and Joseph!" Fee exclaimed, wrapping Nicolette in her arms.

And then all the other Daisies were there as well, arms and legs and bodies merging into a tight circle. Love and concern wafting from them so large that it was almost a visible cloud.

D'Angelo swallowed the lump of emotion the sight caused in him.

Over the tops of the women's heads, four men glared at him.

The women broke apart, and Fiadh whirled to face him. Before he realized what was happening, she'd punched him in the jaw with a closed fist. His head whipped sideways, and he took a step back.

"Oh, feck, that hurt!" Fee said, shaking her hand. Asher Riggs strode to her side, bringing her hand to his face, examining it.

"Damnit, baby. You hurt yourself!" His voice was

dark with barely suppressed annoyance.

"What the hell, Fee?" Nicolette left her friends' sides to put herself between D'Angelo and the others.

"He kidnapped you, lied to us, and then broke your fecking heart!" Fiadh growled.

To D'Angelo's surprise, it was Kent who came to his aid. "She's alive, Fee. She's alive because of him."

A rush of demands to know what was happening came from all of them.

"Perhaps we should do this somewhere other than the staircase," D'Angelo suggested.

His voice carried through the entire entry. Dark. Gravelly. It drew everyone's eyes to him again. They took in his sling and his bandaged hands, and maybe it was because he was injured, but everyone's faces seemed to relax ever so slightly.

He didn't want to care. Shouldn't care. And yet, it was suddenly important to him that they see him as something other than the beast who'd hung in the shadows of their lives for two years. He wanted to be seen as a person rather than a dark figure who'd caused people to bleed on their behalf. But he also needed them to know he would be at Nicolette's side, doing just that all over again if it was the only way to keep her safe.

Nicolette led the little parade of people to the royal chambers. It had been years since D'Angelo had been inside them. Not since his sister had lived in the castle. It brought back memories he couldn't afford, more emotions he was barely containing already.

The women huddled together on the sofas as Nicolette tried to explain what had happened in the prime minister's office. She lost her words, and D'Angelo took over for her, trying to keep the mention of her stepmom down to a minimum because every time her name was said, it looked like Nicolette was stabbed in the chest all over again.

Ronan Hawk, the man who'd hired her stepmom to

travel with them over the last few weeks, sank down on a chair opposite the band and ran a hand over his neat beard. "Fuck." Then, his jaw tightened, and he looked at Nicolette and said, "She loved you, Nikki. I swear on every ounce of my soul. The way she talked about you... She was proud of you."

Nicolette let out an anguished sob. D'Angelo stepped toward her, but Adria already had her pulled up tight to her chest as Paisley rubbed her back.

"Enough," D'Angelo announced, and everyone in the room bristled.

Asher raised a brow. "While we appreciate that you've had our backs from behind the scenes for a long time, Angel—D'Angelo, whatever the hell name you go by—you don't get to dictate to any of us what happens from here."

Kent stepped in between them. "Did we actually get a confession about Landry?" he asked.

Nikki nodded. "The prime minister hired Oliver Maynard to kill me...but he messed up." Another choked sob escaped her, and D'Angelo couldn't stand it anymore. He moved so he was behind her on the couch, leaning in and kissing the top of her head.

"*Stellina*...this is not your fault," his voice was even deeper.

She looked up at him. "God...but it is..." She turned to Paisley, tears running down her face. "I'm so sor-rry, Little Bit... She d-died..."

Paisley shook her head violently, pulling her into a hug that took Nicolette too far away from him again. Paisley whispered into her hair, "It's only the man who did it and the ones who hired him who are at fault, Nik."

"It could have been any of us." Adria's voice was clogged with regret and sadness. "It could just as easily have been Tatiana and the GNVL, Nikki."

"Or Smythe and For Greater Tomorrows," Leya said softly.

"Hell, it could even have been Artie," Jonas added on, his voice gruff.

Fee moved so she was kneeling at Nikki's feet. "It's over now."

"And from what it sounds like from Reinard's men, you beat the living hell out of Maynard. He's lucky to be alive," Holden said, respect and admiration in every syllable.

"Can we all have a go at him?" Fiadh demanded. Asher grunted his disapproval.

"You can watch him get justice at the hands of the priestesses before we turn him over to the U.S. government. He'll never see daylight again," D'Angelo promised.

"It will never be what he truly deserves." Ronan's voice was full of grief.

Nicolette sobbed again. Her friends surrounded her, and D'Angelo loved it as much as he hated it. He wanted to be the one giving her comfort.

But he'd have plenty of time to be there for her. He'd be there for her in the dark when the nightmares came. Nicolette would never be able to erase the mark on her soul from what had happened here. She'd never be able to completely forgive herself for the fact she was alive and her friend wasn't. That she hadn't somehow miraculously known it was her stepmom behind it all along. So, when the dark tried to take her, he'd be the one to show her the way back into the light, just as she'd shown him.

♫ ♫ ♫

It took way too long for the Daisies and their male entourage to leave Nikki and him alone. So long, that he'd started to shift from side to side, wishing he was at full strength and could shove each of the men from the room.

As they left, Kent nodded his head to the door, and D'Angelo followed him into the hallway.

"I trust you aren't leaving her side?" Kent demanded. D'Angelo gave a curt nod, and the former Secret Service agent eyeballed him and his injuries. "You in good enough shape to defend her?"

"No one will hurt her while I'm here."

"They already did," he said, and D'Angelo bit his cheek in order not to retaliate with words or fists, because the man was right. To his surprise, Kent's face broke into a weird smile—half grimace, half humor. "Don't feel too bad. Leya was taken from under my nose, and there won't be a day that goes by I don't hate myself for it. Adria was under my watch when the horde took her. All we can do from here is love them and shield them as much as humanly possible."

He turned and headed down the hall to where Leya was waiting for him, and he stopped to turn back. "You do love her, right? Because if you don't, you need to back the fuck off right now."

A growl escaped D'Angelo's throat, and Kent laughed.

He waved a hand and journeyed toward his fiancée.

D'Angelo stepped back into the suite into a blessed silence.

His phone buzzed, and he looked down to find a series of texts from the *Gran Duca*. They had file after file after file they'd retrieved from the prime minister's computers—lists of mercenaries he'd hired, names of those loyal to the cause. The man had been arrogant enough to think no one would ever come for him—or stupid enough.

D'Angelo's body tensed. He'd been arrogant as well. He'd thought he was prepared for anything, could handle it all alone, and in the end, it had almost killed them both. He wouldn't do it again. He'd join the hunt, but it would be with the others instead of in the shadows. And it wouldn't be tonight.

He sent a text back, letting Luther know he'd be there

in the morning. Then, he sent another to his mom. A simple *I love you* she was quick to return before asking about Nicolette.

D'ANGELO: She's devastated. But strong.

MOM: She's everything San Fiore needs as a queen, but more importantly, she's what you need. I was wrong at the basilica. I'm glad Rhaibele knew to bring you together. You have a heart ten times the size of a normal person's, D'Angelo, but you've been hiding it since your father and sister died. You can't do that anymore. Not only because I don't think she'll let you, but because she'll need enormous amounts of love after the betrayal she's experienced. Together, perhaps you can heal each other.

His jaw ticked, a mix of emotions filling him.

D'ANGELO: I'm sorry you thought you lost me as well.

MOM: Somehow, I knew there had to be more to your story. Maybe the goddesses were whispering it to me so I could be at her side.

D'ANGELO: Thank you for being there for her.

MOM: Enough of this mushiness. Go get some rest. I'll see you tomorrow.

The dark muscle in his chest, that he'd tried to deny for so long, banged and fluttered. Heartache and love twined together. He'd known Nicolette wouldn't be the same person once he got her to the island. She'd be required to be something different, more. What he hadn't expected was for those changes to be wrought over him as well.

He tilted his head as the sound of running water filled the room. His feet followed the noise. The door of the bathroom was ajar, and he pushed it open to find Nicolette in the shower. Her beautiful body, lean and muscled, normally tall and straight-backed, was hunched, face in her hands as more sobs wracked her body.

He reached down, undid his boots, and toed them off as his body protested. He shed the sling and his clothes and stepped into the spray behind her. He pulled her back to his chest, both arms surrounding her, his injured shoulder screaming.

"I've got you," he said softly, and her body shuddered. She turned to face him, arms surrounding him, going up on tiptoes to bury her face in his neck.

"Everything I knew w-was a l-lie," she said.

"Not everything, *Stellina*."

"My dad wasn't who he said he was. My stepmom was a murderer. I'm not even who I thought I was," she said, looking up at him with the saddest eyes he'd ever seen. He hated it. He wanted to go out and do something…wound someone…anyone who'd hurt her. And he would. He'd have every single anti-royalist hunted down and put in the ground or behind bars, whichever worked.

"You are exactly the person you were before. Brave. Strong. Resilient. Beautiful."

She stared at him for a long moment, and then she was kissing him. A tortured, heated kiss that stole his breath and pounded through his veins. Wet and silky and needy. And damn, did he want to pick her up, put her back to the wall, and join them together as they had been on the boat. He wanted to make her lose every coherent thought except the one that screamed his name, but his body wasn't going to allow him that tonight.

He slowed them down, the kisses turning into soft presses of devotion instead of insatiable desire. She looked up at him with those dangerously sad eyes. "I need you."

And he was undone all over again. Just as she'd unraveled him inch by mighty inch for days now, until he'd lost his damn mind and taken what was never supposed to be his and yet now was. He wasn't letting her go.

"As much as I'd like to give you what you need right here and right now, I hate to confess my body isn't exactly in the shape to do it standing in the shower. Take me to your bed, *Principessa*."

She stepped back, eyes going wide and really taking him in. He knew what she saw. The bruises covering him almost from head to toe. The scrapes all over his body from where he'd tumbled over the wall and dragged down it, wearing nothing but a damn gladiator outfit. The gauze on his hands that was now soaked.

She gently lifted his hands, unwinding the cotton to expose the raw muscle and bone beneath them. She gasped. "Oh my God."

She whipped around, turned off the water, and pulled him by the elbow from the shower. She grabbed a towel and dried him and then her off all while he watched with hooded eyes. She scoured the sink and came away with a first aid kit. She pushed him down on a vanity stool, stood between his legs, and then carefully and gently wound more bandages around each finger and then his palms.

When she was done, she laid a gentle kiss on each one, and he felt the salty tears that landed on the clean cotton.

She fell to her knees in front of him. "Nicolette," he growled. And she shook her head, pushing his swathed hands away when he tried to bring her to her feet.

"I thought I lost you…" her voice bobbed. Her eyes fluttered shut and then opened again. "I love you." He nodded, and his throat swelled almost shut as emotions filled him. One torn hand went to her waist, the other to her neck as he took her mouth in his. Soft, slow, a promise. A damn devotion.

"Nicolette Dariana Alberta Fiorani, you are my queen. My love. My life. I pledge the rest of my scarred, dark days to you and only you." She cupped his face, thumbs rubbing the corners of his mouth. Then, she placed a soft kiss on his lips.

"You'll be mine to command?" she asked, her voice breathless, sexy, and even with every bone and muscle in his body sore, his dick still throbbed at the sound of it.

"Whatever you wish…is yours."

She dropped her hand to his groin, and he swelled in her grip.

"This. On the bed where I can show you how you'll forever be the only person who can fill me up, body and soul."

She released her hold, and he let out a sound that was half whimper, half grunt, and her lips quirked up. Pride swelled through his heart at that small change to her expression. He'd offered her a brief moment of light, and that was what he wanted to do forevermore. Make sure she stood and basked in nothing but golden hues where no more shadows could reach her. None other than him.

She guided them to the giant bed on its raised dais, pushed him down on his back, and then straddled him. "Don't move," she demanded. "Let me do all the work."

It went against every grain in his soul, but he did as he was told.

He ground his teeth as she moved gracefully, beautifully, and sensually above him. Her body its own shimmering work of art that he'd gladly worship for eternity. With every move, the pressure built inside him, until he knew he was going to lose control, but there was no damn way he was going over first, not without her.

"Nicolette!" he growled.

And she went off around him, convulsing as pleasure coasted over her face in waves. The most magnificent thing he'd ever seen in his life. He'd attempted to hold his body still, letting her do what she needed, but seeing her like this—feeling her like this—it pushed him past any kind of restraint. His hips moved of their own accord, finishing the last desperate thrusts, until he'd shot into her, and his entire world narrowed to nothing but the vision of her face draped in love.

Chapter Forty-two

Nikki

PROUD

Performed by Lea Michele

TWO DAYS AFTER

Her eyes were swollen and gritty when someone opening the curtains on the floor-to-ceiling windows woke her. She was tangled in D'Angelo, their naked bodies more on display than not. She squeaked, and D'Angelo was instantly awake, arm drawing her behind him as he bound to his feet in a way that had to jar every single part of his battered body.

"Good morning, Your Highness." Cerise's voice was tight.

When Nikki risked looking at the woman, she had her eyes averted. But then they slid to D'Angelo before darting away again with her cheeks turning bright red.

Nikki didn't know if she wanted to laugh or storm in jealousy.

"I'll step outside for a moment," her assistant said. "But we have a busy day scheduled. We have thirty minutes to get you ready and out to the shops if you intend to pick out a dress for the swearing-in ceremony."

As the door had shut behind her, Nikki slid from the tangled sheets and put her arms around D'Angelo. Her forehead went to his chest, and one of his hands went to her waist. His other hand tangled in her hair, drawing her head back until he could look into her eyes while concern welled in his.

And that was when the grief hit her all over again. She'd traded the loss of D'Angelo for the loss of her mother. She had a million questions for Clarissa—or Brita, or whoever she was—and yet she also knew that none of the answers would ever truly give her the peace she sought.

"Lock the door," he said softly. "We'll stay here. You. Me. Skin on skin."

She smiled and barely held back an exasperated laugh. "This is your doing. You wanted me here, claiming the throne."

"That was before I fell in love with you. Now, I don't want to share."

Every vein in her body reacted to his deep voice saying the words she'd always craved. Heat coiled and churned deep in her belly. She wanted nothing more than to spend the day lost in his arms, but there was no way she'd let the sacrifices they'd both made, the people they'd lost, all be for nothing.

"Kiss me good morning, get us through this day, and then we can spend the night skin on skin."

He stared for a long moment and then kissed her. But it wasn't fierce as she'd expected. Instead, it was reverent and tender, heartbreakingly so, bringing unexpected tears.

A knock was followed by Cerise's voice. "Your Highness, we really need to get a move on, and the *Gran Duca* is here for *Signore* Castelli."

His face grew dark, and Nikki's heart pattered. "What does he want?"

"We have some more of the anti-royalists to round up."

"D'Angelo, your body… You can't. I refuse to let

you!" she blustered around the agony the thought of him facing more hands and guns caused inside her.

His finger trailed over her face. "I'm not in any condition to face them myself, Nicolette. But I will be behind the scenes. At the computer and in the shadows. I need to see every last one of them put away before I'll be able to sleep with even one eye closed. I promise, I won't be alone. Never again."

Her eyelids fluttered, and she shuddered before they opened again.

"You'll be back. For the swearing-in?"

"By your side, through it all."

♫ ♫ ♫

Nikki and the rest of the Daisies spent part of the morning in the boutiques lining the main thoroughfare. The army of bodyguards and palace guards who followed them were enough to notify every human in the vicinity of who was there.

Whispers of *"principessa"* filled the streets and the shops.

Nikki's skin prickled. Not so much unease, but discomfort.

Beyond the whispered name, it was the other things she heard that echoed through her chest like an anthem. Voices full of emotion murmured, "Thank Rhaibele they found her," and, "Finally, the curse will be broken." Those words left her almost speechless.

They made her start to believe D'Angelo was right.

The people wanted this. Needed this. Whether it was as some damn symbol or as a real person who could actually make a difference, she wasn't sure. But if it was truly what they wanted, somehow, she'd have to try to be both.

Fee made royal jokes, one after the other, to try and lighten the mood, but there was still a heaviness that lay between her and the band that Nikki couldn't shake. After they'd all found dresses for the swearing-in ceremony and for the New Year's Eve ball the next night and were journeying back up to the castle, it was Paisley who finally broke the tension. She stepped back from the others and twined her arm through Nikki's.

"It's beautiful here," she said quietly.

Nikki's throat bobbed as she nodded.

"I thought being spread across the United States was bad," Paisley continued. "Being on entirely different continents is going to be harder. We'll make it work though, Nik. I promise. For as long as you want. But I'll also understand if you need out. This…" She waved at the castle as they walked through the gates. "Your entire life blew up."

Nikki squeezed Paisley's hand. "Thank you for saying that, but I don't want out. I'm not sure how to make it work yet. But as long as you'll still have me, I want in. I have a feeling I'm going to need the music, and Fee, to keep me grounded in reality."

"It does feel pretty dreamlike here."

They walked in silence a few more steps. "I'm glad you're okay. That you didn't die… I wish…" Paisley's eyes filled, and she shook her head. "I can almost hear her, can't you? She'd say, 'Nikki's always been a damn queen. Now the rest of the world just knows it.'"

A little sob escaped Nikki, and a tear drifted down Paisley's face.

"I'm going to do everything I can to honor her…to ensure everyone on San Fiore knows how she gave her life so I could have mine."

"She would have. In a heartbeat."

And it was true. Landry would have laid down her life for any of them. She just shouldn't have had to.

They'd made it inside the castle where Cerise was anxiously waiting to take Nikki to get ready, but she pulled Paisley into her arms in a hug that was fierce and tight.

"I love you, Paise."

"Love you too, Queen Nikki. Go do your thing. We'll be here for you when you're ready."

They both wiped at tears and stepped away, heading in different directions down the golden hallways. But Nikki promised herself she wouldn't let the band be hurt by this. They'd already suffered too much.

Her brain started to whirl, and as she joined Cerise, she said, "I need someone to help me write a speech."

Cerise's eyes widened, and then she nodded, tapping on the tablet in her hand.

♫ ♫ ♫

The dress she'd picked out had reminded her of the *Regina astrapia* and the palace guard uniforms. It was a short-sleeved, black satin dress that fell below her knees and was accompanied by a midnight-blue cropped jacket with abalone shell buttons glimmering with teals and purples. The royal dresser pulled her hair back in a chignon that draped at her neck, but when the woman offered her the jewelry case again, Nikki refused anything except the two brooches she'd been wearing since arriving.

When she was finally led into the throne room, there was a small collection of people waiting—members of the Old House, the high priestesses, the leaders of the *Cavalieri,* and her friends with the men who loved them. There was one person missing, however. D'Angelo wasn't there. Her heart sank, her stomach twisting with worry, but she didn't have time to ask about him as she was led to the enormous thrones at the front. There, the three high priestesses held Rhaibele's scepter, a gold staff garnished with sapphires and diamonds, and asked her to join them.

She wrapped her fingers around the base, met Alessia's eyes, and tried her damnedest not to freak out. As the Mother Priestess, Rey was the voice of the sisterhood, asking Nikki to take the oath of the San Fiore monarchs.

Ten days ago, she would have run screaming. Seven days ago, she would have denied it. Today, she didn't hesitate. She was doing this for D'Angelo and her dad and Landry. For all the men and women who'd died trying to find her and protect her. She was doing it for an island full of people who believed in the monarchy.

So, her shoulders were back, and her voice was strong as she recited the words Cerise had helped her memorize. "I swear to uphold the laws and beliefs of the San Fiorian people and to be guided by Rhaibele in protecting the hearts and souls of all those who reside on our shores."

And just like that, she was no longer a rock star, not even a princess, but a queen.

When she let go of the scepter and looked out at the room, the gaze of one man caught her attention—D'Angelo. He'd shown up, just like he said he would. The night before, he'd been in the uniform of the palace guards, but tonight he was in the dress uniform of the military branch of the *Cavalieri*. The white jacket was hung with medals and ribbons.

Her breath caught.

He looked like Prince Charming—or some darker, more beautifully crafted Winter Soldier version of the fairy tale. The romantic little girl in her squealed a bit as they locked eyes across the room. She could see the glimmer in them. The promise. The heat. And when she stepped down off the dais, it was his arm that she took.

In that singular moment, somehow, someway, she knew the truth.

The storm had passed.

There was nothing but light and love ahead of them.

Chapter Forty-three

D'Angelo

MASTERMIND
Performed by Taylor Swift

Leaving Nicolette's side that morning after days of being twined together and after both of them nearly dying, had been more difficult than anything he'd ever done as his shadowy self. But he'd also been determined to make each of the men and women who'd turned on San Fiore, their queen, and their brothers and sisters pay. With their leader gone and the files Luther had found, D'Angelo had known it would be easier to do than ever before.

So, he'd gone to the command center, sitting at the *Gran Duca's* side, hacking into computers, obtaining search warrants in multiple countries, and sending out orders. By the time the morning rolled into the afternoon, they'd sent the police after mercenaries in nations around the globe and trusted the *Cavalieri* to pick up the remaining anti-royalists here and abroad.

They were almost done when Luther slid a paper toward him on the table.

It took a moment for D'Angelo to realize what it was. Dated weeks before his father and sister had died, it was a letter from the prime minister to an assassin in Italy, requesting the queen's death be made to look like food poisoning.

The paper crinkled in D'Angelo's hand, his desire to kill the man winging through him all over again.

"He couldn't risk her getting pregnant," Luther said quietly. He cleared his throat and kept going. "There's more. The boating accident with King Sergio…it wasn't an accident either."

"I'll kill him." The words were low and guttural.

"That's not where you're needed, D. Not by a long shot," Luther said calmly. "We may not be a capital punishment country, but you and I both know his life and the life of every anti-royalist we imprison will be hell. Even our criminals love San Fiore. They won't be gentle or kind. No one will. Until the day he dies, he's going to be in pain."

The words Ronan had spoken last night about Maynard came back to him. This time for Massi. The pain he'd experience in jail…it would never be what he truly deserved.

"Look," Luther said, shifting so D'Angelo had to meet his eyes. "There's no guarantee that some faction of the anti-royalists won't raise its ugly head again, or that the dogma they preached won't someday threaten the crown, our queen, or the people we love. But for now, for a moment, we have peace. And the place you're really needed is at her side. That's where you belong."

D'Angelo's chest twisted and twined. He'd promised his mom and Nicolette they wouldn't have to worry about losing him again. He'd promised himself he'd stepped away from the dark and into the light Nicolette had shown him. Luther was right. He wasn't needed in the shadows anymore.

"You need to hurry if you're going to make it to the swearing-in," Luther said, lips twitching with a sudden, unexpected humor.

D'Angelo looked at the time and groaned.

"You'll need this." Luther snapped his fingers, and from behind him, a sergeant appeared with a white dress uniform of their military. When D'Angelo hesitated, Luther kept going. "You aren't undercover anymore, D. If you love her and intend to be at her side, you're going to need to look the part. I'm sure we could find you a tuxedo, but you'd look like a stuffed penguin. This is better. More fitting of a prince consort, don't you think?"

D'Angelo bit back a grunt as the realization of the words hit him. Fuck. What the hell did he know about being a prince consort? *As much as she knows of being a queen*, his conscience threw back. His chest spasmed. They'd have to figure it out together.

As he jerked the uniform from the poor man's hand, Luther chuckled. D'Angelo flipped him off and stormed away to get ready.

Once he entered the throne room, once he saw Nicolette standing holding Rhaibele's scepter and reciting the oath with a strength and solemness every single person in the room could hear, he was relieved he'd put on the uniform. She deserved it. She deserved even more than what he could offer, but what he had would have to do because he wasn't letting her go.

As soon as she placed her hand on his arm, a calm filled him, easing the turmoil in his stomach, easing the bitter losses and allowing him to concentrate on the other emotions that would better serve him. The joy of her. The love he felt.

They were led directly from the castle to the round, pillared chamber of the parliament building where she placed a golden cape around Cosimo Bianchi's shoulder and swore him in as acting prime minister. They'd barely finished that ceremony when they were swept off again, this time heading to the temple where the songs and poems for the third day of the Transition were being performed.

The crowd that had shown up was even larger than normal. While San Fiorians always loved celebrating the Transitions, today it was as if the entire island had shown up, and it wasn't because of the rite. It was to see their queen.

D'Angelo's eyes narrowed when Cerise whispered in Nicolette's ear, a twitch returning to the backs of his eyes. Nicolette squeezed his hand and then rose, going to the temple steps and a podium that appeared from nowhere in front of the Dawn and Night Priestess statues.

No one had expected her to give a speech, and yet the podium and the notes in her hand made it obvious she was. His heart bounced around in his chest, the ache growing in him to wrap her in his arms and keep her safe. Worry growing about what she was going to say, and who had coached her, and hoping his people would see the light that emanated from her like its own star as much as he did, even if she made a mistake.

She looked out at the crowd that, he suddenly realized, wasn't just San Fiorians but also a whole host of the press and her friends. The Daisies were standing near the front, almost within reach, and they were all smiling up at her reassuringly. Nicolette ran a finger over her lapel, and he noticed that next to the plumes of the Regina astrapia brooch was the cheap daisy he'd bought her. His heart convulsed all over again, and by the time she actually raised her head to speak, he already had tears in his eyes and a desire to kneel at her feet in order to pledge all over again to be hers and only hers.

"It is with both a heavy and light heart I find myself on the steps of Rhaibele's temple, accepting the honor of becoming your queen." The crowd clapped, some cheered, but it wasn't the full riot D'Angelo knew his people could offer. They were withholding their judgment, and he wanted to scream at them to show their queen her full due, but instead, he bit his cheek and listened. "Growing up in the United States, little girls are bombarded with images of cartoon princesses who overcome great evils in order to take back their destiny. I never expected that to be my reality." She smiled, and the crowd chuckled. "What's hard to imagine when watching those cartoons is the disappointment the people of those kingdoms must feel when a stranger is brought into their midst to somehow lead them. That disappointment—that hesitancy—is what I know each San Fiorian must be feeling today. I can only humbly ask that you give me the opportunity to prove to you I am loyal, hardworking, and willing to pledge my heart and soul to each of you."

She looked at her band members who were holding hands, and he wondered if they'd already discussed what would happen with her and the Daisies while he'd been out dealing with the anti-royalists.

"As most of you know, I'm one part of the band The Painted Daisies." Cheers went up. "As I pondered today how to balance my old role with my new one, I realized something important. How can I possibly prove to you I will be a loyal queen if my very first act as one is to abandon the people and the promises I've already made? If I leave the women who are my sisters in the middle of a tour we built to honor our fallen friend, it would be a disgrace. Not only for me, but for all of you. Because, you see, my friend Landry…she lost her life so I might live."

Gasps and murmurs ran through the crowd.

"In order to continue to honor her, I hope you'll understand—I hope you'll grant me the clemency—to split my time between San Fiore and wherever my band of sisters needs me to be."

More shuffling went through the gathering. D'Angelo wasn't sure if it was good or bad, and his worn-out body tensed, instinctively taking a step closer in case he needed to haul her out of there if the crowd turned into a mob.

She smiled again. "I promise, no matter where I go with the Daisies, I will always come back to these shores. To you. To San Fiore and the home I intend to make here. Not only because you have crowned me your queen but because the love of my life, the man I want to be at my side for the remainder of my time on this earth, is here as well. His home has become mine, and I'm hoping he will guide me as much as Rhaibele, the priestesses, and our new prime minister."

She turned to D'Angelo and reached out a hand. Her eyes begged him, and he did what he'd told her last night he would always do—go where she commanded. He stepped up next to her and took her hand. She smiled, and even though the sun had already been shining, it was as if it came out from behind the clouds all over again.

She looked from him back to the audience.

"The Castelli family is not only one of the Old Houses. They've also sacrificed over and over again for you and for the island. As priestesses"—she waved to his mom—"as your former queen, and as a *Cavalieri*. I choose D'Angelo Castelli to be mine, but what should be much more important to all of you is that he chose me to be his. And if nothing else I say today can sway your disappointed, hesitant hearts, I hope that simple fact can. Someone you hold dear, a member of your beloved island, has seen me as worthy. Worthy of love and trust. Together, D'Angelo and I stand before you, hoping you'll let us lead a thriving San Fiore into the next few decades."

This time when she stopped, the applause was louder. The shouts and cheers more authentic. Real. But it was still not the joyous, unbound riot he knew his people could make. He couldn't blame them. They'd been through a lot in the last day. But what they didn't know was exactly what Nicolette had been through to be there before them, and he made another pledge, this one to himself, that he would do everything in his power to show his people just how lucky they were to have her.

♫ ♫ ♫

THREE DAYS AFTER

One of the many things his people did well was throw a party. With the Transition between the Night and Dawn Priestesses over after the lantern ceremony in the marina that morning, and the calendar year ending, the celebration in the banquet hall was almost over the top. The tables were laden with food and drink. The music was full of the Billboard's greatest, including many of The Painted Daisies' songs, and the dance floor was packed.

A huge grandfather clock, gilded in—big surprise—gold, had been wheeled into the center of the room with the hands ticking down until midnight. D'Angelo had been in this room many times for many parties, including New Year's Eve, but for the first time in over a decade, he felt an inexplicable anticipation for everything that was coming next.

He watched from the sidelines as Nicolette danced with her friends. They were all in tiny cocktail dresses, long limbs on display. Beautiful bodies moving to the beat, laughter on their faces. The band was doing their best to help Nicolette forget the betrayal of her stepmom and the deaths her role had caused. His throat bobbed as unexpected emotions hit him. Strong feelings for all the women, what they'd been through, and how they were there for each other.

He'd told Nicolette that she was beautiful, brave, and resilient, but it was true of all of them. They'd been through more in two years than most people experienced in a lifetime, and yet, here they were. Smiling. Loving. Giving of themselves to the world. Open and not closed. Fucking magnificent.

Tension radiated through him as four large bodies joined him. Asher and Ronan were on one side, Holden and Jonas on the other. Jonas handed D'Angelo a glass with an amber liquid in it. He hoped it was whiskey. He'd need it in order to stay calm if they started something. He wouldn't ruin Nicolette's night with a fight. In the condition he was in at the moment, he wasn't even sure he'd win.

"Welcome to the club," Jonas said, and all the men raised their glasses in his direction.

"Excuse me?" His gaze narrowed, taking in each of them.

Jonas's green eyes flashed, a smirk appeared on his lips, and he waved his drink at the others. "We're all upstanding members of the Daisies Ultimate Fan Club. Welcome aboard."

D'Angelo didn't really know these men. Not like he knew his brothers in the *Cavalieri,* but he knew a single truth about each of them. They'd die for the women on the dance floor.

When he didn't respond, Asher let out a half-laugh, half-growl and said, "As Jonas said when I joined, we can drink and commiserate over how fucked up it is to watch the woman you love being attacked, and how you'll never, ever feel like you can keep them safe when they're in the public's eye all the damn time. And with Nikki becoming a queen…I guess she's going to be the one out front the most. You're going to need help. Believe me."

His chest clenched. The man was right. He was never going to feel completely safe when she was onstage or in front of a crowd. Even with Landry's murder solved and the anti-royalists behind bars, there would always be people who wanted to see the San Fiorian monarchy crumble. People who would come for her and her family for money or pleasure or just to make a name for themselves. He'd told her as much on the boat when he'd given her an out. Damn…maybe he should have forced her to run away. He could have taken her to some secluded island where he'd have her all to himself.

Ronan saw his expression darken and gave a small shrug. "I asked last month if it ever gets easier. These assholes told me no, and I think they're probably right. It's always going to be hard to watch them from the sidelines, waiting for the worst to come at them."

Holden downed his drink, set the empty glass on a nearby table, turned to them, and said, "You're all wrong. We don't have to watch them from the sidelines, and we certainly don't have to wait for the worst. We get to sweep them into our arms, claim them while they claim us back, and celebrate every breath, every kiss, every fuck. So, that's what I plan to do."

And he left them there, sauntering out onto the dance floor, pulling a smiling Leya away from the others, and dragging her up against him. The two of them moved to a much slower beat than the music called for. Sensual. Making it clear to everyone in the room what they were. Lovers. Partners.

One by one, the other three men did the same. Drinks downed, stepping onto the dance floor, claiming the woman they loved. D'Angelo had already started moving by the time Nicolette turned around to find him in the crowd. They both moved to close the distance between them. She wrapped her arms around his neck, and he pulled her, one-handed, into him, hips colliding, heat already building between them.

A chime went through the room, the music stopped, and everyone started counting down. Neither D'Angelo nor Nicolette said a word. They just listened while the crowded banquet hall practically vibrated with the strength of the voices calling out the seconds left in the year.

The crowd was still at two when his mouth landed on hers. Fuck waiting until midnight. He wanted to make sure they were joined for each second, every heartbeat between the old and the new. They had a lifetime together, and he'd make sure that lifetime was long and pleasurable. They'd have a horde of kids and grandkids. They'd be in this room in another eighty years, celebrating new beginnings if he had any say in it. But this brief moment, the slip of seconds between heartbeats and years…this singular one was special because it was the first one they shared together as one unit, one entity, one soul contained in two bodies.

"Happy New Year!" the room screamed.

Balloons and confetti rained down.

And still, he kissed her. It was more than lips and tongues. Even more than hearts and souls. It was as if they'd slipped into a tangled corner of the universe where Rhaibele had twined them together. The light of a single star eclipsing a black hole and spinning it into something new. Something brighter. More powerful. An infinite beginning without end.

415

Epilogue

Nikki

ENDLESS LOVE
Performed by Stan Walker w/ Dami Im

SIX MONTHS AFTER

For the first time in weeks, Nikki woke and didn't feel nauseated. And that knowledge was pure joy. It made her want to run out and find every kind of breakfast food available and scarf it down. It made her stomach grumble in a way that had the large possessive hands resting on her abdomen shift.

Warm lips found the curve of her neck, scarred palms sliding up and over her naked skin, grazing the wildly sensitive tips of her breasts, and before she could help it, a moan had escaped. "Was that a grumble I heard before the moan, *Stellina?*" D'Angelo's deep voice asked softly as his tongue and mouth danced along her bare shoulder, and his fingers continued caressing her.

"I'm starving."

He rolled them in a flash so she was on her back below him, and he was propped up over her, dark-midnight eyes alight with love and passion and joy.

"You're actually hungry?"

A smile broke out over her face. "Yes, but in multiple ways now."

Her hands trailed down over the rippled muscles of his chest and waist, digging into his sides and trying to bring him down on top of her.

"No."

She huffed out a laugh at the seriousness on his face. "No? You do remember how it usually goes when you say that word to me."

His lips tried to twitch, but he held back the smile valiantly.

"You're hungry. That hasn't happened in weeks. Food first. Sex second."

He was already off her, and she blew out a frustrated breath.

Making love was one of the only things that had allowed the nausea to abate. Maybe it was the adrenaline rush. Maybe it was just the way her body knew to respond to his commands. She wasn't sure which was true, but it was the only thing that helped. For most of the first trimester of her pregnancy, she'd been so sick it had actually caused her to go running from the stage at one tour stop.

She'd been the last one of the Daisies to find her partner, the second to get married in a mad rush, and the first to get pregnant. It felt fast and wild and a bit absurd, but the baby was their own fault. They'd started having sex unprotected from the get-go and had never gone back to putting on a condom. She was surprised it had taken them as long as it had to make a baby. Now, barely six months after they'd first fallen together on the stormy seas, she was not only pregnant but well into her fourth month.

The pregnancy had taken D'Angelo's protectiveness to an entirely new plane of existence. He'd been unwilling to leave her side before, and now it was almost impossible to go to the bathroom without him coming along. Some women would hate it. Some women would beg for space to breathe, but Nikki had breathed alone for too long.

She'd felt the gaping holes in her life as pieces came apart at the seams, and now she simply loved having him with her. Maybe that would change someday, but she doubted it. Her world only felt right when he was nearby.

She finally realized he'd slid into a pair of pajama bottoms and was talking to someone on the phone. When he came back, he was holding her robe in his hands. "Get up, Nicolette. We need to feed the baby before you decide to go back to vomiting."

She rose, let him help her into the robe, and then turned and grabbed the waistband of his pajamas. "You owe me, Kraken. I need to see multiple stars for denying myself now to feed your hungry child."

He chuckled, eyes glittering in that way that happened more and more often, and then he kissed her, fierce and strong as he always did. "*Our* child. And I'll fit in as many visits to the heavens as I can before we have to get ready for the ceremony."

She was being sworn in again today. This time, it would be in front of the entire world as it was broadcast over every news outlet across the globe. After the oath she'd taken in December, her first command had been for the parliament to find out what the San Fiorian people truly wanted. Did they want the monarchy, or did they want it dissolved? A special vote had been held, and the results had been overwhelmingly in favor of the monarchy remaining. They'd chosen Nikki—or at least the Fiorani family—to continue on in its current role. She hadn't known if she'd been disappointed or relieved. In the end, she was glad the sacrifices that had been made hadn't been for naught.

When she glanced at the clock, she groaned. "None. You're going to fit in no trips to the heavens before the coronation. Cerise and the band are going to be here in thirty minutes. They promised me an entire day of massages and waxing and curling."

A rattling outside the door announced the breakfast tray being wheeled in.

He kissed her again. "Your sacrifice for the crown is duly noted, my queen, and it *will* be rewarded. I promise." He nibbled on her ear. "And you know I always keep my promises."

♫ ♫ ♫

D'Angelo was dressed in his white military uniform, the one that made him look like a fairy-tale hero come to life, and she was in a dress fit for a princess…a queen. It was made of gold and royal blue twined together, scattered with diamonds and sapphires. It was extravagant in a way that everything on San Fiore was, and yet simple because it was almost like the robe on the statue of Rhaibele, except without the diaphanous quality. D'Angelo would have had a coronary if she'd used the one the designer had originally suggested.

When the carriage stopped outside the basilica, the crowd was thunderous. The San Fiorians had come out in droves, and the entire island was full of celebrities and dignitaries. Her life had changed in such a short space of time that sometimes it was hard to catch a breath. So much lost and gained. The rips in her soul would always be there, for the people who'd died for this island without even knowing—like her father and her friend—but also for the ultimate betrayal that had cost her the mother she'd loved.

Clarissa—or rather Brita—had written her letters from jail. Nikki had read them, but she had been unable to find the truth in them because what kind of mother would hand her daughter over to be murdered?

Nikki put her hand on the tiny swell of her stomach beneath the gown.

This little bean inside her… She already knew she'd do anything to protect it. She'd give up everything and anything. What she'd never do was simply watch as a gun was pointed at it. So, no matter what Brita said, Nikki knew the truth. Her stepmom hadn't loved her.

When D'Angelo went to open the carriage door, she halted him with a hand to his arm. He turned, taking her in with a furrowed brow. "What's wrong?"

"I love you."

Every time she said the words, she was rewarded with pleasure coasting over his face, like on Christmas, when they'd shared the gobeletti, and he'd told her she tasted like joy. His lips quirked, as if he could hear her thoughts. But when he spoke, it was another memory he recalled.

"The first time you told me you loved me, we had another crowd waiting for us on these same steps, waiting for the procession."

"I said I was falling in love with you, not in love with you. And then, you promptly tried to die on me."

His smile faded, and his hand slid over her cheek, cupping it. "I'm not dying today, Nicolette. I love you with every piece of my beat-up body and soul. I'm not going anywhere without you ever again."

She wasn't sure why her chest was tightening and tears were threatening. Maybe it was the damn hormones. She'd already taken the oath in December. She was already performing the duties of queen. The people had chosen her all over again. But somehow, this formality felt like yet another promise. Or maybe it was because her accepting the role one more time reminded her that, in doing so, she'd also changed the life of the child growing inside her. They'd never grow up wishing on a star for a fairy tale to come true. They'd live it instead.

But darkness came for fairy tales.

She'd seen it firsthand.

"What if—" She shook her head.

"Close your eyes," he demanded. When she hesitated, he brushed his hands over her lashes. "What do you hear?"

Cheers. Laughter. Excitement.

"Happy people," she whispered.

"And what do you smell?" he asked.

"The salt air and the orchids. You."

"And how does it make you feel?"

She let it settle in her chest for a long moment. Whenever they came back to San Fiore and the scents and sounds of the island hit her, she was overcome with the same sensation.

"Home. It makes me feel like home."

He brushed his lips lightly against hers.

"Then, go show the world you've made it yours."

Her body broke out in goosebumps, not only at the words and how they filled her heart but at his warm breath on her skin and his lips so close to hers.

She drew his hand away, and their eyes met.

"I was yours first," she told him.

"I know. And sometimes I still kick myself for sharing you with the whole damn universe. But the truth is, Nicolette, you were born to be our queen, to free us of the curse."

"Your mom said you didn't believe in it."

"Have you had a migraine since you took the throne?"

He wasn't asking because he didn't know the answer. He was asking to make a point. They both knew she hadn't had a single one since December. Maybe it was yet another thing the hormones had caused, or maybe it was truly the curse being broken. She'd never know unless the headaches returned, and she wasn't praying for that to happen any time soon.

"Stop stalling, *Stellina*. Let's go so you can claim your people and your home, and we can go back to bed, and I can bring the rest of the stars down to worship at your feet."

The pretty words lodged in her throat, but she heaved

out a protracted sigh just to taunt him before waving him toward the door. As he turned to open it, she said softly, "All the stars, D'Angelo. I have a whole lot of stress to work out."

He chuckled. "Whatever you command, my queen."

When he turned back to hold his hand out and help her from the carriage, his face was still lifted upward in a stunning smile that few people got to see. She was glad his people had a chance to do so today. She hoped a thousand cameras captured it so they would see he was not the dark shadow hovering around her, as some of the papers claimed, but the light showing her the way.

Their fingers collided, sending the normal zing of energy over her arm and down through her chest. Love and so much more. Souls twining. He assisted her out, the long train of her gown trailing behind her, and when she looked up at the temple, the first things she saw were the Daisies, Jerome, and Tommy, who was recently out of rehab. They were tucked between some of their security, the band's crew, Brady and his wife, Marco and Trevor who'd been invited as guests, the prime minister, and the high priestesses who were all lining the steps. It was a collection of people she'd known for over a decade, and some she'd barely met, and yet all of them were ones she trusted. People she believed in, and somehow, they still believed in her even after the worst had happened. After the secrets and death and destruction that had come and taken some of them away.

Cerise and the others had instructed her that she was supposed to walk up the steps by herself. D'Angelo was to come after her. The queen first, the prince consort second. But the truth of the matter was, she wouldn't have been there on those steps if not for him. She might not even be alive without him. She certainly wouldn't have been convinced to take on this mantle, this crown. This day…this coronation was as much about him as it was her.

And she'd once told him they would do everything side by side.

So, after she'd taken the first step, she turned back and extended a hand.

He frowned, the smile he'd had disappearing because he knew she was supposed to go first.

"You promised, anything I commanded," she said quietly.

His jaw ticked in a way she rarely saw anymore. Him battling duty with what he really wanted to do. Denying himself pleasure. She wouldn't have it anymore.

"D'Angelo," she said quietly.

He reached forward and took her hand in his. His fingers scarred from years of service blended with hers scarred from penance and music, and yet they fit perfectly together, just like every single part of them did.

He drew himself up next to her and untangled their fingers but didn't let go. He placed her hand on his bicep and covered it with his. Then, they slowly ascended the steps together. White and gold. Black and browns and blues. Magnificent colors that melded and blurred, making them one instead of two.

Showing the world what she really wanted them to see.

Not her. Not D'Angelo. But what lay beyond the skin and bone and pretty clothes to the truth…

To the only real superpower that existed on this earth.

To love.

♫ ♫ ♫

Thank you for reading my five little stories that began with a girl who'd started a band for her little sister. The Painted Daisies spun into my mind, took my heart and soul into their hands, and made me work and create in a way I'd never done before. In the end, they left me breathless, and I hope they've done the same for you. The Daisies had great losses and great loves. They battled evil and won in the end, sharing the truth I know to the bottom of my soul, and I hope you know too—that love is the only real superpower. The only thing that can truly heal.

If you're like me and aren't quite ready to let the Daisies and the alpha heroes who stole their hearts go yet, you can read a *series bonus epilogue* for free with a newsletter subscription. ***It gives you a teeny, tiny taste of all the couples five years later in a fun interview with the reporter that started it all.***

https://bookhip.com/JZAHNNL

If you enjoyed the Daisies fast-paced adventures twined with mystery and intense romance and want more like it, check out my **scrappy PI and single-dad in their standalone**, romantic suspense story, *AFTER ALL THE WRECKAGE* (https://geni.us/AATWLJE).

After All the Wreckage Sample

Chapter One

Rory

AM I ALRIGHT

Performed by Aly & AJ

If panic attacks could have babies, I'd be having *quintuplets.* The thought landed in my chest as I pulled my royal blue Honda Rebel into a tiny spot on the street outside my dad's office. It was the last place I wanted to be for more reasons than I could count. Some of those reasons were petty, full of old grudges and teenage hurts, and some were deadly serious.

The deadly part was why I'd swallowed my pride enough to come.

I slammed my foot on the kickstand and swung my leg over the seat before standing in my thick-soled Harley-Davidson boots and pulling off my helmet. I dragged the hair tie from my ponytail, slung it around my wrist, and ran a hand through the dark brown strands.

When I turned toward the small but expensive building that held Bishop Investigations & Security, my reflection caught in the two stories of glittering glass. I cringed, knowing neither my bike nor my appearance would help my cause today. My black jacket was naturally distressed with spiderweb cracks along the leather, and the hole in my black jeans was from a tussle with a cheater I'd been following rather than any designer styling. They'd be the first of many things my father would pick at today. A few more additions to the long list of my mistakes. But two could play at that game. After all, I had a list of his that I could recite too.

I shoved my shoulders back and strode through the doors. The inside of his office was professional and cold. Decked out in steel and gray leather, the lobby was elegantly arranged to impress Dad's clients. As if the surroundings screaming wealth proved he could get the job done rather than the fact he had a good interior designer. But the truth was, as much as it irked me to admit it, Dad always got the job done. Whether the client liked what he found was an entirely different story—one I knew firsthand.

My eyes drifted to my wrist and the black-and-blue fingerprints that had turned darker throughout the day. I tugged the cuff of my jacket down, clamping it against my palm with my fingers. If Dad saw the marks, any chance of asking him for the favor I'd come for would be lost. And I needed him to come through. For the first time in almost a decade, I actually needed my father.

I hated it.

At the desk, the latest receptionist in a long string of Georgetown grad students sat waiting. Each of them used their time with his company to launch a litany of justice and law enforcement careers. His name on their résumé was an exclusive D.C. insider's gold star that opened doors. Too bad I'd never been offered a chance to earn one. Maybe he'd known I would have rather been boiled in acid than sit at that clear glass desk answering his phones.

"Rory," Chanel greeted me with a snip to her tone. Her gym-toned legs below the hem of a gray pencil skirt crossed as she swiveled toward me, purple Prada pumps dangling from her feet. They were the only sign of color in the stark space. She fit into Dad's image perfectly whereas I looked like I'd been dragged in from the biker bar on the edge of Cherry Bay—the town I called home after leaving D.C. a few months ago.

"Dad in?" I asked her, trying to keep my voice light and even.

Her gaze flitted over me briefly, barely withholding her judgment, but I could hear it anyway. The silent *How on earth is this Sutton Bishop's daughter?* Because the only thing I'd inherited from the blond-haired dynamo in a suit who was my father was the cleft in my chin. He was tall with a square face and wide shoulders, whereas I was almost all Mom with honey-toned Italian skin and a lithe, short frame. Dad's green eyes screamed their color even over a distance while the tiny bit of jade that flashed in my brown ones was only visible if you were close enough to kiss me.

Not that I'd been kissed lately. It had been so long, my lips and vagina thought I'd abandoned them.

"He has twenty minutes before he has to leave for lunch on the Hill," Chanel said primly.

It was exactly what I'd hoped for. Dad spent more time wining and dining D.C. bigwigs these days than he did investigating. Although, maybe that wasn't much different from when Mom had been his partner. Back then, he'd brought the business in and she'd executed it… or I did. Right up until the divorce split them down the middle and me along with it.

As I headed for the stairs, I tossed a jab over my shoulder. "Dad has dining with sleazy politicians down to a science. They should give him the oil prospector of the year award."

"First, not all politicians are sleazy. Second, you're one to judge. How's it going swimming with the cheaters?"

My foot stalled on the first step, and when I looked back, her eyes were narrowed. I almost laughed at her quick retort, but then I wondered if her defense of Dad came from a sense of loyalty that went much deeper than an employee-employer relationship. I wondered if Dad had tucked this receptionist into his bed a time or two… or more.

It made me want to heave up the cold mac and cheese I'd called breakfast.

I didn't respond, turning back around to take the stairs at double time.

His office door was open, the low hum of his voice audible if not the actual words. He didn't have an assistant guarding the entrance. He didn't believe in having one. The fewer eyes and hands on sensitive information, the better in his opinion. And if for some reason the nearly perfect Sutton Bishop did need help, the highly paid receptionist downstairs would be tasked with it.

Dad had his chair turned toward the enormous windows looking out at the dome of the Capitol Building. I knocked, and he swung around to take me in. His eyes narrowed ever so slightly before a tight smile appeared on his lips.

"I'll have to call you back," he said into the phone, pausing to listen to the response. "I'm telling you, you're worrying over nothing, Roland. I'll see you tonight."

He hung up and watched as I moved to stand next to the pair of straight-backed chairs in front of his steel desk. The chairs weren't designed for comfort. Dad didn't want people to dally in his office any more than he wanted them lingering in his personal life.

Handsome and brimming with charisma, my father could have been a politician as easily as he'd become a private investigator. He could charm his way into just about anywhere… and anyone. It was a skill Mom said I'd inherited from him, and sometimes, I wasn't sure if it was a compliment or not.

"I'd love to say it's nice to finally see my daughter again, but I'm confident you didn't drive into D.C. on that asinine bike just to visit dear old Dad," he said dryly with a pointed look at the helmet under my arm.

I tossed it on the chair as he came around the desk to draw me into a one-armed hug. A catch and release he'd once shown me how to do while fishing. The nonchalance pricked at old wounds I couldn't afford to let show.

A wisp of pine from his cologne combined with a hint of smoke from his occasional cigar wafted over me. I was dismayed by the temptation to hold on to him longer, to use his strength to buoy me up. To once again be the little girl he'd beamed at when she'd handed him the proof of a certain congressman sleeping with a prostitute. Proof that had cost the man his reelection and his wife.

I gritted my teeth and stepped farther away. If I allowed myself to drop my shield even briefly, the weight I was carrying might slip off and I'd never be able to pick it up again. I wasn't even twenty-three yet, but I had both lives and a business resting solely on my shoulders.

As he leaned up against his desk, he scanned my outfit, his look lingering on the fresh cut and red skin visible through the hole in my jeans. I grabbed the cuff of my jacket extra tight, ensuring it stayed firmly in place.

"To what do I really owe the pleasure?" he asked.

I regretted the cold mac and cheese all over again.

Now that I was here, I didn't really want to make my request. I took a few seconds to run through the numbers in our bank accounts once more. Then, the image of Mom lying in the bed at the long-term care facility settled cruelly in my chest. Her skin was paler than ever before, and her eyes were always shut as a feeding tube, a host of cords, and beeping machines kept her alive. I forced back an unexpected rush of tears. I couldn't afford them any more than I could afford the damn hug to undo me. Tears never solved anything—the saying should have been monogrammed on our Bishop family crest.

"I need a loan," I told him.

I knew better than to ask for money straight up. Dad believed in earning what you got. Struggle built character. It was the one and only thing my parents had agreed upon after the divorce.

Dad crossed his arms over his chest. "How much and what's it for?"

If I said I needed it to cover the added expense of Mom's new facility in Cherry Bay, he'd object. He'd made it very clear he disagreed with keeping her on life support after the doctors had recommended shutting it off and the insurance had stopped paying because of it. But if I said I needed cash to cover Marlow & Co. bills, he definitely wouldn't give it to me. He'd be happy if the business Mom had created after divorcing him disappeared. One less competitor.

After my mistake in high school—getting suspended and almost expelled for stunning a drug dealer in the boys' bathroom—he and Mom had pretty much switched sides. Once he'd seen me as an integral part of their business, now all he saw were my errors.

Because neither of the real reasons I needed the money would sway him, I gave him the fake one I'd come up with on the commute into D.C. "I want to get my master's."

I tried to keep my face impassive through the partial lie. I'd once planned on going to grad school before applying to the FBI, but these days those ideas seemed like Neverland dreams, and I was out of pixie dust. After missing the spring semester because of Mom's accident, I'd transferred from Georgetown to Bonnin University in Cherry Bay where I was weeks away from squeaking out a bachelor's degree. Even though it was less expensive, I'd still had to take out a loan as every penny from the sale of Mom's D.C. condo had gone toward keeping her breathing.

Dad's eyes narrowed as if he was attempting to read me. My face remained stony, but I made the mistake of shifting ever so slightly on one foot, and he caught the small movement.

"You've applied and been accepted to grad school? Where?"

He wasn't buying it. Why had I humiliated myself like this when I'd already known it was a futile effort? Mom's face flashed in my head again, and those fricking tears I never let out threatened once more. I grabbed my helmet and headed for the door before I further humiliated myself.

"Never mind. Forget I was even here," I said.

"I didn't say I wouldn't give you the money. I just want to know the truth."

Gripping the chin guard of my helmet with one hand, I waved at him with the other. "Why does it matter? Your daughter needs a loan. I'm not asking for a handout. I'm not asking for anything I won't pay back. You set the terms, and I'll meet them."

The second he strode toward me with anger flashing in his eyes, I realized my mistake.

He grabbed my arm, demanding, "Who hurt you?"

"It isn't important." It was embarrassing was what it was. A stupid wardrobe malfunction that had let the cheating bastard lay a hand on me.

"Damn it, Rory-girl! How many times do I have to repeat myself? You aren't cut out for this business. You're going to end up dead just like your mother."

"Mom isn't dead!" I growled back, pushing him away from me and taking a step into the hall.

He sighed, the sound full of frustration and sadness. "She is, Rory. Even if, by some miracle, she comes out of it, she'll be a shell of a person. She won't ever be Hallie again."

"Just because you've given up hope doesn't mean Nan or I have," I hissed. "And Mom didn't die because some asshole cheater came after her. She crashed into the Potomac."

I stomped toward the stairs.

"Because someone messed with her car's computer."

As his words sank in, my feet stalled. My heartbeat sped up, doing triple time, as I whirled around to face him. "What?"

He rubbed his forehead. The regret and exasperation on his face were a clear message he'd let something slip he'd never intended for me to hear. I'd repeatedly asked the detective in charge of Mom's accident for the cause, and Muloney had told me they'd never know for sure. There hadn't been another vehicle involved. She'd just gone over the edge and into the river. A submerged tree had pierced the right side of her head, and she'd drowned before the rescue people got to her. They'd resuscitated her, but she'd never woken up. She'd gripped my hand a few times, her lids had fluttered open and closed, but she'd never really been cognizant.

And now it had been eleven months... Eleven months I'd survived without her. But it felt like twenty years. An eternity in which I'd lived in some alternate version of what had once been my life.

"Who told you that?" My words were garbled as pain and fury roared through me. He didn't respond, and it only goaded me further. "I can't believe you! You told

Muloney to cut me out? You're not her next of kin. You don't get to make any decisions about her. You lost that right when you divorced her. Like it or not, I'm the one who's responsible for her now."

"Except you want my money to keep her alive."

"That's not what it's for."

"Isn't it?" he demanded, brow rising again. "I know you've gone through the tiny profit you got out of the condo, Rory. I know you've had to change facilities more than once. This bullshit idea about a master's degree? You and I both know it isn't what the money is for."

God, there were times I hated how good he was at his job. He really knew everything. He always had. It was why clients flocked from all over the Northeast to his doors.

"Keep your damn money. I'll do this alone, just like Mom and I have done everything else for the past ten years, and I'll figure out why someone wanted her dead while I'm at it."

"I don't want to lose my daughter *and* my wife."

"Ex-wife. Your latest girlfriend would hate to hear you call her that."

He blew out an exasperated breath. "You're not cut out for this, Rory," he repeated. "It's my fault you started down this path. I can admit I was wrong. I never should have asked you to do any of the things I did, and Hallie should never have let you coerce her into picking up where I left off.

"Jesus, look at you." He gestured toward me. "You're battered and bruised, racing around town on that deathtrap, for what? An idea that you can be some real-life Veronica Mars? Real detective work isn't anything like that goddamn show."

Each syllable was a hit to my already bruised psyche. Scars and scabs hidden deep in my soul started to bleed. Veronica had saved me. And ever since Mom's accident, my life had taken on an even more decidedly Veronica-like vibe. She'd stayed to help her dad after he'd gotten sick just like I was helping Mom. She'd gone back to running the family PI business, and I'd done the same. The clients and money I brought in weren't nearly enough, though. I was doling out more each month than I was bringing in, and Nan didn't have any extra cash to offer. She was barely getting by on Pop's widow's pension.

I swallowed hard, striking back the only way I could with words I wasn't sure were true but would hit home anyway. "At least Keith Mars loved his daughter. Fake show. Real love. The complete opposite of this." I waved a finger between us and then turned on my heel and headed down the stairs.

He followed me to the railing, calling after me. "Rory, don't leave like this."

I didn't respond.

"You know there are a lot of companies who would give someone with your computer skills a hiring bonus. If you're looking for money and don't want it on my terms, at least consider it. You need to leave this business behind and concentrate on what you *are* good at."

Chanel was pretending not to watch the show as I stormed past her desk, but I saw the smirk, and it only fueled the rage inside me. I wished I could slam the door to the building, but all it did was swing back and forth.

As I stalked over to my bike, the realization that Dad might be right caused bile to hit my throat. Maybe I did need to get some eight-to-five desk job in some corporate office peddling my computer skills. Not because a buckle had gotten caught in a trellis and the cheater had pulled me from it by my wrist, but because a job in a corporate office would pay a helluva lot more than my handful of clients.

But then Dad's slipped admission came back. Someone had messed with Mom's car! Someone had done this to her on purpose. There was no way in hell I'd let that go. I'd borrow money from Tall Paul, the biggest loan shark I knew, before I'd just walk away.

Just like Veronica Mars had once said, this was where I belonged. In the fight. It was who I was. And I could guarantee whoever had done this would regret it.

As I pulled on my helmet and merged into the heavy traffic of D.C. at lunchtime, I wondered how much Dad had paid Baloney-Muloney to keep the truth from me. Was Dad investigating it on his own or was he leaving it to the tiny force that made up Cherry Bay's police department?

If Dad had any information, I'd find out. I had a backdoor into his network that he was clueless to. I'd find out what he knew, and if it was nothing, there were other doors I'd start banging on—or hacking into.

Dad was right about one thing. I'd die before I let anyone get away with this.

Chapter 2

Gage

BROKEN

Performed by The Guess Who

I tapped my fingers along the edge of the Pathfinder's steering wheel, trying to push down the impatience I felt sitting at the back of the car line in front of Cherry Bay's only middle school. I had a long list of things to get done at the bar, which meant I barely had time to manage picking Monte up and getting back to the apartment before opening.

The car in front of me inched forward, and I did the same thing as I scanned the sea of tweens sidling down the sidewalk past the car. No copper-topped waves in sight. Had Monte worn a baseball cap today? I couldn't remember. My younger brother did more often than not. He hated his red hair. Hated the curls more. Hated that kids teased him about being Orphan Annie's twin brother. How the hell they even knew who she was beat me. I'd had to look it up.

"Bubba, I have to pee," a tiny voice from the back seat whispered.

Shit. I glanced in the rearview mirror, meeting Ivy's gaze. My sister's pale blue eyes were just like our mother's, but at the moment, they were wide and desperate. A look I wasn't sure I'd ever seen in Demi's. I'd seen fanciful, whimsical, and even clouded, but never desperate. More often than not, Demi's were strangely serene, even in the face of my anger.

Ivy wiggled in her seat, and panic filled my veins. I definitely didn't have time for a bathroom accident. Didn't have time to clean the car seat, the car, or tame the shamed tears that would flow. It wasn't her fault. What three-and-a-half-year-old hadn't had an accident or two?

"Hold tight, Ives," I ground out.

I flipped on my blinker, zipped out in front of a car in a way that earned me a loud honk, then cut off another car before it could block the driveway of the school's parking lot. After sideswiping the orange cone set up to keep people out, I pulled up along the sidewalk near the flagpole in front of the nondescript square building.

I was in the red zone, but I didn't care as I jumped from the driver's seat and jogged around to help Ivy unbuckle even as she protested. Holding her tightly to my chest, I ran toward the bathrooms outside the gym—smelly spaces I knew well from when I'd attended the school a lifetime ago.

I skidded to a halt outside the boys' and girls' restrooms, debating which to use.

"I don't know if I can hold it," Ivy's small voice squeaked out.

Her alarm raced through me. I rushed into the boys' room. When I didn't see anyone standing at the urinals, I sent a silent thanks to the universe. Two stalls were empty. I'd barely set her on her feet before Ivy was jumping up onto the seat. I winced, trying not to think about what was on the toilet. It wasn't like middle school boys were known for their hygiene. But the look of pure gratitude on her face eased the chokehold that had taken over my chest.

Her ponytail was askew. Little wisps of curls had escaped, surrounding her elf-like face dusted with a light sheen of freckles. If there was anything in my life that could make me feel like a failure, it was her damn hair. How did other parents do it? Every time I picked Ivy up from preschool, all the other girls seemed to have their hair still perfectly assembled—neat and tidy—while Ivy's seemed to come loose the moment I put it up.

How was I, at twenty-seven, even in a position to be thinking of a little girl's hair and where the nearest bathroom was? My life was so far from where I'd imagined it would be that there were days the simple weight of it was like an anvil sitting on my shoulders. I was living the wrong life. With that thought came the spike of anger and frustration that usually followed it. Fucking life. Fucking Demi.

Once Ivy was done, she leaped off the seat, and her face burst into a smile so bright it felt like heaven was shining a beam right down on us. It took every thought I'd just had about living the wrong life and all the rage, and zapped it away. She was worth it. She and Monte both.

"All better?" I asked.

She nodded, slipping her tiny fingers into mine, and we made our way out to the sinks where we both washed our hands. With our damp palms joined, we made our way back to the SUV as Ivy tried to skip. She looked like some malfunctioning robot, but it made my lips twitch upward for the first time all afternoon.

I was definitely going to be late now. But I had help at the bar. River would be there, and he'd pick up the slack by unloading the delivery. Audrey would handle the setup inside, and between the two of them, they'd shoulder the tasks I hadn't been able to get to. It would be fine. It always was.

When I got back to our gray Pathfinder, I lifted Ivy into the back seat and watched as she struggled to buckle up. She was extremely proud of being able to do it herself and would get frustrated if I tried to help. It took her five times as long as it would have if I'd done it, but it all came down to that old saying about teaching someone to fish... No one ever mentioned how much patience and energy it took the teacher to do so.

I hopped into the driver's seat and moved to a spot that had opened up near the school's front office. I left the car idling, pulled my phone from my pocket, and shot Monte a text.

> *ME: Ivy had to use the bathroom. We're parked in the lot.*

A couple minutes went by, and the number of kids wandering past dwindled. The vehicles in the car line beyond the sidewalk started to fade. Still no sign of my brother. He knew the timing was tight from pickup to the bar opening, so he usually did his best to get out quickly. I flipped my phone over to see there was no response.

> *ME: Hey? Did you have practice today?*

I had his basketball schedule taped to the refrigerator, logged into the calendar on my phone, and burned into my brain. But that was the other thing I'd found out the hard way—nothing was predictable with kids.

The principal meandered down from the head of the car line, picked up the cones in the driveway, and set them aside. Three kids tagged along behind him, backpacks weighing them down, phones in hand, and walking while texting in the way teens did despite the warnings that it could be dangerous.

An inkling of something that wasn't quite fear but close hit me in the chest.

Nothing is wrong. Everything is okay.

It was a mantra I lived by these days.

Except last night Monte hadn't slept, and neither had I because of it. His eyes had been shadowed this morning, a sense of despair clinging to him as he'd shoveled in the eggs and toast that his growing body demanded.

"What's the point of even having the visions, Gage?" he'd asked. "I'm useless to stop whatever they show me. Nothing I can do. Nothing you can do. We've both tried."

What if he'd gone on his own to D.C.? That singular thought caused more alarm than any kind of pee accident could.

While waiting for his response, I shoved my hand through the pitch-black of my thick waves. I looked nothing like my brother and sister. They were all Demi— strawberry-blond strands with pale eyes and soft white skin that showed off their freckles. I was Dad from my dark hair, gray eyes, and square chin down to my skin that always carried a hint of tan year-round.

As the minutes ticked away, my anxiety grew. I stabbed out another desperate message.

> *ME: Please tell me you didn't go to D.C. I'm at the school. Ivy is about two seconds from melting down.*

It wasn't Ivy who was having the meltdown. It was me. But Monte would do just about anything for our little sister. When she'd first been born, he used to crawl into bed with me for comfort whenever she was crying, even when it was just a normal *I'm hungry* type of cry.

My phone buzzed with a reply from Monte, and relief washed through me.

> *MONTE: I went home with India, remember? I'm spending the weekend with her to work on our science project.*

My relief was quickly replaced with guilt. Had he told me and I hadn't paid attention? I'd been so focused on his vision, sleeplessness, and growing restlessness that I might have missed him telling me.

> *ME: Are you sure that's a good idea with everything happening?*

> *MONTE: It'll keep my mind off it for a while.*

In my gut, I knew the truth. He was doing this for me as much as himself. He didn't want me hovering over him, worrying. But it was my job to protect him, not the other way around.

I put the SUV in gear and backed out of the spot, heading toward the bar.

The asphalt roads at the edge of town quickly turned into cobblestone streets in the town center. The first village in Cherry Bay had been founded in the late 1700s, but the college that had been built on the bluff overlooking the Potomac in the 1940s was what had put us on the map. It drew students and academics from around the globe.

I hooked a right at the alley between two stone buildings that would have been perfectly at home in a medieval English village and headed into the small parking lot at the back. The Prince Darian Tavern had been in my family for over two hundred years. It had first been a post inn, and now it was a bar and restaurant with a two-bedroom apartment and extra storage space above.

While Dad had leased out the restaurant several decades ago, the tavern had been run by a Palmer since its inception. Between the renovation loans I hadn't known he'd taken out and the pandemic closing us down, we'd been almost wiped out financially. After Dad had died, I'd had to sell the house, and we'd moved into the apartment that he used to rent to college students. We were squished together in a space crowded with furniture that didn't fit, but I refused to get rid of those last pieces of our family history. Selling the Victorian we'd grown up in had been painful enough.

I parked the Pathfinder and waited with gritted teeth while Ivy fumbled with her buckle. My gaze journeyed to the next parking lot over, and my heart skipped a beat at the sight of a dark-haired woman. I could practically feel the energy vibrating from Rory Bishop as she headed toward the doors of the Cherry Bay Police Department. The aura of brave confidence was the same as it had been when she'd been fifteen. A self-assurance that mimicked the fictional heroine she'd worshipped back in the day.

Lithe and edgy in all black, I was hypnotized by the way she moved. Unable to draw my eyes away from her.

How long had it been since I'd seen her? How many miles, years, and traumas had filled the space between us?

I was just about to call her name when Ivy jumped out of the car and landed on my foot. It turned any sound that would have emerged from me into a deep grunt, and I had to catch my sister as she wobbled and balance myself at the same time. When I looked back over to the station, Rory was gone, and something a bit like sadness filled me.

Which was ridiculous. I didn't even know Rory anymore. I'd barely known her as a teen.

I pushed aside any thoughts of her, stepped around the wrought iron staircase leading to our apartment, and headed for the rear entrance of the bar with Ivy's hand in mine. A delivery truck had its door rolled up, and as I'd expected, River was already unloading it on his own.

His wide shoulders flexed as he hefted a case of vodka onto his shoulder. His height and build along with his shaved head, pierced nose, and plethora of tattoos intimidated most people. They had no clue his aura radiated nothing but kindness when all they saw was a scary giant.

River had been working for my dad since he'd been in college himself, and decades later, he was still here. Although I was pretty sure that had more to do with not abandoning me and my siblings than because he needed the job. Not when his art was in high demand around the country.

"Sorry we're late," I offered before looking down at my sister. "Go into the office and get a snack from the snack drawer and your coloring books from the shelf. I'll be in after I help River."

"Can I have a chocolate cwinkle?" she asked, eyes wide, knowing I normally didn't let her have sweets this close to dinner. But with my nerves feeling frayed after the scare I'd just had at the school, I didn't feel like arguing with her.

"Yes, but only one," I said, narrowing my eyes at her.

She grinned and then took off down the hall, her messed-up hairdo bouncing around her.

"Hey, Squirt! Don't I even get a hello?" River grunted after her.

She waved her stuffed otter without ever looking back as she hollered, "Hi, Uncle Wivuh!" her R's lisping into W's.

"I expect a hug later."

I grabbed another case off the back of the truck, hauling it to the storage room above the bar. The dark interior stairs were small and groaned with age, but they were smooth and stained to perfection. Everything in the building might be old, but it wasn't shabby. Dad had made sure of it, and I'd picked up where he'd left off.

While River and I unloaded in silence, my thoughts kept drifting back to the brown-haired dynamo I'd seen next door. A piece of me longed to go back in time to when I'd known her. When I'd had nothing to worry about but internships and college tuition. To a time when I'd been adored by a girl who I'd known would take the world by storm and set some guy's heart on fire.

Last I'd heard, she was at Georgetown, but I vaguely recalled some mumblings late last year about her mom being in a car accident. I hadn't paid much attention to the talk because Rory and her mom hadn't lived in Cherry Bay for almost a decade. Plus, I'd been hip-deep in another of Monte's visions and finalizing the paperwork on Ivy's and Monte's adoptions. I'd barely been able to breathe at the time, let alone think of a young girl from my past.

But now I couldn't shake the image of her.

Why was she in town? Was she visiting her friend Shay, whose family owned the Tea Spot across the street? Or was she visiting her grandmother? Regardless of why she was there, I didn't have any more time now to let my thoughts dwell on her than I had a year ago.

I signed the receipt from the delivery and walked toward the tavern's office. I pushed open the antique wooden door with its beveled glass to find Ivy at a claw-foot table that had been there probably since the tavern had first opened. She was on her knees in a burgundy brocade armchair, draped in a mosaic of color from the stained-glass window that made her seem like one of the paintings of our ancestors hanging on the walls in their gilded frames.

When I got up close to her, the mirage broke, and a chuckle rumbled through my chest. She was covered in chocolate from forehead to chin. It never failed to surprise me how quickly and absolutely she could become a mess when eating. She'd need a full body scrub before dinner.

Which reminded me, I needed to call our babysitter and beg her to come over. I'd expected Monte to be home to watch Ivy, which only reconfirmed I hadn't known my brother would be at India's. Unease settled in my chest once again—a worry I couldn't shake. I was an Olympic champion at worrying these days.

I pulled my laptop from the old captain's desk on the other side of the room and brought it over to the table. I kissed the top of Ivy's head as I set it down in front of her. "Give me a few minutes, Ives, then I'll take you upstairs for dinner. Do you want to watch something while you wait?"

She nodded. "Scooby-Doo?"

Her addiction to the cartoon made me smile. "Sure."

I loaded the streaming service, started an episode, and then looked at her chocolate-covered face and hands. "Don't touch the computer. And wash your hands when you're done with the cookie."

She nodded absently, already watching Scooby and the gang as they scurried over the screen in the opening song. I stepped away, watching her with regret curling through me. She was loved and cared for, but she didn't have a normal childhood. Then again, none of us had been allowed one. Not with Demi in and out. Not with the abilities she'd branded us with.

But we had each other, and that was all that really mattered.

Chapter 3

Rory

NO ONE

Performed by Aly & AJ

My first stop on returning to Cherry Bay was the police department. The building was several hundred years old, sitting at the edge of Main Street and butting up against the acres of green that made up the Bonnin University campus. Even after it had been retrofitted multiple times, the station still had a moody, Gothic vibe with its original stone, brick, and iron mixing in with high-tech cameras, computers, and bulletproof glass.

Harriet sat at the front desk where she'd been for as long as I could remember. Her dark hair was cropped short. She had a lean, toned frame and dark eyes in a narrow face. One of Mom's best friends and the department's dispatcher, Harriet was the first to know everything that happened in town. It tugged hard on my heart that she might have been hiding the truth from me.

"Look at what the cat dragged in," she said with a smile that faded once she saw my glower. "Is it Hallie?"

"Not in the way you're thinking," I said, and relief coasted over her face. I felt a twinge of guilt before I demanded, "What the hell, Harriet? Her wreck wasn't an accident, and you kept it from me?"

Her eyes widened in surprise. "What? No!"

Her reaction seemed genuine which meant she hadn't known either. My teeth gritted as I headed for the swinging half door that led to the desks in the back. "Where is Baloney-Muloney?"

She shook her head, reaching out to stop me. "Muloney isn't here, Rory. He drove to New York to bring his daughter home for Thanksgiving."

My emotions swung back and forth. A part of me wanted to storm into the bullpen, tear up the detective's desk and his computer, and get what I'd come for. Except that wouldn't win me any favors with anyone in the department. It would likely ban me from the precinct forever. The smart course of action was to pull out the Bishop family charm and win him over when he returned. With the way my anger was bubbling and growing, I wasn't sure I'd be able to channel it when he returned.

"When will he be back?"

"Sunday," she said.

Another two days wasted. I was already too far behind on Mom's case. Almost a year too late. Why hadn't I demanded more from him sooner?

"He lied, Harriet. He lied and kept the truth from me. He's lucky I haven't put out a hit on him yet."

"I haven't heard even a whisper of it being anything but an accident. I would have told you." She squeezed my arm again, and we shared a tormented stare before she patted my cheek. "Come to the house on Thanksgiving. Please. I told Kora I wanted you both there. Hallie wouldn't want the two of you sitting alone in a room at the recovery center."

That was the thing no one seemed to understand. My grandmother and I weren't alone. We were with Mom. And I wasn't much for holidays these days. It felt wrong to celebrate while Mom was lying there, but the hope in Harriet's eyes had me swallowing back my automatic no. Instead, I told her I'd talk to Nan about it and said goodbye.

It was a short drive from the station to Shady Lane Rehabilitation and Recovery Center across from the hospital. Both were square buildings built in the fifties, but they'd kept the charm of the town in their stone and plaster facades. Shady Lane was the second facility Mom had been in since the D.C. hospital she'd been airlifted to had kicked her out. Nan and I had moved her here, not only because the staff knew us, but because it didn't require Nan and me to commute in the horrendous beltway traffic. The downside was it cost even more than the last place.

I signed in at the front desk and made my way along the sterile hall to Mom's room. The quiet hum of the machines and the antiseptic smell were almost unnoticeable to me after eleven months of practically living in similar facilities. My grandmother was there, sitting in the same chair she always was, knitting a creation that wouldn't be straight and wouldn't fit right. It was a hobby she'd picked up to fill the long stretches at the side of a hospital bed.

"I was surprised when you weren't here," Nan commented as I strolled in and tossed my helmet onto the loveseat under the room's single window.

Nan's hair used to be as dark as mine but was now mostly white. It was cut close to her head for ease, but it suited her. She was only in her midseventies, but the loss of her parents, her sister, her husband, and now her daughter had aged her in an irreversible way, adding wrinkles that shouldn't have been there.

"Where's the Jeep?" Nan asked, head tilting toward the helmet I'd tossed aside. Technically, the Jeep I'd been borrowing ever since Mom's SUV had been totaled was my grandfather's. Nan had kept it running right along with her green Volkswagen Beetle from the sixties even though she definitely didn't need both vehicles. After twelve years, she still couldn't part with a single piece of him. It was why their closet still held his clothes, and the shed out back of their house held his woodworking tools.

"I had some business to take care of in D.C., and the bike needed to be driven."

I hadn't told Nan I was asking Dad for a loan because she would threaten to sell the cottage again. A home she and Pop had bought in their twenties and was mortgage free, but that she could still barely afford because the property taxes and insurance stretched her meager income.

"You got a new case?"

I nodded. It wasn't a lie. I had Mom's case now.

"How is she today?"

Nan's knitting needles slowed ever so slightly, and she didn't respond right away. When she finally looked up, I saw hopelessness in her eyes. It had been a bad day, and I'd been off on a useless errand.

I went to her, crouching down and surrounding her hands with mine. "What happened?"

"Doctor Huan showed up. She basically said we were wasting time, money, and love holding on to a physical body when Hallie is already gone." Nan choked on the last words, and my anger flared back to life.

How could everyone just give up? I knew the odds. I knew the miracle we were looking for was rare. Mom's lack of eye movement, the lack of any response, and the stupid Glasgow Coma Scale they administered all told us the numbers were not in our favor. But every time I looked at my mother, I felt like she was still there, and I'd read enough stories about people who'd recovered even a year later that I couldn't just remove the life support and let her body die. Not yet. Not when we were still within those miraculous months.

"Screw her, Nan," I said gently. "She doesn't know Mom. She doesn't know us. She has no clue what kind of fighters we Marlowes are."

Nan sniffed, grabbed a tissue from the side table, and dabbed her eyes with it. "You didn't get that fight from the Bishops, that's for sure."

After giving her a weak smile, I winked. "I got my charm from them."

I stood and Nan smiled. "The Marlowe women have been known to make a few siren calls ourselves. You got the best of both families. Which makes me wonder why you haven't been luring any hot bodies to your bed lately."

I laughed and went over to Mom's side, grabbing her cold hand and rubbing it between mine. I didn't answer because I didn't have to. Nan and I had been consumed with Mom's recovery. But even before that, my sex life had been pretty hit or miss. Especially when most of the guys I'd tangled with in high school and college had been overwhelmingly immature. Or maybe it had nothing to do with them but a flash of stormy gray eyes I couldn't forget. Memories of a boy who'd burned himself onto my soul without even knowing it. Without even a single kiss.

A man I'd purposefully ignored since moving back to Cherry Bay.

I wasn't exactly sure why.

Liar, my soul screamed. The harsher truth was that I didn't want him to see me this way. I didn't want him to look at the girl he'd thought could be Veronica-Mars-strong and see her struggling to hold herself together.

I didn't want to be pitied by him. Not him.

I sat on the edge of the bed, moving Mom's legs, massaging them, and doing all the things the physical therapists and nurses had taught us to do. She'd be weak when she eventually came back to us, but she was going to recover. She had to. The Marlowe strength was part of our doggedness. We didn't give up once we set our minds on something.

And it would be a hot day in space before I gave up on the most important person in my life.

♫ ♫ ♫

I spent Friday night and most of Saturday on my laptop in Mom's room, doing what I always did—working on my cases and my classwork.

Normally, whenever Nan wasn't in the room, I talked aloud to Mom because the first doctors we'd seen had said it was important for a coma patient to hear their loved ones' voices. I'd ramble on about the Department of Defense background checks I was running, the cheating partner I was following, or the deadbeat parent I was tracking down for child support. I'd talk about my classes or brag about Nan's latest gardening achievement.

This weekend, my silence hung oppressively in the air.

As I was researching her accident, I didn't want her to relive the trauma if she could hear. The most recent reports insisted she didn't have any brain activity and that nothing I said mattered anymore, but I couldn't believe that because if I did…

I shook my head, concentrating on the final string of code I needed to create a backdoor into the Cherry Bay Police Department's server. I smiled when I got in, covering my tracks as I went, like brushing away footprints in the snow.

There was nothing like the thrill of a good hack in the morning.

If I wanted to, I could tell the department how I'd done it so they'd be protected in the future, and maybe I would. But not until Mom's case was solved.

I rooted around their system, learning the ins and outs, and finally found Mom's file. It was suspiciously thin. I didn't know if it was because Muloney had done a shit job or because Dad had told him to be careful what he put online in case I came looking. Whatever the reason, there was nothing about her car's computer being compromised like Dad had insinuated. The handful of notes were about where the Pathfinder had been towed, the stops she'd made before her trip to Cherry Bay, and people they'd interviewed at those locations. There weren't even photos from the actual accident scene, which raised the hair on the back of my neck. The lack of information made me all the more determined to see Baloney-Muloney when he returned. I wanted photocopies of his handwritten notes and the pictures someone had to have taken.

Turning away from the disappointing search, I pulled up Mom's calendar in our Marlowe & Co. system. There was nothing out of the ordinary for the day of the wreck. She had time blocked for yoga in the morning, a meeting with the DoD about our contract for background checks, and then a client meeting in the afternoon. The only thing that made me raise a brow was that she hadn't referenced a case file for the client meeting. I'd check her physical planner later at home.

Still not prepared to give up, I turned my attention to scouring security footage from the day of the accident. I didn't have video saved from our D.C. condo because I'd wiped the server clear when I'd sold the place, but I did have recordings from our office cams. I was still running security for the wannabe game development company who'd subleased the space from me.

Swiping through the stored files, I found the day of the accident. Mom had worn a black-and-white-checked blazer, a black turtleneck, and dress pants. Formal for her. Likely due to the meeting with the DoD. Her steps were hurried as she headed for the door, but nothing to make me think she was upset. I froze the screen, fingers lingering on her face.

Regret was like a computer virus. It ate away at your insides until nothing was left but spoiled zeros and ones. I wished I'd said something more important that morning. More poignant. More lasting. At least I'd shouted *I love you* as I'd left. But had she felt the full impact of it? Had she heard how much she truly meant to me?

"I miss you," I whispered, and then instantly felt guilty as my eyes landed on my breathing mother lying in the bed next to me.

I swallowed hard. Were the doctors right? Was she gone already? Were the thousands of dollars Nan and I had spent to get her into Shady Lane and keep her body breathing doing anything? Would she ever open her eyes, register me, and talk to me… say anything so I would have something besides *See you at dinner* as my last words from her?

Unexpected tears filled my eyes like they had at Dad's office the day before. *Nothing gets solved by crying, Rory-girl.*

I rubbed my eyes and returned to my hunt for video evidence. Most businesses only kept security cam footage for thirty days unless it was subpoenaed by the authorities. Had the police done that for the places Mom had visited? I'd found none of it on the department's server, so I doubted it. I searched each of the businesses only to be handed more disappointment.

If I'd done this last December, we'd be ahead of the game instead of miles behind.

As the sun sank behind the spirals of the buildings on the Bonnin campus, I kissed Mom's cheek and said, "I love you. Maybe think about waking up, okay? You can hand Dad a healthy dose of fuck-you that would make both of our days."

Then, with a heavy heart, I headed back to the cottage and Nan.

The porch light was shining on two pots of multicolored chrysanthemums that would bloom for a few more days. Nan and Pop's place had always been full of color, almost year-round due to Nan's love of gardening.

The half-timbered style of many of the homes on this side of Cherry Bay reflected the Englishmen who'd built them from plaster, stone, and maple wood that had been on the land before the cherry trees had taken over. Once thatched, Nan's roof was now a bright blue tile, giving it a fairytale quality. The cottage had been remodeled several times over the centuries until it now accommodated three bedrooms, a single bathroom, a spacious kitchen, and a living room.

I parked my bike behind Pop's yellow and rust-colored Jeep inside the detached two-car garage. Nan's Beetle wasn't there. She'd gone to bunco with friends for the first time in months. It was good she was doing something normal, but it also seemed like life was moving on without Mom. Like we were leaving her behind. Giving up.

I gritted my teeth, unlocked the front door, and punched in the alarm code that would have made the CIA happy. I made my way directly to Mom's bedroom which I'd temporarily converted into an office. Once she was better, we'd figure out a new place to do business.

I tossed my things on a chair and went straight to the boxes sitting in the corner. They were Mom's things I hadn't had the heart to unpack yet. It took me two boxes before I came up with her scratched leather day planner. I opened it, and her tight but slightly slanted print caused my heart and throat to squeeze closed. I forced myself to flip the pages until I found the day of her accident. In the two-o'clock slot for the client meeting, she'd written *Space Force, Lincoln Memorial* in a shorthand code that only she and I knew.

I sat back, drumming my fingers on the pages. I'd closed all the outstanding cases, and we definitely hadn't been working with anyone from the Space Force. Why hadn't she logged it into our case files? She'd been nervous enough to use our shorthand code instead of writing it out. Unease filled me. Was this what had caused someone to mess with her car's computer? Had the person she'd met done it, or had someone hacked their way in? There were only a couple of ways to get into a car's systems—the easiest through the online navigation or by attaching a device to the car's computer directly. If it had been the latter, the evidence was probably gone. Crushed with the totaled car at the junkyard.

Irritation and impotence whirled through me. Had Dad checked it out before the car had been picked clean and then destroyed?

I turned toward the window and the quiet street outside, searching for peace or answers or a wormhole into the past. The lantern-shaped streetlights barely shimmered through the fog that had rolled in from the Potomac River.

What the hell did Dad and Detective Muloney have that proved it hadn't been an accident? And why hadn't they been able to find out more in the eleven months since? For all his faults, Dad was damn good at his job, so if he didn't have more, it was either because he wasn't inclined to go looking, or it was hidden deep. Neither was an answer I liked.

I looked down at the day planner again, absentmindedly flipping pages until it fell open to a month before her accident. More coded notes, but this wasn't our normal one. A stab of pain slid through me as I realized she hadn't wanted me to be able to read it either. That stung more than anything Dad had said to me yesterday.

On the other side of the page, she'd drawn an icon of some sort. It almost looked like the Avenger symbol, except instead of an A and an arrow, there was an A and an S with a zig-zagged line inside the circle. I snapped a picture, loaded it into a search engine, and went down a rabbit hole trying to find anything that looked like it.

My phone rang, and I glanced down, tempted to ignore it, but then guilt ran through me. My best friend had left me several messages over the last two days, and I hadn't returned them. Instead, as often happened when I was on a case, I'd lost sight of anything but the trail I was following.

"Hey! I was going to call you."

Shay snorted. "Liar." But there was no malice to it. Not anger or frustration either. She was exactly the forgiving angel she'd always been. "I need my wingwoman tonight."

I groaned internally. "Shay—"

"Please. You know I have a good feeling about this one. But…"

She didn't trust herself. Not after the last cheating bastard who'd stomped all over her heart and then had the audacity to say it was her fault.

"Where am I meeting you?"

She hesitated, and I knew what she was going to say before it even escaped her lips. "I know you've been avoiding it…him… But I didn't want to make it feel like a date, so I agreed to meet up with Devlin and his friend at The Prince Darian."

I didn't know which part of her statement elicited more twists and turns in my chest—where she wanted to go or the fact that it would be a foursome.

"He's bringing a friend?"

"I promise I'm not trying to set you up."

"Two couples in a bar on a Saturday night… definitely not at all date-like."

She chuckled. "This is just Devlin and me trying to get a feel for each other without Dad hovering around us at the café."

Devlin was new to town and the campus, carrying his newly appointed associate professor's title like a badge. His visits to the Tea Spot where Shay worked for her dad while going to college had increased until the guy was practically eating every meal there. She'd begged me not to go all "Rory" on him, but I'd still done the basic search. Enough to know he didn't have any priors and no complaints had been filed against him at his last college.

"What time are we doing this?" I asked, and my friend literally squealed. It simultaneously made me feel worse for neglecting her and made me smile.

"If you'd answered my texts, you would've had more time. They're meeting us in thirty minutes."

I put a hand to my messy ponytail, flattened from wearing a helmet, and then rubbed my makeup-free cheeks. I didn't need to look in a mirror to know they were pale and lifeless and that my eyes were shadowed after months of tossing and turning instead of sleeping. This was certainly not the way I wanted to stroll into the tavern for the first time in years. Definitely not how I wanted *him* to see me for the first time in years.

"I look like I've been on a stakeout."

"Come over. I'll have you fixed up in ten minutes."

The debate within me was strong. But I couldn't abandon Shay. Not again. So, I hung up, grabbed the keys to Pop's Jeep, and left a note for Nan before walking out the door. The Jeep smelled like oil and ancient vinyl. Like salt and sea and rust. The scent was one more reminder of things I'd lost. A grandfather who'd been one of the only people in my life to truly spoil me. He'd been gone two years before Mom and I had moved in with Nan the first time. We had stayed barely a year, but those months had branded themselves on my soul just like a certain gray-eyed boy once had.

A gray-eyed boy I wasn't prepared to see again.

I wasn't ready to walk into The Prince Darian.

But I'd do it because Veronica Mars's words were true. The people who really deserved your time, faith, and love were the ones who came through even when you hadn't loved them enough. And that was Shay for me. I'd always been more caught up in my tragedies than hers. So, if she needed me, I'd be there.

If that meant seeing Gage Palmer for the first time in seven years, I'd just have to take the hit and hope I could get up and walk away when it was over.

KEEP READING AFTER ALL THE WRECKAGE ON AMAZON NOW
https://geni.us/AATWLJE

Message from the Author

Thank you for taking the time to read *The Painted Daisies*! The series started as an idea about a girl who'd started a band for her little sister. Once it had spun into my mind, the entire group took root and wouldn't let go of my heart and soul until I brought them to life. They made me work and create in ways I'd never done before. In the end, they left me breathless, and I hope they've done the same for you. The Daisies had great losses and great loves. They battled evil and won in the end, sharing the truth that I know to the bottom of my soul, and that I hope you know too—that love is the only real superpower. The only thing that can truly heal.

If you go searching for the Regina astrapia bird, San Fiore, or the goddess Rhaibele and the religion she spawned, you won't find any of them. They were made up for the purpose of this story, but I had more fun than I could ever imagine creating them. I'm working out a way to share the history of San Fiore with you in a fun way. We'll see if it happens.

All my books are inspired by music, and there's usually one song that becomes the novel's anthem. For *Royal Haze*, that song was Taylor Swift's "Mastermind." I hope the way Nikki and D'Angelo brought each other from the shadows into the light will leave a mark on your soul. I hope the way their story of resilience was mixed with music leaves you with memories and emotions you feel every time you hear one of the songs on the playlist from now on.

If you like talking about music, books, and just what it takes to get us through this wild ride called life as much as I do, maybe you should join my Facebook readers' group, **LJ's Music & Stories**, and the conversations happening there. Hopefully, the group can help *YOU* through your life in some small way.

Regardless if you join or not, I'd love for you to tell me what you thought of the book by reaching out to me personally. I'd be honored if you took the time to leave a review on BookBub, Amazon, and/or Goodreads, but even more than that, I hope you enjoyed it enough to tell a friend about it.

If you still can't get enough (ha!), you could also sign up for my newsletter (http://bit.ly/LJEmoGive) where you'll receive music-inspired scenes weekly and be entered into a giveaway each month for a chance at a signed paperback by yours truly. Plus, you'll be able to keep tabs on what's coming next in my bookish world.

Finally, I just wanted to say that my wish for you is a healthy and happy journey. May you live life resiliently, with hope and love leading the way!

Acknowledgments

I'm so very grateful for every single person who has helped me on this book journey. If you're reading these words, you *ARE* one of those people. I wouldn't be an author if people like you didn't decide to read the stories I crafted, so THANK YOU!

In addition to my lovely readers, I must also acknowledge these people:

My husband, who lived through months of silence while I crafted and shaped my most challenging endeavor yet. Every time I got frustrated and was ready to give up, he kept pushing me forward. I love you, honey, more than all the words in all the universes combined. Here's to you being a "kept man" someday, my love.

Our child, Evyn, owner of Evans Editing, who remains my harshest and kindest critic. Thank you for helping me create this series while I cried, and ranted, and moaned. Somehow, the child became the teacher, and I'll always be grateful for that. For you. Love you, kiddo.

The folks at That's What She Said Publishing, who took a gamble on me, this wild idea I had for a series, and then were determined to see the best in all of it even when I chewed my lips to smithereens, worrying that it would fail. You have no idea what it means to have this endeavor supported with such certainty, calm, and confidence. Thank you.

My sister, Kelly, who made sure I hit the publish button the very first time and reads my crappy first drafts, still loves my stories anyway, and is never afraid to say, "You can do better."

My mom, who tells me the truth, even when it hurts her to do so, as she beta reads my stories and then loves them enough to buy them repeatedly and reread them over and over.

To my dad and my father-in-law, who are my biggest fans and bring my books to the strangest places, telling everyone they know (and don't know) about my stories.

The talented Emily Wittig, who made the perfect covers for this heart-wrenching series.

Jenn at Jenn Lockwood Editing Services, who is always patient with my gazillion missing commas, my hatred of the semicolon, and scattered deadlines, but always leaves me feeling like I've done something amazing by simply writing a book.

Karen Hrdlicka, who ensures the final versions of my stories are beautiful and reminds me hyphens aren't always optional. You're a beautiful soul that I'm grateful to have in my life and for the friendship we've formed over books, teaching, and just life in general.

To the entire group of beautiful humans in LJ's Music & Stories who love and support me, I can't say enough how deeply grateful I am for each and every one of you.

To the host of bloggers who have shared my stories, become dear friends, and continue to make me feel like a rock star every day, thank you, thank you, thank you!

To a host of authors, including Stephanie Rose, Erika Kelly, Kathryn Nolan, Lucy Score, Hannah Blake, Maria Luis, Jami Albright, Annie Dyer, and AM Johnson, who have shown me that dear friends are more important than any paralyzing moment in this wild publishing world, MWAH!

To all my ARC readers and the Daisy Detectives who have become sweet friends and true supporters, thank you for knowing just what to say to scare away my writer insecurities. An extra special shout out to Stephanie F., Rikki B., Bex, Michelle F., and Carli C. who go over and above to make me feel like a queen in my own bookish world and to share my books with others.

Leanne J., your Painted Daisy quilt will forever hold a special spot in my home.

Leisa C. and Rachel R., thank you beyond words, for being the biggest cheerleaders, partners, and friends I could ever hope to have on this wild ride called life.

I love you all!

About the Author

Award winning author, LJ Evans, lives in Northern California with her husband, child, and the three terrors called cats. She's been writing, almost as a compulsion, since she was a little girl and will often pull the car over to write when a song lyric strikes her. A former first-grade teacher, she now spends her free time reading and writing, as well as binge-watching original shows like *Wednesday, Ted Lasso, Veronica Mars,* and *Stranger Things*.

If you ask her the one thing she won't do, it's pretty much anything that involves dirt—sports, gardening, or otherwise. But she loves to write about all of those things, and her first published heroine was pretty much involved with dirt on a daily basis, which is exactly why LJ loves fiction novels—the characters can be everything you're not and still make their way into your heart.

Her novel, **CHARMING AND THE CHERRY BLOSSOM**, was *Writer's Digest* Self-Published E-book Romance of the Year in 2021. For more information about LJ, check out any of these sites:

www.ljevansbooks.com

FaceBook Group: LJ's Music & Stories

LJ Evans on Amazon, Bookbub, and Goodreads

@ljevansbooks on Facebook, Instagram, TikTok, and Pinterest

Books by LJ

Standalone

After All the Wreckage

A single-dad, small-town romantic suspense

He's a broody bar owner raising his siblings. She's a scrappy PI who's loved him since she was a teenager. When his brother disappears, she forces aside years of pining and family secrets to help him.

The Last One You Loved

A single-dad, small-town romance

He's a small-town sheriff with a secret that can unravel their worlds. She's an ER resident running from a costly mistake. Coming home will only mean heartache…unless they let forgiveness heal them both.

Charming and the Cherry Blossom

A contemporary, new adult romance

Today was a fairy tale…I inherited a fortune from a dad I never knew, and a thoroughly charming guy asked me out. But like all fairy tales, mine has a dark side...and my happily ever after may disappear with the truth.

Perfectly Fine

A Hollywood, second-chance romance

He's a charming, A-list actor at the top of his game. She's a determined, small-town screenwriter hoping for a deal. They form an unexpected connection until secrets ruin their future.

My Life as an Album Series

My Life as a Country Album — Cam's Story

A boy-next-door, small-town romance

This is tomboy Cam's diary-style, coming-of-age story about growing up loving the football hero next door. She vowed to love him forever. But when fate comes calling, will she ever find a heart to call home? Warning: Tears may fall.

My Life as a Pop Album — Mia & Derek

A rock star, road-trip romance

Bookworm Mia is trying to put years of guilt behind her when soulful musician Derek Waters strolls into her life and turns it upside down. Once he's seen her, Derek can't walk away unless Mia comes with him. But what will happen when their short time together comes to an end?

My Life as a Rock Album — Seth & PJ

A second-chance, antihero romance

Recovering addict Seth Carmen is a trash artist who knows he's better off alone. But when he finds and loses the love of his life, he can't help sending her a host of love letters to try to win her back. Can Seth prove to PJ they can make broken beautiful?

My Life as a Mixtape — Lonnie & Wynn

A single-dad, rock star romance

Lonnie's always seen relationships as a burden instead of a gift, and picking up the pieces his sister leaves behind is just one of the reasons. When Wynn enters his life just as her world is disintegrating, their mixed-up pasts give way to new beginnings neither of them saw coming.

My Life as a Holiday Album – 2nd Generation

A small-town romance

Come home for the holidays with this heartwarming, full-length standalone full of hidden secrets, true love, and the real meaning of family. Perfect for lovers of *Love Actually* and Hallmark movies, this sexy story intertwines the lives of six couples as they find their way to their happily ever afters with the help of.

My Life as an Album Series Box Set

1st four Album books plus an exclusive novella

In the exclusive novella, *This Life with Cam*, Blake Abbott writes to Cam about just what it was like to grow up in the shadow of her relationship with Jake and just when he first fell for the little girl with the popsicle-stained lips. Can he show Cam that she isn't broken?

The Anchor Novels

Guarded Dreams — Eli & Ava

A grumpy-sunshine, military romance

He's a grumpy Coast Guard focused on a life of service. She's a feisty musician searching for stardom. Nothing about them fits, and yet their attraction burns wild when fate lands them in the same house for the summer.

Forged by Sacrifice — Mac & Georgie

A roommates-to-lovers, military romance

He's a driven military man zeroed in on a new goal. She's a struggling law student running from her family's mistakes. They're entirely wrong for each other…except their bodies disagree. When they end up as roommates, how long will it take before intense attraction shatters their resistance?

Avenged by Love — Truck & Jersey

A fake-marriage, military romance

When a broody military man and a quiet bookstore clerk end up in the same house, it isn't only attraction that erupts. Now, the only way to ensure she gets the care she needs is to marry her.

Damaged Desires — Dani & Nash

A frenemy, military romance

A grumpy Navy SEAL reeling from losing his team fights an intense attraction for his best friend's fiery sister. Until a stalker put her in his sights, and then he'll do anything to protect her, even if it means exposing all his secrets.

Branded by a Song — Brady & Tristan

A single-mom, rock star romance

He's a country-rock legend searching for inspiration. She's a Navy SEAL's widow determined to honor his memory while raising their daughter. Neither believes the intense attraction tugging at them can lead to more until their futures are twined by her grandmother's will.

Tripped by Love – Cassidy & Marco

A broody-bodyguard, single-mom romance

He's her brother's broody bodyguard with secrets he can't share. She's a busy single mom with a restaurant to run. They're just friends until a little white lie changes everything.

The Anchor Novels: The Military Bros Box Set

The 1st 3 books + an exclusive novella

Heartfelt reads full of love, sacrifice, and family. The perfect book boyfriends for a binge read.

The Anchor Suspense Novels

Unmasked Dreams — Violet & Dawson

A second-chance, age-gap romance

Violet and Dawson had a heart-stopping attraction they were compelled to deny. When they're tossed together again, it proves nothing has changed—except the lab she's built in the garage and the secrets he's keeping. When she stumbles into his dark world, Dawson breaks old promises to keep her safe.

Crossed by the Stars — Jada & Dax

A second-chance, forced-proximity romance

Family secrets meant Dax and Jada's teenaged romance was an impossibility. A decade later, the scars still remain, so neither is willing to give in to their tantalizing chemistry. But when a shadow creeps out of Jada's past, seeking retribution, it's Dax who shows up to protect her. And suddenly, it's hard to see a way out without permanent damage to their bodies and souls.

Disguised as Love — Cruz & Raisa

A chemistry-filled, enemies-to-lovers romance

Surly FBI agent, Cruz Malone, is determined to bring down the Leskov clan. If that means he has to arrest or bed the sexy blond scientist of the family, so be it. Too bad Raisa has other ideas. There's no way she's just going to sit back and let the infuriating agent dismantle her world… or her heart.

The Painted Daisies

Interconnected series with an all-female rock band, the alpha heroes who steal their hearts, and suspense that will leave you breathless. Each story has its own HEA.

Sweet Memory

Paisley and Jonas's opposite-attract, second-chance romance.

The world's sweetest rock star falls for a troubled music producer whose past comes back to haunt them.

Green Jewel

Fiadh and Asher's enemies-to-lovers, single-dad romance.

He did it. She'll prove it. Her body's reaction to him be damned.

Cherry Brandy

Leya and Holden's opposites-attract, forbidden, bodyguard romance.

Being on the run with only one bed is no excuse to touch her… until touching is the only choice.

Blue Marguerite

Adria and Ronan's second-chance, frenemy romance.

She vowed to never forgive him... Not even when he offers answers her family desperately seeks.

Royal Haze

Nikki and D'Angelo's bodyguard, on-the-run romance.

He was ready to torture, steal, and kill to defend the world he believed in. What he wasn't prepared for… was her.

Free Stories

FREE with newsletter signup

https://www.ljevansbooks.com/freeljbooks

Perfectly Fine – A Hollywood, second-chance romance

He's a charming, A-list actor at the top of his game. She's a determined, small-town screenwriter hoping for a deal. They form an unexpected connection until secrets ruin their future.

Rumor – A small-town, rock-star romance

There's only one thing rock star Chase Legend needs to ring in the new year, and that's to know what Reyna Rossi tastes like. After ten years, there's no way he's letting her escape the night without their souls touching. Reyna has other plans. After all, she doesn't need the entire town wagging their tongues about her any more than they already do.

Love Ain't – A friends-to-lovers, cowboy romance

Reese knows her best friend and rodeo king, Dalton Abbott, is never going to fall in love, get married, and have kids. He's left so many broken hearts behind that there's gotta be a museum full of them somewhere. So when he gives her a look from under the brim of his hat, promising both jagged relief and pain, she knows better than to give in.

The Long Con – A sexy, antihero romance

Adler is after his next big payday. Then, Brielle sways in with her own game in play, and those aquamarine-colored eyes almost make him forget his number-one rule. But she'll learn… love isn't a con he's interested in.

The Light Princess – An old-fashioned fairy tale

A princess who glows with a magical light, a kingdom at war, and a kiss that changes the world. This is an extended version of the fairy tale twined through the pages of *Charming and the Cherry Blossom.*